Tamara Goranson holds a Ph.D. in Clinical Psychology and Neuropsychology as well as Adjunct Professor status at the University of Victoria in British Columbia.

She published several academic pieces before she turned to writing short stories, creative non-fiction, and historical fiction, winning 3rd prize in the 2019 Vancouver Island Writers' Association annual general contest for her non-fiction piece, 'A Voice in Time'.

Tamara lives in Victoria with her husband and two daughters. When she is not writing, she enjoys spending time outdoors hiking in the Canadian wilderness.

www.tamaragoranson.com

 instagram.com/tgvikinggirl

Also by Tamara Goranson

The Voyage of Freydis

The Oath of Bjorn

THE FLIGHT OF ANJA

TAMARA GORANSON

One More Chapter
a division of HarperCollins*Publishers* Ltd
1 London Bridge Street
London SE1 9GF
www.harpercollins.co.uk

HarperCollins*Publishers*
1st Floor, Watermarque Building, Ringsend Road
Dublin 4, Ireland

This paperback edition 2022
1
First published in Great Britain in ebook format
by HarperCollins*Publishers* 2022

A catalogue record of this book is available from the British Library

ISBN: 978-0-00-852656-6

Printed and bound in the UK using 100% Renewable Electricity
by CPI Group (UK) Ltd

MIX
Paper from
responsible sources
FSC
www.fsc.org
FSC™ C007454

This book is produced from independently certified FSC™ paper
to ensure responsible forest management.

For more information visit: www.harpercollins.co.uk/green

For my daughters,
Tavania and Taralyn

Freydis returned to her farm and livestock, which had not suffered from her absence. She made sure all her companions were well rewarded, since she wished to have her misdeeds concealed. She stayed on her farm after that.

Not everyone was so close-mouthed that they could keep silent about these misdeeds or wickedness, and eventually word got out. In time, it reached the ears of Leif, her brother, who thought the story a terrible one.

Leif then took three men from Freydis's company and forced them all under torture to tell the truth about the events, and their accounts agreed in every detail.

Saga of the Greenlanders, c. 13th century, translated by Keneva Kunz

Prologue

FREYDIS

Summer, 997 AD

As the *goði* of Greenland, my brother, Leif, is a respected man – a man who has always been revered. When he crooks a finger, men come running.

Today his mood is foul; his eyes are wild, as though with fever. When he dismisses his men with a rumbled shout that shakes the longhouse beams, disturbing dust, I flick a glance at the open door. The little bairn inside me kicks as if to announce there is no moon daddy rising to protect us, no Red Raven here on Greenland shores.

By the gods, I've had my fill of angry men.

"I'll ask one more time," Leif barks. "What happened on Vinland shores?"

"Your sister, Freydis, wanted to purchase the Icelanders' ship to transport the trading goods from Vinland back to Greenland. The Icelanders reacted badly, and she insisted I

1

avenge her honour," Thorvard of Gardar, my so-called husband, says in an oily voice. "Am I now meant to pay the price for her misdeeds? She was the one who incited conflict between the Icelanders and Greenlanders. She was the one who insisted I axe them down."

"He lies," I spit.

"Slander has its consequences," Leif says as he pushes back from his counting table.

Thorvard's thin lips slide into a tight grin. He lifts his chin, assuming victory. Outside, we hear a scream followed by the whizzing hiss of whips digging into flesh. I lower my head, feeling a tightness in my chest as I try to stop my hands from trembling. These men are being tortured to clear my name. Bludgeoned so they will talk.

Leif draws himself up, squints as he glances out the open door. "I swear to you, I'll whip your men until their bones break to get to the truth," he thunder-rumbles. "If that doesn't work, I'll brand them with my fire irons until they speak. Listen to the three of them out there crying for mercy."

I slurp a breath. "Thorvard was the one to steal the Icelanders' ship and drag me back to Greenland against my will. Why won't you believe me?"

"Enough, sister!"

"He was the one who axed down your fighting men in their sleep! The men were too ill to sail. He killed them in a helpless state."

Leif's eyes wander over to Thorvard as the hearth fire burps out sparks that fizzle-fall. "I should raise the gallows and hang you on the spot for not giving my people the opportunity to defend themselves."

Thorvard blinks. "Your sister is a hot-headed bitch who

2

bedded a *Skraeling* man on Vinland shores," he counters in a disdainful voice. "She now carries his troll in her womb."

Leif's gaze falls across my pregnant bump. He clears his throat and waves his hand in an effort to banish Loki, the trickster god. "I shall wait to see if Freydis births a changeling or a bairn before I deal with her and give her the punishment she deserves."

"Thorvard is the wicked one! He is a crow feeder. He calls himself my husband, but I am only his trophy wife whom he likes to insult and abuse. When you break his men, you will learn the truth. I swear to you, brother, you will call me 'innocent' before this day is through."

"You are no innocent, Freydis," Thorvard says with a stiff half-smile.

Outside, another scream rends the air, shrill and sharp. In silence, Leif turns his back and wanders into the shadows of the longhouse and pours himself a horn of ale.

"Do you not see your sister's insolence?" Thorvard fish-flaps.

Leif's drinking horn is halfway to his lips. He pauses when he hears approaching feet, scowls when three bloodied men, who can barely stand, are pushed inside with raw slashes crisscrossing their backs.

"Speak or lose your tongues," Leif demands. He spiders forward.

"Freydis did nothing wrong," one of them blood-mumbles. His eye is black. His lip is fat. There is a laceration on his cheek, dripping blood.

"Thorvard is the one to blame," a second one lisps in breathy whispers. His nose is broken. He has lost a tooth. "He murdered the Icelanders and killed your Greenlanders and dragged several of the women outside and had them slaughtered."

3

The third man blinks wildly. Leif's man prods him fiercely in the back with his knurled weapon. "Speak, you fool!" A harrowing whine slips out, wolf-wild and scared.

Thorvard glares. "You cowards," he spits. His face is pasty pale and full of malice. Panic shimmies through my bones.

With the flick of his wrist, Leif clears the room so that only Thorvard and I remain. "Thorvard, this does not bode well for you," he whispers in a solemn voice. "If you were tried at the *Althing* for killing my men, the clan would banish you to the north."

There are tingles in my breasts, bolts of pain shooting down my back. I cusp my belly and hold my breath. The baby twists. When I glance down, the fabric of my apron dress worm-wiggles over my hump of rippling flesh.

"By law, it is your right to bring this case before the *Althing*," Thorvard retorts in an angry voice, "but consider this: your sister is pregnant, and the child isn't mine. I, too, could speak against her at the next *Althing* and accuse her of adultery. I could have her condemned to a life of exile. She and her bastard child would starve or freeze to death if they were banished to the northern lands."

The wind whistles through the door. My knees start shaking; my bones lock up. I study Thorvard: his greased-back hair, his well-manicured hands, his luscious furs.

"You will lose face if you spread the rumour that I conceived a child with someone else. People will question your manhood. Already no one believes you can sire a child after all these years."

"The miscarriages were your fault," Thorvard quips.

There is a swell of grief that rumbles in, pounding at the rock wall around my heart. I try to summon my one last sword in a voice as calm as stagnant water. "Your relationship with Ivor, your overseer, could be disclosed."

Leif's head shoots up. He shifts his gaze between the two of us. Then he says, "Accusing Freydis of being unfaithful would be your ruin, Thorvard. I would advise you to lay claim to the bairn for the sake of your own reputation."

Thorvard fingers the ornament hanging from his beard. His eyes are such a deep obsidian black that if one looks at him, one could lose oneself and fall into a panic.

I glance into the rafters.

Thorvard paces back and forth. "I'll lay claim, but I won't raise the child," he finally says in a dragon whisper that dispels the wafting hearth-fire smoke.

"I'll keep the child," I start to say. Thorvard cuts me off.

"If it is a boy, the child will inherit my farm when he comes of age."

Leif cracks his knuckles with a bone-snap pop. "What will you do if it is a girl?"

"If it is a girl, Freydis can have her, but when it comes time for this so-called *döttir* of ours to marry, I want to be the one to receive the bride price."

Leif sniffs. The room falls silent. "I won't bring your case in front of the *Althing* if you agree to name the child as your own, but you must also agree to these terms: You must never speak ill of my sister. You must never attempt to banish her to the north, and you must never go near her from this day forth. What is more, you must give me all the trading goods you brought back from Vinland – the wine and grapes, the timber and all the pelts from both ships. I will allow you to keep your farm, but you must agree to separate from my sister and set her up on her own lands."

"This is robbery!" Thorvard snarls. He kicks over the water skins.

"I also want a herd of sheep."

Thorvard's jaw tightens; his face turns an ugly shade of red. "I will never agree to what you ask."

"You insult me, Thorvard. As the *goði* of Greenland, I could order your lover's death. I could make Ivor sing as I pull his nails out one by one. I could set his muscled body on a pyre and watch him burn. Don't you think it would be better for him to die with honour than to live with shame?"

Thorvard pales. Leif's face turns to stone. Thorvard's body goes very still.

"The bairn must be raised to think I am the *faðir*," my troll of a husband mutters. "The child must never know the truth about what happened on Vinland shores."

"You will be *faðir* in name only," I snarl like a wolverine.

"The child must visit me every month at full moon," he insists.

"*Neinn!*"

"Freydis, don't be difficult," Leif warns in a voice that tunnels low. "The child can visit on feast days. I'll be the chaperone."

"I won't have it."

"Thorvard, you must swear an oath," Leif announces, ignoring me. I glare at him. Leif must think he has protected me from the wolf, Fenrir, the goddess, Hel, and the Midgard Serpent, Jörmungandr, all at once. He couldn't be more wrong.

I feel Loki's presence in the room.

On the night of my *döttir*'s birth, there is a blood moon sparkle-dancing across the sea, spilling moonlight tears. My labour is long and difficult, but when she finally slips into this world, screaming loudly, I think my heart will burst. She is Achak's child, with a full head of hair, raven-coloured, perfect in every way: cheeks round and full with nut-brown skin and tiny fists clenched up tightly in a ball, as though she is prepared to fight.

I name her Anja Freydisdöttir.

By the time she has five summers to her name, Anja can draw a heavy bow string, shoot an arrow straight, and track rabbits faster than the shepherd boys. I teach her how to skin her catches and cure the hides. Together, we honour the spirit of the animal like Achak taught.

Her *faðir*, Achak, becomes a distant moon memory, a falling star that once careened across my sky. I never mention him. I swore an oath. To break it would be too dangerous.

I wear *moccasins* on feast days when Anja visits Thorvard's farm. She always returns with gifts from him, and he is generous. He gives her snow-bear pelts and narwhal tusks; soapstone bowls and silken fabrics dyed from madder root; seabirds' eggs and fresh capelin to roast on an outdoor fire; seashell necklaces and precious stones. When I try to warn her that Thorvard is a wolf, she won't listen. Thorvard has ensnared her, and she is mole blind.

When Anja comes of age, Thorvard gives her a set of carved statues of the gods made from walrus tusks. It is her most treasured possession. She likes the one of Freya, goddess of love and beauty, best. When I refuse to place the statue on the longhouse beam above her bed-platform, she calls me "Freydis". Not mother. *Freydis.* I am just grateful that this child of mine who stops up my breath – this *döttir* who has helped me find the softness I thought I'd lost – still chooses to live with me instead of Thorvard of Gardar.

May the gods protect her.

She is Raven's *döttir*.

She is my everything.

Part One

SHE MUST RISK EVERYTHING

Chapter One

MEADOWLAND MAGGOTS

Harpa, 1012 AD

The smoke from the hearth fire snakes lazily into the rafters of the longhouse and tickles the blackened beams before cloaking the statue of Freya – the goddess of love, beauty and desire. She comes to collect fallen warriors to take them to live in *Folkvangr*, the grandest of her halls. The carved walrus-tusk figurine, shrouded in clouds of white, intrigues me with her hair gathered in a bun, swept back as if pulled too tightly, her eyes bulging and swollen and popping out of the ivory.

Freydis glares at me, as if chastising me for being disrespectful, but she, too, has her weirdness. She always goes outside to stare up at the moon god, Máni, with his pox-marked, wan, white-pearl cheeks.

I sometimes wonder if Freydis becomes a *mara* when she slips out of the longhouse after the stars come out. Such a terrifying wolf monster makes a body contort, a person's teeth lengthen into points, one's nails sharpen. If I knew Freydis was a *mara*, I could understand why she is always so irritable in the mornings.

Freydis stirs the pot of seal fat before she plucks the wooden spoon out and points it at me as the steam wafts up:

"Anja Freydisdóttir, where are you off to now?"

I stand perfectly still, remembering what *Faðir* said, holding his words inside like a squirrel hiding nuts, worried that she will see what I am thinking. He knows Freydis keeps me stuck at home, sheltered. He thinks I am worked too hard.

"*Dóttir*, you must be back before the moon is on the rise."

Freydis's voice, weighted down by worry, shatters the peacefulness in the longhouse. I taste the bitter tang of resentment, wishing I was back on *Faðir*'s farm. If only I had the courage to voice the words: *I am not your* dóttir! *I have never been. You raised me for a price after my real mother died in childbirth on Vinland shores. I am not as blind as you think.* Faðir *told me everything.*

"Don't fret, I'll be careful on my walk through the meadowlands," I manage to say as I collect my quiver and bowstring from the wall hook and grab my herb basket off the bench.

"*Dóttir*, listen," Freydis implores. "A herd of musk ox was spotted at the entrance to the fjord. Be on the lookout. Avoid travelling near the rocks."

Her warnings have become as predictable as the tides.

"If you're not back before I see the moon, I'll send Seth out to look for you."

The shepherd boy will never find me. I know the hills too well.

Freydis wipes her brow with her forearm, and a strand of her red hair falls into her eyes. "Take pity, Anja. I'll fret otherwise," she says as I pluck my mantle off the hook and slip outside.

There is a smell of springtime freshness – of growing things, pungent and popping. I quickly climb the narrow path that winds through the hills up towards the cliffs that meet the sea. At the top of the bank, I spot the sheep far off in the distance, their white forms grazing near the fence separating our farm from Uncle's. Beyond that, Uncle's longhouse sits on a raised ridge that slopes down to a cold blue ocean where the white-tipped waves lick pans of ice.

The wind picks up, moaning; the grasses rustle-hiss in the harsh breeze. *Harpa,* the first month of summer, is almost over and there are still patches of melting snow, dirt-streaked and icy, dotting the rolling hills.

I make my way across the ridge and down the slope, picking my way over the rock lichens and mosses, looking for young, tender angelica stalks and listening to the wheeling sea birds and chirring insects sweeping through the meadowlands. Freydis's image floats in fog before my eyes. Does she not realize that with almost fifteen summers to my name, I am a grown woman capable of defending myself? Does she not realize that I can hunt better than most men? She is always doubting me, unlike *Faðir.* He knows my worth. He would have me live with him if he and Ivor were not away so much arranging to trade their goods. I know he doesn't want me left alone with his thralls and stable boys. I've tried to tell him that I know to be careful and guard my virginity to increase the value of my bride price and the *morgen gifu.*

A patch of roseroot catches my eye. As I lean down to harvest the stalks, I find my peace as my fingers pluck out the plant and pinch off the yellow blooms. Roseroot is not angelica, and it will not help with digestion or a runny nose, but I want to bring some to Helga. She can place a clump beside her bed to ward off evil so that her little ones can sleep and her husband won't lose more hair.

I stand and shoulder my bag and lift my herb bundle. The sun is directly overhead, leaking light through puffs of clouds tendrilling apart like carded sheep fleece. When I glance up, a rabbit suddenly leaps across my path, startling me so that I almost drop my herbs. Without any conscious thought, my fingers pluck the air to catch them up as the rabbit hop-zips through swishing grasses, high and thick, and darts into a patch of tuckamore. Further up the hill, the sound of men's voices drifts in my direction amidst the bug-swarm hum. I scan the slope, seeing only patches of loamy green grasses hidden between scattered rocks. At a higher elevation, there is a breath of movement. When two bobbing heads emerge from the bank of fog slithering between two big boulders, I draw in air. I know these two. Grimr and Loki are Corpse-Lodin's sons, and their reputations stink like sloughs.

They move like wolves in search of sheep, their guffaws cut short by a burst of foul language. A sudden surge of wind knifes through my mantle and whistles into nothingness. I've no desire to be caught out here alone with these two brutes. *Faðir* wouldn't approve of it. Freydis would be beside herself.

"Anja Freydisdóttir, we have need of ye," Grimr calls. His voice screech-scratches like the swooping gulls.

With my chin tucked low, I dodge behind a bush, but my mantle gets stuck in thistle weed. I rip it free and continue moving, trying not to swallow bugs as the panic bites sharp like a thousand ant stings.

My senses sharpen. Just ahead at the base of the slope, the

rolling surf kicks up spray as it slams into the seaside rocks and vomits out a foamy scum, yellowed at the edges. Tossing a look behind my back, I will my legs to pick up speed when I see the brothers coming for me at a run. Fear twists through me. The slope is steep; the rocks swirl around my feet. Without stopping, I take a running leap and jump over a low-lying shrub and narrowly miss taking a tumble before my feet half-skip, half-hop down the bank.

Keep going, run! I tell myself as the slope becomes a lime-green blur, a smudge of mud and dirt and tiny pebbles underfoot. Someone is shouting. Voices echo down the slope. I hold my arms out, balancing with the basket as I careen down the hill, heels sliding on slick rocks that begin to roll. Behind me the brothers are quickly gaining speed.

"Freydisdöttir, slow down!" the shorter of the two Corpse-Lodin brothers cries as I tumble onto a grassy stretch overlooking a windswept beach. He grunts and reaches for me and pulls me back, panting heavily as if no amount of air could be enough. With a sideways twist, I wriggle free.

My thoughts ping as I toss a glance to my left where a bank drops off to a beach below where the water is crashing into shore. My ears are popping; my vision blurs.

There is no time to think, no time to plan. Veering sideways, I propel myself over the bank and pull with me an avalanche of loose pebbles as my ankle twists. Instinctively, I toss the basket and try to brace myself against the fall, but my balance falters and I half-slip and land on the rocky beach, winded and shaken.

I smell their dirty tunics even before I can fully lift my head. Both wear rough, shit-stained homespun wool trousers. Grimr, a boy not much younger than me, eyes me harshly as Loki leans down with his thick, tattooed arms and pulls me roughly to my feet. I wince. Grimr sneers as he rubs his hand underneath his pimply nose to remove a stream of snot.

"Look, brother," he says. He has pox marks covering half his face. "She is truly a wild one, like Freydis."

Loki smirks. "Wilder, by the looks of things."

Poxface hawks a gob of spit into a patch of nearby shoregrass. "By Odin's beard, they say this one is cursed. Take care when you touch her, brother."

I feel my fists ball up. There is a knife stashed inside my boot. My bow and quiver hang heavily against my back. I reach for the knife.

"Didn't Freydis put a hex on Thorvard's men and kill them in a fit of rage when she went *a vyking* to Vinland shores? If this one is her *döttir*, I'd be wary, brother."

"The wench was cleared of all wrongdoing, if you can recall," Loki puffs.

Poxface slops a breath. "Freydis's brother is the *goði* of Greenland, and he protects her. We all know that, but I've heard tell that Freydis is a witch and that this girl, here, is not her child by birth."

"This is true, brother. Thorvard of Gardar took a *Skraeling* lover to his bed and sired this wench, but Freydis, Thorvard's former wife, did not approve."

"I thought Freydis axed the *Skraeling* woman down in a fit of jealousy after she gave birth."

"She did," Loki snorts, as if he knows it all. "That makes this one here a dead woman's child."

"If you ask me, Thorvard should have fed the ravens with Freydis's blood if she murdered his thralls and stole his newborn child."

A raw anger shoots through me, pulsing and humming. I

want to scream at them and call them on their vicious lies. Freydis is many things, but she certainly is no murderer. Poxface eyes me quickly.

"The *Skraeling* woman probably deserved to die," Grimr continues. "Watch yerself, brother. If Freydis is a murderess, her so-called *döttir* might be just as bloodthirsty. Where there is a wolf mother, wolf teeth are near."

Loki cracks a tiny smile. I have the urge to fly at him and wring his throat until I see Poxface reaching for his hunting knife. My own weapons hang heavily from my back. What good are they against two of them?

"Look at Anja's hair, brother," Poxface threatens gleefully. I feel my eyes grow wide, my legs become jellyfish. Poxface piddles phlegm through a crack in his front teeth. "Her hair is so black and thick and smooth, she must be half crow. If we sheared off her mane, we'd git new rope."

Loki shoots me a stained-tooth grin, and I step back. "I agree, brother, but that bitch-dog, Freydis, might yelp a bit."

Poxface looks half-crazed. "I don't give a snow-bear's turd what that she-wolf thinks."

I am careful to keep a deadpan face, but the anger threatens to geyser up. Poxface unexpectedly grabs my arm and pushes me in the direction of his brother.

"I'll thank you for taking your hands off me!"

"The murderer's *döttir* speaks," Grimr pants excitedly as he leans in closely. He has halitosis of such stench that I snag a breath. "We'll have to tell *Faðir*."

"*Faðir* wouldn't give a rat's arse. He's always drunk."

"Then we'll have our fill of her before he gets his turn," Grimr gloats. "I'll enjoy listening to her voice-box break."

"My uncle is Leif the Lucky," I cry when I register what they are about to do. I try to struggle free, but Loki's grip tightens. "My uncle is Leif Eiriksson! He is the *goði* of Greenland, the clan chieftain."

"Leif Eiriksson saved your mother from a life of misery in the north, but he can't save you," Loki says as he wraps his grimy hands around my neck and pushes me down into the sand.

Panicked, I try to scream, but my throat is as dry as summer wind. When I catch a glimpse of Poxface unclasping his hooded cloak and throwing it quickly onto the mucky ground, I find my legs and begin to kick, realizing that my knife is gone.

Poxface wears filthy trousers, calfskin shoes, and a tunic with a low-hanging belt from which is clasped a pouch of cracked leather, a sax, and a utility knife.

"Untie your apron dress," he orders. I flinch when I see his blotchy face, and a chilling scream slips out, pinging up and down the beach, floating up into the hills.

Loki clasps me so tightly from behind that I am winded. The set of keys dangling from a chain around his thick, ropey neck begins clinking as he fumbles with his trousers. "Shut up!" he orders in a gravelly voice.

Oh gods! I will be shamed and violated and left for dead!

I kick with all my might, but my captors are too strong and quick. Grimr falls on top of me and knocks the wind right out of me. I feel the weight of him, heavier than a dead walrus, squashing me as his groping hands snake-slither here and there. Another scream rises in my throat, but his mucky, stinky hand finds my mouth, and he smothers me, and I gag against his stench and struggle to draw in air, wriggling and twitching and trying to shake him off. He is too strong. He crushes me.

In a tangle of limbs, I lurch forward and drag up my shieldmaiden arm and poke my finger into Grimr's eye. He yelps, pulls back. I struggle free, but Loki towers over me. My breath comes quickly as I claw for the quiver on my back.. When Loki slaps my cheek, I reel backwards and cry out in pain and touch my face, cupping my cheek protectively. Through stars, I see a hunting knife which Poxface uses to rip open my bodice and expose my breasts. He goes to touch them, and my hands fly up to swat him off, but he grabs my wrists, and I am helpless to stop him from throwing me harshly to the ground and fondling me. Bile rises in my throat, building like a massive wave.

They turn me over and lift my skirts, and I taste the grit of sand between my teeth. Just as I am bracing myself for a backward mounting, there is a sudden shout from up the hill.

"You boys are far from home," Uncle calls down from his horse on the upper banks. He is dressed in black, wearing furs, and his image floats into my periphery as I scramble out from underneath and begin scampering back up the bank. "Best get ye home. I've just come from your *faðir's* farm. He wasn't there, but I'm sure he requires help to milk the cows. The villagers tell me you now have the biggest herd."

Behind me, I hear a faint, whispered laugh. My head jerks around.

"We've the biggest herd because our old man is always stealing things from lesser men," Loki chortles low so that only his brother and I can hear. His face is flushed.

"He steals when he isn't drunk," Grimr mutters in reply. He grins at me, and I feel the grime of him still fondling me.

"Come, niece," Uncle yells.

My ankle is throbbing, my cheek is sore. I feel blood trickling from my nose. With shaking hands, I try to claw my apron dress together against the chill as I continue staggering up the bank. As soon as I reach the top, Uncle extends his hand, and in one easy tug, he lifts me onto the back of his handsome steed. "Didn't I warn you, niece, about the dangers of walking alone in the meadowlands?"

Something in me shifts, all slimy, as I adjust my grip around Uncle's waist and feel the gushing guilt spilling into me. Maybe I am too headstrong. Maybe I should not be wandering the hills alone.

I am not even settled when Uncle suddenly kicks his horse and we lurch forward. "I'll not speak of this again," he mutters solemnly. "You are of marrying age, and Thorvard and I have been trying to find you an honourable match. As you know, it has been difficult because of Freydis's reputation and the rumours about what happened on Vinland shores. You can't change the destiny that was ordained for you by the Norns, but you can protect yourself from those who want to dishonour you. I will continue in my quest to find you a wealthy husband only if you do your part." He cranks his neck and eyes me harshly, and when he registers my clammy brow and stricken look, his face softens. "By Odin's eye, you wouldn't want to be shackled to a shepherd boy for your entire life – some lean simpleton who likes to think himself a man. *Neinn!* You are an Eiriksdóttir. You deserve to marry well. You must tame this wild spirit of yours that is always trying to break free and do things on your own. One day you'll find yourself in peril, and I won't be there to rescue you."

The wind whips his hair into my face. Above our heads, the seagulls are screeching loudly as they dip low.

"No one will pay the bride price we are asking if you become pregnant as an unmarried maiden," Uncle continues in his sternest voice. A hard wind rises with a sudden force. "Hear me out, Anja Freydisdöttir: From this day forward, I don't want you to walk alone in the meadowlands."

He must feel my body stiffen. "It is my only joy," I mumble. "Even Freydis allows me to go into the hills on my own."

"Hush now, niece. I will discuss it further with Freydis. You will be with your mother soon enough."

"She is no mother to me," I manage, gathering strength.

Uncle spurs his horse. "Freydis has tried to give you a comfortable life here on Greenland shores," he says, tossing the words over his shoulder. "It has not been easy for her, considering that Thorvard disadvantaged her. She has sacrificed much for you."

"She has sacrificed nothing," I mumble into his back.

"Quiet," he says so harshly that his horse whinnies.

I square my shoulders and sit taller in the saddle, but resentment leaves a sour taste, and I have the urge to spit. Uncle hasn't been there when Freydis's mood is foul. He has not had to hear her rants or hear the skunk piss she sprays at *Faðir*. I rarely see him because of her.

Uncle tilts his shoulders forward, and I feel his muscles harden, his skin perspiring through his tunic beneath his furs. "You will need someone who will not be intimidated by you. No tepid man will have you, niece."

"I don't want just any man to have me, Uncle. He must be brave." The words come butterflying out, and I snag a breath, surprised by how quickly I can say what Uncle wants to hear. This talk of husbands is getting old. I will offer almost any sacrifice to the gods if I can hold onto my freedom just until the next *Jul Blot* comes.

It is not long before the longhouse and the byre, the smokehouse, the smithy, and the storage sheds come into view.

The familiarity of our farm threatens to compromise the firm control I've managed to maintain. The last thing I want is for Freydis to fret and fuss like she always does.

"Your bodice is in a state," Uncle says awkwardly when we finally stop and he is helping me slide off his placid horse. When he takes his own fur mantle and wraps it firmly around my shoulders for modesty, I feel my face flush hot.

"Will you tell Freydis what happened?"

"*Neinn*," he says, but he is so annoyed, he can't look at me. At the door to the longhouse, he stops and turns and forces me to enter first.

In the great room, I am met with the enticing aroma of well-cooked stew. There is a man standing in front of the hearth fire with his back to us, talking in a loud, brusque voice. On the pinkie of his left hand, he wears a large lapis lazuli ring that speaks of wealth – perhaps the wealth of a merchant who comes from across the northern sea. Freydis is sitting stiffly on her dais, listening to him pontificate. When he grabs a breath, she quickly stands.

"Come, Anja," she chirps. "We have a guest."

Chapter Two

BLOODSHOT EYES, BLOOD-ORANGE SKIES

At the sight of his face and well-dressed form, I draw in air and force myself to step back into the shadows. Quickly, I grab Uncle's arm. "What is Grimr and Loki's *faðir* doing here?"

Uncle's face is inscrutable as he takes me by the elbow and steers me forth. "Corpse-Lodin must have business here. Stop fretting, niece."

Olafur Corpse-Lodin is an old man, seasoned by years of hardship but dressed in the finest furs. Around his neck he wears a string of beads with a runic brooch featuring a red glass gemstone. When he steps forth, he grasps Uncle's wrist and forearm in greeting before sliding his gaze in my direction. Before forcing myself to bob my head, I study his thinning, long hair and his scraggly beard, peppered grey and covering a pointed chin.

"Olafur is here to discuss the sale of sheep," Freydis says dryly. "He claims to be desperate to purchase my best ram."

"Freydis has no intention of selling that ram," Uncle says

matter-of-factly. Corpse-Lodin lifts his eyebrows. "The beast in question established dominance on this farm a long time ago. It is not up for trade."

"I told your sister I'd pay twice what the beast is worth."

"Owning that animal would not serve you well at this time of year. The tupping usually occurs late in the summer around *Tvímánuður*."

"Isn't that unusual? My sheep breed all year round," Olafur says as he flicks a strand of his uncombed, matted hair over his balding spot. He has a bulbous nose marked by battle scars, and the bags under his slitted eyes are smudged purplish-black. He licks broken lips and strips my body with his eyes.

"Come here, Anja," Freydis says curtly, searching for the herb basket I should have in my possession. When I don't move, her eyes sweep over me. "You came from collecting herbs in the meadowlands, did you not, *döttir*?"

"I did," I manage weakly. Beside me, Uncle bristles.

"Anja took a fall. I found her at the bottom of a hill," he says in his deep baritone. Freydis blanches and scurries forth. To avoid her, I quickly dodge behind the loom. I am aware that Corpse-Lodin is watching me, and I fumble with my furs, attempting to hide my torn bodice.

"You should go clean up," Uncle mutters as I snake-slip between two rows of posts running the length of the longhouse. I am almost at my bedchamber when Uncle's voice stops me cold: "Anja, you'll return for dinner and do your duty and help your mother serve the meal."

I slowly turn. Freydis blinks. Her face is flushed.

"The maiden should join us now," Corpse-Lodin says. He is studying me with his rheumy eyes.

"Supper is a long way off," Freydis declares in an unnatural voice that seems to come from far away.

"Well then, mistress, I hope you'll tap one of your kegs of wine. I hear tell that your Vinlandic wine is very good."

The mice scurrying in the walls catch my attention, and I push my way through the partition into my dark bedchamber. I can barely feel my breasts, numb from the groping, and my knees are scraped and bleeding. In the other room, Corpse-Lodin is guffawing like a donkey. The faces of his two sons skip across my thoughts like chucked stones skimming the surface of a lake. I can still smell their stink, still feel their groping fingers touching goosebumped flesh, still hear their chortles ringing in my ears like the salty waves of a churning sea, swishing and pounding into shore. When I look down, my hands are shaking, and I feel the cold creeping up my back.

Corpse-Lodin is drunk by the time dinner is served, but not too drunk to admire my clean *hangerock*. It was a gift from *Faðir*. The linen has been died blood red.

"Did I tell you, Leif, that I recently purchased a thrall valued at twelve *ore*?" Corpse-Lodin sniffs.

"Why did you pay so much?" Uncle asks. "No thrall of mine is worth five hundred yards of homespun cloth."

"I was in need of a new bed slave," Corpse-Lodin says. He takes another gulp of wine and then reaches over me to grab a chunk of bread. I catch a glimpse of his rotten teeth and smell the stench of his sweat. When I pull back, Freydis tosses a look and frowns. "Thorvard advised me to go see his man, a merchant by the name of Kjaran who has a fine collection of bed slaves up for sale. I understand his women are shipped from Norway once a year."

"I've heard," Uncle replies dryly. "Doesn't Kjaran breed sheep as well? Perhaps you could obtain your ram from him? They say he barters fairly, for what it's worth."

"I will approach the man," Corpse-Lodin mumbles as he stuffs another piece of seal meat into his mouth. He glances up, slurps in the blubber, and starts chewing loudly. "Even though I talk of bed slaves, it's a wife I seek."

"I've heard," Leif says.

Corpse-Lodin smears the seal grease off his lips and leans back and gropes his crotch. Then he turns and spits a string of seal fat on the floor. My stomach churns.

"I stopped in at your farm," Uncle says as he picks at his stew. "I wanted to offer my condolences. It's always difficult to lose a wife, but you are fortunate that the illness didn't spread to your kinsmen."

Freydis sits up taller in her chair: "May your wife enjoy an afterlife in the holy mountain of Helgafjell."

Corpse-Lodin nods. His eyes are bloodshot; he slurs his words.

"Will you send raiding parties to plunder the northern regions during *Sólmánuður* and *Heyannir* again this year?" Uncle asks as he takes another bite of stew.

"There is much profit in it," Corpse-Lodin sighs. "I'm sure I'll return with many pelts and ivory pieces and narwhal tusks. Every year, I sell the tusks for many times their weight in silver. Narwhal tusks are in great demand."

"For their magical powers?" Freydis asks.

"For curing melancholia and neutralizing poison, as only one such as yourself would know."

Freydis's hawk eyes turn cold. Uncle cautions her discreetly with his hand. In his drunken state, Corpse-Lodin pays no attention. "Perhaps I should fetch my own cup from my horse's saddle bag," he says as he spears another piece of meat. "'Tis made out of narwhal tusk to negate the effects of any poison slipped into my drink."

Uncle stops eating. "Despite the rumours being spread, my sister would never poison you."

"Good," he says. "Tell her to pour more wine then." He makes to stand but almost falls. Instinctively, I reach out to steady him. His breath has a strong, sweet, musty smell – the smell of belches, the smell of death.

"Leave him be, Anja," Freydis mutters sternly. She quickly stands and clears the trenchers, and I unstick myself from his elbows. Corpse-Lodin is so drunk, he sways unsteadily on his feet. When he manages to sit back down, another stinky burp slides out in a deep rumble.

We are still not rid of Corpse-Lodin by the time the bats come out and the midnight sun sinks into the western sky. When Corpse-Lodin leaves the longhouse to go and relieve himself, he leaves the door open and rays of golden light stream down from a marbly, blood-orange sky.

"Leif, do you not think it's time to take him home?" Freydis asks as I begin collecting the drinking horns. Her mouth is set in a grim line, and she looks fatigued with her badger eyes.

"He'll not be able to steer his horse."

"Then take him to your farm next door. You're the *goði*! You must know how to deal with difficult men like him. I'll not have Anja listening to that buffoon all night."

"We can't afford to anger him."

"I don't give a rat's arse if I offend that piece of dung!"

"Calm yourself, sister. I might want to strike a trading deal with him. Corpse-Lodin is a shrewd merchant when he is sober. I've heard he is quickly amassing wealth."

"His raiding is notorious," Freydis snaps. "Magnus recently told me that he takes pleasure from counting up the women he rapes before he sets their longhouses on fire."

"Freydis, you exaggerate," Uncle chastises. "Be reasonable. You've always had an eye out for trouble."

"I'm telling you, brother, it's what I heard."

"I, myself, do not always believe what I hear. You, of all people, should know that. When you returned from Vinland, did I not listen to your tale? Was I not fair? Did I not support you? By the gods, Corpse-Lodin likes to drink and blister ears, but he has done nothing inappropriate."

The room is spinning. I slink onto the nearest stool. The weight of the day's events is taking its toll. All I want is to be excused.

"Anja is tired," Freydis says as Corpse-Lodin stumbles back into the room and weaves his way over to the nearest bench. He is stooped over, old-man-like, backlit by the bloated, midnight sun.

"I'll stoke the fire before I retire," I manage as I haul myself up. Uncle clears his throat.

"You'll stay with us until our guest has left."

"My leg is sore," I plead in a voice that avalanches into a whine.

"Let her be," Freydis murmurs as I hobble in the direction of the kindling box which contains heaps of peat moss and some of the last remnants of Freydis's Vinlandic wood. On the way, I stop to pick up an empty jug, but as I am lifting it, Corpse-Lodin reaches out and pulls me close.

"I'll take a horn of ale," he says. He is a bibulous fool. I glance at him disgustedly. I cannot shake the smell of him off me: the piss and bile, the wine, his sweat.

"Uncle, we are almost out of ale," I sputter, trying to pull myself free of him.

"Are you a gambling man, Corpse-Lodin?" Uncle asks, eyeing us. "Freydis will challenge you to a game of *hnefatafl* if you are up for it?"

"Not now, surely?" Freydis says as she rises stiffly. She quickly comes towards me and takes the empty jug from my hands. In the process, she tugs me free. There is a soreness flaming down my back, a buzzing throb in my ankle and in my knee. I set my jaw, waiting for further instructions.

"Let's place a wager on the game," Uncle says dryly. "Freydis will play for a stack of pelts from your looted stores. If she loses, you can take a thick-haired goat from her."

Freydis shoots a quiverful of ghost arrows into Uncle's chest.

"I'm in no state," Corpse-Lodin mutters irritably. "Besides, if I play, Freydis would have to wager more than that to make the game worth my while."

"Just name your price," Uncle says indifferently.

"My price is always fair," Corpse-Lodin grins licentiously as his eyes sweep across my chest. A shadow falls across Freydis's face.

"*Hnefatafl* would take too long, and it is growing late," Freydis says in a voice as cold as the ocean waters after the ice melt.

Corpse-Lodin wheezes in a wad of snot. "How is it that you learned how to play *hnefatafl*?" he lisps. "It's such a game of strategy."

"Anja plays an even better game," Uncle quickly says. "I can't beat her. She seems to have a mind for it."

"Women shouldn't play games that require them to conquer things," Corpse-Lodin mumbles as he gestures for me to bring more wine.

"To conquer kings is what you mean," I stammer, and Uncle frowns. I feel a flush moving into my cheeks.

Corpse-Lodin drops his elbow to his knees and lets his head fall into his hands. When he begins to rub his temple with his thumb, Uncle quickly pulls Freydis and me into the shadows where the moths are sleeping on the posts.

"When Corpse-Lodin passes out, the two of you will have to help me drag him to his horse."

"Anja can barely walk," Freydis breathes.

Behind us, Corpse-Lodin is muttering and swearing as though speaking to shadow ghosts. Uncle turns. He looks perturbed.

"Come, Corpse-Lodin, it's time to leave," he decrees.

Freydis's face is awash in eerie light cast by the glowing embers of a dying hearth fire. She blinks as Uncle marches up to Corpse-Lodin and hooks him by the elbow and hauls him up, swearing underneath his breath. I scramble up, knowing without being told that it is my job to clear a path.

Just as I am moving past the *hnefatafl* board that sits illuminated in whale-oil lamp shadows, the light flickers, scattering gaming ghosts. It is almost as if the board whisper-shouts, as if unseen giants who are worthy opponents are shivering expectantly, waiting for me to overlook what is crucial. The king has a clear path forward unless he is blocked.

I feel the urge to make the move and win the game in Loki style until I hear Uncle's words jiggling around my head, almost as though he is taunting me:

No tepid man will have you, niece.

Behind me, Freydis swears. I snag a breath and make the move.

Chapter Three

BONE DEALINGS

I n the coming weeks, the weather suddenly turns warmer. Freydis and I work side-by-side planting herbs and shearing sheep, but she is tight-lipped and irritable. I can't begin to guess what ails her, so I leave her be. Her burdens are not mine to carry.

On the day Uncle sends his messenger to fetch me, the goats are birthing kids. The messenger is a boy-man-child, all legs and arms. His voice is high and scratchy, about to break. When Freydis sees him, she glances at my mud-splattered apron dress.

"The *goði* said he has an important message for Anja Freydisdöttir. He needs her to attend alone."

Freydis closes her eyes. "Leave then," she says to me. Her hands are shaking; her face looks grey.

"You'll be hard pressed to manage the goats without me," is all I say.

"Go," she breathes. "Your uncle doesn't like to be delayed."

I follow the messenger across the newly tilled fields, feeling the faintest tremor in my chest, an excitement building in my bones. I can't stop thinking about why Uncle wouldn't come for me, himself. He knows what we go through at this time of year.

As soon as I arrive in his counting chamber, Uncle sits back and inspects me. His arms are crossed, he tilts his head, his face is as hard as iron ore. There is a tiny spider crawling across his boot. "Thorvard is asking for you."

Something eases in my gut. I can scarcely speak. I swallow carefully, fingering the fabric of my apron dress. "You know how much I long to see *Faðir*, but the goats are birthing, Uncle, and as you know, a first-timer's udder doesn't always bulge and it's sometimes difficult to tell when the delivery is getting close. Freydis will need my help if she is to make any profit from the sale of the kids this year."

"Freydis's overseer can help. Magnus is competent."

"Freydis will want to know why I've been summoned. Spring is such a busy time, and this is not a feast day."

Uncle laces his fingers together and studies me in silence, and I try not to breathe. "You know how Thorvard gets when he hasn't seen you for a while. Freydis always disapproves of your visits to Thorvard's farm so I've told her I will accompany you."

"Is this about my betrothal?" I ask, tasting defiance in my tone. I have no desire to be married off. Having a husband would only keep me in the women's room, and I like the freedom to wander into the meadowlands and collect my herbs.

Uncle stands. "Thorvard is expecting us," is all he says. "I've asked my thrall to bring the horses round."

Outside, Seth is calling for the sheep. Quickly, I collect myself. Uncle goes to retrieve his sword and gather up a sack he's packed. When he returns, he brings me a basket for collecting herbs.

Uncle's men are waiting for us by the gate. There are questions forming in my head, itching more fiercely than mosquito welts, but I bite my tongue. I am pleased that *Faðir* finally called for me. The last time I saw him was at the end of the harvest season during the feast of Winter Nights when the veil between the worlds was thin. *Faðir* hallowed the last sheaf in the field and then relinquished his land to the ghosts and trolls for the winter months. His great deeds were toasted, and he had his *skalds* tell tales of old, including the saga of his voyage to Vinland across the northern sea. On that night, we honoured the ancestors and Hela, the goddess of the dead, and Mordgud, the guardian of the underworld, and Nidhogg, the corpse-eating dragon, and Hlin, the goddess of grief.

Then the snows came and the route between our farm and his was blocked, so I was forced to miss celebrating the *Jul* and the Feast of Ostara with him. For many months, I have been cooped inside a smoky longhouse with Freydis and her thralls, listening to the howling wind and missing *Faðir*, missing the life that could have been if Freydis hadn't rejected him. He says he tried to love her, that he was a good husband and a good provider. All he ever wanted was to keep our family together, but Freydis stole me away from him. She gained a farm in payment for the care of me after my real mother died, because he had no one else who could look after me. When I think of it, my stomach sours.

"I am anxious to see *Faðir*," I mutter into Uncle's back. He doesn't turn.

We ride hard, turning our backs from the sea to follow a path that leads through lush meadowlands full of hardy plants: broad-leaf fireweed, bog blueberry, heather and mosses in a wealth of colours that spread across the stony soil and sandy riverbeds. I can't seem to settle even when Uncle lets me stop to collect a bundle of mayweed flowers which will be useful for mixing a digestive to combat flatulence. Later, when I am forced to leave behind a clump of comfrey because the long, hairy, deep-green leaves, tucked along the ridges of a riverbank, are too hard to reach, my mood turns sour.

That night we camp at the mouth of a river that splits into a slow-flowing channel with muddy banks. The men are jovial as they sit around the outdoor fire, but I am tired. After pinching off the mayweed flowers and setting the stalks to boil, I still can't fall asleep.

"When morning comes and you are weary, all will be as burdensome as ever," Uncle says. "Your mother will manage the birthing fine." He sits down beside me as the outdoor fire sizzle-spits.

"The overpowering odour from Anja's herbs will help drive the bugs away tonight," a man by the name of Hrut announces as he swats away the mosquito swarms.

"That concoction is sure to cleanse any body of venom and pestilence," Arild pipes up. He is the youngest of Uncle's men – a strapping brute, tall and broad-shouldered with plates for hands. He is standing in the firelight brushing his fine horse, a black stallion with a diamond-shaped splash of white on its nose.

When the men aren't looking, Uncle leans in closely. "Watch yourself around that one." He flicks his chin in Arild's direction. "He is known for deflowering maidens, and I won't let that happen on my watch."

I am struck by the way Uncle sets his jaw and looks at me with the midnight sun haloing him golden. Arild is handsome, but he is no threat. Uncle doesn't realize that Freydis has trained me to defend myself. Still, I barely sleep that night surrounded by Uncle's wolf pack, these men whose farts and burps give off such stench that even the mosquitoes disappear.

Arild is already up when I rise at dawn to make the porridge. He steals a glance and tosses a half-smile, and I busy myself with the water flasks. "Thorvard of Gardar gifted me with a horse last year," he sputters, almost shyly. "Your *Faðir* is a generous man. I did nothing to earn the prize. Truly, I am well-favoured by your family."

I lower my eyes and say nothing. There is a coolness in the springtime air.

"I would hope that your goodly mother thinks highly of me as well," Arild continues. I glance at Uncle who is just getting up.

"I should go," I manage nervously.

"Your *Faðir*'s horse means the world to me," Arild says. I nod, feeling the heat spreading in my cheeks. "I will be a great breeder one day, a man deemed worthy enough to take a high-born maiden for a wife. I could give a woman the freedom she desires." His eyes meet mine.

When it comes time to serving the gruel, I give Arild extra, and he looks at me as if we share a secret, as if our brief exchange meant something more than what was said.

That day, I can't seem to dismiss Arild from my thoughts as we pass through clumps of blooming, spiky, yellow-flowered gorse on the way to *Faðir*'s farm. Arild rides ahead on his horse with his head held high and an axe swinging from his belt. For a moment, I wonder what it would take to care for such a man and then I give my head a shake. I want more white-water rapids before I settle down and claim a life of oblivion.

When, at last, we enter *Faðir*'s yard, we are greeted by a group of thralls who are working over a cauldron cleaning debris from sheep's wool, newly shorn. The steam from the soupy broth puffs up into their sweat-soaked faces as they heave heavy sticks of woollen fibres in and out of dirty water. Beside them, the wool carders are seated on the ground, chatting as they brush and clean the fibres. When Uncle calls out greetings, *Faðir*'s clansmen stop their work and come to welcome us to Gardar.

In the quickly gathering crowd, Uncle is the centre of attention. He smiles and nods, listening with his *goði*'s ear. I wait and wait, letting frustration fatten and impatience shimmy through my bones. When Ivor, *Faðir*'s trusted overseer, finishes telling Uncle all the news and finally acknowledges me with a nod, I grab Uncle's arm.

"Will you come in to see *Faðir* with me? I am hesitant to go inside alone. *Faðir* doesn't like it when I appear unannounced."

"You're being foolish, Anja," Uncle replies, but he seems to be weighing what he should do. When he glances up, he meets Ivor's stare straight on. "It seems strange that Thorvard isn't here."

Ivor looks around, frowning as if he is trying to remember where he saw *Faðir* last.

Without another word, Uncle guides me towards the open door of the longhouse where it is dark, and inside some orb-weaver's web is dangling from the top of the lintel, half-destroyed. I am so excited that my mouth tastes of linen, my armpits stink.

The great room is dimly lit by a hearth fire that runs between two rows of benches ending at an elaborately carved dais which has been covered over in rare, sought-after pelts. On either side of the dais, two pillars rise into the rafters. *Faðir* is sitting on the dais. In the dim light, his scarred face looks stern as he pulls on his braided beard and toys with the beard ring holding the hairs in place.

There is a woman who is kneeling and whimpering at *Faðir's* feet – a thrall who is poorly dressed in a garment of coarse, undyed fabric with no ornamentation. *Faðir* yanks violently on the fetters around her neck. As I beetle closer, I notice a vicious welt on her cheek that marks the beginning of a nasty bruise. Clearly, she is a thrall of the lowest status.

"Greetings, my good brother!" *Faðir* calls upon seeing us. "I owe you thanks for bringing Anja to my farm. I hope the path was clear of ice and snow. Spring is certainly late this year." He flashes the warmest smile, and my heartbeat quickens and tears well up.

Faðir is oblivious to his snivelling thrall. He turns to Uncle: "You arrive in a timely fashion to advise me on how to deal with this mewling piece of property who beseeches me to have pity on her useless son."

Uncle eyes the thrall. "'Tis within your right to flog her if she has been disobedient."

Faðir nods. The whiskers of his chin brush against the fox pelt that hangs forebodingly around his neck. The thrall keeps kneeling at *Faðir's* feet. Her chest is heaving. Her shoulders shake pathetically.

"Take heed, brother," *Faðir* sighs. "Thorfinn Karlsefni will soon set sail for Vinland. I was asked to provide him with as many able-bodied men as I can spare. In front of others, I ordered this thrall to present her only son. Apparently, he is a strapping brute, a good workhorse, but my thrall is refusing to relinquish him. She does not want him to sail to Vinland shores."

Uncle chortles softly. "I say that you should flog her for publicly defying you. Where is the boy now?"

"I've sent my huntsmen to find him. I'll order him to present himself to Valbrand, son of Falgeir, whose ship is sailing with Karlsefni's fleet."

The thrall moans in agony.

"Silence!" *Faðir* orders. She flinches and lifts her chin. When I see the purple around her eye and the broken skin on her cheekbone, crusted over with dried blood, I quickly look away. Beside me, Uncle huffs.

"Thorvard, she is not worth any more of your time. We have other matters to discuss."

Faðir flicks his tattooed arm to have the woman removed. As she shuffles past, she tries to appeal to me, but it is not within my power to grant her mercy.

"Anja, come here, my child," *Faðir* gestures. I step forth into his waiting arms and kiss him dutifully on both cheeks. He smells like sage. "How you've grown! Truly, you are a maiden now."

I feel tears welling to hear the gentleness fleeing in his voice. There is yearning for how things could have been, a rustling, faint and soft.

"Thorvard, why have you summoned us?" Uncle asks impatiently. "Prithee, speak. I'm a busy man."

"I suspect you are eager to know the bride price?" *Faðir* laughs.

A burst of panic and annoyance needles through me, but I stand there quietly glancing between *Faðir* and Uncle, anxiously clasping my hands together to stop the trembling, trying desperately to find my meekness.

"Have you managed what I said you couldn't?" Uncle asks as he scans the room. The firelight flares and illuminates his thin face.

Faðir is silent. He turns and smiles before helping me get settled in a chair. "I've made an alliance with one of the most important and wealthy families of the clan," he says as he moves to a side table and retrieves two gilded drinking horns amid a medley of flasks and pewter bowls. He hands a goblet of wine to Uncle. "Now we can be assured of receiving powerful support in our dealings at the local *Althing*."

"Is the groom the man I recommended?" Uncle asks, and I stare at him as if he is a stranger, wondering why he didn't tell me that he had a man in mind for me to marry. My anger is a tick digging deeply into my flesh, festering somewhere underneath.

"When you sent your messenger to inform me that he was looking for a wife, I learned all about the Christians he captured and brought to Greenland shores as thralls. Apparently, one of these men, who calls himself a 'monk', is now trying to convert the entire clan."

"This 'monk' should be whipped."

Faðir laughs. "It would be entertaining to watch."

"My sister will not be pleased to learn of this," Uncle says, scowling.

Faðir chortles softly. "All hail to Freydis! We are sending her *dóttir* into a den of Christians, but she'll find some way to avoid the punishment of the gods."

Uncle stands and wanders over to the only window where a beam of light filters in through the smoky haze. Without turning, he addresses me.

"This is an opportunity, niece," he begins, but he cannot look me in the eye. "I consider the groom worthy. He is wealthy enough and eager to bed a young wife. I believe this match will suit the family well."

The shock of everything – the anticipation, the expectation and disappointment – drops like a heavy weight. Uncle has kept this news from me, and he never keeps secrets. There is a ringing in my ears like the buzzing of a mosquito swarm. "I want to know the value of the *mundr* that will serve as my bride price," I manage. *Faðir* laughs. Anger flashes over Uncle's face.

"The groom offered a half-dozen oxen, horses with bridles, and a herd of goats," *Faðir* says, eyeing Uncle.

"What else?" Uncle asks from the shadows. He takes another sip of wine. My stomach churns.

"The groom also pledged a count of shields, spears, and swords as well as twelve bars of iron. He has offered compensation for Anja's virginity in hides."

Uncle sniffs. The silence moults poison. "You are most fortunate, Thorvard. The bride price is a good one."

My body sways as I stand there waiting and shivering and forcing myself to bite my tongue. *Faðir* slowly clears his throat. He looks formidable in his rich mop of skins. "As Anja's *faðir*, we agreed that I would get the *mundr* in its entirety."

I want to spit on them and hurl up the contents of what I last ate as I listen to them discussing their business dealings with my bones.

"I demand half of the bride price," Uncle grunts. "She was raised by Freydis on my farm."

"You swore an oath, brother," *Faðir* says, blinking. "What is done can't be undone. You'd bring on the wrath of the gods."

A shadow passes across Uncle's face. For a moment he is silent. Then he rakes his eyes over me. "Niece, this is something to celebrate," he says, but his voice sounds strained, as if he has swallowed shark.

"Anja will do well by this arrangement," *Faðir* announces brusquely. He turns to me. "To find you a match has been difficult, *dóttir*, but I have managed it. Your groom has offered more than your weight in silver, which means you have been well provided for, after that sordid affair on Vinland shores."

"I am grateful, *Faðir*," I lie.

"Wedding celebrations usually are week-long affairs near harvest time," Uncle snaps.

"'Tis true, good brother. We should plan to taste the bridal honey-ale during the autumn month of *Haustmánuður*." *Faðir*'s voice echoes through the great room. He sounds jovial. "We can announce the official engagement as early as the upcoming *Midsumarblot*."

I am suddenly itchy, as though something is nipping at my skin, lice-like. The *Midsumar* Feast is only one week away.

"What say you, niece?"

When I look at Uncle and observe the richness of the furs draped around his neck – the short guard hairs of the harp-seal pelt, glossy in the firelight – my resentment swells, and I feel unequivocally duped and betrayed by him all at once.

"Until the groom's name is revealed, I can't comment on the match."

Faðir frowns and takes another sip of wine. "Freydis would spit in our faces if she were here. *Döttir*, you are nothing like her. Thank the gods! Your uncle and I sense that you respect our judgement and that you will submit to our will. I've spent many sleepless nights thinking about how to arrange for such a match."

I square my shoulders, lift my chin. "What is the name of my groom?"

Uncle coughs. "Thorvard will tell you. After all, he wants more than his fair share of the *mundr*, and all he did was arrange for the betrothal. I now know what caring for you is worth." He drains his goblet then quickly strides across the room. Without even looking back, he stomps outside and leaves us in the company of one lone fly zip-zipping around our heads. When the door blows shut, it is once again dark inside, and I swat at the air and miss the fly.

Faðir takes a moment to collect himself. In the silence, the fly is a nuisance as it circles round and round our heads before flitting from one longhouse post to the next. I follow the pesty thing with my eyes, waiting for it to land. When *Faðir* releases a heavy sigh, I glance at him. His eyes are as bright as sparkles twinkling on a lake in summer. "Your uncle hasn't changed a bit," he whispers in the smoky air.

"He didn't tell me what this meeting was all about."

Faðir gives a weary nod. When he stands, he wanders over to a bed-platform stacked with a rich assortment of comely furs and pulls out an elaborately carved birchbark box, ochre red and covered with etchings of the moon and sun.

"Before I tell you the name of your betrothed, let me give you this," he says as he fiddles with the birchbark lid. At his prompting, I lean in to take a closer look and see a pair of caribou-bone earrings, elaborately carved, sitting on a bed of moss. Each earring has an intricate, incised design of two ravens with their wings spread wide as they soar across a moonlit sky.

"They were your mother's," *Faðir* stiffly says.

When I see the intricacy of the *Skraeling* workmanship, my breath catches, and it is as though I am drowning in feathers, touched by the gnarled fingers of a spirit woman who has seen too much grief. *Faðir* never speaks openly about my dead birth mother, the *Skraeling* woman who was his lover on Vinland shores. I imagine the gentle softness in her face and wonder if she cherished these earrings with their red-ochred ravens and the circle moon – the perfect moon – when she was alive.

"This is my bridal gift to you," *Faðir* says in a muffled voice, choking up.

"I'm grateful, *Faðir*," I manage. There is an emptiness, a hollowness, a surge of sheer despair when I imagine my birth mother, the *Skraeling* woman I will never know. How I wish I had had the chance to be raised by her and not the cruel impostor with the dragon fire inside her who stifles me with her overprotective mothering. By the gods, it isn't fair that Freydis Eiriksdóttir spun a cocoon around me and prevented me from spreading my wings and taking flight. I am still the caterpillar.

There is a yearning so raw, my breath snags and my thoughts swirl like kelp swishing back and forth in murky seas. I snap the box shut, and the noise sounds like a thunderclap. *Faðir* sees the sadness squatting in my eyes. He reaches out, takes up my hand.

"You wanted to know the name of your betrothed? He is a horse breeder – a merchant in the making. I assured him that you are capable of bearing sons."

Faðir gently takes the birchbark box off my lap and opens the lid and plucks out the earrings. With tenderness, he slips them into my lobes and smiles at me just as the bothersome fly, with its iridescent wings shimmering greenish-blue, lands on my arm.

"What is the name of this horse-breeder who is to be my wealthy groom?"

Faðir licks his lips and smiles, and I shiver like a newborn foal.

"I am certain you have heard of him, *döttir*. His name is Olafur Corpse-Lodin."

Chapter Four

WHERE BLACK FLIES SWARM

S hock, the cold sting of it, scuttles through me, and the venom of fear kills thought, mutes speech as it coils around my throat. I tunnel into myself, feeling too stunned to notice that one of *Faðir*'s thralls – my favourite – is waiting by the door.

"I was told to check on you," Astrid meekly says. *Faðir* quickly stands. When he goes to pour himself a drink, I find my legs and dart out the door. As soon as I step into the yard, Astrid blinks. "The *goði* of Greenland bids you well and reminds you to express your gratitude to your *faðir* and the gods."

Fat tears well up. "Tell my uncle that I've no desire to speak to him."

For a moment, Astrid gawks. Then she bows her head respectfully.

That night I attend the feast that is held in my honour. I am forced to sit between Uncle and *Faðir* in the stuffy great room where the cacophony of voices blends with the music the throat singers and jaw harpists make. *Faðir* notices that I have no

45

appetite for the well-cooked rack of lamb he usually serves when I visit, but he says nothing, and I ignore him.

When Uncle finally breaks off talking to Ivor, he leans in closely. "Why do you look so sullen, niece? I thought you'd be pleased. After all, it has taken some time to arrange this betrothal to the horse breeder. He is very wealthy, or so they say."

"Shall I pour more ale?" Ivor interrupts.

"I'll take a horn of wine," I sniff, knowing that *Faðir* reserves the wine for only his most important guests.

Ivor's brow furrows in consternation. When he looks at me, I lean back in my chair and notice the runic inscriptions on the wood shadowed in the firelight.

"Are you upset that I didn't tell you on the ride out to Thorvard's farm?" Uncle asks as he draws a breath. *Faðir*'s ears are sharp. He breaks off his conversation and turns to us. His eyes are dancing, full of life.

"Leif, I have well considered my *döttir*'s worth, and I had to use my charms to accomplish the impossible. Many in our clan are still of the opinion that Anja's heart was bewitched by Freydis and that any marriage to her would only end in disaster."

"You exaggerate, Thorvard," Uncle scoffs. "What are these gossip-mongers saying?"

A bat flutters into the rafters in a tornado of wings. *Faðir* glances up. "They predict Freydis will kill the groom to keep her talons gripped around her only child."

Uncle chortles low in his chest. "She could use a simple stave."

I let my eyes scan the crowd, and I see the *skald* seated on a bench with his lyre beside him nestled in a bed of straw. The raven earrings dangling from my ears feel heavy. With shaking hands, I reach up and touch the etchings and feel the moon, wondering if *Faðir* will ask to hear the saga of his Vinland voyage where I first learned about the mother whom I lost. She is but a *Skraeling* ghost, a breath of wind, a pile of bones.

Faðir rises and shouts over the medley of voices in the hall: "Let's toast my brother-in-law, the *goði* of Greenland. Leif Eiriksson and I have much to celebrate after discussing an important matter which will be disclosed soon enough. May the gods bless our friendship." He lifts his drinking horn. "*Skál!*" he shouts.

I wince and see Corpse-Lodin's drunken face, his bloodshot eyes, my unhappy life. There is a sick feeling rising acrid in my throat as I try to inhale deeper and deeper breaths. Uncle slips a hand underneath my elbow and helps me up. I draw my furs around my neck and stumble towards a bedchamber at the back of the longhouse where the air is damp and the smells are sharp, where the ethereal wash of firelight dances up the walls, where the swirling smoke hides in dark shadows. I shake my head and begin to tremble, feeling the rumble of the clan celebrations slipping away, fading into nothingness.

Dizzily, I grope around and crawl up onto the bed-platform and find my snow bear hide. I am choking under the hands of two snot-nosed men who have the power of turning themselves into wolves, who will surely violate my body and crush my bones. A clan cheer rumbles through the walls, and I picture the tug of a smile at *Faðir*'s mouth.

The one you trust can disappoint the most.

The thought comes unbidden, slipping through my mind like a water snake wriggling through cloudy silt and disappearing behind the rocks.

I trusted. That was my first mistake.

When I wake the next morning, a headache thrums. In silence, I rise and tiptoe past the sleeping Norsemen who are sprawled out on the rushes that line the floor, sleeping in clumps of two or three. I would take any of them as my husband, even the balding one who smells like sheep shit.

Uncle and his men are already waiting in the yard. When Arild sees me, he brings my horse. "*Góðan morgin*, maiden," he says with a pleasant grin. Ignoring him, I turn my attention to the sweet warbling trills of the springtime birds, to the robin mothers feeding baby birds.

Faðir comes staggering out of the longhouse with a horn of wine in hand, grinning at Uncle and slurring words. When he tries to say *Far vel*, I am cold and heartless, barely there.

We ride out into thinning fog drifting across the land in spindly wisps. The horses climb at a steady pace out of the valley and find the cliffside path trailing alongside the stormy sea. Staring into the waves below breaking hard against the jagged rocks, I feel like steering my skittish mare over the edge into the cold, rumbling sea where I know I would find my peace. The thought sticks and wriggles, worming deeply. Behind me, Arild calls. His voice is stolen by the hissing wind.

"Let's veer inland until we cross the river," Uncle shouts as he reins in his horse close to mine. When he gallops off, I hang my head and my mare slogs on, and I am jerked back and forth in a slow, monotonous rhythm.

We leave the cliffs and as soon as we make our way down into the river valley, Arild gallops up to me. "Is your horse groomed to your liking, Anja Freydisdóttir?"

I stare straight ahead and shift my weight. "My horse is a

good one," I mumble into the springtime air that smells of rot and wet.

We cross the river without incident, and as our horses are wandering through the meadowlands, Uncle spots some yarrow buried amongst a tapestry of blooming wildflowers with purple petals. "Look, niece, there is that patch of herbs you needed most. We'll stop so you can fill your basket with your medicines."

"I've no need of yarrow anymore."

Uncle cocks his head.

"Yarrow relieves burning pain and no amount could bring relief."

Uncle looks uncertain. When he whistles for Arild, I dismount my horse and wander off. In my periphery, I see the two of them bending their heads together, and the heat of a cold anger beetles through me, and I start to run.

When I finally stop and turn around, Arild is talking to my horse.

I am exhausted by the time we arrive back at Freydis's farm. My legs are cramped and stiff, and my back is sore. Before entering the longhouse, I feel for the earrings deep in the pockets of my mantle. They are warm and smooth in my palm, my only bit of joy against the heart bruises I sustained.

Freydis is sitting in front of a blazing fire, spinning wool. At the sight of me, she stands. When I see her hopeful face, the anger and resentment flare and grief pulls me into black waters where Jörmungandr, the sea serpent, lives.

"What's your news, *döttir*?" Freydis asks in a cautious voice.

She comes towards me as I push past. Behind us, Uncle grunts a greeting, and Freydis turns.

"Is my *döttir* betrothed?"

"She is, sister, but not to the man we thought."

My hands are suddenly cold and clammy. I clasp them together to keep them still. When I turn back, Freydis is scowling.

"I thought Anja was to be betrothed to Arild Alfson, the horse breeder's son?"

Uncle's eyes flit between us. My brows shoot up. Uncle coughs. "Sadly, his family didn't agree to the match. Your reputation and the rumours about what you did on Vinland shores disadvantaged her."

There is chilling silence as a log in the fire splits in two and throws out sparks. Another wave of anger ignites faster than the driest moss. Something ripples through me, searing reason, devouring pain. I smell the stench of cooking hides, and my stomach sours, and I chew into a fingernail, gnawing at the nailbed until the skin begins to bleed. Uncle's eye is twitching uncontrollably. Freydis lets out a low, agonizing wail that is shrill and wretched, as if her spine is cracking, as if she is birthing wolves.

"Be quiet, woman!" Uncle says sharply. "The thralls will hear."

Air tiptoes up through Freydis's chest. "Tell me the name of Anja's betrothed," she foams in a voice so cold that icebergs shiver.

"I sent a horse breeder – a wealthy man – to Thorvard's farm to buy a ram."

Freydis's face drains of colour. Uncle stares at her wretchedly. "Your *döttir* is betrothed, woman. You should be pleased after all this time."

"*Neinn!*" she roars.

"Anja will marry Olafur Corpse-Lodin. It has been arranged," Uncle says as he tugs at his leathers. "Thorvard has done well by her. At first, I thought the bride price and *morgen gifu* was underwhelming, but when I cornered Thorvard, he finally disclosed what was truly offered for Anja's hand. It was such a noble sum that in the end, I agreed to the match. Think on't! Olafur offered us twenty snow-bear pelts for Anja's virginity. In addition, we are to share half of what Corpse-Lodin takes in from his raiding and looting this summer. The arrangement is better than we expected, sister. Anja will want for nothing."

"Brother, you are as fickle as the weather," Freydis screams. "You betrothed her to a licentious brute!"

"Settle down, Freydis. Surely even you would agree that the number of pelts offered for Anja's bride price is generous."

"What of pelts?" Freydis sniffs. "These don't matter. Her betrothed is old, and he drinks too much."

"What would you have had me do?"

"You should have had me there," Freydis snaps. "I refuse to have my *döttir* married off to some old snake just to make you and Thorvard rich."

"Hold your tongue, sister," Uncle snaps. He attempts to take Freydis by the elbow and move her out of earshot, but she shrugs him off.

"I've had to hold my tongue for many years. I've had to lie to save my *döttir's* life!"

"You stubborn, pig-headed fool," Uncle spits. "I've had to defend you all your life. That *Skraeling* affair on Vinland shores could have been our ruin. It almost destroyed Anja's chances of marrying into wealth."

"That *Skraeling* affair was my life!" Freydis cries. "I lost everything on Vinland shores. Thorvard cheated me. He stole from me."

I raise my chin and taste tear salt slipping down my cheeks as the questions inside me resume their hot-pool bubbling – questions that feel as unnerving as listening to ice crack on a frozen lake, a wildfire tearing down a hill. "I need to know the truth," I manage in a voice that cracks. "What happened on Vinland shores?"

"You tell her, Freydis," Uncle replies. He pinches his nose between his thumb and index finger, and his eyes half-close. "Tell your *döttir* what came to pass. Tell Anja the sordid tale and risk cutting her off from her inheritance."

"I won't!" Freydis screams.

I retreat into the shadows, listening to them blame each other in a clash of tongues. All I want is moth wings, speckled brown and feathered at the tips, with red-orange lines so I can flutter-dance into the moonlight and leave all this behind. Uncle's voice is rising, stirring the dust on the beams. "If I could send you both back to Leifsbidur, I would, sister. You know it."

"Would you truly send us back, brother? Prithee, you wouldn't dare! You would risk too much. Think on't. Thorvard would be able to claim my lands and take back my sheep and steal my lumber. I know you, brother. We have argued about this for years. You won't allow me to divorce him. You would have to pay too much. I should have fought to stay behind in Leifsbidur even though more innocent men and women would have died."

"Leifsbidur," Uncle scoffs. "I doubt it stands."

As darkness falls, I find myself battling trolls with blood-stained trousers and fangs for teeth. The visions linger, flicker, pop. I observe their complexity, the way they morph into even more horrific scenes where I am fighting frost giants who are dragging me off into their cavernous pits and strapping me to bedposts to torture me.

When darkness falls, I float above myself, feeling only a flat, empty numbness that dulls the pain. In the black, empty void, there is the absence of anything solid, the absence of ice and fire, water, air. The world goes deadly silent and deadly still, and I watch myself, lost in fog, searching for the part of myself I thought I knew, the part of myself I know I've lost.

Chapter Five

TANGLED STORIES, SHAMELESS LIES

I wake in the cold, quiet hour before dawn after dreaming of owls devouring mice and men. Very quickly, it all comes flooding back – my uncle's silence, Freydis's knowledge that I was to be wed, my betrothal to a drunkard with brutish, abusive sons. Shivering, I stare into the rafters.

Uncle is gone. The fire is out. There is a woolly taste in my mouth. Freydis is leaning tiredly against the back post of her bed-platform. Her eyes are closed. Around her shoulders she wears a tattered shawl as grey as the pallor of her face. When I get up and start clambering about looking for the drinking jug, she drags herself out of bed.

"I didn't know Thorvard when they married me off to him," she begins. Her voice is but a whisper. When I glance at her, she is staring blankly at the wall. "Our union was for political manoeuvrings to enhance my family's fortune. As newlyweds, we were expected to forge a workable relationship after our wedding night. Like you, no one asked me to consent to the match."

She is hidden in the shadows. Her figure is a smudge against the wall, her words a sliver of wood underneath a nail.

"At least *Faðir* was honourable," I mumble, feeling one lone tear slipping down my cheek. Impatiently, I brush it off.

"Thorvard was no honourable husband," Freydis says with sudden venom.

"Honourable or not, now you are free of him," I say, feeling as though I am swallowing sand. "You manage your own lands and you have your own flock of sheep and herd of goats and cows. You sell your wool at market, and he lets you. He treats Uncle with the respect he deserves, and he has never abused you. Don't you see? Your situation is not like mine. Olafur Corpse-Lodin is of the wicked! He is a malt-worm who has sired two monster sons who tried to debase me in your fields."

Freydis's brow constricts. "How did they debase you?" she asks sharply.

"I was walking in the meadows when the Corpse-Lodin brutes attempted to ..." I hesitate. The words are sticky cobwebs in my throat.

"Did they violate you?" Her voice is shaking. Her tone is weak. When I don't answer, she snags a breath. "Sheep's dung, we must undo this match." She can't look at me. "Sons often lurk in their *faðir's* shadow, but *döttirs* must unobtrusively walk one step ahead. By Óðinn's beard, this is Thorvard's doing! He has undone me once again. Before the gods, I swear to you, we will set this right. Thorvard will not win again so easily."

"What will you do?" I ask pathetically.

"I'll tell your uncle to cancel the marriage contract. By the gods, I'll insist on it." She wanders over to flint the fire. Her hands are shaking. She makes three attempts before the flint sparks and she uses it to light a tinder bundle.

"*Faðir* will protest the loss of the bride price."

A piece of wood catches fire. Soon the fire is snapping as though hungry and exploding tree-sap sparks are flying here and there. Freydis pulls back before she rises and motions me in the direction of the *hnefatafl* board. "Anja, you won't marry Corpse-Lodin. I won't allow it," she says as her delicate fingers pluck a white defender up. The ivory piece is scratched and lacklustre in her hand. "The villagers have called me a murderer capable of doing brutal things. By the grace of Thor, I'll earn that title and use my sword to show Thorvard how much I value my *döttir*'s life!"

The room feels suddenly stuffy, way too hot. I shrink back against the wall. "You won't hurt him?" I croon pathetically.

"Who?" Freydis asks, sharply.

"*Faðir*," I say pitifully.

A sudden draft stirs the hanging herbs. Freydis throws her head back and releases a brittle laugh.

"How now, mother?"

"How now? How now, Anja Freydisdóttir?" she repeats.

"*Faðir* has not misused us, mother. He doesn't even know about my dealings with the Corpse-Lodin brothers. I didn't tell him. I shouldn't have mentioned anything."

"*Neinn!*" Freydis rasps. She lifts her eyes. The white king she is holding slips between her fingers and crashes down and destroys the positioned pieces on the board. "Thorvard of Gardar won't abuse you like he abused me."

I hear heart thumps thwacking in my ears and feel the weight of everything in my chest. When Freydis speaks again, I study her eyes, the way she flits them here and there. "Anja, you are my *döttir* whom I fought hard to keep. You'll not live to repeat my story."

She goes to take up my hand, but I yank it back. "Promise not to harm *Faðir*, who is innocent in all of this," I plead in earnest. "Truly, I tell you, he is not to blame. With the help of the gods, he tried to find me a husband and make a match. He doesn't know that Corpse-Lodin is of the wicked. He doesn't realize he has brutes for sons."

"You are blind, *döttir*," Freydis says as she begins to pace. When she passes under the smoke hole, the sunlight streaming in catches up the shine of her long, red hair. "Thorvard of Gardar has misused us both."

"*Neinn!* He has been good to me. He has cared for me my entire life."

"Before the gods, I'm exceedingly weary," Freydis declares. Her breathing is building like an ocean swell. "May the one-eyed Óðinn share his vision and may Loki leave our midst. Thorvard of Gardar views you as his property and that is all."

"It is not like that! He'll break the contract when I tell him what was done to me. He would never let a husband abuse me."

"He doesn't care," Freydis mewls.

"I'll cry mercy, Freydis!"

"What dribbling nonsense! I swear to you, he'll marry you off to punish me."

The *hnefatafl* board swims before my eyes, and I right the pieces, restore the king.

"Come now, Anja, let's take a walk and think this through. Before you were born, they forbade me to tell you the saga of your birth, and I was afraid of losing you, but now it seems I have no choice. We will walk together until the moon comes out."

I gawk at her. "*Faðir* tried to love you. He wanted us to live together on his farm, but you were the one who wouldn't have him. You were the one who was difficult. You were the one who took me away from him. He told me!"

She flinches. "Anja, by the gods, you don't know the all of it. You have it wrong."

"I don't," I spit. "I see it clearly. I see who and what you are!"

Freydis's lips are quivering. "May the gods help me. I didn't realize he had such power over you."

I see sorrow squatting in her eyes and something dark and tangled. She begins to hum her garbled words, the ones she learned in Vinland. The beat is strange and unnerving. As I grab my mantle and my bow, I feel a headache coming on.

In the yard, I catch a whiff of spring and smell the scent of growing things. Overhead the brilliant sun sparkle-dances across the path that skirts around some low-lying shrubs where the nesting birds are chirping wildly, singing throaty mating calls. The path narrows as we trudge through tall grasses that lick our ankles, before we veer off to follow a caribou trail leading to the beach. When we reach the shore, the tide is coming in and hundreds of tiny rock crabs are scuttling across the sand. Eventually, we find a sheltered spot where we sit cross-legged looking out across a vast stretch of endless sea merging into a cloudy, tarnished, silver sky.

"My *döttir*, I've kept many secrets from you for far too long," Freydis begins in a voice as smooth as liquid silver. Overhead, the seagulls screech. "I thought that keeping my silence would offer protection, but now I see that I was wrong. I've made sacrifices to every god, and still Loki has had his fun with me."

She picks at her mantle and hangs her head. The wind wails and moans. I scrutinize the wrinkles that line the edges of her eyes and see only *Faðir*'s lonely life. A sudden gust lifts the edges of my apron dress, and I scramble to force the linen down.

"You must learn the truth, but please know this: I kept your birth story from you for your own good. Thorvard would have killed us both."

I hate the way she always paints *Faðir* as if he was monster born. All I care to learn is my birth mother's name. I want to feel the moment when she tells me, the moment she admits she raised me for a price.

"It was an arranged marriage," she begins. "My own *faðir* betrothed me to Thorvard of Gardar, a man of wealthy means thought to be honourable. Your *grandfaðir* was a caring man who loved me well. He thought the match would be advantageous."

When I hear her speak, I imagine wading into the churning sea and succumbing to the freezing cold and drowning quickly in the depths.

"Thorvard was an evil and abusive man who was eager to have a child, but I had difficulties conceiving. When I lived with him, he took every opportunity to beat me." She shudders, and I can't even look at her. I notice the birds skirling overhead as she scoops a breath. "I had a chance to escape from Thorvard, and I took it. Two Icelanders by the names of Finnbogi and Logatha helped me sneak away on a longboat bound for Vinland shores. Logatha was my dearest friend. She, too, hated Thorvard of Gardar."

"By the gods, the *skalds* say you were eager to kill the Icelanders and that because of you, a river of their blood spilled into the sea. They say you murdered them and stole their ship."

"Anja, *döttir*, this isn't true! Haven't you been listening? Thorvard was the one who stole the Icelanders' ship. He was the one who axed them down."

"I'll not listen to your dribble anymore," I yell as I pick myself up off the sand. There is a rush of anger, a wave of grief. I'm sick of her pathetic tale, tired of my pathetic life. The wind blows cold against my face. Just ahead there is a green string of slimy kelp, tantalizing for the sand flies, rank when I snag a breath.

"Stop, Anja!" Freydis yells from behind my back. "I've not told you all of it."

The world around me spins; the seagulls screech. I want to tell her what it was like for me when I was growing up. I want to talk about my loneliness. I want to tell her that the other girls were cruel and that is why I walked alone in the meadowlands. I want to harvest sunbeams and leave moonbeams behind.

"You ruined my life," I scream. "I had no *faðir* because of you!"

"*Döttir*, by the gods, you must listen. Your *faðir* loved you. You are half-Beothuk, Greenland born!"

I am drowning in seaweed, swallowing waves and chewing fish. Her words get tangled in my head.

"Listen, Anja Freydisdöttir!"

"I want to know more about my Beothuk kin!" The ancestors speak in the cadence of the wind. They say: Be like the ever-moving tides and listen to the incoming story, the pounding surf of gritty love.

A rumble of a sob emerges from somewhere deep. Freydis approaches and tries to rub my back. It feels like her hand is a jellyfish sucking at my skin.

"Prithee, Anja, I will tell you everything, but first know this: Thorvard was a jealous, vengeful man who silenced me when you were born. For years, I was afraid of him, but I am not anymore. I won't let him marry you off to an abusive man, even if this means I must relinquish you."

I stare at her.

"You are worth more to me than the sun, the moon and all the night stars combined. When they placed you in my arms after you were born, there were moonbeams sparkling in your hair, and I felt your *faðir* with us, as if he heard the call of the raven. He spoke to us and his message was carried on seagull wings across a great stretch of water, and all I could mutter was: *Anja, my beloved child.*"

"You should have stayed with him."

"Your *faðir* tried to keep me near, but fate intervened. One cannot change one's destiny. I was always meant to be your mother, and you were meant to be my child, but I had to fight to keep you. I can't imagine how I'll be able to let you go."

"Corpse-Lodin owns me now. *Faðir* sold me for a price. He, alone, did well by me."

"Hush now, Anja. The two of us will dupe Thorvard of Gardar. I know of a Viking expedition that is Vinland bound. Your uncle, Thorfinn Karlsefni, has been called by the gods to lead this voyage across the northern sea. You could sail with him."

I gawk at her. "How?" I ask. "I hardly know the man. He and Aunt Gudrid have been married for less than a year, and I doubt they want the responsibility of protecting me."

"When Gudrid was widowed after her husband, my brother, died, she faced hardship until she found Thorfinn Karlsefni. She knows what it is like to be female born, and I am certain she can help us. Her husband is a helmsman of good repute who is on the lookout for women to assist with the meal-making, sheep-tending and the like. Think on't, *döttir*. If we could somehow manage to sneak you on board one of Karlsefni's longboats, Corpse-Lodin, that grave worm, would lose out on marrying you, and I could send you back to Achak and your Beothuk kin."

When I register her intentions, I stand. "You'll be exiled for this," I mutter as I struggle to collect myself. She shakes her head.

"By the gods, I'll make certain no one knows I was behind the plan." She draws a ragged breath.

"What about Aunt Gudrid? She will tell Uncle. If she discloses our deceit, you will be exiled to the north."

"*Neinn*," Freydis whispers into the wind. "Gudrid has had her fair share of heartbreak, and I doubt she would wish you ill if she knew you were betrothed to such a man as Corpse-Lodin. Besides, she owes our family a debt, considering she is the widow of my dear brother, Thorstein. After he died, your Uncle Leif allowed her to keep Thorstein's farm."

"This is a fool's errand."

"Hush, my child. Óðinn and Freya will protect you, Thor will give you strength, and Loki will help us dupe them all. I'll make sacrifice to all the gods for your protection, but you must steer clear of Gudrid and Karlsefni until you arrive on Vinland shores, do you hear? At that point, you can find your aunt and tell her all that has come to pass."

"This means I'll have to leave Greenland."

Her face drains of colour. She steps closer. Reluctantly, I let her take up my hand in hers. For the first time ever, I study the vicious scar creeping from her thumb all the way up to her elbow, the white ridge of puckered flesh. For a moment, I think of her terror, and everything sinks away. How could it be? *Faðir* has disappointed me, but he is no Thor. I try to picture the dragon in him breathing fire, uncurling its tail and lashing someone with a vicious thwack. The wind hisses, sending bursts of ripples across the sea

"When you arrive in Vinland, you must find a way to travel to the Beothuk village that lies just east of Leifsbidur," Freydis breathes.

"Leifsbidur?" I repeat.

Freydis's hands are cold. "*Já, döttir.* That is where you will find your kin. Your *faðir* won't expect it. I can't imagine how he will feel."

What do I care, I think, as some vulture inside me takes flight.

That night, after we have spoken more about me leaving Greenland, I am so exhausted, I slip into my bedchamber without bidding Freydis *góða nótta*. I can hear her feet shuffling around the longhouse, followed by the click, click, click of her steel striking flint. Then silence.

In the wee hours of the night when the hazy midnight sun is trickling in through the open door, I rise and see Freydis's dark shadow leaning against the lintel. Her mantle is draped around her shoulders and her red hair is spilling out of her hood.

"What are you doing?" I whisper in a voice that feathers across the room.

"I want to see the moon." Her eyes are glassy in the wash of light.

Before I can move, Freydis slips outside where the crickets are chirping and the sea breeze moans. For a long time, I stand listening to the night noises – the creepers and the crawlers, the crackles of the dying fire. In the stillness, there is an empty feeling, almost as if the fates are whispering my name and calling me out into the moonshadows. Almost as if I hear the ancestors weeping for me.

Chapter Six

FOXBITE AND SNAKE TATTOOS

As I crush herbs to take aboard Karlsefni's ship, I savour the scents and reflect on the last few days, which have felt ludicrously normal: visiting Helga and helping Magnus around the farm, using my bow and arrow to shoot at targets under Freydis's watchful eye, trapping and skinning a plump little rabbit to make a pot of stew. Yet, everything is different.

Freydis won't let me be. When I grow tired, she insists on showing me more shieldmaiden moves; she makes me grapple with her until my muscles shake. Then she shows me how to use my knife to kill a man and defend myself against a beast. She natters non-stop, telling me things I already know, like how to survive on little to eat, and how to determine if water is stagnant, and how to discern if a mushroom is edible.

"Nothing can prepare you for the hardships you will face on Vinland shores, but trust your instincts, *döttir*. Trust your intuition most of all."

"The gods will protect me," I tell her solemnly. I don't

mention that I look forward to living among my birth mother's kin as a valued member of their tribe.

"Vinland is a godless land, but you will survive if you follow my instructions," she replies.

By the time the end of the week arrives, Freydis has not managed to find me passage on board one of Karlsefni's ships. She is as elusive as the moon when she leaves the farm on a Thursday at sunrise. In her absence, I collect my herbs and organize what I will take on my *vyking* voyage across the sea. The afternoon sun is bright and hot, but I stay indoors, anticipating the feeling of being free of this blasted farm where I have been stifled in my youth, living under Freydis's rule, living a life of lies.

When I catch the sound of horses entering our quiet yard, my hands drop the bundle of mayweed, mugwart and comfrey I am holding, all thoughts of crushing herbs forgotten. If it is Uncle coming to fetch me – or worse, if it is Corpse-Lodin coming to take another look at what he bought – I'll have no protection in Freydis's absence.

I sit, hands shaking. The panic flares as the room shifts, and my breath quickens, and my vision blurs. The deep rumble of a man's voice reverberates through the yard. Instantly, I am across the room, hiding behind the open door. When I sneak a peek, I see Freydis dismounting from her large gelding in the company of a Norseman who is about six feet tall with a balding head and tattoos scrolling up and down his massive arms.

"I've ridden all this way. Show me what you have, woman," the man demands.

I release a breath. My shoulders drop.

"I have many goats. Certainly, I can spare some if you need," Freydis coos. Her skittish horse whinnies. When she turns around, her voice arrows towards me, snagging me before I can retreat inside. "*Döttir*, come meet Jelani Arnarson. He is a helmsman who will be sailing with Karlsefni's expedition to Vinland shores."

A roar explodes inside my head. There is everything riding on the way I present myself. I cannot afford to overstep. My legs are quivering. I am suddenly out of breath.

"Did I mention that I've come all the way from Norway, where I met the king?" Jelani brags, squishing me like he would squish a bug. "The king, himself, instructed me to bring him looted treasures. He wants ivory tusks and bog iron, luscious furs, and grapes for making wine. They say I can find all of this and more in Vinland. If I return to him with all these trading goods in hand, he has promised me a great reward. He has promised me a gift of lands!"

Freydis smiles, but she is wringing her hands and there are beads of sweat on her brow.

"Freydis Eiriksdöttir, if you have provisions to spare like you have said, I'll bring you back a load of wood," Jelani continues, speaking fast.

"The deal is fair enough," Freydis croons, "but I'd also like a barrelful of Vinland grapes for making wine."

"I see you like to barter," Jelani says. His laugh is as harsh as a sea lion's bark. "As the sister of the *goði* of Greenland, you are a wealthy woman of some repute. I'll bring you back your grapes, but first let me see the provisions you have to spare."

"Don't you trust me?" Freydis asks. Jelani rubs his balding head.

"I am low on trust. One of my thralls tried to dupe me in the past. When I discovered his deception, I had him flogged. You see, good woman, honesty and integrity are what are most important in this world. I'll happily trade with you, but I'll tell you this: I always know when people are trying to use me to get what they want at my expense." He flashes Freydis a charming smile.

"I, too, am low on trust," Freydis says as she composes herself and looks Jelani squarely in the eye. "I hope we will be able to assist each other."

The helmsman sizes up our farm. "Freydis, you appear to be someone who will be able to supply my ship. Tell me, do you have chickens to spare? I want to take them for the eggs."

When Freydis dares to glance my way, her look lends me strength. "This farm can certainly provide you with all the goods you need to travel to Vinland shores," she quickly says, "but trading is not the only reason I brought you here. I was riding out to see my brother on this very morning to discuss the *vyking* expedition that is Vinland bound. You see, helmsman, I have a vested interest in seeing if the settlement of Leifsbidur still stands. Perhaps you've heard of it? My brother founded the colony in Vinland when he first discovered the place. That was many years ago."

Before Jelani has a chance to speak, a flock of sheep make their way into our yard accompanied by our shepherd boy. The bleats are loud, the sheep get underfoot, and the three of us are forced apart. I reach for Freydis's sack, and she relinquishes it as we make our way over to the byre. At the entrance, Freydis shouts to Magnus. The tall, brawny overseer emerges from the back with a rag in hand. His hands are filthy. He wipes them off.

"Magnus can provide you with all the goods you need," Freydis informs the helmsman as she stares down at the snake tattoo creeping up his arm. The overseer steps forward and reaches out to grasp Jelani's forearm in greeting. Freydis tells him that Jelani is planning an expedition across the northern seas to Vinland shores and that she is interested in backing his mission and providing him with the goods he needs.

Magnus nods. "I trust you have men to help transport and load the supplies our farm can spare?"

Jelani sniffs and rubs his head. "I've just arrived from Norway, but I'll make the arrangements within the next few days. Óðinn, the god of gods, must have led me to this farm. I see there is much bounty here."

Freydis turns and smiles at me. "Come, Jelani," she demurs, tossing the words behind her back. "As I said, making trading deals is not my sole motivation for inviting you here today. You must come with us to the longhouse where the three of us can speak in private about an important matter."

Jelani looks around one last time before he hustles forward to catch up to us. He follows so closely that he doesn't notice he is splattering the back of my *hangerock* with the mud his boots kick up. He is an ass, I think, but I bite my tongue when Freydis takes up my arm and steers me forth.

When we have just about reached the longhouse, Freydis turns and ushers Jelani into the dark interior, where it is springtime cool with an earthen smell.

"Please come in," she says as she shuts the door behind us. A moment later she goes in search of a drinking horn like a puffin during nesting season. When she finds the one with the gilded rim, she pours the helmsman a generous portion of her best wine. "Can I be frank with you, helmsman?" she purrs as my eyes grow accustomed to the dark. "I hear tell that you are recruiting women who would be willing to travel overseas."

I stand there picking at my *hangerock*.

"*Já*, but I've not had much luck. Females are generally reluctant to set sail with foul-mouthed sailors whose rowdiness and sordid behaviour could easily lead to trouble. I don't have to tell you that life on board a ship is wretched. We don't have tents so we sleep outdoors underneath the stars, and there is always the chance that Rán will pull my storm-weary thralls into a watery grave. All told, the *vyking* life is a hard life. May Thor protect us."

"Helmsman, you give the impression of being honourable. Because of this, I put my faith in you. You see, I have a female thrall who would be interested in sailing with your crew, but I want to ensure she is protected. She will do well by you. I am confident this thrall of mine will not be lured in by the selkies nor does she have a selkie lover. I would know if such a seal shapeshifter shed its skins to take on human form in my own home. Indeed, this is not the case. By the gods, I can assure you, helmsman, this thrall of mine is a good woman who is eager to go *a vyking*. I would be willing to let her sail away with you for a price."

The helmsman's ears perk up. "Your timing, good woman, could not be better."

Freydis smiles. When she glances at me, I'm careful to keep my expression flat. Freydis is known for her bartering. She is known for dealing for a price.

"Anja, fetch more wine," she orders in the calmest voice. I do as I am told, keeping the two of them in my line of sight.

"Tell me, how much do you want for her?" Jelani asks as I uncork the jug. Freydis ushers the helmsman to the place of honour at the hearth. When he gets settled, Freydis takes up the drinking horn I offer and hands it over to the helmsman. "My thrall is not for sale, but I will lend her to you if you agree to give her freedman status once you arrive on Vinland shores."

Jelani slowly lifts his free hand and crooks his elbow and rubs his head. His brow furrows into knots.

"This girl has been with me for many years," Freydis says. "You can't imagine how surprised I was when she told me how eager she was to take a *vyking* expedition across the sea. I, too, was eager to go exploring when I was her age."

Jelani gulps down his wine. Freydis sighs: "Good helmsman, I am worried for her, that is all."

"I won't let the men misuse her. 'Tis a promise," Jelani announces with a burp before he reaches up to rub his head again.

"My good man, you are most honourable," Freydis chirps, "but seafaring Norsemen are prone to using women hard. If I should let her go with you, how can I trust that you will keep her safe?"

Jelani steals a peek at me with eyes the colour of cold water. "Good woman, you mustn't fuss. Your thrall will be well protected in my care, but I feel compelled to offer some advice. You might do better to sell her off as a concubine or an *ambatt*. I'm sure she'd fetch a pretty price."

At his words, I feel squeamish, like I have stepped into an ant hill and the wee buggers are biting as they crawl up my leg. Freydis pales. She grabs for a high-backed chair. Jelani twists his body and shuts me out.

"I've heard tell that an old man – a widower in these parts – is looking for a comely maid," he says. "It might be wise to speak with him. I'm sure you could sell her off for a goat or two."

Freydis's eyes narrow into slits. Jelani is oblivious. He takes another giant gulp of wine.

"Here's the thing," Freydis mutters. "This poor thrall's mother died in childbed, and I've raised her as my very own since she was small. Others criticized me for it, but I was a lonely woman in need of company after my husband died. Now that I've grown old and grey, I worry about what will become of her. She has no inheritance – no *heiman fylgia* or dowry to be held in trust. If truth be told, I do not need her anymore, but I won't sell her to my neighbours who would only laugh at my stupidity for taking her on as my own all those many, many moons ago."

I lower my chin and stare at my feet, unsettled by the lies she tells. Memories of what the *skalds* used to say about her puff out like cooked barley in porridge. They say she lied about the abuse she endured at the Icelanders' hands. They say she made *Faðir* fight a *holmgang* to defend her honour.

"What say you, thrall?" the helmsman asks, startling me. "Do you want to come with me to Vinland shores?"

Before I can even snag a breath, he turns back to Freydis, and I have no voice again. I am a girl ignored.

Jelani's bald head, sporting knotwork tattoos, is glistening in the sunlight streaming in from the smokehole. The beams cut through the smoky haze and illuminate flecks of ash and dust that flutter-dance into the shadows. "Thor's hammer, did you tell her that sailing is not for the faint of heart? She better not be one of these wenches who gets seasick easily!"

Freydis sighs. The helmsman frowns. With vigour, he rubs his balding head, and I can't help but see a red patch welting.

"I've spoken with her about the life she can expect. Trust me, helmsman, she is sturdier than she looks. Did I mention that she is able to carry a heavier piss pail than my shepherd boys? I've even trained her how to hunt and fight. Perhaps she'll snag a white falcon for you to bring back to the king of Norway himself."

Jelani flashes a smile that reveals a missing side tooth before he scrutinizes me from head to toe. He is suddenly sober. "My good lady, I hate to ask, but I'll need some goods for the care of her."

"I thought you were paying me? I thought you said you needed thralls? Of course, if you say nothing to my kin about taking her on board your ship, I could do well by you. I could supply your ship. Our chickens lay the finest eggs."

Jelani rubs his head again. I shift in place, wishing for this foul business to be done. When I look up, there is worry nesting in Freydis's eyes.

"God's bread, I pray that Loki doesn't have a hand in this," the helmsman frets.

"Loki? What does the trickster god have to do with me wanting to stock your ship?" Freydis asks. She shifts in place and wrings her hands.

"I should carve a stave on my breasts in my own blood to protect myself against female foxbite," Jelani mutters without looking up.

"It might be wise," Freydis snaps.

"If I discover that the two of you are double-crossing me, I'll smite her down with my own sword," the helmsman fumes. He spits a gob of muck onto the ground.

"Prithee, good man, calm yourself," Freydis chides.

"As I said, I'll take her on, but if she is lazy ..."

"Truly, I tell you, she isn't lazy! By the grace of the gods, she has been my greatest joy." Her voice snags. My head snaps up. Jelani's eyes lock onto mine.

"Let me see the palm of your right hand," he says.

"My palm?" I repeat, confused. Jelani sniffs. "If there is a blood stave, I won't take you on board my ship. Truly, I tell you, something feels off in all of this."

"Please, good helmsman, this is nonsense," Freydis reassures. "If you take this thrall *a vyking*, you won't be cursed. All I ask is that you keep this arrangement to yourself. I don't want my kinsmen to know that I stocked your ship and that you took my thrall on board your ship."

Jelani prickles. "I beg pardon?"

"I've no wish for my clansmen to learn that this good maiden achieved freedman status by sailing west under your watchful protection," Freydis says in a calm, soothing voice. "Just imagine if word got out that you are offering freedman status to anyone who agrees to sail with you to a barbaric land where the risk of being eaten alive by giants or swallowed up into Hel's underworld is of great concern. As it is, no female wants to sail with you. Even so, it is difficult to gain freedman status, and if you are offering that for free, all the thralls might suddenly leave their posts and sail away with you. Truly, you wouldn't want to be the cause of a mass exodus of female thralls. Can you imagine? The chieftains here in Greenland wouldn't like you very much for stealing their bed slaves."

"Sheep's dung, I see your point," the helmsman mutters as he fiercely rubs his head.

"Then it is settled," Freydis sighs. "When you take my thrall on board, you must only say that she is a maiden from the islands who is eager to go *a vyking* with your crew. Come now, helmsman, today an opportunity presents itself."

Jelani heaves another heavy sigh. "What did you say her name was again?"

Freydis coyly averts her gaze, but her face turns red. Jelani flicks a glance at me. Just as he is about to question us, we hear Seth calling for the sheep.

"If you don't want my thrall, I'll find another helmsman," Freydis says, recovering.

"*Neinn*, I'll have her," Jelani snaps. "She should present herself to my ship right before the *Midsumarblot* so we can load her gear. Karlsefni's expedition sets sail the day after the festivities."

There is a sudden pang, a biting realization as I watch my life on Greenland shores disappear like puffs of mist being licked up by the rising sun spilling across the meadowlands. Freydis bobs her head in deference as the helmsman slowly stands.

It is late in the afternoon when we accompany Jelani to the byre to discuss the goods he needs to stock his ship. I milk the cows and listen in as Freydis gives Magnus instructions and Jelani itemizes what he needs. As the three of them begin discussing what can be spared, I feel my throat close up, my stomach sour. What if the helmsman is Loki in disguise? What if I am following him into a trap? The knowledge that I will soon be leaving Greenland stings and itches like a horsefly bite, and I can't help but think how much I've yearned to be anywhere other than Freydis's farm. Then a feeling squirms through me, skipping across dreams and settling like dust into a pool of loneliness.

When the bartering is finally done, Freydis and I see Jelani off. The sun has dipped behind the hills, and in the distance, the sea looks rough. In the blustery breeze, Freydis's *hangerock* flaps wildly against her legs as she collapses against the well.

"I am not sure about him," I tell her solemnly. Behind us, the grasses swish. Freydis's face is a map of worry lines.

"Escaping with him is your only choice, *döttir*. Come. We have much to do before the moon comes out."

The wind snaps her words up, tossing them up to Sól. I look up. Sól is the sun goddess who, it is foretold, will be killed by a monstrous wolf during *Ragnarök* after giving birth to a *döttir* who will continue her mother's voyage across the sky.

The irony of it is almost laughable.

Chapter Seven

RAVEN'S DÖTTIR

I n the morning, Freydis drags me from my bed and steers me into the yard where she forces me to grapple with her once again. In her eyes, there is smoke and fire and something dark. Her wildness is growing, webbing around me, smothering me and dredging up panic.

"The eyes. Go for the eyes, *döttir*," she screams when I fail to deflect her blow. "Block it faster! Counter quick!"

"I can't," I mutter as I narrowly avoid getting hit. "I'm tired. It's time for me to attend to my herbs."

"Forget your herbs," Freydis pants.

We go again. In two quick moves, she bests me and hits me in the back. I swear. She wipes the perspiration off her brow.

"Vinland isn't an easy place to live, *döttir*," she breathes between broken breaths. "You have to learn to be vigilant without my help."

She pulls me up and makes me try the moves again. I hate her for it.

When we are done, my muscles ache and my sword arm is shaking and weak from overuse. Freydis looks battle weary and defeated. Disappointment slithers through her; there are nesting snakes in her eyes.

"Never let your guard down, Anja. You must always keep a knife hidden in your boot to stay prepared." She leans in closely. "The forests in Vinland are full of hidden dangers. Have your bow and arrows ready at all times."

"I promise," I say as I pick up my weapons.

"I am worried for you," she whispers in a ghost breath that spawns a flood of fears.

"I am capable," I say bitterly. She should know by now what I can do. She was the one who taught me the shieldmaiden ways. She was the one who kept me away from the women's room.

"Your *faðir* will marvel at what has become of you."

"He doesn't care," I spit, and the floodgate breaks, and Freydis comes and takes me in her arms, and this time I let her rub my back.

The day before Karlsefni's group is set to sail, Freydis challenges me to a final game of *hnefatafl* in the evening after the chores are done and the thralls have all gone to bed.

"We should offer sacrifices to the gods. May Óðinn guide you and may Thor give you strength," Freydis says as she shuffles a knucklebone into place and squeezes out my knight. I can't seem to concentrate with all the worries in my head.

"'Tis not up to the gods," I sputter. "When I leave Greenland, I'll only have myself to rely on, as you have said."

Freydis stops her play and glances up. "You must place

yourself in the hands of the gods and use your wits at all times. I wouldn't trust Jelani until he proves himself. In any case, when you arrive in Vinland, you'll have to go in search of the Beothuk on your own. I've reconsidered it, and I think you should avoid telling your aunt what you are all about. The woman is always seeing visions and she'll try to discourage you from leaving the settlement of Leifsbidur. May Loki, the trickster god, inspire you to find a way to dupe her."

She knows she is asking me to achieve the impossible.

"Don't fret," she whispers when she sees that I am terrified. She sits straight-backed in her chair with her long fingers hovering over the game board. Head swimming, I relocate my king to avoid getting captured and try to imagine what it was like for *Faðir* living among the Beothuk. I try to picture him with my birth mother, taking meals in the company of her tribe.

"When you arrive in Leifsbidur, you must find my dearest friend, Logatha," Freydis mutters. She looks as though she is seeing ghosts. "If she is still alive, tell her you are Raven's *döttir*. Ask her in secret to help you make the arrangements to rejoin your Beothuk kin. If Snorri is there, he can take you to Achak's village, which lies a good two or three days' walk west of Leifsbidur. Snorri is a Greenlander, and you can trust him. The Beothuk will surely welcome Raven's *döttir* back into their fold."

"Raven's *döttir*?" I whisper carefully as if my birth mother's name is sacred, as if she is my guiding light. I am surprised that Freydis has disclosed the name. I can't seem to find my tongue, to ask the questions I want to ask. I can't seem to see through the blur of welling tears. Something stirs inside, strange and beautiful, formed in whispers, lived in secret, wished for on stars.

"The Beothuk will be surprised to see you, I'm sure of it,"

Freydis continues in a trance. Her voice floats away like a puff of smoke snaking through the air, thinning into wispy tendrils.

I try to picture my Beothuk mother, wondering if I share her looks, wondering if she, too, enjoyed collecting herbs, wondering if she was a healer. Through mist, I slip into a ghost kingdom, a place of "what if" imaginings where I picture the life I would have had if circumstances had been different. When I glance up, the yearning comes again. All I ever wanted was to belong to a family, to wake and be surrounded by siblings, to have both of my parents sitting around the same hearth fire. If the gods have fated it, I will soon be living among my birth mother's kin as a valued member of their tribe.

"Don't fret," Freydis mutters again. She seems distracted and barely present. "The Beothuk are not as threatening as you think. When you tell them who you are, they will take you in and teach you the ways of the ancestors. They will welcome you."

I stare at the *hnefatafl* board and the knucklebone pieces on the table, listening to the silence as Freydis takes her attacker and rolls it between her thumb and index finger. In the firelight, her hands begin to shake. "You needn't be afraid of the Beothuk. They cover their clothes, their weapons, their canoes and even their bodies with red dye extracted from rocks and soil found in great abundance in their land. They even paint the skin of newborns red. Don't be offended if they ask to paint your skin red as well."

Freydis stares down at the gameboard. Then she makes one final, unexpected move and traps my king, and the game is over. She has won at *hnefatafl*, but she will be losing me, her so-called treasure, the *döttir* she stole from a dead woman's bed because her womb was barren and she needed me to make herself whole. Fie on it! She robbed me of a life. She left my *faðir* when I was young and raised me to think that I was hers. She said that *Faðir* always wanted me, that he treasured me despite the distance between us. I was a fool to believe her. I am still a fool for trusting and hoping she can save me from the marriage bed.

Standing quickly, I scurry to place another piece of precious wood on the dying fire. Freydis's red hair pools around her shoulders as she plucks at her woollen shawl, pulling it closed across her chest. In the firelight, my shadow flickers and splits off from Freydis, wavering and ethereal.

"You are Raven's *döttir*. You must remember that," Freydis breathes into the silence.

The name is a gift, a precious pearl I toss into the air. An image takes shape, swirling in the hearth-fire smoke, rising into the rafters. I see my birth mother and the beauty of her smiling eyes, her smiling face.

"I swear to you, you are more beloved than you know. Achak will know what to do," Freydis sighs, but her voice is a swishing wave that washes into a bleak and barren place where nothing grows. Everything suddenly falls into place – the earrings *Faðir* gave me with the etchings of the two ravens with their wings spread out, soaring high across a moonlit sky. These were Raven's earrings, a gift from *Faðir*, the only connection to her that I have left. I am suddenly eager to find this Achak who knew my birth mother well.

"I envy you for being able to go back to Vinland," Freydis whispers in a weary voice. "Óðinn's ravens – Huginn and Muninn – will protect you if you only ask. They bring the wisdom gifts. Look for them in spirit form when you are abroad and know that I have made sacrifices to the gods and sent them to you. If we are lucky, the gods will allow them to report back to me and share all your news. Truly, *döttir*, when you see the raven, know that my spirit is with you."

My thoughts melt into puddles of anger that I can't mop up. This so-called mother is an expert at shielding her heart with toughness, at numbing her pain with work. She has always been reticent about her past and now that I am about to leave, she suddenly has a change of heart? By the gods, what should I ask her?

"I beseech thee, Anja, please remember me in kindness. I tried my best to give you a life."

I bow my head, feeling a discomfort building, a headache coming on.

"May the gods guard and protect you on your journey back to Achak's tribe."

"I need to sleep," I say as I lean forward to snuff out the whale-oil lamp.

"I will miss you, *döttir*."

"You should be able to manage without me. You've managed this place on your own before."

"The place means nothing," Freydis says, but her voice catches.

When I turn around, she shields her face from view. For a moment, I just stare at her. Then I grab my sheepskin throw off the bench and head in the direction of my bedchamber.

That night I toss and turn and hardly sleep. Freydis wakes me at dawn, and we eat in silence as the sun comes up nested in a smattering of pink, wispy clouds. I am suddenly struck by the thought that this will be the last time I watch Freydis putting a fire out, the last time I see her flitting around the longhouse, the last time I sit around her hearth. A lump rises in my throat.

When I pull the longhouse door shut behind me and leave my childhood home one last time, a flock of eiders is foraging by the water and a guillemot is swooping low over the inlet. Mother speaks, but I am too tired and woolly-headed to turn around. I can't – I won't – look behind me. I know I'll miss the byre, the sheep, the chickens in the coop, the thralls, the blacksmith and even the haughty shepherd boys. Thoughts of Helga and her little ones blossom in my head, and I come unspooled fighting off the grief. There are so many things I wanted to say, so many moments we could have shared.

"If the gods look favourably on you, you'll be able to begin again on Vinland shores," Freydis says as she gathers her skirts together and begins to trek up a steep incline. Her loose hair is knotting in the wind. As I trudge behind her, I notice a streak of silvery white in the red.

"Sól is bidding her brother, Máni, the moon, goodnight. 'Tis a good omen," Freydis breathes as she tosses her head back and looks way up. "'Tis rare to see both the sun and moon in the morning sky."

I feel for the raven earrings hidden in my mantle and picture the moon etchings carved on bone. The wind whistles past, and I hear the whispering of the ancestors and picture Raven's face, red-ochred and glistening in the morning sun. Her spirit bids me safe travels back to Vinland shores where her people wait and where Freydis's name is surely whispered with a curse.

~

It's a two-day walk to the beach where the ships are anchored. The pastures are loamy and lush at this time of year, and the birds can't stop chirping and tweeting long enough to eat a worm. My favourite resting spots – the cove where the grey horizon melts into the blue-grey sea where the ice chunks float; the fast-flowing river where Freydis taught me how to fish; the sheep grazing high in the hills; the sunshine highlighting the sparkles in my favourite slab of rock – get tucked away in my heart, but the memories gnaw as though I am walking in a fevered sleep, only half-alive. I cocoon myself in silence while Freydis talks and talks. There is a strangeness between us. Both of us know that my life is over and yet, it begins.

As soon as we begin our descent to the beach where Jelani instructed us to meet him, we see the string of longboats lying in the wet mud of the landwash, anchored to the rocky shore. The ocean stretches far in front of us, flat and glassy, and the beach is a picturesque long stretch of sand. Freydis stops and squints against the glaring sun.

"Listen to the music. The *Midsumarblot* feasting has begun." She tries to sound upbeat, but her voice catches. In the distance, groups of Norsemen are milling around like moving ants. There is a burst of laughter followed by a cow-horn blast.

"Can you smell the meat roasting over the open fire? Perhaps we should wait for nightfall before we approach." She points to the festive tents on the upper banks that flank the shore, and my stomach grumbles noisily.

"If we don't go now, I'll lose my will."

We find Jelani standing by the ship's starboard barking orders to a handful of weary-looking Norsemen who are working hard to load his ship. His longboat is the last in line, anchored far away from Karlsefni's ship.

"You, there, watch that crate!" Jelani yells at a heavy-set Norseman who is attempting to drag a barrel on board. "Be careful not to scrape the strakes."

Another sailor, thin as a blade of grass but strong as a block of ice, hoists a sack of barley over his shoulder. He is grimacing underneath the weight, and there are sweat stains underneath his arms. On the beach there are crates containing chickens and goats to supply us with fresh eggs and milk. The animals are skittish. Their clucks and bleats compete with the screeching seagulls that are circling the ships, catching wind-currents, dropping low.

Freydis picks her way down the embankment. I am slow to follow, alive to the ordeal that awaits me and reluctant to submit entirely to the plan, even though Freydis implores me to hurry. I can hear the singing waves as they swish into shore, beckoning me closer with their gentle rumbles. My eyes snap up when the helmsman shouts:

"Kjaran, take yer beastie away from here and keep her in yer company 'til daybreak. I'll not have that piece of shit mucking up my floorboards!"

In the distance, a merchant is struggling to control a crazed sheep. His arms are waving to and fro. *"Far vel!* I've sold her to thee fair and square, Jelani. She's all yours to manage now."

"Come back here, you piece of goose shit," Jelani bellows harshly.

The merchant is a fat man with a full beard who is wearing elaborate jewellery to show off his wealth. He fixes Jelani with an ugly stare. "With the gods as my witnesses, you promised to purchase her," he bellows so loudly that his jewellery jingles. He backs away from the starboard side where Jelani stands. "For the love of Óðinn, I've given thee no cause to renege on the deal. 'Tis as I said. I warned you fairly. Now throw me down the axe you promised, for I must be gone."

"You seagull-brained, conniving bastard," Jelani gripes impatiently. "I won't pay for damaged goods. Look at that animal farting and voiding. For gods' sake, man, we haven't even left Greenland and that creature is a nuisance. I'll not take yer blasted sheep with me all the way to Vinland shores. She wouldn't last a day at sea."

"I had no knowledge that this sheep would be so skittish around water," the merchant shouts defiantly. "There are witnesses here who would say that you purchased her willingly. Now give me the fine axe you promised and let me pass. There is a festival on, and I have people waiting."

"You have people waiting!" Jelani screams indignantly as he vigorously rubs his balding head. "You brainless twit. Take yer beastie with you, or I'll have my men slit yer throat."

"You cheat!" the merchant screams as he goes to reach for the tether that trails behind the sheep. Without warning, the beast kicks back and narrowly misses hitting the merchant in the eye. In the process a spray of sand flies up, and Kjaran yells so loudly that two muscled Norsemen stop their work and stare.

"I'll tell the other traders about what you did to me," the merchant rants. "Forsooth, I'll ruin your reputation before this day ends. When you return to Greenland, I swear this: no one will want to trade with you."

Jelani tosses a low-throated chuckle before he catapults over the gunwales and runs at the merchant with such agility and speed that all of us are caught off guard. The merchant's eyes pop wide as Jelani pulls back and pummels him with such a violent swing that the merchant is knocked to the ground. There is a high-pitched shriek, a bark, a shout.

When Jelani goes to deliver another punch, several Norsemen with muscled shoulders step in to hold him back.

"You'll pay for this, helmsman!" Kjaran shouts as he struggles to right himself and shake off the sand.

One of Jelani's men darts forward and grabs hold of the guiding rope to prevent the forgotten sheep from running free, but the animal is agitated and it shits again. Kjaran is halfway up the hill when Jelani releases a foul-mouthed curse and loses his footing and narrowly misses falling into a heap of steaming dung.

"May Óðinn's eight-legged steed shit in your path, and may you slip in the dung!"

The merchant disappears over the embankment and the music swells. Freydis doesn't waste any time. She ploughs ahead with the clear intention of reaching Jelani before he becomes too preoccupied. I scramble after her with a sickened feeling in my gut.

As soon as Jelani sees us, his face softens. "Seems as though your thrall's first task will be to attend to this cursed sheep," he begins. His shirt is all askew; his eyes look crazed. He draws in air and rubs his head. "The animal apparently hates the water."

Freydis clucks her tongue and shakes her head before releasing a bloated sigh. "You are a fine helmsman, I can tell," she panders. "It appears you have expertise in loading ships, but you need some help taming skittish beasts. Trust me, this sheep will settle and get used to being on a swaying ship within three days of setting sail. In my experience, the animals always do."

Jelani smiles. His dimples pop. "Good woman, take your thrall and go enjoy the festivities," he says in a tender voice. "She is not on duty yet, and she won't be needed until tomorrow at the break of dawn."

I lift my chin and stare at him. *What a pompous ass*, I think as I snag a breath and find my buttery voice: "If it pleases you, helmsman, I'll put myself in charge of this poor sheep on my return. I can see you've had enough of her."

Freydis smiles. "Jelani, I wish you well tomorrow. May Thor's hammer protect you. I'll offer many sacrifices to the gods for your safe passage through rough waters."

"Much thanks, my good woman," Jelani says distractedly. He flicks a glance up the bank. "All this talk of gods is making me weary. Don't be fooled. The gods use us as pawns. They like to laugh at our expense. Even now they have determined the outcome of this *vyking* voyage to Vinland shores. Truly, I tell you, don't make a sacrifice. It would be a waste."

I steal a glance at Freydis and see a heavy scowl moving into the folds of her forehead. She always worries when anyone snubs the gods. It is insulting, she says. It brings bad luck, she thinks.

Jelani is oblivious. After he takes my gear, he climbs back into the longboat and waves us off. Without another word, Freydis grabs my arm and steers me to the far end of the beach where there are numerous tidal pools hidden amongst the rocks.

We find a relatively dry spot nestled between two gigantic slabs of slate-grey rock that shelter us from the cold blowing off the sea. Shivering, I pull my woollen mantle tightly closed. Freydis does the same. She is still agitated when she takes her finger and begins to draw in the sand.

"If you want your scythe to stay sharp," she says without looking up, "carve these signs on the sharpening stone with your knife."

When I say nothing, Freydis sighs. "I shan't sleep knowing that Jelani has rebuked the gods. It could go badly for all of you.

Give me your palm, *döttir*, so I can draw a stave to keep you safe at sea."

I look out across the water and feel the salty breeze on my skin as she takes up my hand and traces symbols on my flesh.

"Remember all that I've told you, *döttir*. Vinland is a vast wilderness, and it is easy to get lost. Always keep track of the positioning of the sun. This will help orient you in the trees so you can find the Beothuk settlement which is located directly west of Leifsbidur."

The cold digs its way into my bones. Above our heads, a stream of smoke from the feasting tents spirals into the sky, carrying with it a whiff of roasting meats. My stomach rumbles; my insides weep.

"I have bread and cheese," Freydis says when she sees me gazing up the hill. She adjusts the hood of her mantle as the panpipes mingle with the sound of a trilling flute and the booming thumps of a hide-covered drum. "I should go and fetch us something to eat from the tents."

"It isn't safe," I mumble. "Someone will see you and there will be questions."

Freydis sits so closely that I feel her warmth seeping through her mantle. Without intending to, I conjure imaginings of my real mother with a red-ochred face.

"You'll be all right," Freydis says, and the calmness of her voice startles me. "Do you want to hear Óðinn's saga one last time?"

I barely nod.

When she begins, the rhythm of her voice stirs up memories as dry as the marsh reeds rattling in an autumn breeze. As I listen carefully to the rumble of her voice, the way she stresses words, the way her tone grows softer before it builds again, I try to savour the memories of days gone by. I see our farm, the life we shared, the daily grind of milking cows and herding sheep, the evenings spent sitting around a smoking fire. The stories shared.

"Óðinn's quest for wisdom – his sacrifice – was honourable, but it cost him an eye," I sigh deeply when her saga ends.

"You can think about his losses or his gains," Freydis whispers as she takes up my hand in hers. I feel a strangeness in my chest, as though there is a new aching wound, a ripped-open scab that is bleeding and bleeding. Freydis draws in air and finds her voice: "If we dwell on the losses, there is only sadness and regret, but if we think about the sacrifice as a way forward to seek some gain, we can endure the pain. Leaving is the only way, *döttir*."

The whispers of the sea swell, and something deep inside me cracks. I feel the grief swelling in my chest, begging to be released.

"Hail Thor, son of Óðinn," Freydis whispers quietly. Her voice falters. "O Lord of the Hammer, may my *döttir* honour your legacy as we prove once more that we will not be broken."

The noise from the festive gathering – the drums, the songs accompanied by the *lur*, a burst of laughter – carries me into the world of sleep. As I sink down, I become an oyster-catcher using my strong bill to smash open molluscs on the rocks. I become a raven with sleek, black wings who swallows Sól and becomes her *döttir*, who sits on Óðinn's shoulders to pass the time.

Give me the raven earrings, some spirit walker says as it tries to rouse me. I fight my way through the fog, a white swirl of mist that envelops everything, but I have a hard time surfacing. I hear a soft, low voice, and the cadence pulls me in, and I suffer from a melancholy that keeps me stuck in mud-puddles of drowsiness. Freydis is asking for my leather pouch. She holds out her hand,

and there is resistance until I remember that *Faðir*'s earrings are hidden deep inside the pocket of my mantle, hidden far away from the groping hands of a mother I hardly know. She insists on taking up my pouch and inspecting the contents – my sewing needle, my fire steel in its ornate mount, my hunting knife.

"Some Beothuk tribes are nomadic. Finding Raven's people might be like trying to find a lamb in a blizzard," she whispers into the night, and I snap awake, shivering.

"What if they have moved their village for the summer?" The words slip out, mumbled, through a yawn.

"Do not venture through the wilderness on your own. It is too dangerous," Freydis says in a solemn voice. "Remember to ask for Snorri. He has long been in the service of our family here in Greenland." I sit up straight. Freydis pays no heed. She is not herself. "As I said before, Snorri will know where to find the Beothuk. I'm sure of it."

She does not tell me what to do if he is dead. She does not tell me what to do if I can't find my birth mother's people or if I can't find this place called Leifsbidur. In the hazy light, I see only the darkness of a hard journey, only the struggles I will face while I am all alone.

"I don't want to go," I suddenly blurt out, panicking.

"I can't come with you, *döttir*. I need to protect our lands from falling into Thorvard's hands. I need to protect your uncle, Leif. Thorvard will try to accuse him of being behind the plan to set you free."

"I'm scared," I say pathetically.

"I know," she whispers almost inaudibly. She looks away. "I should have sent a red tapestry with a runic message for you to carry to Achak. O gods, what does it matter? My gift to him will be you. With your easy temperament, you would have made some Greenland farmer or noble *skald* or talented musician a happy man. You could have gifted me with grandchildren in my old age."

"You should have told me about *Faðir* right from the start," I manage, trying to force the iron weight of terror off my chest.

Freydis sucks in air. The fingers of her left hand work their way into the folds of her *hangerock*. The tide is washing in. The *midsumar* sun, which shares the sky with a sick-looking moon, is blurring orange, flaring red. "Before you were born, I lost your *faðir*. I didn't want to lose you, too."

The words slide out as easily as a water snake slides through sand, and we sit there looking out across the sea where a patch of fog is rolling in. The *Midsumarblot's* festivities are at their height; the crowd emits a boisterous cheer. Directly above our heads, we hear the swish of whispers tangled up in snatches of half-word mumbles.

"Let's move you back to Jelani's ship," Freydis mutters as she glances up. She places a finger to her lips and motions for me to collect my pack as she holds out a hand and helps me up.

In silence, she nudges me out of the alcove of rocks that shelters us from the incoming tide. The water level has risen so much that we are forced to remove our foot coverings and wade through the water to make it to the other side of the beach where the boats are anchored. In the distance, Jelani's longboat is bobbing gently in the shallows with its silent hulk rising out of the water. It sports a massive, frightening figurehead in the shape of a dragon that has empty, wooden eyes and flaring nostrils and a curled tongue.

"Sit over there against that rock in front of Jelani's ship," Freydis says impatiently. She quickly points. "I have something I must do."

The hazy light from the midnight sun casts eerie light across the beach. "I'll come," I mutter sleepily.

She shakes her head, but she seems to hesitate, as if she has been dreading this storm-cloud moment that sits between us, hovering. "I don't deserve understanding or forgiveness, Anja, but I swear by the gods that I've spent my entire life trying to protect you from the howling wolves Loki was constantly placing in my path. I have sacrificed everything, and I would gladly do it all again if it meant I could keep you here and change what has come to pass and bring your *faðir* home to us." She takes a breath. Her eyes are vibrant orbs in the wash of eerie light leaking from a sickened midnight sun.

"On the day you were born, the moon shone down, and I dried my tears and you gave me life again. Truly, you were a gift from the gods, more precious to me than any sparkling rock mineral or snow-bear pelt. All through my life, I have loved you fiercely, loved you bravely, loved you when it was hard to do so on my own. I am grateful, my *döttir*, for it was you who filled the cracks in my broken heart and taught me how to love again."

She pauses. The weakened sun picks up the red brilliance of her hair. I close my eyes and feel the tickle of the midnight sun fondling my skin and casting flickering shadows across my eyes.

"Now that the time has come, I don't know if I can relinquish you," Freydis mumbles from somewhere far away.

"You must," I say. The wind is cold against my back. My stomach grumbles. My legs feel weak.

"My bones are getting old, *döttir*. I am not sure if I can bear to say *Far vel*."

"You are Freydis Eiriksdöttir," I say. "Your blood is thick. Your heart is tough."

She tosses a glance my way. "You have your mother in you, Anja Freydisdöttir."

There is a feeling that threatens to break my soul, a wildness in me that rises up, something in her look that almost breaks me. She doesn't deserve my pity after all of her dishonesty. Even now, she believes her lies are the truth.

"If your *grandfaðir* had only lived," Freydis continues in a voice that tremble-cracks, "he would have protected us. I know it, Anja." A sudden, cold ocean breeze whistle-flutters across the rocks. In the dead of night, the shadows dance across the beach.

"I don't hate you for the choices you made," I manage in a careful voice.

She studies me and a breath slips out.

"Wait here, *döttir*," she says. Her voice breaks apart as she looks at me, as if she is seeing me for the first time, as if she is remembering the child in me, as if she is pulling for every little memory, as if I am already gone from her. As if she is no longer.

Chapter Eight

GRASS SHADOWS

I watch her slipping into the grasses lining the bank where the silence sits and swallows everything. A midnight sun is dribbling oranges across the placid surface of the sea, spilling speckles of muted light across the row of ghosted Viking ships. With a heavy yawn, I bow my head and draw my mantle closed. When I finally fall into a restless sleep, I dream of snow bears and dragons rearing up with fiery breath. In my sleep, I am helpless to defend myself. A soundless scream escapes, and I am yanked back down with stardust, sliding down moonbeams flecked with silver and twinkling sparkles. In spirals, I fall into the moment, blinded and disorientated.

Behind me there is a sudden noise.

"Behold, if it isn't my little thrall, Anja," Jelani whistles low. He is so drunk, he is swaying like alder branches in the wind. I duck behind my rock, and still my heartbeats, snag a breath.

"I've been looking for you for quite some time," Jelani slurs when he spots me. The helmsman, smelling like dead fish and wine, holds an ornately decorated sword in his right hand and a flask of spirits in his left. When he stops to take a swig, I jump up, as agitated as a skittish colt. In two quick strides, he has me locked against the rock.

"By Óðinn's beard, I've a suit against thee, thrall," he says in a drunken drawl. "Have you not heard what the villagers say about you and your witch of a mother?"

"There is no truth in that," I snap, wiping his spittle from my face.

"Are you merry?" he blubbers weirdly as he dances around me. "I am merry 'cause you will marry!" He holds up his bottle and takes another swig. When he turns, I have just enough room to dodge around him, but his limbs are suddenly agile, his reflexes quick.

"You've deceived me, you little wench," he mutters. With a heavy, unexpected grunt, he reaches forward and yanks my hair and pulls me back so violently that I wince in terror, yelp in pain. "You wanted to avoid marrying the Corpse-Lodin widower, and you thought you'd escape by leaving Greenland shores on board my ship? May the gods curse you, you little fox! Your mother betrayed me with her serpent's tongue. Forsooth, her fangs are venomous!"

"You've got it wrong," I stammer.

"Corpse-Lodin was betrayed, Thorvard of Gardar was cheated, and I have been made the fool!"

"Mother didn't mean …"

"I'll make them pay me for the return of you or perhaps I'll sell your body off. With a chunk of silver ingot in my hands, I can do many things. Poor little fool! It must come as a surprise that you got caught."

I try to wriggle free, but he blocks me.

"I was duped, you lying mammet," he snarls as his spine snaps straight. "I swear that you and your slut of a mother will be punished for your deceit. By the gods, I'll have the two of you tried at the *Althing* and banished to the north. By Óðinn's beard, I'll not be treated as though I am a knave. *Neinn!* I'll show you what I am made of. You will fear me by the time I'm done."

Jelani's handsome face is mottled red. I can smell the stench of a sickly sweetness on his breath. He sways a little and pulls me with him. I have to grip his elbows to keep upright.

"Your *faðir* seems desperate to have you matched," Jelani announces to the sky. There is a sudden chill, a knowing deep inside my gut.

"For the love of Thor, I don't understand why so many would happily kiss that braggart's arse. Thorvard of Gardar has boasted about your bride price all evening long."

He lets me go so that he can retrieve his flask and take another swig. In that moment, I quickly scoop up my pack that lies forgotten in the sand.

"Don't wriggle away from me, you little mouse," Jelani yells. His face contorts into a scowl and he steps in front of me to block my escape. "You are betrothed, are you not?"

I try to keep my face as still as stone.

"You treat me like goose shit and expect not to be held accountable? I think not! You ingrate! You disobedient, untrustworthy girl! By the gods, it makes me mad. Your *faðir*'s only care was to marry you off to a wealthy man, yet you scheme to escape the union he arranged?"

In a breath, he has the tip of his brandished sword pointed at my neck, and I pull back in shock, reaching for my hidden knife. Jelani lunges, but his aim goes wide. Instinctively, I half-duck and then my feet scramble to right myself and I start to run.

Despite his drunkenness, Jelani grabs for me, and his grip is strong and powerful. When he twists my arm behind my back, there is a surge of stink, and I deliver a backward kick that catches Jelani off guard. He yelps in pain and I kick again, and he swears and falls onto the hard-packed sand.

I hear the drum of my heart thudding as my hands, slick with sweat, fumble in an effort to grip my knife and flick my mantle behind my back. I am sharply focused, meticulous in the way I move, alert when the world around me suddenly stills. I catch movement in my periphery – a shadow morphing into Freydis's form as she emerges from the shrubs running the length of the upper banks.

"Move!" she yells as she runs towards us with a two-handed grip on a sharpened spear aimed directly at Jelani's heart.

The helmsman's eyebrows arch in shock. Frantically, I dodge into the sand as Freydis allows her spear to reach the full extent of the shaft. When she drives her spear into Jelani's chest and impales him, the force of her thrust is so powerful that the helmsman is lifted off his feet. He tries to snag one last breath, gurgled and wet, before his body crashes to the ground and he spills blood across the rocks, turning the shallow tide pools crimson. Freydis is as quick as a jackrabbit. In a frenzy, she rushes forward and begins tugging to extract her weapon from Jelani's chest. There is a burbling sound, a little hiss of air. For a moment, all goes deathly quiet, deathly still.

With my senses pinging, I begin to register the pops of Freydis's muffled voice, the faint whispers of the waves washing into shore then sloshing back. The volume increases. Freydis's voice becomes sparks of lightning through thunder-booms, heaving with Thor's anger.

"Anja, quick! Help me get this helmsman into a sitting position. We must lean his body against your sleeping rock."

Freydis rushes towards me with a strange fierceness in her face, a twitching in her right eye. When she pushes me with her bloodied hand, I am still half-dazed, in the grip of imagined frost giants.

"*Döttir!*" Freydis snarls as fiercely as a she-devil. In shock, I stare at her.

"You murdered him!"

A darkness envelops her. The villagers' accusations fill my head, and I see her as a she-wolf. Perhaps she is a Midgard Serpent in female form.

"Go grab his drinking flask. We'll place it in his lap," she orders. The smell of death oozes from Jelani's corpse – the stench of urine, the tangy smell of blood.

Freydis pushes me, and I stumble forward to manage what she asks. There is a ripe, rotting stench coming from somewhere up the beach, a rancid, seaweed smell. Soon the carrion eaters will come to eat the helmsman's flesh. Already the seagulls are screeching wildly and sweeping low.

Together, we drag the body into place, lugging and tugging and grunting with the effort. His blood-soaked, sand-stained shirt is salted against his skin; my hands are sticky from his gore. Freydis plucks Jelani's money pouch, full of silver, from his kaftan and turns to me.

"We might get lucky. When they find him, Kjaran might be blamed for his death. We will make it look like he is the murderer."

The memories of Freydis's warrior cry ring ghost-like in my ears. Glancing up, I see the meagre light thrown from the midnight sun bleeding across the glassy seas, and something tentacles across my skin. Freydis has killed a man. She has killed a man! For that, she will be banished to the north where she will freeze to death or slowly starve or die of loneliness in a world of white.

The panic bubbles, blisters, pops. And me? I'll be married off to a fattened worm, a warty dragon, a hungry beast. Thorvard of Gardar will see to it. In fact, he will insist on it.

My legs crumple, and I throw up.

"For the love of Thor, hurry up," Freydis mutters as I wipe my mouth off with a handful of grass, slick with dew.

"Sheep's piss! Our lives are ruined," Freydis moans pathetically. "You won't escape the marriage bed."

I puke again.

The midnight sun crests above a hilly peak. I lift my chin. There are splotches of dried blood on my apron skirt, dark black splatterings along my sleeve. The horror bleeds inside my chest, and I sink down into the dew-soaked grass and claw at myself in agony.

"O gods, my *döttir*! What have I done?" Freydis wails as she kneels beside me. Her breath is hot against my face. "Corpse-Lodin's sons are swines. They will misuse you, and then it will be his turn."

"My fate is sealed," I croak, and the thought punches, an choke on blood.

Freydis's shadow dances in the sh
speak, but I silence her with n
her eyes.

"Anja, this can't be happenii
won't allow it." The midnight sun
into the sea. A sudden thought dev
flickers and sputters like a drowning

"I know of another way for me to leave this place," I breathe.

We hear a noise behind us. Freydis quickly stands. Her eyes dart behind her, sharp and hard. The path is empty, ghosted only by grass shadows.

"There is a thrall whom we must find," I whisper in a halting voice. "She has a son. He is Vinland bound against his will, and his mother yearns to keep him home. If we can find him, I might be able to take his place."

"Take his place?" Freydis repeats, her eyebrows rising. I barely nod.

"I could pretend that I am he," I mumble.

Freydis stares at me. Her face is a map of worry lines. "I would kill again to keep you safe."

"I know," I whisper solemnly.

The midnight sun emerges from behind a mess of clouds and shines down weakly on the two of us. I feel as if something dark and deformed inside of me has been plucked out, and I can finally see. I have met Freydis's shieldmaiden, her warrior self. I now know the woman who raised me. I now know my worth.

Chapter Nine

KNUCKLEBONES

We have the gods on our side. That is what Freydis says when we finally find the group of tents belonging to Thorvard's thralls. Most of the tents are dark, but we hear voices coming from a few. Freydis and I crouch down low behind a boulder in the tall grasses that line the field. In the dim light, I catch sight of someone hauling water into a tent.

"Praise Óðinn, I think it's her," I whisper with a knowing rippling through me, faster than any startled garter snake. A youth scampers behind the woman, clinging to her in the shadows.

"Take care, Anja," Freydis cautions as she tugs on my mantle to prevent me from bolting forth. "There are others who are still awake, and we don't want to be recognized."

The grasses swish as a gust of wind blows through the field. Then all goes still. With my heart thudding, I grasp Freydis's hand, and the two of us creep out of our hiding spot. When we reach the back of the thrall's tent, we try to push ourselves into the shadows as we listen to a woman muttering to a boy inside. Freydis flicks a worried glance over her shoulder and gestures for me to approach the front entrance that faces the festive grounds. Just as I am about to pop out, a Norseman walks by, shuffling his feet and dragging up a cloud of filmy dust, chalked orange in the midnight sun.

Freydis tenses and pulls me back. At the end of the line, the Norseman turns around and begins patrolling past the thrall's tent once again. Inside, the voices stop. I hold my breath. As soon as he is gone, Freydis fingers me in the back. "Go!" she whispers urgently.

We slink around to the front entrance where the two of us are fully exposed. Across the way, there is another tent. In the pre-dawn stillness, a shiver crawls up and down my spine, and my vision clouds. In my agitation, I almost trip.

"Who goes there?" someone asks from inside the tent in a voice as dry as rustling reeds in wind. I take a breath.

"By the grace of Thor and Óðinn, we have searched high and low to find you," I begin. "We understand there is a boy who does not wish to go *a vyking* with Karlsefni, the helmsman who is set to sail to Vinland on this very day. If this is true, we have a plan to keep him here on Greenland shores."

Slowly, the tent flap opens. A head pops out. The thrall looks scared. Behind her, we hear fierce whisperings coming from a lanky youth with a black head of hair. He is protective of his mother when he steps out and glares at us, owl-like. There is a sheen of sweat on his upper lip.

"Please let us in," I plead.

The woman pushes her son aside. Her facial bruises have turned an ugly purplish-black, and one side tooth is missing. She hastily beckons us both inside.

"My name is Anja Freydisdöttir," I begin in a shaky voice.

"Good lady, we know who you are," the woman lisps as though her tongue is swollen. In close quarters, her smell is strong.

"May Óðinn be with all of us," Freydis murmurs. She pulls the tent flap shut and rapidly blinks to adjust to the dim light inside. "I come to ask a favour and give a gift."

The thrall's eyes flick between us. I clear my throat. "I'm betrothed to Olafur Corpse-Lodin, a man whom I do not wish to marry."

Freydis slips her hand into the crook of my arm, and the boy's brows constrict.

"Your owner, Thorvard of Gardar, has arranged for my betrothal, but I wish to break the contract without him knowing. The only way I can do that is to sail to Vinland on board one of Karlsefni's longboats."

The thrall's eyes come to rest on the black, bloody splotches on my apron skirt. Beside me, I can feel Freydis shaking, though the heat in here seeps into my skin.

"We've heard tell that Thorvard's treatment of his thralls is dishonourable," Freydis says. "Thorvard's treatment of my *döttir* has been just as harsh. He betrothed her to a wicked man, a drunken sloth with brutes for sons. Dear woman, my *döttir* will soon be stuck in an abusive marriage unless we work together to save our children from their respective fates."

The thrall says nothing. The orange shadows from the midnight sun dance diagonally across her face.

"We have a far-fetched plan, a daring one," Freydis continues, breathing hard. "Your son could save my *döttir* and simultaneously, he could save himself. If my *döttir* exchanges places with your son, she can escape the marriage bed and sail away to Vinland shores and your son would be free to stay here in Greenland."

The thrall's face stays blank.

"You must think we are visiting from *Folvang*, the field of dead people, but this is not the case," I rasp, glancing sideways at Freydis.

"You and your son could stay together," Freydis intones. "You would not have to relinquish him to the sea monster, Jormungandr."

The thrall's eyes tear up, her face crumples and her shoulders begin to shake.

"By what magic have you come?" the thrall's son queries as his mother's knees give out. He half-catches, half-squats beside her as he strokes her back. He glances up. "You are the *goði*'s niece, are you not?"

"*Já*," I say. "I am Anja Freydisdöttir."

"What madness is this?" he asks as he tries to help his mother up. "Taking the place of a thrall won't be easy. You would be beaten to death if you were discovered. As for me, I'd be killed."

"It will not come to that," Freydis quickly reassures. The boy's mother glances up. Her face is as grey as newly shorn, washed wool.

"It is almost time for the ships to sail," Freydis pleads. Outside the early morning birds have begun to chirp. Their rippling trills come in short, loud bursts. "One of you will need to be on board a longboat before the sun is fully up."

The boy's voice hasn't changed. When I look at him, there is sudden, overwhelming fear, and I feel the beginnings of a headache coming on. How are we going to dupe Karlsefni's crew? I look nothing like the boy standing in front of me.

"This is a daring plan," the thrall begins. She can't stop her blubbering.

"Daybreak will soon be here, and we have much to do. Prithee, tell us, where was your boy told to go? What was he told to bring?"

"I was told to report to Valbrand, but I have not met him," the thrall's son says. "His longboat is the third ship in the line."

"'Tis fortune's fool that you've not met your helmsman," Freydis murmurs, but her tone is sharp. "Tell us all you know so that we can plan."

"I was dragged in front of the great Karlsefni, the man himself, and told to report to Valbrand on the morning following the Midsummer feast. Thorvard will punish me if I don't show."

Freydis mutters to herself as she peers through the tent crack. When she turns back, she reaches for the thrall's shaking, work-hardened hands. "If your boy has not been seen by his helmsman – this Valbrand – it is likely that our ruse will work."

The thrall looks scared. Air ladders up her nose. "Praise Loki, but it will be difficult to dupe the helmsman. Your *döttir* wears a robe and shift."

"It's not hard to switch things around," Freydis sputters. "My *döttir* has her own deerskin breeches and woollen socks and leather boots. As for her hair, we will have to cut it off."

The tent suddenly feels too hot. The air is tight. There are too many of us cramped inside a tiny space. Freydis disentangles herself from me, and my legs begin to shake.

"My good woman, if you could hand me your sharpest tool, I'll cut off my *döttir*'s locks right now and stop worrying about the way she looks. Hair is not worth the fuss I've given it in the past."

Almost instantly the thrall passes a dull-looking blade into

Freydis's hands. I close my eyes. "Hair will grow," she whispers softly in my ear. With a few quick snips, my hair is gone.

"Time is passing," the boy pipes up.

When the thrall parts the tent flap to better see, the sunrays creep inside and jab my chest like thrusting spears. The thrall draws in air through her broken teeth. "What of my son? Prithee, what is to become of him?"

"I'll take your boy back with me to my farm where I'll give him food and shelter and work to do as my thrall. I'll do all this if you never mention that we traded children, not even if Thorvard threatens you. It would be our ruin."

The boy scrutinizes me as if he is trying to ascertain who will bear the greater loss and who will be able to comfort Freydis best. Already I am strangely jealous.

"Mark my words," Freydis announces to the boy, "I'll treat you as my trusted stable-hand. Occasionally, I'll even try to arrange for you to meet your mother in secret, but the opportunities might be rare. From this day forward, you must never come looking for your mother. It would bring suspicion on my house, and I don't want trouble, do you hear?"

The boy nods, and I release the breath I've been holding. I see her warrior heart. She would peck through ice to protect me even though we don't share the same blood.

"'Tis honourable, this guardianship you offer," the boy's mother mutters. There is a noise outside. Freydis's eyes grow wide.

"Thorvard's other thralls are up," the boy whispers almost inaudibly.

"'Tis too early," the thrall moans.

"Let's exit out the back," the boy says as he frantically scrambles to unhook the tent peg from the ground. He glances out before directing us to crawl underneath. I am the first to wiggle out and smell the summer air.

There is no one stirring in the tent next door, but all of us are on high alert as we carefully make our way down the bank to Valbrand's ship. Already there is movement on the beach, a commotion brewing around Jelani's ship. I stuff the panic down and turn to Freydis who hastily reaches out to anoint me with the sign of Thor's hammer.

"I will miss you, *döttir*," she says with a shaky smile. Her voice wavers like the rolling sea, and I taste the salt of one lone tear.

"You taught me how to fight and how to be strong enough to stand alone," I whisper into the crisp morning air that smells of budding flowers and growing things.

"Be strong enough to stand alone, be yourself enough to stand apart, and be wise enough to stand together with your kin when the time comes," she whispers urgently. "May the gods go with you. They will be your protectors now."

I bow my head. My legs won't move. We hear the sound of a Viking horn echoing across the beach, through the grasslands, up the path.

"Go, that is Valbrand's call," the thrall's son urges in a desperate voice.

"Go you must, *döttir*! All will be lost if you stay too long."

I turn, and Freydis's fragrance lingers: the smell of earth and sun and wool and sheep. I hear her voice: *Show no fear. Adapt. Know your weaknesses. Survive each day.*

At the entrance to the beach, I am forced to crawl over washed-up pieces of driftwood, and I worry that my knees will buckle, that I'll lose my nerve, that somehow I'll betray us all.

When I look back, Freydis is no longer. The path is empty. The grasses sway.

It is not long before I find myself seated on the planks of Valbrand's longboat with several pale-faced young men who smell like fish and sweat and wet sheepskin throws. When the stern-faced helmsman unexpectedly begins barking out orders to the oarsmen, he startles me, and I jump. Someone sniggers, someone farts.

Valbrand is of medium height with a foreboding appearance. He wears a musk-ox pelt lined with wolf fur around his shoulders, and when he commands his men to row the longboat forward into the fjord, the fibres of it shimmy in the ocean breeze.

When the festive tents are only a smudge ghosting the horizon, I feel for *Faðir*'s raven earrings and my breath catches, and I release a rumbling snort that morphs into a wet, gurgled laugh. I am in Loki's clutches until one of the overseers – a short, burly taskmaster by the name of Berger – kicks my foot.

"Hush, boy!"

Another burst of laughter pushes its way up from my chest and curls into chortles before escaping through my nose. The overseer throws me an evil eye.

"Valbrand will throw you overboard if you keep that up."

Digging my nails into my palms, I force myself to stop as the ship rolls over another wave. The wind is chilly. My back is cold. The shore begins to blur. The cliffs look small. A group of Norsemen hoist the greased and well-oiled wadmal sails. Soon we are sailing at a fast-paced clip with the sails billowing wildly in the blustery breeze. There are two majestic auks soaring overhead, accompanying us out to sea. Berger points them out, but his voice is ripped away by the wailing wind as the floorboards groan and the mast begins to creak.

Staring down at the churning sea, I can't seem to stop the shakes. I see *Faðir*'s face in the depths – Freydis's face, bold in strife. Memories of Jelani's dead body, of Freydis's spear, of the risks she took, of her sacrifice. The images hover like insect clouds. I have lost the only home I have ever known. I have lost my guardians, the only clansmen who knew my tale, the only kin to profit from protecting my lonesome bones.

As the longboats sail forward, I get lost in the monotony of staring out across the sea and trying to spot pods of humpback whales heading up the fjords. Herds of caribou roam the bluffs and flocks of seabirds fly in formation close to shore. I need to crawl across men to do my chores, and I always struggle under the weight of the drinking pails. When they ask me to milk the goats and muck out their crates, I am barely able to manage the grief that swells.

Berger, the overseer, is a suspicious taskmaster. His scrutiny feels as unpleasant as stepping in dog shit. One day as we are sailing under clear-blue skies, he confronts me while I am eating my noonday meal.

"How come the peach fuzz on your chin still hasn't grown, boy?"

I steal a glance at Almarr, a stout, muscular, sun-burned Norseman who is hunched over his trencher eating noisily.

"What say you, boy? By Ýmir's frosty balls, yer mother must've been a washerwoman who scrubbed yer young cheeks way too much when you were small. Seems strange that nothin' grows there on yer cheeks."

An uneasy feeling destroys my appetite. Almarr lifts his head. "Leave him be," he says as he swallows a mouthful.

The overseer tugs on his bushy beard. "Is it true that Valbrand promised all his thralls freedman status just for sailing with him to the *Skraeling* lands?"

"He promised me," Almarr grunts as he spits out a piece of bone and picks it up to inspect it with his dirty fingers.

"He should keep his thralls like he keeps livestock," Berger smirks. "With his animals, he works them hard until butchering season."

"That's what you do with yer woman, right, Berger? You work her hard," a Norseman named Gisli guffaws.

"Harder," Berger retorts. His smile reveals a missing side tooth.

When he lowers himself into an easy squat, he looks me squarely in the eye. "By Óðinn's beard, I bet you haven't had a woman yet. Perhaps we could give 'im Sigrid tonight when we hit landfall?"

Sigrid, one of the three women on board, is sitting to my right. She is a homely looking, tight-lipped thrall.

"It's my turn to get a piece of Sigrid's flesh tonight," Gisli barks.

Just then, the watchman shouts: "Ice! Dead ahead!" In the chaos, Gisli and Berger scramble up. When they are out of earshot, I reach out to hold Sigrid back. She flinches, startled.

"I've some herbs for you to stop a pregnancy. You'll need to put them in your tea," I say as I dig out the pouch I wear around my waist.

Her face looks hard, and I am suddenly wary.

"Trust me, Sigrid. My former master taught me the ways of a healer."

"I see," she says, but her voice sounds dead and flat.

"I want to help."

She stares at me. All around us the men are shouting and heaving ropes and manoeuvring sails. "Leave me be," she mutters. "It would be best."

We stay on board that night, anchored in some pretty cove bordering massive cliffs. The ale is flowing heavily, and the men get drunk. Berger asks me why I refuse to piss overboard, and I ignore the man's vulgarity. Afterwards, when the hour grows late, I hear the sound of shuffling feet and a muffled scream, a body being dragged across the deck. In the shadows, Sigrid moans in terror and begins to beg for someone to come and help.

"Why aren't you in line for that stupid cow?" Berger asks. I glance around. Gisli and three of his friends are taking turns mounting Sigrid, who lies naked beside a pile of ropes. My stomach sours. Without thinking, I stand up.

Berger winks at me from across the fire. "Go easy, boy," he guffaws. "If you're too eager, you might release your seed prematurely. It's less enjoyable that way."

I turn my back on him and stare out to sea, feeling a rush of heat in my cheeks. When Sigrid cries out again, I brace myself against the gunwales, listening to the lapping water hit the strakes.

"Will it be your first time, then?" Berger asks. His voice cuts sharp, and I turn back. Berger's image wavers in the smoky air rising from the cooking fire on board. Beside him, Valbrand yawns. I feel my fists ball up, a sweat break out.

"I find little value in womanizing while I'm out *a vyking*,"

Valbrand says in a sleepy voice. He tosses a glance down the deck before taking another swig from his drinking horn.

Sigrid screams again.

My gaze focuses on the endless stretch of ocean that sparkles in the moonlight. Behind me, Berger snorts. "Listen to them coupling. By the gods, I miss my wife."

"Piss off, Berger," Valbrand growls as he suddenly springs awake. "Boy, stop staring. You'll go cross-eyed. Either take your place in line or take the night-time watch."

"I'll take the watch," I mumble, and Berger frowns.

"Leave off, Berger," the helmsman grunts. "The boy is young. He has never sailed before. He'll find another chance to become a man."

That night I have difficulty settling. Memories of Sigrid's whimpers come in waves, attacking like stone shards piercing flesh, like carrion birds plucking out human eyes. Her screams mix in with the singsong voice of the goddess, Freya, whose stone statue sits in the rafters of the longhouse back on Greenland shores:

You have disappointed me, child. You have failed to defend an innocent, a Norsewoman who needed protection. Why didn't you plead with this helmsman to stop the men? Why didn't you try to save her yourself? You should have tried.

I try to cry out, but I choke on seawater, realizing that a sea monster has swallowed me whole, and I am sloshing around in its belly, bleeding out.

Some time in the middle of the night, Almarr wakes me with a kick. "Get up, boy."

The deck rumbles with the sound of men snoring – the gurgling, guttural, vibrating snorts; the heavy, nasal-sounding puffs. In the shadows of a large sea trunk, I spot Sigrid curled up tightly in a ball. She is surrounded by two other women. I can see their hair spilling down their backs. In silence, I watch Almarr settle into his sleeping sack. When he falls asleep, I dig out my stash of crushed-up rue and hellebore and carefully step over the backs of the sleeping men.

Sigrid snaps awake as I am placing the herbs in the folds of her cloak. "I am sorry that the men ..."

Wordlessly, she draws the hood of her mantle over her head. For a moment, I stand there looking down. There is a cold wind blowing off the water and thousands and thousands of stars twinkling brightly in the black.

In the coming days, Valbrand's foul-mouthed crew grows more and more restless. I try to be discreet when I seek out Sigrid's company, but she and the other women want nothing to do with me. They are like ghosts in their brokenness, and I am keenly aware that the mask I put on to hide my sex is a flimsy one I must protect.

At night the boardgames come out, the ocean is flat and the sunset casts glorious ribbons of vibrant oranges and yellows across the water's surface. When I sit down to play a round of *hnefatafl*, the knucklebone piece feels foreign in my sweaty hand, but there is also a warm familiarity that brings me comfort, breathes back life.

When Berger sees what I can do, he places several wagers, and I don't disappoint when I easily win three successive games.

"Where did you learn to play *hnefatafl* so well?" he asks when we find ourselves on watch together.

"My master taught me." I fiddle with the leather sheath that holds my knife.

Berger sniffs. "If you keep winning, you'll make me rich." He studies me with his flat, green eyes. "If you play again, I'll wager more, but you better win, or I'll send Gisli to deal with you." He winks, and I step back from him, trembling.

Two days later, the weather worsens, and the wind picks up, and we are driven far off course. When we accidentally loop back to the flat-stoned land believed to be Helluland, Valbrand's mood is foul.

"Stop rowing like old women," he barks at his oarsmen. "You'll cause the longboat to keel."

I scramble out of his way, and he ignores me as he continues to fling out insults. Once I make it to the other end of the ship to where Berger is stationed, I peer overboard.

"After sixteen days, I'm ready to get off this godsforsaken boat," he announces bitterly. Far off in the distance, we see a ridge of black. When the lookout turns, his face looks panicked.

"Look yonder at those massive swells. We shouldn't stop. The wind will push us into those rocks."

"The animals are agitated and badly in need of a walk on land," Berger retorts in an impatient voice. "Can't you find a place to set down anchor for the night?"

Valbrand leans forward from his station at the helm. His brow is furled, his cheeks are red, his eyes look fevered, his scowl is grim. When he barks out orders, the men respond. Beside me, Sigrid draws in air.

"By the gods, the swells are growing so high that I feel sick," she mutters underneath her breath. "If they send me down into the belly of the ship to tend to those blasted sheep, I'll puke again."

"If you want, I'll do your chores."

"May the gods smile down on you."

For two more days we sail forward, and all of us are kept busy managing the flapping wadmal sails. By the time someone spots a vast, forested land on the starboard side – Markland, if I have it right – even Valbrand looks relieved.

"They say that trolls live there," Almarr tells me as we work together to uncoil the rope that holds the anchor.

"I hope to find me a giantess who looks like Sigrid," a thin reed of a Norseman by the name of Ofeig grunts.

"Not me," Gisli says. "I want something better than that stupid cow. I'm sick of Sigrid. I want to trade her in for some other whore."

I throw a glance behind my back. Sigrid is nowhere to be found.

"Take the boy with you when you go ashore," Berger lisps as he helps to haul in the wadmal sail. I snap awake.

"He tarries," Gisli complains as he flicks a slimy look my way.

"The boy is green," Almarr says. I glance at him. "He needs some direction, that is all."

Above our heads, the seagulls squawk. Almarr ignores them, and Gisli guffaws. "Should we call you his *fosterfaðir* from here on in?"

Almarr scowls. "Go piss yourself."

That night the mead flows heavily and the bonfires on the beach lick the air and throw out sparks. I steer clear of Karlsefni and Gudrid's fire, and that is easy enough to do with all the men crawling around like ants on shore. In the sky, there is a vast array of dazzling stars that hold my attention until the men grow rowdy and start telling stories about their raping and their pillaging. In the firelight, they morph into a pack of wolves. What if they discover who I am? What if Aunt Gudrid recognizes me? What would her husband, Karlsefni, do?

I am vaguely aware of the bats scooping up bugs and flitting back and forth into the trees as I make my way up the beach and find a place where I can sit and be alone. The moon is rising over the water, splattering the glassy ocean with beams of silver light. Gazing out across the sea, the whispered memories come unbidden – memories of the longhouse I left behind, memories of Helga and Magnus and our farm, of Uncle and Freydis and the dogs. I smell roasted herring cooking on the scroll-iron in our longhouse. I see the statues of the gods perched on the beams around my bed.

Behind me, an owl calls unexpectedly, and the spell is broken by Berger's voice: "Here is our boy!" he exclaims when he sees me resting against a piece of bleached-out driftwood glowing white in the moonlight. He is panting heavily. "What are you doing with your back to the trees? Any beastie could leap out and eat you."

"I like it here," I stammer.

"They have a game of *hnefatafl* going. May Óðinn help you find your way to victory. Come. I want to bet on you." He offers me his dirty hand to yank me up. I begrudgingly take it.

On the way back down the beach, Berger talks non-stop until we arrive at the first of a half-dozen bonfires where I am introduced to another helmsman's crew. Eyjolf is a giant with a scowling face and a scraggly beard. He grasps me firmly by the arm before we sit down to play our first game.

I win easily. My opponent is replaced by a grumpy-looking Norseman with a lazy eye whose name I forget as soon as the boardgame starts. Three more times I win at *hnefatafl*. I am oblivious to the gathering crowd until Valbrand, himself, expresses interest in playing against me. Behind us, the tide is coming in.

"They say you have a knack for winning," the helmsman says as he stares at my breast. I feel the heat rising in my cheeks. There are a few hecklers at the back. Some burly Norseman is discussing who plays best. The helmsman eyes me hard. I bow my head. "You are one of mine, are you not?"

"The boy comes to us from Thorvard of Gardar," Berger says above all the noise. Just then the crowd parts and Karlsefni, my uncle, staggers forth. He is nursing a horn of ale in his hand, and he is clearly drunk.

"Valbrand, my friend, I hear talk that you are playing a game of *hnefatafl* against a lowly thrall. Perhaps I'll bet on him instead of you."

I keep my head down when I hear my uncle's voice. I can feel the heat coming off him.

"It seems odd that Thorvard of Gardar taught his thralls to play this game," Valbrand muses, ignoring Karlsefni. My heart knocks against my ribs.

"Thorvard treats his people well," Karlsefni slurs. My skin prickles when he stumbles forward. I feel my heartbeat thumping in my throat. "Where did you find the time to learn how to play this game, boy? Didn't you have any night-time chores?"

I swallow deeply. My mouth is dry.

"Speak!" Karlsefni slurs.

"This is the one whose mother complained about being

mistreated at Thorvard's hands," Valbrand says without looking up. He spits a gob of phlegm into the sand where the firelight flickers, the mosquitoes swarm.

Karlsefni calls for another horn of ale. As soon as someone brings him one, he wanders off, and I release a heavy breath.

"Swine's piss, couldn't one of you offer me a horn as well?" Valbrand spits.

Eyjolf laughs. "Gellir," he shouts, "bring the helmsman a drink of ale."

Valbrand makes a glib remark. There is a rumble of laughter, a brief exchange.

"Which side do you want to play – the king's guard or the opposing force?" I ask, struggling to keep my tone even.

"Give me the king," Valbrand says, and I relinquish the treasured piece. The crowd falls silent. We begin the game.

I am halfway through a play when Berger coughs. He is standing behind Valbrand with his hands folded over his barrelled chest. He coughs again, and I glance up. Valbrand studies the placement of the knucklebones on the *hnefatafl* board, and Berger's eyes lock onto mine. For a moment, I feel confused. Berger's look is strange. When I see the subtle gesture he is making with his head, I almost miss it. The crowd stirs expectantly.

"It's your turn," Valbrand says as he removes one of my knucklebones. I bide my time before easily capturing one of the few pieces Valbrand has left.

In the dim firelight, it is hard to see. The mosquitoes begin nipping at my ankles, and I swat at them and scratch a bite. Valbrand is in a fine position to move his king to a corner square. There are two possibilities – one that will lead to my win and one that will likely disadvantage me.

Berger won't look at me, and I can't help feeling that he wants me to do the impossible. I make my move. For a moment there is silence. The men, who have gathered at my back, moan audibly.

"By Óðinn's beard, I won!" Valbrand exclaims as he moves the king down the board. He stands up so quickly that the knucklebone pieces go flying, and I am forced to go in search of them in the sand. All around us, the men are either swearing or cheering and calling for more ale. Some are swarming around the helmsman and patting him cheerfully on the back.

In the moonlight, I scramble to retrieve the last *hnefatafl* piece, but someone snatches it up before I can get to it.

"Karlsefni doesn't like Valbrand. He bet on you, if you must know," Berger whispers as he hands the piece over. Our eyes connect. He studies me.

"And you? Who did you bet on?"

"I bet on Valbrand. I thought he would be the safer bet."

Somewhere in the trees, an owl's call floats towards us; its hoots are soft and soothing and rhythmical.

"I played to win," I mutter softly in the night. I can't look at him. He would see my lie.

"Truly, boy, winning or losing doesn't matter. Clearly, you knew how to play their game."

"I played to win," I repeat.

"I'm sure you did," Berger says. He cracks a smile.

Chapter Ten

WIND-MURMURS

We leave the next morning at the break of dawn under a cloudy, ominous-looking sky. As the oarsmen struggle to turn the ship into the churning seas and drive her forward into the wind, the seagulls circle around the mast, screeching loudly. No one mentions my skill at playing *hnefatafl* or my loss to Valbrand, but I feel as if I have gained some notoriety, a type of unspoken respect among the crew. Even Gisli lets me be.

By noon, the wind is howling, and Valbrand is glancing uneasily at the sky. "There's a storm brewing," he shouts as the ship pitches and rolls through the waves. When he sees me, he throws out orders, and his voice swells in the wind. I brace myself, legs spread wide apart, as a massive wave slams against the strakes. For a moment, I hear Freydis's voice telling me she had it worse.

During the next lull, I scramble to make my way across the planks towards the ladder which drops into the belly of the ship. As the ship rocks back and forth, I carefully climb down until I reach the lowest rung where I come face to face with Sigrid. Her face is shadowed, she looks fatigued, her eyes sport a fire inside. A flash of lightning lights up the sky, followed by a thunderous boom. Almost instantly, a blast of rain drenches us. When another storm wave suddenly rocks the ship, the hull shudders and creaks as the full weight of the storm descends.

Rain buckets down as the animal pens begin sliding across the planks in a chaotic swirl and the goats and sheep bleat crazily amidst the shouts of men. When the longboat plummets into the trough of another massive swell, Sigrid grabs for me, and we brace ourselves and look up to where the grey-black clouds are gathering thickly overhead. The ship lurches violently in the howling wind, and a rush of water is swept overboard.

"May the gods save us," Sigrid yells into my ear before she pushes off me and struggles to make her way into the hold. I hesitate, making certain that she has found something to grip before I turn around and quickly return to the upper deck. There, I am hit with another blast of water as a tremendous wave surges overboard.

"Hold onto something, boy," Berger screams above the noise of the pelting rain. There is another bolt of lightning, a thunderous boom. In front of me, an oarsman who is struggling to pull down the sails loses his footing and falls and hits his head against the deck. Instantly, three others scramble to help him up as another massive wave rocks the ship.

The mast squeals. Flashes of lightning rip through the sky followed by loud peals of thunder and a wave so wild, it rivals the tallest mountain I have ever seen..

"Thor's hammer strikes!" some Norseman yells.

I throw my shoulders into the wind, but just as I am struggling to find a handhold on the gunwales, I lose my balance and my body is propelled down the deck. With a frantic cry, I grope for anything that will stop me from being thrown overboard as the ship begins tilting dangerously and I am spun and tossed and bumped along. I swallow water and my arms flail wildly. A shrill scream escapes. Instantly, I am pushed so hard by a giant wave that I stumble-kneel. With a frightened yelp, I try to keep myself from being flung into the churning sea, but my body starts careening down the deck at a break-neck speed.

Berger is shouting as I fly past. With a tremendous grunt, he reaches out and clasps my wrist and shoves me towards the mast as the lightning flashes, white in grey.

"Tie yerself to it," Berger orders as his voice trails off.

The ship moans and groans as a succession of planks are ripped apart and a handful of unlucky crewmen are tossed into the raging sea. I grip the mast with clawlike strength, bracing myself against the howling, hissing wind that plasters my clothing against my skin.

The ship is driven into the sky and carried up the rolling swells. In the chaos, Valbrand battles to regain control, but his shouts are torn away as the ship plummets low before climbing again into the black. An instant later, Berger flies past with his arms and legs outstretched. Instinctively, I reach for him, but all I grasp is air. His body is eaten up by the angry swells.

Behind me someone releases an ear-splitting cry. We climb. We plunge. It starts again. With a wild surge of strength, I wrap myself around the mast and cling to it and close my eyes. I pray, "God of the sea, O great Njörðr, please wait patiently for your wife. Skadi is coming. Please don't drown our ship with your tears, I beg of you!"

The prayer has barely left my lips when the next wave sweeps over. I hear a tremendous crack. The mast lurches forward, lurches back. My body moves with the swaying mast as another blast of wind whips my hair into my face, blinding me.

When the mast breaks free, the force of the water from underneath surges up, and I am suddenly propelled forward and flung into the hungry sea. My body stiffens. I gulp a breath. Down I sink, and the water slurps me up like a *kraken*, the beady-eyed, huge-nostrilled sea monster shaped like a giant squid.

Far down in the deep, I hear Freydis's voice calling, telling me to kick with all my might and try to swim. Then a whoosh pushes me up and out. Just as I manage to resurface and gulp in air, another wave hits me from behind. Once again, I am plunged into the murky depths where my body is carried past the ship's debris and driven forward in the storm-tossed seas. Barely conscious, I am vomited out just before I run out of air.

Hel bids me enter her churning gates before another upsurge pitches me forward once again. In the raging seas, my body connects with a wooden plank, and I use it as a makeshift raft and let myself be carried forward on top of another rolling wave that flings me into the darkness, into the deep.

I am barely conscious, barely alive. My head goes under one more time and I brace myself, waiting for the blackness to claim me, waiting to meet my fate, hoping to hear the voices of the nine *döttirs* of Ægir and Rán coming to rescue me as I am pushed forward into the sea.

When I come to in the weak morning light, I find myself lying on a desolate stretch of beach strewn with driftwood and bulbous seaweed, clumped and crawling with sand fleas. The crashing surf pounds against the shore and aggravates my throbbing head so that I nearly vomit until I half-sit up. The wind is tossing the angry swells and driving the rolling waves into shore. I try to move, but the shivers come. The sea has spat me out onto a no-man's-land, a nameless place where I am all alone.

When I sit up, another rush of wind shoots icy daggers through my wet woollen mantle, matted with coarse, pebbled sand. There are bruises and scrapes along my shins, a nasty cut snaking down my arm, half a seashell sticking out from a laceration on my knee. I pluck it out. The wound trickles blood. With numb indifference, I lift my chin and gaze across the bleakness of a wind-tossed sea where a blast of ocean spray is somersaulting into the air before raining down on a massive boulder that marks the entrance to a bay. Squinting into the greyness, I see no wreckage in the choppy waves, no *vyking* ship bobbing in the deep.

With frozen fingers, I feel my face and lick my lips. All I taste is salt and sand and bloody spit. Behind me there is a line of tall spruce trees stretching all along the beach. Trolls must be hiding in the underbrush, tracking me with their yellow eyes, waiting for me to come to them.

I try not to think, but the panic rises and carries me into a sea of worries where I drown again. There are dragons squatting in my head, breathing fire, burning all. The seagulls are crying out to the forest beasts who are tracking my sweet and salty scent and eyeing up my skinny bones. My vision blurs.

Oh gods, there is no one here! No Valbrand or Berger. No Sigrid. No one at all. The ocean must have swallowed up my entire ship!

For an instant, I listen to the sounds of the screeching gulls and crashing waves, to the lonely wind music that stops up my heart. There is nothing on this stretch of desolate beach. No

Norsemen. No foul curses. No movement of any kind. Wrapping my arms around myself, I listen until the sound of the moaning wind become monotonous.

When I try to stand, the ground is a moving swell of sandy waves. With effort, I look up and belch up seawater, tasting salt. The ocean roars as if to mock me, and the surf hisses and churns up frothy foam.

Be strong enough to stand alone, the wind whispers in my ears. I reach down deep, seeing bands of light in my periphery. *You must find water or you will die of thirst.*

I begin picking my way towards the gnarled and twisted trees, misshapen from the force of wind. The forest is dark and thick, the trees as tall as giants, wondrous in their greenery. My eyes well up until I hear something rustling in the underbrush.

Clawing at the pockets of my mantle, my fingers unexpectedly find *Faðir's* raven earrings. When I look down, the carved ravens seem to blink into life:

You must thank Thor, the Thunder God, for doing battle to keep you safe, even though Óðinn is the greatest protector of them all. When you get settled, offer both gods a sacrifice.

Freydis's voice is in my head, as if her spirit follows me. I scan the beach. In the distance, there is an overturned, unopened seachest that calls my name. I look again, afraid that Loki is playing tricks. The wind tickles a tidepool, and the water ripples wildly. How can there be nothing but rocks and sand that stretch into an endless sea?

Before long, I am pushing my way over to the chest, grunting from the effort. When I see a rock crab scuttling across the sand, I feel something stir awake, and I find my strength and approach the seachest and lift the lid. Inside, there is a Norseman's axe, a longbow made from yew and several tanged iron arrowheads. In my giddiness, I perform a silly dance, but I am as wobbly as a jellyfish, and my sealegs almost give out on me. When I take a tumble in the sand, a flock of birds rises from the treetops in a poof of wings.

After that, I stick courage to my chest and get up and hike into the quiet woods where the trees are dense and the silence hisses. Two steps in and I am directionless, but I will myself to notice the enchantment of the place: the green, growing plants, the smell of loamy earth. There is a wealth of medicinal plants in the undergrowth waiting to be discovered and harvested. Up above, the giant trees form a canopy of leaves that call to me, inviting me to learn their names.

The strangeness of the vegetation popping out of the forest floor, amidst the brown and dry and dead, yanks me forward. On instinct, I look for troll droppings and animal scat. When I can't find any, I wander further in and feel the poke of fear and the thump of heart booms rattling against my ribs.

At the sight of raindrops trapped in the curled folds of some large-leafed plant, the tears well up, but I hold them back and quickly manoeuvre the plant into place so that I can drink. As the shadows flicker across the forest floor, I nock an arrow just in case.

The bugs are bad. I swat at them while studying the endless stretch of trees leading further into the forest darkness. The tree-trunk sentinels are silent when I catch the movement from a dance of leaves. The forest seems to come alive, and I hear a hint of mirthless laughter in the trees, as if the tree spirits are mocking me. Everything feels futile in this place where the wilderness envelops me, breathing me in and trying to decide how to spit me out.

The silence pulls me into the vastness of the green, and I am tugged forward into the stillness. It is not long before I stumble into a small clearing at the end of which is a shallow stream gurgling over slimy rocks. All thoughts of danger are banished as I rush forward and begin to drink. Over and over I cup my hands as a cloud of black flies drops lower and hovers just above my head.

My vision blurs as I slowly stand and scan the trees. Batting away the branches, I hack my way through the underbush and wonder about the wisdom of returning to the beach until I realize that one glimpse might unnerve me to my breaking point. How would it feel to end my life by thrusting the point of an arrow into my heart?

The longbow suddenly feels too heavy in my shaking hands. When I feel the urge to slice open my outstretched arm and watch the liquid trickle out, a moan slips out:

Go, you must!

The sound of Freydis's ice-crystal voice morphs into the call of a red-winged blackbird, and I let myself fall into the memories. I float into our longhouse where the hearth fire is leaping high and where the billowing smoke is drifting out through the smoke hole. When I glance up, the memories show me a moonless sky.

For a moment, I am lost again and my thoughts scatter like seeds sown in summer wind. Then a strange bird calls. Its trilling is so harsh and mystical that I lift my bow. I am ready to make a kill until I realize there is nothing there, that there is only an endless stretch of trees with branches reaching out to point accusatory twig fingers and to whisper leaf messages through a web of roots slithering along the forest floor. My breathing falters. A twig snaps.

In fear, I follow the stream for a while before finding a deer path that continues to snake uphill. The ground is covered in wild blueberries, deliciously sweet and large. Repeatedly, I bend down to pinch off handfuls which I stuff into my mouth and chomp noisily. I am alive to every movement, vigilant to every sound.

My spirit settles when I reach the top of the hill and see a meadow the length a maiden could walk with a slow heifer between high noon and supper. There is a look-out on the other side. When I venture a little further in, I jump back in surprise when I stumble across a dead caribou, freshly shot, with a finely constructed spear protruding from the creature's back. Already the flies are swarming the carcass. For the love of Loki, what manner of nonsense is this?

The crows swoop down. An entire flock. They caw at me when I kick the caribou with my foot to verify that it is real. The caribou's dead eyes stare back at me unnervingly. Breathing heavily, I lean down to inspect the fine construction of the shaft, its carvings depicting special symbols I can't read. These aren't any Norseman's runic inscriptions. These are completely strange.

Peeling back the deerskin covering that lines the handle of the spear, I discover that it is made of elk horn. At the tip, there are dangling feathers and strips of some strange animal's fur. It takes some effort, but when I yank the shaft out of the carcass to inspect the spearpoint, I find that it is shaped like a long, narrow awl, and it is as sharp and heavy and unwieldy as any a Norseman would use. There is even a tanged end to facilitate hafting. The workmanship is remarkable.

Suddenly, I hear the huff of an animal in swishing grasses. Then I hear a drawn-out woof followed by a wet puff and snort. I turn and look. My body stiffens; my senses ping.

A black bear of medium size is lumbering towards me through the grasses on all fours. Its coat is a glossy black and flies are swarming around its eyes. It suddenly stops and sniffs the air.

With the utmost care, I slowly begin to back away. The bear looks up and releases another anxious wuff that overpowers the sounds of the buzzing flies, the chirping birds, the hissing wind, the swishing grasses, the snapping twigs below my feet. The bear's ears lie flat against its fur.

When the bear suddenly releases a low-throated growl, I grab for my spear, but the bear homes in on me. In my terror, I clasp at air.

Instinctively, my hands fly up to protect my face, but the bear knocks me to the ground, and I hear a pop and snap. Groaning, I try to right myself, but the bear loops back and takes another swipe, and its claws dig deeply into my back so that I scream in pain and half-roll over, half-scramble into the grass.

Terror propels me to hoist myself up onto my hands and knees, but I can't seem to move fast enough. The smell of the bear's rancid breath and its stinky fur choke me up as it lets out a deafening roar that shakes the ground. When it rears up on its hind legs, panic seals my throat, and I lose my balance and fall backwards and twist around and try to scramble up, but the bear comes crashing down, landing heavily on my back leg.

With a guttural groan, I try to swipe at the wild beast, but the bear's sharp claws dig through my back. There is vicious pain and blood and fear and dirt and sweat. My vision narrows, and I force myself not to faint. Panic flints the fight in me as the bear's beady eyes blink down on me. As I haul myself up off the ground, my arms curl around my head.

The fearsome thing is in no mood to relinquish its victim so easily. Once again, it rears up and releases another deafening roar, the sound so shrill that the crows – a blur of black – fly off with frenzied caws. In a flash, I am rolling into the grass, panting and moaning and crying out to the ancestors, but the bear's shadow falls on top of me. Effortlessly, it flips me over and swipes its claws across my chest, and I release another scream as my arms fly up and the bear's fangs clamp down in bone-crunching agony.

Drawing on the strength of Thor, I reach for my fallen spear with my good arm and see a swoosh of black, the bear's massive incisors dripping saliva, its lolling tongue. In that split second, I manage to raise my spear and stab the tip into the creature's eye. Reeling backwards, the bear releases a long, low-pitched growl before it begins to paw at its eye pathetically.

It seems like my body splits in two. A part of me yearns to die; a part of me yearns to fight. Cringing, I grab hold of my spear with my good arm and haul myself up and turn, half limping and mad with terror. The bear's bloody eye socket has partially blinded him, but his sense of smell is keen.

I can feel the wet, sticky blood sliding down my back. My leg feels broken. My arm is crushed. Blinking, I use my good arm to lodge the end of the shaft into the ground with the pointed end facing up. Then I turn. The bear is pawing the air in search of me, roaring so fiercely that terror tentacles through me, slipping lower in my gut as I brace myself and wait for the bear to charge.

There is a confusing whiz. A buzz of movement in my periphery. The bear releases a vicious roar and runs at me, and I roll into the grass to avoid being crushed by the forward thrust of the bear's heavy weight as it impales itself on my spear.

The jarring pain radiating from my arm and chest and back fans out quickly. When I peek through splayed fingers and see the bear's black form, I release a breath I didn't even know I was holding. There is fog. Or is it dust? Or am I climbing into the clouds? Perhaps I am travelling to Niðavellir, the first of the nine worlds where the huge dragon, Níðhöggr, guards the bubbling hot-springs. Perhaps I am falling into the living well. Perhaps I will find myself floating in a stream down a mountain to the plains where I will solidify into frost and ice.

My body floats towards the bear, and I imagine arrows raining down from Asgard as I slip into an ethereal state of nothingness. In the haze, I can dimly make out the outlines of many red faces leaning above me and murmuring softly, their voices wobbling and cutting in and out. I try to push them away, but I have no strength, and my vision dims, and my head is filled with swarming flies. I brace myself, knowing that I am helpless to defend myself, knowing that this is the end, knowing that I cannot and will not show my fear.

Chapter Eleven

RAINBOW-COLOURED CAVE MIST

S leep. Muddled sleep. Wooziness and pain. I try to talk, to groan, but I can't force out any sound. Every bone in my body hurts, from my broken ribs to my back and arm and aching chest. I slip in and out, drifting past islands, hazy and wave-like. When my eyes flutter open, I see the backs of men conferring with each other as they stand around a roaring fire spitting out a spray of sparks. My head pounds; my wounds throb. There are strange ripples of sound, words I can't understand.

Someone comes to give me a drink of foul-tasting liquid, and the bitter scent makes me gag. Falling into the otherworld of dreams, I try to protect my head, but I can't seem to move my limbs. I am frozen ice. I am falling snow. I am twinkling starlight and sparkling sunbeams. I am guarded by the moon.

Later, when a scream slips out, I have a vague impression of being in a darkened cave lit by torchlight. The red faces come and go as they please. They must be trolls. *Neinn*, they must be giants. The faces slowly disappear, and I dream of ravens eating my flesh in the company of other carrion birds and scavengers beaking up the blood spilling from my mangled flesh, tasting the sweetness and the stickiness of it, savouring the iron tang.

The birds' mocking screeches fade into a different sound – a soothing trill, a warbler singing in my ear. A haunting tune crescendoes to a roar, but I can't seem to focus long enough to follow the melody to completion. Before I sink deeper into sleep, I hear the flutes and lyres and cow horns making the ethereal music of my people – the jumble of multiple melodic lines.

Freydis floats into my dreams in a sea of white where she is flanked on either side by ravens with broad, black wings and curved beaks croaking gibberish. In a mystic swirl, the scene morphs and melts. Freydis is standing before a roaring peat-moss fire. Her face looks serene. Her red hair is crowned with a halo of rainbow-coloured mist.

It is time to wake, döttir. *Come and be with your mother's people.*

Her voice becomes a haunting melody, a sad, familiar tune strummed on a lyre, played on a flute.

My head is all muddled.

There is a tall, fair-haired Norseman standing at my bedside. He wants to re-dress my wounds, to bind my forearm and my wrist, to treat my leg. Wincing, I try to wake, but sleep pulls again. Its sweetness shields me from the vicious pain, the agony.

The Norseman smears a foul-smelling paste across my shoulder and down my left arm before he tells someone that he'll need more pine sap to make a tincture. Startled by the warmth of his touch, I try to pull away, but the pain is so sharp, I think I yelp. He steadies me.

By Óðinn's beard, who is this healer – this man who is skilled in herbal magic? Who are the other fur-clad grim reapers who speak of death as they sit around a roaring fire? I lose track of how frequently they come to re-apply the salve, a mixture of arnica and sage, I'm sure of it. I get confused. The smell is strong.

The pus seeping from my injuries won't stop oozing, and I worry they will turn septic until someone comes to tend to my wounds. I am vaguely aware of the smell of burning herbs, of someone touching me, of someone else leaning over me.

"See the angry red claw marks on her back?"

"They look much better than they were."

My ears are full of water. Someone is speaking Norse, but the sound morphs and twists, and there is a salty taste.. I feel the presence of the trickster god in the room, as though Loki is taunting me and playing tricks. Perhaps I have taken my last breath. Perhaps my *hamr* – this lifeforce within me – is shapeshifting in the mist, ready to be scooped up by the gods. Surely, my soul has not started its journey into the realm of the dead? It cannot be! I have my *hugr* – these fuzzy thoughts, my broken mind.

Someone with a wrinkled face leans in closely, and I feel his *hamr* touching mine. His eyes are smudged with black. The rest of his face has been painted red. There is a raven's feather dangling from his hair, and there is a smoky smell wafting off his skin, as though he is a growing thing. I try to speak, but the words come out in fits and starts. Snakes are crawling underneath my skin; a hot iron is searing into my wounded flesh.

In my periphery, I catch the scratch of movement. A bird-hop shuffle. A low gurgled croak. My raven spirit grows in the mist, all silver-black and iridescent pearly-blue. It croaks again when its beady eyes meet mine. The raven is my *fylgja* – my attending spirit that lets me know I live with the second sight. It has travelled on ahead, this part of me that is not dead.

When I finally stir awake to the sound of voices arguing in the dark, my newly awakening mind is as foggy as the morning mists rolling across the meadowlands. With effort, I turn my head, but the room begins to spin, and I need to brace myself until the place comes into focus.

I am in a cave. There are eight of them. Warrior-types. All wearing red. The tallest has a luscious fox fur draped around his neck and feathers and shells tucked into the braid trailing down his back. He is talking to a short, stocky man with red tattoos scrolling across one side of his shaved head. This one is wearing nothing but a loincloth and leather boots. Another with straight, black, free-flowing hair leans in closer to the fire to warm himself.

By the gods, I am in a den of *Skraelings*, lying here helplessly on a bed of scented pines!

Tremendous pain shoots across my shoulders and down my back. I bite my lip and try to quell the brimming tears. Just in front of me, I hear whispers morphing into an argument where the pebbly voices ebb and flow like swishing tides. When I lift my head to better see, the backs of two Norsemen come into view.

"Considering her injuries, she won't be able to travel, Bjǫrn. Show some reason, man! You must return with us before the winter comes and you get trapped inside this cave. The weather could quickly turn at this time of year."

The speaker is a bearded man of middle age who, from all appearances, looks like a fearsome hunter. I catch a glimpse of the axe hanging from his belt, glimmering in the firelight. He continues in a voice as smooth as butter:

"Bjǫrn, you must let go of guilt. The shaman will give her a sleeping potion to end her life. Believe me, she won't feel a thing. Afterwards we'll bury her honourably so the animals won't find her remains and rip her body to pieces in this cave."

"I won't leave her. 'Tis my duty to stay here as long as the maiden breathes."

"As I said, we'll build a rock cairn so that her bones are protected. Come, my boy. Be reasonable. You must end this madness! If we leave tomorrow, we'll be lucky to arrive back in time for the great caribou hunt. Think on it, Bjǫrn! Use yer head!"

I try to protest, but I don't have the strength. A painful spasm shoots through my arm. The limb is hot and swollen and as heavy as a giant rock. *Damn them to Hel! How dare they think of killing me! I'll scratch their eyes out and bite them like a wolverine!*

"I can't leave her, Uncle, so let me be," the younger Norseman says as he runs his fingers through his thick blond hair. In the shadows, he clenches his clean-shaven jaw and spits a wad of phlegm onto the ground.

"Your mother always called you pig-headed," the older man mutters angrily. "Truly I tell you, this cursed girl won't survive the week."

"She will," he says. "I'll re-dress her wounds."

"Her flesh has been ripped to shreds, and she cannot walk! Did you see her back? May Thor save you from this hopeless fight. After she dies, you'll be stuck in this godless place for the entire winter on yer own."

The younger man flicks a glance in my direction. I quickly close my eyes.

"Our Beothuk brothers are anxious to leave, my boy. Listen to them arguing. They are beginning to resent your stubbornness. May Óðinn help you see the situation for what it is. We don't understand your care for a girl who is mostly dead. Look at

Askook. He and Megedagik quarrel daily about when the birds will begin to migrate south. All of us are anxious to get back after being gone for several months. Besides, your mother and your sisters likely need our meat, and Nashushuk will worry about you."

"My mother and my sisters can fend for themselves! They are capable," the younger Norseman replies stubbornly. "'Tis as you said. You should get back. The caribou will be migrating in greater numbers this year. Nashushuk will be organizing the great caribou hunt, and he will need your help."

"Our brothers don't want to miss out on the *Mokoshan*. The feast comes but once a year."

"The Great Spirit will direct the movement of the herds. Only men like Askook believe that he must be there. He says his good fortune depends on how many caribou he spears."

"Do what you will, Bjǫrn. For my part, I intend to go back to the Beothuk settlement. We can leave you some supplies for wintering in this cave, but you'll have to jerk yer own meat. Afore the gods, I don't agree with your decision to stay, my boy, but I'll tell your good mother where you are and that you are safe. I doubt she'll be happy."

"She is never happy."

"If you survive, you'll have to journey back next spring after the snows melt. With any luck, you'll be able to meet up with the harp seal hunters during their first run of the season."

Every muscle pains me. My skin feels as though it has been stretched across hot rocks. My head is throbbing, and I am quickly tiring. There is searing pain in my shoulder that radiates upwards into my neck. When I look down and see the claw marks running parallel across my chest, my gorge rises. I smell rancid animal breath and hear a bear snorting in the dark. There is a surge of panic, and the walls waver; the firelight dims. I taste the iron tang of blood.

The man named Bjǫrn quickly turns, and the shadows cast by his tall frame shimmy in the flickering firelight. I start to slip into a foggy haze that mists up from the floor of the cavern, spreading white puffs that plume then waver, grow then shrink. A creature breathes from underneath.

In front of me, the two Norsemen start to disappear into the greyness of the rocks, and clouds of white slurp them up.

Sometime later when I wake, I have trouble focusing. A hazy beam of sunlight swirls around me, wrapping me in a wash of light that changes, spinning and breathing as it climbs up the walls of the cave. It feels as though my insides have been ripped apart and my arm is being punctured with a hunting knife where the blade keeps hitting bone. I imagine pulling a bear's incisor from my flesh, and I try to moan, but no sound comes out. The cave is quiet. A cold dampness is seeping off the rocks.

From far away, I hear a flute. On the edge of thought, a bird pokes its long, pointed beak into the sweetest of flowers before fluttering away so quickly, the air hisses. When I force my eyes open, the warbles of a little thrush lace the air before the ethereal shapes of minstrels begin parading around my bed. I follow them through Freydis's longhouse until I get lost and the last remaining musician calls to me.

He paddles me out to my uncle's waiting ship, but the longboat suddenly becomes a death barge that sails into a storm-tossed sea.

There is a loud noise. I snap awake.

I am burning up with fever, frazzled and disorientated. My eyes are blurry and sensitive, and I hurt everywhere. With little strength, I pinch myself to check to see if I have flesh, that I have not changed into the form of a bird. My raven *fylgja* croaks.

I allow my eyes to scan the cave. Directly in front of me, a broad-shouldered Norseman – ropey muscled, with blond hair falling forward in his eyes – sits hunched over a piece of gnarled wood with a carving knife held in his big-knuckled hands. He is concentrating as he nimbly works the piece, and the firelight dances across his face. Slowly, he extends his legs to warm his toes against the fire, but when a firelog snaps and splits in two, he glances up.

I shimmy down into my hides.

"You have slept long," the stranger says.

I nod. When I go to rise, he moves like a huntsman on silent feet. Instantly, he is by my side.

Another surge of pain shoots through me. In a woozy, muddled state I watch him ladling something out for me. The liquid is foul-smelling. When he lifts my head to help me drink, I flinch. Pull back.

"The concoction comes from stewing the young needles and catkins of white pine. It'll help relieve the pain and decrease the swelling," he says in the voice of a healer. I watch him move, all cat-like. "You've much healing left to do. The drink will help."

"You should use yarrow," I manage in a rasp that sounds more like clinking shards of ice.

He turns around and blinks at me. It takes great effort to fill my lungs and push out air. "Yarrow stops the bleeding," I say, pausing to snag a breath. "It's good for broken bones."

He stares at me as though I am unworthy of being heard.

"I've also made a poultice from the inner bark of spruce," he mutters. "It stinks, but I need to re-dress your wounds."

When he goes to touch me, I pull away. "I've sacrificed much for you," he mutters, biting back anger. "I think the gods fated me to care for you, yet you reject my help."

I look down and see my puncture wounds. The chewed-up flesh. The bloodied scabs. "What is this place?" My throat feels like it's been pierced by a hundred arrows, a thousand spears.

"You were attacked by a beast," the huntsman says without looking up. "Afterwards, we carried you to this cave. It's not far from where we found the wreckage of your ship." He carefully places my swollen arm underneath a soft fur hide. Even so, a hot river of pain shoots down my arm, rips through my wrist, tears across my hand and sets fire to the fingertips of my right hand. The room spins. The Norseman is oblivious. He squints when he examines my other arm, which has been wrapped tightly in a piece of hide that stinks.

"The hurt is everywhere," I manage, wincing.

"As well it should! That cursed bear bit you through to the bone. It's a wonder he didn't take half of you with him before rearing up again and clamping down."

There is no air, only tingling, hot, searing pain. Through hearth-fire smoke, I see dark shadows stretching wildly on the rocky wall. There is a creature pacing on the other side of the firepit – a bear that snorts and stomps the ground.

From somewhere deep, a pathetic noise bursts forth, a cry that fizzles out, a hiss of air. The Norseman stops his ministrations and leans in so closely that I'm forced to stare into his ocean eyes.

"Don't fuss," he murmurs softly. "That bear is dead. Your spear lanced him and our arrows finished him off."

I feel the warmth of the Norseman's breath on my face before I turn from him and cover my eyes with my good hand.

"The Medicine Man advised me to regularly apply certain types of poultices. I'll have to prepare another chamomile and white meadowsweet concoction for your left arm to guard against infection. The injuries were deep, but the Medicine Man cleaned the wound. Then he stitched you up, but it was a messy job. I'm sorry for the pain he caused, but it looks as though he saved that arm. Your other arm is hurt as well, but there is less damage. The bear's claws were sharp. Its nails cut deep."

I can't look. He moves lower to inspect my leg. There is a sudden shyness, a reluctance for him to lift the blankets and examine all my injuries.

"I suspect you can't remember how loudly you screamed when the Medicine Man popped your shoulder back into the socket? We thought you were possessed by the spirit of the bear."

I experience another painful wave, a twinge so fierce it feels as though I am being stabbed. Who is this Norseman who is so familiar with my body, so knowledgeable about where all my bruises and my injuries lie?

The annoyance festers, flares. In silence, I endure his prodding. After some time, he moves to the other side of the cave where he retrieves a stone pestle before throwing his shoulder into grinding down a generous bunch of herbs. I watch him work. When my eyes drift across the herb bundles strewn across the floor, I only recognize some of them.

"I've given you alder bark tea to guard against the spread of blood wounds. Juniper boughs were used in a sweatbath to protect against evil influences," the Norseman says without looking up. "I'm now preparing a poultice made of dried dogwood bark."

When he returns, I let him spread the paste onto the swollen puncture wounds on my shoulder where the skin around the scab is beginning to turn a sickly shade of yellow and purple-blue. The Norseman's face looks serious, as though he wants to tell me something I won't like.

"I'm going to turn you on your other side so I can better reach your back. It will hurt, but I need to re-apply some of this paste to guard against the spittle dragons. It stinks, but it is for the best."

It takes all my effort not to sob. In silence, he moves me slowly, and his hands are warm against my throbbing skin. When I am settled, he begins working the ointment into my wounds, and I bite my tongue against the pain. Over my dead body will he call me weak.

"You bled so much, you came close to death," the Norseman mutters as he does his work. "The Medicine Man splinted your leg. It was so misshapen and twisted after your battle with that bear. At first, we thought you'd never walk again, but I have hope. The Beothuk figured the bear's heavy weight came down on you and almost crushed the bone." He pauses. There is water dripping off the cavern walls, plinking into the woozy puddles in my head.

"If you stay still and rest, the sharp broken bones inside your leg won't slash the muscle. Our Medicine Man told me this. He is a great healer who is revered by all. I wish he would have stayed with us."

My mouth is as dry as a ball of sheep's wool ready for carding. "The wrappings are too tight."

"They told me not to loosen anything, but what do I know? I am a hunter, not a healer. In any case, you'll have to stretch. We can't afford to have your muscles stiffening up, and I don't need you to be difficult. You are too heavy for me to carry."

My chin begins to tremble, and I turn my face into the wall.

"We should send sacrifice to Eir, the healing goddess, so that no pus builds up. If your wounds begin to fester, I'll not be able to help you much. The slashes across your back are open wounds that aren't closing up as fast as I would like."

He continues nattering about what he has done to treat my injuries, and I stiffen up, rattled that he knows so much, irritated that he won't shut up. His angular jaw is silhouetted in the firelight. His eyes shine brightly as he works.

"Your back is mauled. There will be ugly scars," he says as he uses his thumb to probe the hot skin surrounding the lacerations on my arm. The smell of him is smoke and herbs.

"I need water," I manage. A rush of heat moves into my cheeks.

The Norseman scrambles to fetch a cup. When he returns, he helps me half sit up. I drink and drink until I am attacked by another sharp, shooting pain which is broken apart by a period of short relief before there is another surge of agony. The Norseman's brows contort.

"My name is Anja," I rasp weakly as he lowers me back into bed.

"Anja, is it? Your ship must have been a long way from home."

I wheeze as I try to suck in air and start to squirm, and his brows contort. He waits for my pain to subside before he begins to apply another strong-smelling salve to my wounded chest. It is as though he is impervious to the intimacy of touching me.

"Is the pain unbearable?" he asks in a voice of feathers, as if he is trying to establish trust. His breath is warm against my face.

When he pulls back, he hesitates. "I couldn't help but notice that you were wearing breeches when we undressed you. We found it strange. Do maidens not wear skirts in your village?"

For the love of Loki, this man is bold! I slurp a breath and feel the jabs of a million spears. "The story is a long one," I rasp.

"Truly, I've never seen a maiden with hair so short."

Our eyes connect as I gather up my breath. "I was travelling on a *vyking* ship, and it was best I travelled as a boy."

"Where are you from?" He looks at me with eyes that melt my ice and something shifts inside, all soft and spongy, as if I am walking through pond silt.

"Greenland," I whisper. The fire crackles and Freydis rises in the flames and glares at me and spits out sparks. I curse myself for my stupidity.

"You must rest now, Anja from Greenland. Óðinn has spared your life and Thor continues to protect you through me. If you should wake and I'm not here, you mustn't worry. I need to hunt."

My eyes feel heavy from the exertion of talking. "Is it *Sumarr* still?"

"It is *Tvímánuðr*, corn-cutting month. The days are growing shorter. This cave is draughty. It can't be helped." He tucks the hides underneath my feet. "Tomorrow I'll go to check my traps, but I promise to return by nightfall. I'll stoke the fire before I go."

I choke on air. The Norseman towers over me. "Do you have a name?"

"Bjǫrn of Vinland," he says as he fingers a talisman dangling from a leather cord around his neck.

"Vinland?" I ask, incredulously.

"'Tis the place," he mutters. His dimples pop. "Your longboat sank. We searched the shores. You were the lone survivor, as far as we could tell."

In a swoosh, it all comes back: the terror and the helplessness, the waves of panic, the awful fear. When I hear the vermin scuttling somewhere close, I claw for air.

"My clan hails from a place called Leifsbidur," Bjørn continues.

There is a burst of hope, a nervous feeling in my bones. I gawk at him.

"Two months ago, I travelled south from my settlement to meet up with hunters from a Beothuk tribe. You would know the Beothuk by another name. The Norse call them *Skraelings* or Red Men because of the red-ochre markings on their skin."

I hear the voices of the ancestors in the rock and see my unknown kin rising like ghosts in fire shadows. There is the wise woman. Her eyes are glistening. There is *Grandfaðir* sharing stories about a wolf. I see a child flinting fire.

"Many moons ago, I left Leifsbidur and travelled to the Beothuk village where I joined my friends for the harp seal hunt. We followed the herds to their breeding grounds and scored many kills. After that, half of us took the spoils back home while the rest of us went in search of whatever hunting we could find. We walked far under mostly fair skies for many days. My Beothuk kin say that the Great One smiled down on us when we discovered that the hunting is plentiful in between this point and home."

My slurped words twist: "How did you find me?"

"One afternoon, we scored a kill and when we went to retrieve it, we found you battling a ferocious bear. Óðinn and his ravens must have led us to you in your time of need. You were badly injured and barely alive. When our Medicine Man saw the extent of your injuries, even he …" He breaks off and averts his eyes as a flush moves into his sun-kissed cheeks.

"I survived," I try to say, but the words get muffled by a painful cough, thin and wheezy. Bjǫrn leans forward, and I wave him off. His palms are calloused; his touch is warm.

"Against the advice of my Beothuk brothers, I made the decision to carry your injured body into this cave where we had set up camp," Bjǫrn says as soon as my cough subsides. "There was much arguing about what to do. At one point, you cried out for some raven spirit – some shapeshifter – to help you survive a battle against a giantess in Hel's underworld. It frightened my Beothuk brothers, but I took it as a sign."

A moan rises in my chest. The shadows grow and growl and stretch into bears with orange eyes. Bjǫrn anchors his body over mine. His eyes dig deep.

"Anja, that bear cannot hurt you anymore. Your leg will heal. I'll see to it. Both of us will walk out of here. Both of us will make it back to Leifsbidur."

"You'll be rewarded by the gods," I manage as the air drizzles out of my aching chest. I close my eyes. My heart thunks so loudly, I am sure he hears.

"My reward will be your healing," he simply says. "Now you must try to rest."

Somewhere behind us in the belly of the cave, there are water spirits dancing to the sound of dripping plinks.

"I can't," I say. "The pain is bad."

Chapter Twelve

YULE LOGS AND SAGAS

T he days pass in a blur. I drift in and out. One day I wake to silence and searing pain and a cold breeze stirring up leaves at the entrance to the cave.

"Huntsman?" The word slips out in a gurgled wheeze. When I manage to prop myself up, a surge of pain builds like an ocean wave. "Are you here?"

A weak beam of light spills into the belly of the cave. There is no one sitting around the firepit. No *Skraelings* waiting to attack. There are no wolves, no trolls, no bears or shadowed beasts. The ashes from a long-snuffed-out fire are sitting in the firepit, white as snow. The chill is damp. There is an autumn smell.

May the gods curse him. He has left me alone to die.

I taste the warmth of a rising anger twisting around me and cutting off my air supply. *Sweet Óðinn, how did it come to this? I survived a shipwreck and a bear attack, and now I'll die alone in this hewn-out rock tomb that is nothing but a home for bats.*

When I push back the furs to examine the splinting on my leg, my stomach groans, and the nausea comes in waves. In the corner of the cave, there are stacked cords of firewood. For a moment, I sit and stare, knowing what I have to do. Unless I want to suffer death, I must keep warm and fed and dry.

I gingerly ease my weight out of bed. When I stand, my good knee locks. Teetering dizzily, I see bursts of light that rain down stars. My arms start flailing; a yelp slips out. When I glance up, a dark shadow fills the entrance to the cave. Bjǫrn blocks the light. He has a string of white-tailed rabbits hanging from the pole he is balancing on his shoulder. "What is happening here?"

I close my eyes. He takes a breath. "Your bones are weak. Your leg will snap!"

"I needed heat."

He drops his rabbit pole with a thwap. In a few quick strides, he is across the room. "May the gods give me patience," he says as he helps me get back into bed. He tucks the hide around my feet. "I've given Óðinn a promise to be your keeper, but you're a stubborn fool. What were you thinking? If you try to walk too soon, you'll rip the stitches, and you wouldn't want me to stitch you back up. I'm not good at it." He pauses, and I try to shift away from him, but I am sweating from the mere effort of moving. "Loki must be laughing at my expense. I am a stupid man for giving up my whole life for you. I can't help someone who refuses to help herself."

"I didn't think," I murmur as the tears well up.

"You could have fallen!"

I struggle to pull the covers up underneath my chin, and he stands abruptly and walks across to the firepit where he begins to set a fire. When he is done, he squats and stares into the firelight. Above my head, I hear the bats.

"Your stubbornness will be your curse, Anja from Greenland," Bjǫrn whispers tiredly.

I slink down further into my bed and close my eyes and wonder about the holy mountain of Helgafjell and wish that I was there playing *hnefatafl*.

After Bjǫrn skins the rabbits, he roasts the meat and brings me some, but I am woozy and half-asleep, and his shadow dances on the wall, gyrating in ghost-wild ways until it wiggles into the shape of a carrion bird that wants to tear my bones apart and pick out my eyes.

The dark smudge morphs again, and I get trapped in a worm's cocoon where everything seems sleepy and slow. In a trance, I sense a blackness coming closer and then I feel the horror of its bloody fangs, its snapping jaws, its drool dripping onto my broken arm. It has a furry brow and one missing eye – an empty socket with some spirit presence lurking in the darkened depths. The bear releases a low-pitched growl, and I fall into the empty void, spinning and twirling into the darkness of some creature's maw.

Hail Thor, son of Óðinn. O Lord of the Hammer, give me the courage to honour your legacy. Make me shieldmaiden strong. Give me strength to kill this bear, to rip its spirit from my bones.

Panicking, I fall into a black and bottomless pit where I am held down by the paws of a large black bear with sharpened claws. With arms flailing, I struggle to resurface, pushing with all my might as I try to fight off the furry, one-eyed monster with barnacles stuck in its stinky fur. I am nothing in a nowhere place, a lost soul floating in the depths of some cold sea.

Bjørn's voice creeps through mist in a loud boom-crack that bounces off the wavering rocks. I allow myself to be carried up, as though I am a fish being dragged on a line.

"Focus, Anja! I am here beside you! We are in a cave."

With a heavy thunk, I fall back into myself like a selkie shedding skin. Bjørn's face floats above me, and I blink to bring him into focus. His blue ice-chip eyes are large pools of soothing light. From somewhere distant, I hear him speak my name again, all tangled and wobbly, all jumbled and disconnected. Slowly the cave's vaulted ceiling comes into view. Bjørn is sitting beside me with worry lines criss-crossing his forehead. I feel his hand holding mine, the rough warmth of it.

"I've returned," I finally manage, sputtering. The shadows from the flickering fire playfully work their way up the wall.

"The Medicine Man said it might take some time for you to conquer the bear's spirit. He was here when we found you, but he was anxious to return to his people before the snows set in."

The Medicine Man? Who is that? I look away, feeling another surge of pain shooting down my leg.

Bjørn drops his eyes. "In the spring when you can walk again, we'll leave this place, and I'll help you walk back to my settlement. We will need to pass through the Beothuk village. The terrain isn't always easy to navigate here on Vinland shores, so the trek will be difficult."

The wall shadows twist again. Freydis morphs into a raven soaring across the marshlands before fading into the blackest of skies. In a burst of light, she reappears again, but then the darkness in her rises. Suddenly, she drives the shaft of her spear into a bear's furry chest. When the blood spurts out, it comes from Jelani's body, and I watch it pooling in a bone graveyard where crows gather and ravens speak.

Bjǫrn's hand is warm. I close my eyes. When the visions try to come again, I iron up and push them down.

I wake in the hazy light of a late afternoon to the sound of hauntingly beautiful flute music floating towards me from somewhere deep inside the cave. The trills crescendo before there is a pause. Then the music slurs into a fluid phase and the notes seemingly bleed together, slipping into delicate and soothing sounds that help me distance myself from pain.

When Bjǫrn's shadowy figure emerges from the back recesses with his flute positioned against his lips and his nimble fingers adeptly moving across the holes, I watch him from underneath my hides. His music builds again in a series of fast, frenetic trills, and I am transported back to the meadowlands in Greenland where I reach through fog and catch memories of some shepherdess singing in the fields. There is a sudden yearning, a homesickness that makes tears well up.

"You have a gift," I say, speaking softly to his back.

"I'll play some more for you tonight. Shall I recite a verse as well?"

I gurgle a little laugh. "Are you a *skald*?"

"*Neinn*, but my uncle was before he died. He left me his flute."

I struggle to sit, and Bjǫrn tries to help. My clothing hangs on me, and my leg feels like a brittle twig. My arm is not much better. The open wounds refuse to scab over, and there is a constant throbbing in my lower back.

"Your injured leg is more difficult to manoeuvre than a herd of grazing caribou," Bjǫrn sighs, and his dimple pops. I wiggle free of the tangled hides that line my bed, and he glances at my injuries. "I wish I could give you something to stop the pain."

"The white meadowsweet has been helping."

Bjǫrn goes to retrieve a pulp that I watched him make from cattail root. Just outside the entrance to the cave, the wind picks up and we hear the dry, brittle tinkle of leaves dancing across the rocks and eddying with a building rattle in the whistling wind.

"Winter is coming. I have to salt the fish," he says, but his voice sounds tight.

"I'll help," I say. I feel as exhausted as a salmon swimming upriver during spawning season. Bjǫrn tosses a glance my way.

"You can't," he says. "You are too weak."

"I'll help," I repeat. He knows I am not strong enough to stand alone, not brave enough to stand apart.

The days wear on. Bjǫrn works hard to stockpile food and collect firewood for the winter months. He brings back rabbit and deer and caribou, wild goose and duck. As he scrapes and cures and tans his hides, I use the berries, roots and herbs that he has collected to make poultices and tinctures, teas and salves. He is patient when he explains the uses of various resinous tree saps and berries that are new to me, but he speaks as if I know nothing, as if it is his responsibility to teach me all.

"This is a pulp made from spruce tree tips and bark placed in a piece of soft caribou hide. Wrap it around your injured arm, and it will be particularly helpful to relieve pain."

"The warmth is as soothing as the hot pools on Greenland shores," I mutter as the blue-black light of darkness falls. Bjǫrn can barely keep his eyes open as he struggles to light a fire.

There are dark smudges underneath his eyes; his shoulders slump.

"I'll go out hunting and foraging again tomorrow."

"We have enough. When the snows come, I can go out and help you. It would go faster if there were two of us."

Bjørn's head shoots up. "Don't be foolish," he says as he tries to flint the fire again. He fails, and a curse slips out. "The entrance to this cave also needs to be boarded up in order to keep the blizzards out."

"I can hardly feel the cold from here."

"Not yet, you can't, but if I don't block that entrance, the blizzards will freeze us out. As it is, I'm worried about how little firewood I have collected to get us through winter. We'll need some more."

I glance at the mounting pile of logs on the woodpile. "Surely you've collected enough wood already?"

"Greater men have died because of their lack of preparation for the snowstorms that hit these parts."

"I know," I say miserably.

"You don't," he snaps. He blows on the meagre fire before leaning back. "I can't work any harder or any faster. You're injured, Anja, but you'll have to push aside your pain and pull your weight. Our survival depends on it. I'll keep hunting and you can gut the catches. I trust you know how it's done?"

My eye begins to twitch. He must think of me as highborn. He digs his fists into his eyes, and I fall silent.

"To survive out here has everything to do with a man's perseverance and his skill."

"Then I'll pray you become an even better hunter than you are." I steal a glace and regret the jab. "Trust me, if I could walk, then I would hunt."

"No girl can hunt."

"I am not as feeble as you think."

"I never called you feeble."

"You make assumptions, Bjǫrn, without knowing everything."

"I'm tired, Anja," is all he says.

From that point onwards, I make sure to pull my weight. The caribou hunting is good, and Bjǫrn bags a giant bull with the largest antlers I've ever seen. We celebrate by gorging ourselves on roasted game and cloudberries mixed in fat.

One evening, I find myself thinking of Freydis, and I wish I had a *hnefatafl* board to pass the time. When I mention the game of strategy to Bjǫrn, he shrugs his shoulders and tells me he is not familiar with the game. He is carving in poor lighting, squinting as his knife tip makes a groove. After a few moments, he pauses and unkinks his legs and stretches them out in front of the blazing fire.

"Do you know any sagas, Anja?"

"I do," I mumble sleepily. A firelog splits in two and sends out winking, blinking sparks. Bjǫrn quickly snuffs them out with his big toe.

"Baldr's saga is my favourite," he says. He glances up. "As you know, Baldr was killed by a mistletoe arrow, but he was resurrected when the tears of his mother, Frigga, turned the red berries white. I always wondered about that story."

"What part?"

He holds out his whittled piece of wood to study it in the firelight. "The part about his mother, Frigga. I wonder how it would feel to lose a child, only to see the child eventually come alive again."

He should wonder how it feels to lose a mother, how it feels to have her people come alive again. Freydis ladybirds into my thoughts. She is no Frigga and *Faðir* has no tears. *Oh gods, I've forgotten what everyone looks like on Greenland shores. I've forgotten everything before the bear, before its eyes, before its tears of blood, before its …*

I paw through my furs to feel for the raven earrings that *Faðir* gave me as Bjǫrn leans back and gazes into the fire. When he begins to rattle out a soulful tune, the lyrics are so soft and sweet that I slip into the dreamworld where the ancestors roam.

"This woman you sing of, the one with the ginger-coloured hair, is she a god?"

"*Neinn.* She was a Norsewoman who lived among the Red Men from a Beothuk tribe. I wonder if your people knew her."

I feel my brows crinkle. "The ballad is a sad one."

"*Já.*" He gently wraps his wood carving in a piece of rabbit fur. "Uncle taught me the verse before he died."

"Tell me more about the Beothuk."

"I've mentioned them to you before. They are enamoured by the colour red. Like the song says, the Beothuk huntsman must have fallen in love with the Norsewoman because of the colour of her hair."

"But in the end, she was separated from him?"

"*Já.* That's how the ballad goes."

"You know so many ballads. How do you keep track of them?"

"I think it's in my blood."

"Yes, it must be." In the shadows, the fire flares. I take a breath. "I'd like to meet these Beothuk."

Bjǫrn tilts his head back and looks through the smoke hole at the moon. There is a red splotch creeping up his neck. "If all goes well, we will be able to meet up with my Beothuk brothers next spring."

"My leg will get better," I mutter, leaning back.

Bjǫrn stands and stretches. "I'll board up the entrance to our cave tomorrow and fill the cracks with a mudplaster that you can help me make. We'll have to stuff some sod into the gaps between the lintel and the rocks."

"I hope your efforts will help warm me up. Even wearing all my furs, I can't seem to feel my toes."

Bjǫrn shoots me a worried look.

"Don't worry, huntsman," I quickly say. "My injuries are healing well."

Bjǫrn finishes crafting his wooden door to close off the entrance to the cave just before the first snowfall comes. The arrival of winter marks the onset of a different routine for the two of us. Bjǫrn still goes out to check his traps, but he returns by noon and then he works on fixing tools and fixing gear and fixing me. The knowledge that I've wrecked his life and prevented him from returning to his people itches like a mosquito bite.

One evening, Bjǫrn comes over to my bed to inspect my wounds and he finds pus oozing from the zigzagged stitches laddering up my arm. "We'll need to watch this closely. It could get worse."

When I don't reply, Bjǫrn pulls out a raven's claw from underneath his jerkin. Before I can say anything, he begins chanting, and his incantations build to a peak as his voice pecks out words I can't understand. Above my head, a bat swoops down, which startles me.

"Are you going to place a runic whalebone in my bed?" I try to smile. My lips are dry.

"I would if I had one," Bjørn says in a clear, strong voice. He reaches for his whittling knife.

"Tell me about your family, Anja." His head bends low over his carving piece. There is a sudden awkwardness, a sickly fear.

"I have no family."

"You had a clan?"

"They sent me here," I say, but I am so unnerved that I almost fall backwards into the fire. Instantaneously, Bjørn springs up.

"Careful now. You are still unsteady on your feet." He takes me by the wrist and settles me onto a stool. I glance up at him.

"My mother's name was Raven," I continue dizzily, "but she is dead. They say she walked these shores."

Bjørn lowers himself onto the ground and resumes carving.

"I need to return to her Beothuk village that lies close to Leifsbidur." My mouth is dry. Bjørn stops his work. His brows shoot up.

"Are you certain that Raven is a woman?" he asks me carefully. I must look distressed because he gazes at me long and hard. I can hardly find enough air to speak.

"Do you know of Raven and how she died?" I manage. The words feel sticky and unpronounceable. My palms are sweating; my hands begin to shake. I endure another bout of shooting pain.

"You mustn't fret," he sighs when he sees the expression on my face. "I can take you to the Beothuk village. I know it well."

Our eyes connect. There is a burst of hope that feels as though I am standing underneath a cascading waterfall. Outside the wind is howling. There is a whistling hiss as it slips underneath Bjǫrn's fancy door.

"My *faðir* lived in a Beothuk village once," I manage in a squeaky voice. "Perhaps the village you speak of is the same one?"

"Perhaps," he says, but he looks confused.

"I have a pair of Beothuk earrings," I continue as my heartbeats send arrows into my ears.. "I wonder if you might recognize the design? Perhaps you know the carver?" I stand on unsteady legs and hobble over to retrieve my pouch from my bed, but my hands are clumsy, and I fumble with the leather ties.

When Bjǫrn sees the earrings, he tilts them so that the firelight illuminates the intricacy of the design.

"Have you seen anything like these before?"

"*Neinn*," he says, but his voice falters when he glances at my face.

"Will these be useful to show the Beothuk? Perhaps someone in your Beothuk village will know who made these? It is important to me that I find the carver. I am sure he knew my mother. Perhaps they shared kinship?"

I look down at my trembling hands and try to remember the hazy faces of the *Skraelings* who were present in the cave when I first woke up. There is a sudden memory of a tall, thin man with red markings scrolling down his face. I remember him leaning over me. What if he was someone Raven knew?

Grief comes, unbidden. We sit together in silence. I watch the curled shavings from Bjǫrn's wood carvings feather-falling to the ground as the fire crackles, snaps and pops. A whisper of chilly wind moves through the cave, announcing the arrival of the first blizzard outside.

"You must heal so that I can take you to this Beothuk village," Bjǫrn eventually says.

I lean forward just as a cramp tears through my leg. "I hope we won't have to walk too far."

"It's far," he says, glancing up, "but as long as your skin doesn't rot and you can move, we should be fine."

"How did you learn to care for the sick?"

"You taught me," he says. He cracks a smile.

"I doubt I am the first person you've treated with your medicines."

"*Neinn*," he teases, "but you have been the most difficult."

By the time the winter solstice comes, Bjǫrn and I are feeling more hopeful about my recovery. When he returns from checking his trapline one evening, he brings back a string of ptarmigan.

"Here," he says. There is an awkwardness about him as he tries to suppress a grin. I cock my head. The ice clinging to his frozen leggings falls in clumps to the cave's slate floor.

"You didn't meet with any trouble, did you?" He shakes his head, and I wait patiently for him to draw out something from his furs. When he hands me a Yule log, I stare at it, and my hands begin to shake.

"I decorated this miniature log with sprigs of fir and holly to remind us both of Baldr and our folks back home. Truly I tell you, I've no wild boar to mark this feast day. This simple token will have to do."

Freydis's face drifts like snow into my mind, and I pinch myself and try not to cry. For a long moment, I stare at him. "What is the midwinter feast without something to mark it?"

Bjǫrn begins to remove his snowy leggings, but his fingers are red and stiff and cold, and he is slow.

"Here, let me do it," I say, placing the Yule log aside and bending down. As I am helping him unclasp the ties on his boots, I catch sight of the nasty bear scar running down my arm, and the panic rises in my throat. I can feel the bear's incisors crunching bone, its wet saliva drooling down.

"Your injuries are healing nicely," Bjǫrn says.. I give a little snort, and Bjǫrn swipes his nose with the back of his hand. "Skaði, the avid winter huntress, has arrived. It's bloody cold outside."

He shoots me a wobbly grin before he cups his hands to his mouth and blows on his fingers to stir back warmth. "My family always marked the *Jólablot* with drinking, feasting, songs and games after making sacrifices to the gods and the ancestral spirits."

"We did that too." Helga and Magnus and Seth and all the farmhands drop into my thoughts like lacy snowflakes gently fluttering down.

Bjǫrn glances at the Yule log. "Dusk is falling. On this very night, the wolf of darkness will catch the sun, and she will be doomed and swallowed and devoured whole."

"The solstice marks the return of life. The sun goddess will birth her new self – her *döttir* – who is essential for the return of light and life. Tonight marks the darkest night of the year after which Sól, in the form of her *döttir*, will once again ride her chariot across the sky."

Bjǫrn's face is flushed from the cold outside. "Sól will rebirth herself from the darkness of the wolf's belly, and Sól will return to her former glory in the form of her *döttir*, the new sun."

A realization dawns. "Come, Bjǫrn. We must mark Sól's

return." My spirit sings as I begin to gather the spruce boughs from the ground where they have been placed to catch up the mud.

"I suppose you want to weave the greenery into a circle," he asks as he leans down and we begin to help each other twist the boughs into a wreath. I toss a grateful smile as Bjørn reaches into his pocket and pulls out a short piece of twine to tie the ends together.

When we are done, we make our way back to the door and throw it open to a whoosh of cold that slithers up my legs. In the pale blue light, it is eerily peaceful and deathly silent and bitterly cold. Even the gods have abandoned this land of frost giants.

Looking out across the vast stretch of whiteness, I watch the snowflakes gently fluttering down as the light slips away and the first winter stars appear. Bjørn is leaning against the doorframe, and his breath sends up plumes of mist into lavender blue winter sky. I can feel his warmth against my back, against my neck. Turning, I take the wreath from him so that he can light a tinder bundle. There is a little hiss when the bundle ignites, and a sliver of smoke rises in the air. A few moments later, the wreath is set on fire.

Bjørn helps me fling the burning wreath, and we watch it careening wildly through the air before it finally lands in a pile of snow. Standing together, we shiver in the crisp, cold air as we watch it burn. Afterwards, I peer out across the white expanse of nothingness.

"'Tis a place of beauty, is it not, Anja?"

"'Tis dangerous, too," I mutter as I lean down to scratch my injured leg that feels wooden and heavy and stiff and sore. The winter day slips away. Bjørn crosses his arms and shifts his weight against the lintel.

"When I was a wee lad, the ancestral stories were my favourite part of *Jólablot*."

Wincing, I endure another wave of throbbing pain that works its way down my leg and back. "'Tis good to remember the traditions of our people."

Bjǫrn towers over me. I am suddenly struck by the height of him as he draws me back inside. For a moment, I find myself staring up into his handsome face, and my breath catches, and I see beyond his toughness. I see the sacrifice he has made to stay with me, the strength in him, his resilience.

Bjǫrn reaches over my head to push the heavy door shut behind us, and it creaks as though protesting. "May Thor protect us from destructive powers and clear a path for us to rise, just like he did for Sól." He pauses. In the dark, his eyes are glistening orbs as he scans my face. "Remember how Thor slaughtered his precious goats before reviving them with a blow from his hammer? Mother used to make me dress in goat's fur for the re-enactment ritual." He chuckles, reminiscing. "I hated it. If we had goat skins to wear tonight for the *Jólablot*, I tell you this: I would be hard pressed to put them on!"

He is close enough for me to reach out and touch the stubble on his chin. In the dark, he reaches out and clasps my hand.

"I have another gift for you." His breath is hot against my cheek.

I let him pull me back to the firepit where he sits me carefully on a stool before he scampers into one of the cave's alcoves where I hear him fumbling in the dark. Within moments, he returns with an elaborately carved walking stick. His eyes are dancing; his cheeks are red.

"I whittled the tip out of antler bone, and I carved a healing rune on the wood," he simply says. He seems embarrassed. I pick up the walking stick and admire the detailed animal images that he has carved, his workmanship, the feel of it.

"I do not have a gift for you."

Bjørn bends his head over mine and gently takes the walking stick in his hand to show me the carving of a raven on the back. "Just learn to walk again," he whispers in my ear.

A draught of wind whistles through the cave, and I sense the presence of the ancestors passing through.

Chapter Thirteen

FIRE AND ICE

The cold weather brings frost and snow and blowing bits of pelting ice. In the perpetual darkness of the cave, we tuck in as the snowpack builds. Each morning, I make sure to wake before Bjǫrn to take the waste out and stoke the fire and roast the fish and haul in snow for melting and drinking. The daily routine, the steady sluggishness of it, wears on my spirit and fatigues my bones.

One month after *Jólablot*, we wake to clear blue skies and brilliant sunshine bouncing off the sparkling snow. "I think I'll go ice fishing," Bjǫrn says as he pushes his feet into his sealskin boots. "I promise to return by dark. The trick will be to find a patch of ice that is still thin enough to break through."

"You should take your axe, Bjǫrn," I murmur as I stir the fire.

"It would be wise for you to keep that leg propped up instead of working on your herbs. The crushing can be done later when I get back."

"May the gods go with you," I sputter irritably.

"You make it sound like I am abandoning you." He squares his shoulders underneath his bulk of furs and picks up his spear.

"I could come with you."

"You need to heal," is all he says. When he opens the door, he lets in a blast of cold that crawls up my hides and makes me shiver so that I quickly tug my furs together at my throat. For a moment, I am tempted to stay seated on my stool at the fireside, but then I follow him out, half-limping towards the stream of light that crawls inside. Standing at the doorway, I watch him snowshoeing down the hill. Right before he reaches the treeline, he turns, and I wave him off.

For the remainder of the morning, I try to keep busy sorting herbs and drying sculpins and cooking the herring that I haul in from the frozen cache buried just outside our door. At midday, I take a meal before nodding off. When I wake, I build a fire and the blaze comforts me until I begin to think about the wolf of darkness eating up the sun and casting the light into the realm of Hel. Then my thoughts take on a life of their own, and the worries come, niggling.

The voice of the fire is my only company, and for a while, I listen intently to the crackles and pops and hisses echoing through the cave, the noises that have become so familiar, they bore me. Wrapping my arms around my shoulders, I strain my ears, listening for the clunks of Bjǫrn's return outside our door. I hear only the steady chatter of cave drips, the sweet-nothing noises of the wind, the slight movements of bats and mice in shadows. Evening is coming. Beyond the door, I imagine the swirling whiteness covering Bjǫrn's tracks in the wilderness.

To quell the angst building in my bones, I struggle up to go in search of firewood. Bjǫrn's woodpile fills one full wall. He has stacked the wood so that it is within easy reach, but even so, if I want to build a roaring fire, I will be forced to make several trips back and forth.

When I am finally done, I sit back and stare into the glowing flames and feel the warmth of the fire on my face. Then I watch the sparks shooting up through the air hole in the rocks. Beyond that, a gibbous moon is on the rise in an ice-blue winter sky at dusk. Bjǫrn still isn't back. What is keeping him? He talks so much of tree wells that I begin to wonder if he has fallen into one. The panic swells. My heartbeats thunk. I hear singing through the hissing logs, see spirits dancing in the fiery flames. My raven *fylgja* croaks three times.

Go, my child. Go and put your raven earrings on.

The earrings are tucked away in the stiff folds of my salt-wrecked leather pouch which has become buried in the furs at the foot of my bed. As soon as I catch a glimpse of them, I begin to shake. So much has happened since Thorvard gave them to me. So much has changed. I am not the same. I have walked in death's shadow, and I am no longer afraid of the coming of *Ragnarök*.

When I put the earrings on, I am conscious of how heavy they are in my earlobes, how easily they sway back and forth, how easily they get tangled in my hair. With a heavy grunt, I slowly hoist myself up with the help of my walking stick and go in search of a piece of twine to tie my hair back.

As soon as I enter the alcove at the back where Bjǫrn stores his gear, I lose the light and stumble against a rocky ledge that feels like a bench of sorts. Patting my hands over the tools and weapons, I suddenly come across the soft smoothness of a stack of birchbark beside which lies a drinking horn and something else – a slingshot that I almost drop. When I push the weapon back into place, I tentatively reach out and my fingers come across a frayed piece of twine. Without thinking, I tug at it with such force that it comes undone and a hide falls down and quickly unravels at my feet. There is a flare of annoyance as I reach down.

My hands touch fur.

I withdraw in shock.

A black, furry form swipes the air; claws connect with flesh. I am trapped inside a rock cavern, gasping as the spirit bear rises on its haunches and paws its way into my mind. The catapult tumbles off the shelf. I scoop it up and scuttle backwards into the light.

"Who goes there?"

Mucus clogs my throat. I scan the cave. There is a faint rustling sound. I feel the presence of the bear, large and looming, and a scream slips out, and I lunge for it. The bristly fur brushes against my skin, and I swat it off. When I spin around, the shadow drops on all fours and sniffs the air in search of me. Its image flickers in the firelight. All I see is its lolling tongue hanging out and slurping up ethereal mist.

Instinctively, I draw back. When I catch a glimpse of the bear shadow rearing up again with its lips pulled back, I wave the air in front of me. Nothing seems to unnerve the bear. I smell the creature's rancid breath, the stink of its flea-filled fur, the stink of my own clammy sweat.

Terror fills my bones, and I bawl out the huntsman's name and scramble backwards and almost slip. When I lose my footing, I fall backwards on my bum. Towering above me, the bear begins to roar, and its bloody eyes blinks once, blinks twice. On the third blink, I notice its black, cavernous eye socket with ravens spilling out.

There is whirling white smoke filling up the empty cave,

slithering higher into the rocks. My hands fly up to protect my face. Through shaking fingers, splayed wide, I steal a look just as the bear emits another vicious growl. Instantly, I shimmy backwards

"Stay back!" I shout, and my scream echoes through the cave, reverberating off the jagged rocks in loud, discordant echoes.

There is a sudden jolt of pain before the bear releases a tremendous growl that shakes the ground. Startled, I crab my way backwards and spider through the dirt, unable to determine what is real, unable to stop myself before my hand accidentally slips into the roaring fire.

Pain. White hot. A burning sensation underneath the skin. I suck in a sharp breath and bite back stinging tears as an anguished moan slips from my throat. When I see the ugly, red, blotchy burn on my hand, my stomach lurches and I almost puke.

The bear hide is puddled in a discarded heap just outside the alcove. With a heavy grunt, I scramble up and make my way towards the door and lift the latch and step outside and thrust my injured hand into the snow. The image of the black bear unexpectedly pops up in my mind, and I bite my cheeks to suppress a scream. In the pale blue sky, the moon shines down, illuminating a vast stretch of white. There is nothing moving in the trees where the shadows sit. Even the wind has lost its voice.

"Bjørn!"

My shout echoes in a pop that dances through the frosty air. Pain, grisly and pinching and sharp and hot, is radiating from my burn. Gritting my teeth, I examine the flaring redness before my knees go weak. Every part of me is muddied from scrambling across the stone floor. There is a dead leaf matted against my shin.

I search the trees. The panic swells. Without another thought, I turn around and make my way back inside and close myself off to the numbing pain and memories. In a frozen state, I retrieve the bear hide and spread it out and begin tossing logs onto it. When I think I have enough to build a bonfire, I drag the hide across the floor and lift the latch and pull the mound outside. There is sweat dripping down my back and the noise of a thousand buzzing flies inside my ears. With shaking hands, I light my flint and start the biggest bonfire that I can make.

By the time the fire is roaring, it is pitch black outside and the air is windless and very cold. I study each cluster of tree shadows but see no signs of Bjørn snowshoeing through the white. The darkness presses in on me even as the bonfire flares. The silence threatens to swallow me.

I shout his name, and my scream echoes across the silent fields of glistening snow. In the stillness of the winter night, nothing stirs. The silence grows. I feel my skin prickling as I struggle to embrace my courage.

Even before I spot him emerging from the treeline, I hear the swish of his snowshoes crunching over a patch of ice-encrusted snow. His frozen body is hunched over so that it looks as though he is old and stooped. With a frightened yelp, I clasp my furs closed and begin making my way down the bank.

"Stay back!" Bjørn calls out hoarsely. "You'll slip and fall." The lower half of his garments are rigidly stiff with ice, his eyelashes are almost frozen shut, the furs that cover his face and chin are ice-frost mist.

"Frostbite," he wheezes as he struggles up the icy bank. His hair is dripping icicles. I hold out my good hand and pull him up so that he falls into my waiting arms. He is so wooden that I can barely manage to hold him up.

"I can't feel my toes," he moans as we inch our way into the cave. I get him seated on a bench and work to pry off his frozen furs, his buckskin breeches, his leather boots. His toes are as white as mushrooms, and his feet are red and chafed.

"Let me be," he mutters, and I pull back. I had thought that to have him here, alive, would bring relief, but the look of him makes tears well up. I turn away.

"Help me strip off my shirt," he whispers as he clutches my one good arm. His teeth are chattering; his touch is cold.

It takes two of us to manage it. When I pull a warm, furry hide off his bed and toss it around his shoulders, he shivers violently.

"I made it back," he says as he tries to flip back his dripping hair.

"You are a knave for making me worry so!"

I lean forward to grab a rabbit fur off a bench. Taking care, I begin weaving it between his toes. As soon as I am finished, I cup his feet in my hands and begin to blow on them to bring the blood back into the toes.

"You'll have to immerse your feet in water to thaw them out."

He lifts his head and sees my burn. "By the gods, what happened there?" He points, and I avert my gaze.

"I fell," I mutter as I shift in place to dislodge the cramps from sitting. My burned flesh is still weeping, and I purse my lips and rise to go in search of water to soak his feet. I feel his eyes following me.

"I broke through the ice of a frozen lake," he mutters, speaking fast.

My breath catches. "You stupid fool."

"Let me see your hand," he says. When I ignore him, he

heaves a heavy sigh. "There aren't many maids who would have thought to light a fire to guide me back."

I place a bowl of lukewarm water at his feet. He lowers his foot into the water and bends his head in close to mine.

"I brought back fish," he grins.

"You brought me grief."

Bjørn draws in air. "It all happened very fast. I saw a good fishing hole, and I was careful. I took the bundle of hemp rope from my pack and looped it firmly around my waist before securing the other end to a tree on shore. Then I ventured out with my axe in hand and my fishing spear on my back. I was watching where I placed my feet when I suddenly heard an unearthly, grinding noise. Truly, I tell you, I didn't know the ice would crack."

"I wish you had never gone."

"I used the hemp rope to pull myself back into shore, but my leggings got wet and froze against my skin. Afterwards, I could hardly walk. Fie! Fear is a dangerous thing. I thought I'd die."

"Your frostbite is very bad," I whisper without glancing up.

"I've seen other men – Beothuk hunters – who have lost their fingers and their toes. I worry it will be the same for me."

"You won't lose anything," I say, but I have difficulty swallowing, and I know he sees my shaking hands.

"I was tempted to curl up in a ball and give in to death but, in the end, I thought it best to keep moving. Then I caught sight of your bonfire. That's when I forced myself to carry on. I told myself that I needed to stay alive for you." He lifts his dripping foot out of the water. I take it up in my lap.

"If you had died …"

"I didn't, Anja."

"You could have, Bjørn." He winces. I study the redness of the foot resting in my lap. "This salve will help alleviate the burning and itching from the frostbite. If your flesh starts oozing pus, we'll know it didn't work."

"Anja," Bjǫrn says awkwardly, "I'm sorry for scaring you. I should have been more careful. I shouldn't have ventured out across that stretch of ice."

"It's no use feeling badly about what has come to pass."

"'Tis wise advice," he mumbles, eyeing me.

Chapter Fourteen

NIGHT STALKERS

The days grow longer, the drifts start to melt, and the sea ice begins to shift and break apart. My injured leg feels more like a piece of dead wood than a limb, and no amount of alder bark salve brings relief. I begin worrying that I won't be able to hike across Vinland to reach my birth mother's tribe and that we will miss crossing paths with the Beothuk harp seal hunters we are supposed to meet.

"We should leave before the snow is gone," Bjørn grunts as he is sharpening an arrowhead one bright, spring day. He pauses to scrutinize his work before he gently runs his thumb down the edge. "By the gods, I'm of a mind to fashion you a sled. You could sit in it and rest your leg and I'd pull you across the flatlands, at least until we skirt the bogs."

"Could you manage it?"

"Manage what? Pulling your heavy weight or fashioning a fancy sled?"

I grin without looking up.

Bjørn stops his work. "I'll go out into the bush first thing tomorrow to find a tree to chop to make the sled. If I'm lucky, I might even find us something good to eat."

"Please don't bring me any more skins to tan. I need to concentrate on my herbs. I want to make more poultices and salves for travelling so I can manage the hike back to Leifsbidur."

Bjørn tilts his head. "I didn't think there would come a day where you would be healed enough to walk out of here. You've worked hard, Anja."

"Game shot in the paunch often escapes from the hunter only to die a lingering death."

"You won't die, Anja. You are strong enough. If the fates allow it, we will make it back."

Above my head, I hear the screeching of the bats.

Bjørn leaves me once again. When he returns, he is dragging a tree trunk behind him, which he de-limbs and cuts into a pair of runners to make a sled. I haul in snow for melting water and attend to all the other chores. His insistence on crafting something that he can pull me in uses up all his time, and I try not to resent him for it. Once the sled is built, he instructs me to put some of the tree resin in a pot and cook it carefully so that it doesn't boil.

"You'll have to help," he gruffly says when the resin has thoroughly turned to liquid so that a sort of thread trails behind it when the stirring stick is lifted. "The resin will make the sled easier to pull so that the runners slide across the crusty snow."

"There may not be any snow left by the time we leave."

"There is always snow at this time of year," Bjørn replies, but he wears a scowl. Maybe he doesn't like me challenging him.

We work together, and the days slip by, and the sled gets finished before the snow begins to melt. After that, we pack up our things and sort out our gear, and Bjørn goes hunting one last time.

On the day of our departure the air is cool and crisp, and the robins and nuthatches are chirping noisily in the woodlands. Far off in the distance, the sun is cresting over the ocean and spilling light across the land, painting the budding trees in a wash of light.

"I'll check the cave one last time," I announce as I turn back to go inside. At the cave's entrance, I stop and tilt my head back and look way up. There are patches of dirty snow sitting in the rocky grooves, a bunch of crocuses peeking up through the lime green moss.

"Don't linger, Anja. I want to head out before the sun is fully up," Bjørn says as he stops to smell the air and to listen to the sounds of new life waking up in the woods. "Who can guess the ways of the gods and why they gifted us with this cave? May the fates be kind as we journey forth."

"We must trust in the gods to keep us safe. I have offered sacrifice to Eir, who is the chooser of life and death, and who gave me protection and helped me heal. No matter how dire the peril that comes, I know she will help." I toss the words behind my back as I slip into the cave with the mosquitoes hissing around my head.

How strange it is to be standing in this rock cavern that has been stripped bare of our gear, a place of darkness that served as our sanctuary for many moons. In the quiet, I lift my eyes and feel a draught coming from the belly of the cave. Shivering, I glance down at my crippled leg before firmly taking hold of my walking stick.

"I need your pack," Bjǫrn says as he comes up behind. I feel the heat of him at my back, and I linger just a little longer. "The gods always smile on brave women, Anja."

I limp toward the firepit where the grey-white ashes sit as though the cave has been empty for many months. I can't trust myself to speak. Not so long ago, I was lying in the rock depression just over there. In the dim light, I can just make it out.

Bjǫrn clears his throat. "It's time," he says.

"You've lost a winter because of me." The words hang heavily between us. As I flick a glance around the cave, Bjǫrn leans down and hoists my pack.

That morning, as the sun shines down, twinkling off the patches of ice and snow, Bjǫrn pulls me behind him in the sled. When we hit the first patch of bare, frozen ground, he reefs on the cord and the sled jerks forward, and he curses underneath his breath. When I volunteer to walk, he shakes his head.

"I can manage until we reach the river." He removes his furs, and I see patches of sweat seeping through his linens.

When we hit the frozen boglands, there is a wealth of lichens and new-growth herbs poking up through the dirty snow. I yearn to stop and ask about their medicinal properties, but Bjǫrn seems eager to move on.

"You're heavier than a caribou," he grunts as he gives the sled a tug. The guilt wells up. When he glances over his shoulder and sees my face, his eyes soften. "Thor will give me strength. He has put your life in my hands, and you have no reason to doubt my strength. You should enjoy the ride. You may never again be treated like a chieftain's wife."

I feel a flush of heat in my cheeks when I think of Freydis back on Greenland shores operating her own farm. Ironically, she is still a chieftain's wife and she has never been treated as well as this. I close my eyes, and her image floats before my eyes.

We continue to follow a deer trail before turning north and skirting a chain of bogs in a valley full of half-melted snow. Bjørn navigates a way around clusters of tuckamore and dwarf spruce trees budding in the springtime sun, until we hit a rocky stretch that leads up a hill. Then Bjørn makes me get out and walk.

"It's too rocky and uneven here," I say, but the words stick like sap in my throat.

"It can't be helped," Bjørn quickly says. His forehead is gleaming, and he has stripped himself of all his furs.

The sun is at its peak when we finally finish navigating all the hills and make our way down into a river valley where the rapids are cascading over a series of jagged rocks. The air misting off the water is nippy; the ground is still covered in frost and snow. Without a word, Bjørn drops the rope tethered to the sled..

"Praise Óðinn," I say as I lean down and rub the prickles in my foot. As soon as I am able, I make my way over to the water's edge, where I spot a beaver dam stopping up the river.

"I found some cow-parsnip shoots," Bjørn calls from up ahead. The roar of the water almost drowns him out. "Are they edible at this time of year?"

"Come back here and show me and rest a while."

"Not yet," he calls. I watch him enter a patch of thigh-deep snow and disappear into the bush.

When we lose the sun, the cold seeps underneath my furs. In front of me, the river snakes into the trees in a rush of chattering gurgles. I don't hear the huntsman return until he is practically standing over me.

"When we leave this place, we can enter those woods down there where the snowpack hasn't melted yet." A plume of mist dragons from his mouth.

"You'll strain your shoulder pulling me."

"The snow is deep. I can manage it." He blows on his hands to warm them up and scans the bank across the water as I scratch an itch. When I lift my eyes, I see that he is tense and weary.

"The insects are bad here."

"We've got bear grease mixed with mint to stave them off. You should smear your face and your arms."

At the mention of bear grease, the bear's image pops up, and my breathing snags, and I can't seem to make out the shapes of things. The terrifying roar of rushing water morphs into the sound of snuffling bears standing in river water, catching fish. The snorts geyser to a roar.

"Anja?" His voice tinkles stars.

I blink repeatedly.

"Here, take this." Bjørn's voice comes from far away. He forces me to look at him as he thrusts a smooth river rock into my hand. "This pebble is for remembering the beauty of this place."

"Help me find myself," I whisper. My heart thumps loudly as I draw a breath and finger the smooth, speckled stone he has handed me. "I doubt I can manage many more days like this."

"You'll have to try. Either that or both of us will die."

The river roars. A downed log floats by before it gets crushed. On the upper banks, the snowbanks are at their deepest. Bjørn scans the trees.

"There is better snow up there," he says.

We follow the river as it ribbons through the forest for the rest of the afternoon. When Bjǫrn begins to recite some saga I don't know, I nod off until a heavy jerk of the sled wakes me. In front of us, there is a caribou picking its way through the snow. Bjǫrn draws out his arrow before I have time to dislodge the spear. When he misses such an easy shot, he cusses loudly and scares off the birds.

"My muscles are weak from the pulling," he gripes.

I stare at him.

"You should stay awake. You could have been the one to take that animal out. Didn't you say you knew how to hunt?"

I have no words. My leg is throbbing. My pride is hurt.

For the remainder of the afternoon, I keep my bow and arrows at the ready, hoping to show him what I can do and praying that I will be able to prove my worth and demonstrate my hunting skills.

It is still light outside when we come out of the heavily bushed area and are rewarded with a spectacular view of a stunning lake. From there, it is only a short stretch downhill. We arrive just as the sun is setting. Bjǫrn is so bone weary that he barely has any strength left to set up camp. I pull my weight and build a fire and draw some water while the mosquitoes buzz around my ears.

That night, we sleep back-to-back. My bug bites itch, and my useless leg is stiff and sore. In the middle of the night, I bolt awake and sit up straight to check my arm after dreaming that the skin covering the scar has split open and begun to bleed. When I glance down to check, the puckered skin around the old wound is intact; the arm is fine.

The birds wake me with their lively chirping and their mating trills just as the sun is coming up. I am alive to the poplar smells as I drink in the freshness and study the lake mist hovering just above the water. Bjǫrn, with his tousled hair and the handsome protrusion on his throat jiggling up and down with his every breath, is snuggled underneath a bundle of frosty hides, and his stubbled face looks serene. Without waking him, I slowly rise to go and fetch water. When I return, Bjǫrn is squatting by a crackling fire, cooking grub.

He hands me a piece of fish, and we eat in silence as the sun crests over the wide expanse of lake, twinkling and sparkling like thousands of tiny stars. I shade my eyes. The huntsman stands. There are red rope burns and welts beetling up and down his forearms, a bug bite swelling near his eye. "I'll scout ahead."

When he returns, his face looks grim. "There's no more snow. You'll have to walk." He glances at me anxiously.

"I can manage," I say, trying to keep my face as still as stone. Without a word, Bjǫrn turns from me and begins to douse the fire as I start packing up our things. He bats the smoke away and winces before he calls to me.

"I think we should leave the sled behind. It's no good to us if there is no snow."

All around us, the robins are busy plucking worms among the cones and needle-tufts that line the ground.

"Perhaps you should drag the sled behind you for one more day," I say, but I can hear the smugness in my voice, the kind of tone Freydis used to use on me.

"*Neinn.* I am anxious to meet up with my Beothuk brothers, and that bloody thing will only slow us down."

I glance at him, careful to keep my face blank. The bugs are swarming around his head. "I won't be able to carry a heavy pack."

"I won't ask you to. I'll give you the lighter one."

When I think about leaving the sled behind and how long it took for him to make it, I get all twisted up. I can't help but worry that the hike will be impossible for my injured leg and that eventually Bjørn will give up on me as well. When I speak, my voice is hard.

"I will always be in your debt."

"Fie," he yells as he snuffs his nose with his sleeve. His tone startles me, and I stand there helplessly as he begins to rearrange the items in our packs. A sharp pain shoots down my leg.

"Where is the dogwood salve?"

He hands it over and swats a bug. "These bloody mosquitoes. Only bear grease can stave them off."

I touch my arm and feel the scar ridges and bumpy, mottled flesh as Bjørn wipes away his insect blood. When he sees my shaking hands, I pull out the pebble he gave me and turn away. The dark whirlwind inside me spins me in the direction of bear memories and pulls me down into the black, but I rub the stone and plant my feet and listen to the birdsong spilling from the trees.

We emerge from the woods and follow a trail through pristine wetlands dotted with wildflowers and a series of scattered marshes where the waterfowl are abundant. The views are spectacular. When I see a mosaic of herbs growing amongst the rocks, my spirit sings. Even though Bjørn doesn't let me stop, he tells me about the properties of the plants, and we discuss his understanding of the trees.

After a half-day's trek and a long, steady climb into a cluster of scattered larch, I need to stop. My leg is a throbbing inconvenience. Bjørn studies me. The dappled pine shadows flit across his face.

"There is a shallow river up ahead that we must cross. After that, you can rest." He leans down to inspect my leg. Afterwards, he takes my elbow and helps me hobble forward, and I lean on him and use his walking stick.

When we finally reach the crossing and I see how swiftly the current is flowing, I feel the familiar swell of panic rising in my throat as Bjørn paces back and forth.

"The current is strong, but the water looks shallow enough," he mutters underneath his breath, but I feel cold shadows when I see him studying the river crossing and scrutinizing the bank on the opposite side.

He makes me go first so that he can catch me if I fall, he says, but every step is dangerous. The freezing-cold water rushes past, pushing at my wobbly legs. Beneath my toes, I feel the slime-covered rocks, slippery and treacherous as I scramble to find a place to put my feet.

There is a bone weariness enveloping me as my cramping muscles begin to shake. The river swishes, swirling and gurgling as it rushes past, and the water is cold as it licks my toes. Bjørn holds me up by the elbow so that I don't fall, and when we make it to the other side, he leans down and clamps his teeth on his hunting knife to free up his hands so that he can dig through his pack. When he pulls out a piece of dogwood bark to quell my leg pain, I try to smile, but fatigue fills my body, and I can't seem to find the strength.

"This looks like a good place to set up camp for the night," Bjǫrn says as he shields his eyes against the sunshine that is skipping across the water and twinkling and blinking more brilliantly than rockcloud gems.

I rub my leg, worrying that we did not walk as far as Bjǫrn would have liked. There is a deep yearning to sink into sleep where I can close myself off from the pain shooting down my leg, from the roar of the river that mocks me.

"I'm going rabbit hunting so that we can eat," Bjǫrn announces into the air. He shades his eyes with his hand as he scans the riverbank. His leggings are still damp from our river crossing.

"Don't be gone too long."

"Anja, you are a worrier. I promise I'll come back with meat."

In silence, I watch him adjust the quiver on his back before he begins to make his way up the riverbank. At the top of the ridge, he turns and waves.

By the time I wake, darkness has descended and there is a springtime coolness in the air. The bats are swooping low over the rushing water that snakes into the blackness of the trees. Bjǫrn's pack is still sitting where he left it. Without standing, I reach over and lift the flap to find our pelts. For a moment, I can't make sense of it – the claws amidst the fur, a darkened smudge of a hairy pelt. Pulling back, I tug my arms into my chest and stare at the rolled-up hide that comes tumbling out of the overstuffed sack.

I snag a breath and touch my cheek. My hands are cold. Somewhere up the bank, a screeching owl hoots in two short bursts followed by one long call. I feel the chill creeping into my bones, a wave of fright ant-crawling down my spine. My body tenses. I snag a breath. When I look up, the bear hide has formed itself into a ball.

"Bjørn!" I yelp. I think I hear him return my call from somewhere far up-river. His baritone is a low boom that rises over the sound of the river rapids. I wait and call again, but there is nothing but river chatter and water splashes and bugs zipping through the air. There is a whoosh of air. A warmth of something breathing down my neck.

I whirl around.

My startled scream echoes across the gush of the river. There are shadows romping through the trees, slinking sideways through the bush. The creature disappears in a shaft of light and re-emerges in a sunset flare.

My mind must be playing tricks. The tears well up. I can't see straight.

With shaking hands, I peck through the folds of my mantle and find my grounding rock and palm it. *This pebble is for remembering the beauty of this place. There is nothing here. You are safe.*

I half close my eyes and force myself to reach out and touch the hide. Black hair falls forward in my face. I call on the gods, but there is only dizziness and swirling trees and flying rocks and winged creatures descending with their talons poised. Ducking, I angrily paw for the pack and grab the hide and drag it up towards my chin. Instantly, the eyeless creature growls so fiercely that I pull back. There is a smell of blood and vomiting, of bear stink and putrid breath that smells like death.

Through mist, the creature goes to dig its incisors into my arm, and I try to yell but no sound comes out. Panting, I try to throw the hide off my back and get away, but I am a frozen in a block of ice. From far away, I hear the moan of a wounded animal whimpering, and I pull back. The sound is coming from my mouth.

"Bjørn?" I call out again with a quick bark of laughter.

There is nothing moving downriver, nothing crawling out of the bush. I squint. In the worm moon shadows that flit across the water and end where the boulders sit, nothing stirs. There is only blackness. Only fear.

Groaning, I force myself to stand. As soon as I am balanced, I spot a log hidden in the grass and limp towards it, but I have to clench my teeth against the biting leg pain that nearly cripples me. When I've managed to collect enough sticks and logs, I call on the gods to help me build a roaring fire. Then I call out his name again and again, until the river rumbles and shuts me up. In the silence where the shadows lurk, I feel thousands of dangers all at once.

I sense their presence even before I see them: their silhouetted outlines and prowling forms, the glint of their yellow eyes. When the pack of wolves circling on the upper banks begins to howl, I reach for my hunting knife. The leader is mounting a boulder with the slow ease of a predator that knows how to trap and kill its prey.

With my free hand, I grab for my walking stick and take up position in front of the hissing fire. Directly in front of me, the wolves release another menacing howl from their station on a rocky outcropping lining the riverbank. With hands outstretched, I half-listen to their eerie howls as I imagine their canines ripping me to shreds and their maws tasting the meat of me and crunching through my brittle bones.

In the flickering firelight, I catch a glimpse of the leader's eyes and pointed fangs, its hackles and upright ears, its lolling tongue, its speckled brown and greyish fur. When it catapults off its rock-slab throne into a patch of grass, I look past the fire shadows, past their eerie glow, but all I see is dark foliage with no movement of any kind.

In one quick move, I plunge my walking stick into the fire. As soon as it catches fire, I wave the torch above my head. The wolves on the upper bank release an angry howl, and I scuttle backwards, aware of the threat hanging over me. All along the water's edge, nothing moves. Not even yellow eyes.

Thor, Lord of the Hammer, help me throw this flaming fire torch and set these beasts on fire. Protect me from their dangerous fangs.

I twirl around as the fearsome pack leader emerges from a tuft of grass lining the riverbank just upstream. The fire rages, releasing a woody campfire scent. The wolf's menacing form disappears into the smoke, and I draw back. Through the flames, I see the wolf picking its way across the river rocks, flicking its tail up as a visible sign of authority. He is the alpha homing in on me, expecting me to run. There are hot tingles in my feet, rooting me solidly to the ground.

The other wolves suddenly leap off the bank and start closing in on me. Their lips are curled, their teeth are bared, their ears jut out horizontally. I feel the heat of the campfire on my skin as I face the terror of the pack.

The wolves draw closer. The fire flares. With a sudden surge of strength, I jab my fire-stick at them with all my might. There are yelps and howls as fur catches fire. One of the wolves is driven into the fire and is engulfed by flames until it leaps and rolls and releases a loud, pathetic sound. I watch it scamper towards the river, whimpering. In the chaos, the other wolves go running off, scrambling quickly into the grass. The leader appears on the other side of the flames. Its eyes narrow into slits.

By Óðinn's eye, come and get me, you mangy beast! For the love of Thor, I'll strike you down and set your fur on fire so you can't devour my salty flesh so easily.

I lunge, and my torch finds its mark. When I brand the wolf, it begins to yelp.

There is a chorus of howls as the wolves regroup and come for me. One attaches itself to my mantle and gets entangled in the folds. Wildly, I swat at it with the stick. I don't let go. In my periphery, the fire flares as the wolf leader makes ready to pounce again. Just as I turn, it flies at me.

Behind me there is a hissing sound as an arrow sizzles past. I wince and scream all at once. There is a whoosh of air, a tremendous thud. Through splayed fingers, I see the wolf's lifeless form falling sideways with an arrow sticking out of its hairy pelt. In the shadows, the other wolves scatter up the bank.

Bjǫrn leaps towards me and grabs my burning walking stick and begins to pelt the wolf on the head. I look away and focus on listening to the burbling noises of the river, the gush of the rapids swishing over the many rocks. The ground starts to swirl. There is a burst of light. Flames lick up the shadows. I smell seared hair.

Bjǫrn's baritone rises from the land of the giants where life is slow and cumbersome. He is muttering mysterious words, throat-gargled and rhythmic, as though he is chanting to the spirit of the animal that lies somewhere between the realms where murkiness mixes in with clarity. I know this prayer. Freydis taught it to me.

When he is finished, he looks up with eyes that flash with a mix of concern and awe and something else.

"You were gone too long," I say. I taste the release of terror in my mouth.

Strength and power radiate off Bjǫrn, as though he is waiting and willing to fight off the spirit enemies lurking around us with legendary, bone-crushing moves. He is filled with the blood of Thor; his face is a thunderous storm.

"I shouldn't have abandoned you in this wilderness, Anja. With Óðinn as my witness, I swear to you, from this day forward, you will always have my allegiance and protection."

A cool spray is blowing off the water. I feel for my raven earrings in the pockets of my mantle, and there is a soothing comfort. I have so many questions, so many threads to weave together, but at least the wolves are dead.

Chapter Fifteen

RIVER THIEVES

I sleep next to Bjǫrn under the bear hide to benefit from his warmth, but when I wake early the next morning in the drizzling cold, I am shivering. We do not speak about the wolf encounter as we eat our morning meal. The roar of the river gods is conversation enough. After we finish eating, we do not linger long. The weather is worsening, and Bjǫrn is eager to set out.

"I'll find you a new walking stick in the bush," he says as we both stare sombrely at the charred remains of the one he carved.

"I'll need one," I say numbly. He can't look at me. "Your carvings won't be forgotten, Bjǫrn."

He shrugs and hocks a wad of spit onto the ground.

At first we follow the river that twists and turns through a pristine valley where thickets of speckled alder rise from waist-high grasses. There, Bjǫrn finds and prunes a branch that becomes my new walking stick. I use it to help me hobble across a flat, marshy plain that stretches as far as the eye can see. Doggedly, I follow Bjǫrn, and we travel under a cloudy sky that smells of rain. The ground is muddy and strewn with lichen-covered rocks and larch scrub that make it hard to navigate, but I don't complain. Nothing good would come of it.

It is past noon when the trail we have been following suddenly peters out. Just ahead, our way is blocked by a thick patch of tuckamore that appears to be impassable. We have no choice but to backtrack to a river cutting through a bank of rocks. I am fatiguing quickly; my leg is swollen and aching. My blistered feet are sopping wet.

"We'll need to cross this pissing river at this point," Bjǫrn announces to the wind.

I unclip my mantle and roll it up carefully, securing it to the base of my pack with some rope. It will only be a hindrance when I attempt to wade across. When I look up, Bjǫrn is staring across the water. His brow is furled..

"Come eat something," I call to him as I rifle through my heavy pack. He waves me off.

A rainy drizzle turns to steady rain. At the bottom of my pack, I catch sight of the raven earrings and pluck them out. There is a power to them, as if they are singing in my palm. Óðinn's ravens stare up at me, and I call on them and feel the tug of the ancestral spirits gathering round. I run my thumb over the etchings and think of my life and how it might have looked if I had stayed in Greenland. Then I picture my birth mother. I wonder if she looked like me. Was she tall or short? Thin or plump? How about her hair? I am sure it was raven black like mine. I shiver, noticing the rain pelting down, noticing the green of everything.

Bjǫrn is pacing up ahead. It seems like we have hardly rested when he calls to me. With a heavy sigh, I replace the earrings in my pack and brace myself when a sudden gust of wind plasters my buckskins against my legs. Bjǫrn approaches as the rain starts up and sluices down.

"Give me your foot coverings. 'Tis best not to get them wet. I'll put them in my pack." His voice is lost over the rumbling swish of big water. "It is shallow here, but the current is strong and powerful."

"You go first," I grumble. Bjǫrn flicks a glance.

"I'll follow you. It worked before."

I wave him off. "Let me sit here for a moment and catch my breath."

For a moment, he hesitates. Then he turns and enters the water. At first, he is sure-footed as he picks his way across. The water creeps to his hips. Just when he makes it to the half-way point, the wind picks up, and it begins to pour. For a moment I look away. As I am bending down to ensure that the flaps are securely fastened on my pack, Bjǫrn loses his footing and is swept away.

I scream when I see him go under. A moment later, he surfaces, but he is caught in the swirling rapids and hurled downriver. There is a burst of panic as I scramble down the riverbank and try to spot his moving form.

"Bjǫrn!" I yell as he disappears around a bend. Without thinking, I half-limp, half-run back up the bank where I blindly begin picking my way through the tall, wet grasses, scrambling quickly to follow him as I run along the bank and he floats downstream. His form is barely visible through the branches of the poplar trees that line the bank.

I round another bend, and when I glance sideways, I have lost him. The rain sheets down. Terrified, I pick my way up a hill only to discover a look-out point that gives a clear view of the water.

When I look down and spot him, Bjørn is trying to right himself in the shallows on the opposite bank.

"Thank the gods, you didn't drown!" I shout as a shiver runs through me. I can hear the air whistling through my lungs, the panic cresting in my voice.

"The current is stronger than I thought," he calls as the rain slows down.. "You'll have to come to me. Does it look safe enough from where you are?" His words get lost in the rush of swishing water, in the sound of wind and rain. Bjørn sleeks his hair back with his hands.

"Mind your footing and go slowly," he shouts, and the river gurgles in agreement. "If it gets too deep or you can't press on, you must turn back."

The water is cold, and the gooey mud sucks at my soles and gets lodged between my curled-up toes. As I pick my way over the rocky riverbed, I shift my pack and feel the rush of the current pushing at my legs.

"Take care, Anja! The water is growing deeper with every step."

Bjørn's voice gets lost in wind moans and plinking raindrops. Without warning, the current suddenly shifts and swirls and pushes me so violently that my knees buckle, and I lose my balance and topple backwards. Within moments, I am hurtling downstream at breakneck speed.

I am whipped against hidden rocks that scrape my knees and tear my shins. There is such a powerful undertow that I get sucked down and my head goes under until I surface in the rapids, but the heaviness of my pack pulls me under again and again as the current shoves me along at tremendous speed. In a panic, I twist as my body bops down, bops up, bops down again.

I try to dog-paddle into shore, but I feel my body being pulled into the depths. In a desperate struggle, I relinquish my pack to the river gods. As soon as I am cleared of the weight, I am pushed forward at great speed and funnelled downstream until the current whips me into a large eddy where there is a piece of dead wood sticking out of the riverbank. With some effort and much luck, I manage to grab hold of it before I am launched into the current once again.

Dangling from the branch, I resist the tug of the eddy's current and gasp for air. In one quick move, I just barely manage to shift my weight and prevent my good shoulder from being wrenched out of the socket. In my periphery, I see Bjørn's frantic figure come tearing down a deer path that runs the length of the riverbank.

"Over here!" I scream.

Bjørn flops down beside me and tries to grab my arm, but the branch begins to split. To sag. To drop. There is a sudden crack.

"Take my arm," he orders as he strains his muscles to grab hold of me. The branch jerks and drops me lower into the current. When I look down, the gurgling water rushes past.

"I'll have to get some rope," Bjørn shouts.

"Don't leave!" I cry. I can't quite see him as I shift my weight on the branch. My shoulder is slowly giving out. The branch sags lower and then bounces up.

"Thor is with you! Find your strength," Bjørn yells as he briefly disappears from sight.

Just as I am about to be swept out of the eddy and flung downstream, the huntsman reappears with a piece of rope that he swings wide. With luck, I manage to grab hold of it, and he yanks me just enough so that he can grab hold of me and pull me over the muddy bank. When he turns me over, I have no feeling left in my legs. He leans in closely. I reach up to touch his face.

"You are shivering," he whispers as he helps me rip off my water-drenched hides. There are newly carved scrapes and cuts peppering my shins and thighs. Even my good arm is dripping blood. When I wipe my nose on the bear hide, I leave behind a slimy stream of snot.

"Here, take this. It'll stop your teeth from chattering."

He hands me a piece of dogwood bark. There is a surge of panic, a sinking feeling in my gut.

"The pack is gone," Bjǫrn says soberly when our eyes connect.

"Neinn!" I cry.

"It's gone, Anja," Bjǫrn repeats.

A moan slips out. I've lost my hunting knife, my sleeping hide and the mantle that I use for warmth. I've lost my steel and flint and my sewing needle and some sinew thread. By Óðinn's beard, our food is gone! And my herbs!

In a flash, I remember the raven earrings at the bottom of my pack, the only item of my birth mother's that I have left. I see the etchings of the ravens, the moon and stars as clearly as if I am cradling the jewellery in my palms. I've lost Raven's earrings. *Faðir'*s gift.

"Your pack was swallowed by river thieves."

"We can find it?" I manage pitifully.

"We can't," Bjǫrn snaps irritably. He is silent for a moment, and then he flicks a look into the bush. "Your pack held all the meat I jerked."

"Damn the meat!" The burn of a hot rage bubbles up. My throat is scraped raw from the screaming. My bruises throb. I am barely aware of my surroundings, barely aware of anything.

I let Bjǫrn help me up. Every muscle is quivering with exhaustion. Bjǫrn has no choice but to hold me up around the waist. With soothing words, he talks to me, but I don't hear anything as we hobble into the woods looking for shelter, leaning into each other for extra warmth.

That night, I sleep curled in Bjørn's arms, shivering and dreaming of sea monsters and bear-like creatures that team up with demon-possessed fish with razor-sharp teeth that bite so hard, I lose my leg. A huntsman tells me that I am a bloody mess. Then a frightening apparition comes to tell me that I have no business living on Vinland shores. The ground morphs into a marsh that puffs out heavy fog, and I take the shapes of a broken longboat smashed apart, a mermaid drowning without a home.

When I finally wake in the early morning hours, Bjørn and I are sharing the bear hide and lying underneath a rocky outcropping close to the river's edge. A movement in the woods startles me. Instinctively, I reach for my spear. My hand hits stone. The sound of more twigs snapping makes me look again as a large, well-fed buck comes into view. Its majestic form moves quietly through the lime-green grasses that brightly pop after all the rain.

"Bjørn, wake up!" I whisper fiercely as I jab him forcefully in the ribs. The deer's ears shoot up; its eyes dart back and forth.

The huntsman springs awake and fumbles for his bow before he quietly slips out from underneath the overhang on his hunter's feet. The river is bubbling over the noise of the early morning birds. I watch him quietly nock his bow and take aim.

He takes the buck out in one clean shot.

Bjørn works hard to de-flesh and de-grease the deer hide. The flies are bad, and my bruises hurt, but it is my guilt that pains me most of all. It is because I lost my pack that we must spend long days fishing and gathering berries and smoking meat and curing hides. The two of us are often so tired by the time dusk starts to fall that we can barely keep ourselves awake. By the gods, it seems like everything is a struggle in this wilderness, where all we see is the river knifing its way into the trees, beyond which lie brooks and ponds and heavy stretches of tuckamore.

"How many deer hides would it take to replace the mantle that I lost?" I sputter one evening as we are sitting around a smoky fire.

"The hunting is good here," Bjǫrn says as he works to sharpen his butchering knife. "With another four to six, it could be done."

"I worry about summer coming."

"We likely missed the harp seal hunters."

The bugs are chirping. Bjǫrn stands and stokes the fire. His figure flickers in the smoke. "If we stayed here, I could mix some wood ash and animal fat to cure the pelts. I could also carve some antlers to replace your knife."

When I stay silent, he takes a breath: "I've a mind to scold the river for you, but that will not bring your earrings back."

"We should leave this place," I say in a brittle voice. "We need to reach the fjord."

Bjǫrn jerks his chin towards his pack. "We have hides to keep you warm, and I can continue to hunt as we go along."

"Your hunting eye is keen," I try, but my throat constricts.

"My eyes see things that yours cannot."

I sit with my back propped against a fallen log, gazing up into the pitch-black sky. When I spot a falling star, the magic of the moment is overshadowed by a sudden grief. I can feel a change coming, a sense that life as I know it is almost done and that I am about to lose what I have come to know. Soon there will be another ending I must face – an ending amongst all the losses I didn't want.

～

In the morning, we rise early and hike south at a steady pace over flat terrain dotted with trillium and other wildflowers and plants I don't recognize and Bjørn can't name. After a hard day's walk, we suddenly emerge from the tuckamore onto a valley floor that holds a pristine lake.

"The Beothuk will help you learn the names of all these plants. While I have never liked the Medicine Man, he knows his herbs. As the tribe healer, he might be willing to share his wisdom."

What man has ever been willing to share his wisdom? What man would ever care enough?

"I need to rest my feet," I say, squinting against the sun.

Bjørn stops and bends down to examine the animal scat embedded in a set of tracks. When he stands, he stretches tall. "I need a swim." His face looks grimy; his smell is rank.

"I'll race you," I tease. He glances at my injured leg and suddenly, we are laughing, and the pain eases up. Bjørn nudges me before taking off at a run, and I follow him, half-limping, half-hobbling down the bank.

The placid lake is so flat and glassy that it reflects the brilliance of the egg-blue sky. I stumble down the beach and find a place to discard my foot coverings underneath a rocky ledge. The cold of the water stops up my breath, and I shiver. When I turn, Bjørn comes plunging off a cliff.

"Come in, Anja! The lake is warm," he calls as soon as he

surfaces and spots me. The golden sun bounces off his sun-bleached hair.

I shield my eyes against the brightness and remember the hot pools on Greenland shores, the one that borders our little farm. Bjørn begins to swim towards a patch of reeds. "The water will soothe your aching bones," he calls over his shoulder.

The water is a tranquil mix of emerald blue lapping gently into shore. I wade in further, trying to adjust to the cold. When Bjørn stands, his naked back faces me and I see beyond the beauty of his bulk. I see his wild spirit and the way he loves this place, this outdoor living, the dangerous and unpredictable. He is always exploring, never still.

"Aren't you coming in?" he calls before he lowers himself into the water and dives down deep. I lose sight of him until he pops up again, splashing and teasing in a garbled voice dripping with laughter. Teetering, I lose my balance and fall in. In the serene glassiness of the lake, he tries to convince me to swim out to him. My refusal is met with another splash as the silky water embraces me and turns me into a mermaid's child with hair as black as octopus ink. Soon I am shedding my shirt and breeches underneath the water and feeling the warmth of the sun against my back.

I quickly wash the dirt from my skin and hair, and work the grime out from underneath my nails, but when I look down, I am startled by the bear's mark of ugliness: the discoloured welts running up and down my arm, a cord of scars across my chest, the purple-black patches of skin on my thighs and legs. *What will my mother's people say? What if they reject me because of my ugliness? By the gods, I'd hate for them to pity me. I hate that fate has cheated me.*

Bjørn swims towards me, and I quickly dog-paddle into the middle of the lake. I feel his gaze on my back, studying my puckered scars. It is one thing to have him see my nakedness while he is tending to my wounds. It is something completely different to be naked in the lake with him, where I feel like a scaly-skinned selkie, a changeling who is only half-successful at switching her repulsive seal skins for maiden's flesh.

Bjørn smiles, and I can't speak for fear of blubbering. Because of him, I am lucky to still inhabit this broken body, still fortunate enough to have these weakened bones.

"Think I'll go fishing," he calls. In the sunshine, his dimple pops.

By the time Bjørn has caught and cleaned the fish, the evening sun is bleeding into the horizon and splashing pinks and reds across the placid lake.

"You've been in so long, I'm sure your skin is all wrinkled and waterlogged," Bjørn says as I come to take my place at the fire. He watches me wringing out my hair as the mosquitoes hum above our heads. When one lands on my goose-pimpled arm, I squish it and leave behind a trail of blood.

"Move closer to the fire. It'll smoke them out," he advises practically, and I do as he says.

After we eat, we sit together and enjoy the peaceful sounds of the lake at twilight: the lapping water, the quacking ducks, the chirping insects in the grass. Bjørn shares an impressive display of knowledge about the wildlife in these parts, and I grow sleepy and draw comfort from his company. Far off in the distance, a raven disappears into the fading light as a patch of clouds rolls across the horizon and covers up the dying sun. In the opposite corner of the sky, there is a blood-red moon climbing above Bjǫrn's blond head.

Beside me, Bjǫrn's face almost seems to come alive as he reaches for the talisman around his neck. "Did you hear that raven's call?"

"It is a gift from Óðinn," I murmur softly, glancing up. "It is said that Óðinn's own ravens, Huginn and Muninn, will perch on the shoulders of our greatest god tonight and tell him all that they have learned. Perhaps they will whisper about the two of us."

"What will they say?"

"They will say we are richer for having shared this day together."

Bjǫrn looks out across the lake. I can tell he is amused.

Chapter Sixteen

THE BROOCH AND THE RAVEN CLAW

For two more weeks we hike inland across stark headlands dotted with brooks and ponds, black spruce and fir. My leg and back are always sore, but I manage to navigate a valley forest of balsam fir with their tops wind-pruned, their lower branches ghosted down from snows long melted. At times we get lucky when Bjørn spots a trail frequented by some type of large animal, which makes the hiking easier. More frequently than not, we are forced to trudge through sedge meadows of waterlogged peat. I trail behind Bjørn, who seems to never tire, and keep my eyes focused on his feet.

Eventually, we encounter a chain of smaller lakes which Bjørn acknowledges as looking familiar. We attempt to follow them, veering north. After encountering a few dead ends, Bjørn squats down to study the depressions in the moss, and his mood turns foul. When I catch him scanning the flat terrain, my worry blossoms into fear.

"Are we lost, huntsman?"

He says nothing and gestures to an opening in the bush that allows us to continue to move across some very difficult boulder-strewn slopes. At the top of a steep incline, the ground levels off and the vegetation dwindles to larch, and the walking becomes easier.

"It is nearing the summer solstice. My Beothuk brothers should be here by now. They'll be anxious to get back home with all the meat from the harp seal hunt. If we don't show up at the meeting spot, they'll assume we're dead." Bjørn's voice sounds flat, but I sense his angst when he picks up his pace.

"If we miss them, can't we travel onwards by ourselves?"

Bjørn stops and comes back for me. "It won't be possible. Soon we will cross a mountain chain which will require us to hike uphill for two whole days. If we manage that, we'll reach a massive fjord where the huntsmen should be waiting with their canoes."

"Canoes?" I repeat.

"Canoes are boats made of birchbark which sit low in the water," Bjørn clarifies. "We will canoe back to a Beothuk village that lies close to the mouth of the fjord."

"Is it impossible to get there on foot?"

He glances at me worriedly and shakes his head. "If you can't press on, I don't know what we'll do."

"My leg is sore. In addition to the muscle pain, these blasted mosquitoes have feasted on me, and the itch is bad."

"Why didn't you tell me about your leg?"

I look away, embarrassed. "I didn't want to slow us down even more than I already have."

He glances up into the alder branches that are swaying in the gentle breeze. The insect chorus is a long, drawn-out melody of zips and zings. "If we go slowly, will you be able to make it to the fjord?"

I nod. The wind tousles his long blond hair, and I try to throw a reassuring smile. He keeps his face blank; every muscle in his jaw is tensed.

After that, I need to lean heavily into my walking stick as we make our way around more thickets of speckled alder and waist-high grasses swaying in the summer wind. When we enter a forest of old balsam fir that edges up into a ridge of cliffs, the hiking is nearly impossible. Bjǫrn waits for me and pulls me up the rocky incline with his work-hardened hands.

Three days later, when we finally come into a clearing around supper time, Bjǫrn tilts his head back to examine the position of the sun. My stomach knots when I see his furrowed brow.

"We should be on the other side of this mountain range by now," he mutters irritably.

"Don't you recognize this place?"

The twitch in his jaw is telling. "All is well, woman," he snaps. I catch the beginning of a flush moving into his cheek and shift the weight off my sore leg.

"I may have turned us in the wrong direction," he says almost flippantly. "We should hike back to that lake we saw yesterday."

Deep in the forest, a raven begins to croak, and I feel dark shadows in my bones. In front of me, a smudge of black moves through the trees. Bjǫrn cocks his head. "Óðinn's ravens have been with us since the beginning. After our journey ends, they will continue to travel the world."

"They have travelled the world already," I breathe.

"Perhaps we should ask them where we are and how come we haven't hit the mountain range yet."

A shudder runs through me. "I thought you recognized this place?"

Bjørn looks sheepish. "I was hungry for fresh meat," he says.

"Stop being the trickster, Bjørn."

"Stop shouting, Anja. You'll scare the ravens off."

When I say nothing, he flicks a glance at me. "I saw a few caribou disappearing into the woods a few days back," he begins, and my insides roll. "I decided to follow them, but I lost their tracks. I swear to you that I was tricked by Loki. He led us here in the form of a caribou. We have strayed off course."

"Off course?" I groan.

"Truly, I have been a rogue. I'm a huntsman with a vulture's eye."

"I hope the vultures eat your bones," I snap in a voice that ratchets upwards. "How long have we been lost?"

He shrugs, and I feel hot tears welling.

"We'll rest here overnight," he says as he begins to unload his gear. "Tomorrow, we can retrace our steps through the woods."

"You snake charmer! I've trudged behind you despite being in agonizing pain. Truly, I've hobbled behind you for days on end!"

"Peace, I pray you. I shouldn't have followed the caribou."

"By the gods, if we are lost, then we are doomed. Just look around at this nothingness. Have you forgotten that I've been bitten by a bear? Have you no pity? Have you forgotten my injured leg? The gods are making a mockery out of us."

"Hold your tongue," Bjørn whispers viciously. His face turns mottled red.

"You selfish rogue! You thirst for some hunter's trophy prize so that you can brag. 'Tisn't fair," I say, sniffing. "You're a hare-brained fool who is too proud! By the gods, Bjørn, you should have told me that we were lost. I know how to navigate by the sun, the moon, and the stars. I am as fine a tracker as the likes of you."

"'Tis a great noise you make," Bjǫrn grumps as he turns his back on me.

"O ye of little faith! Dost thou not believe that I have tracking skills? I'm probably more capable than any other maiden you've ever met."

"Truly, I tell you, I don't know too many maidens."

My breath comes out in ragged snatches. "You bastard! You followed the caribou, hoping that you could score a kill? Are you never satiated? You are always blaming me and my wounded leg for slowing us down. Now it will be on you if we arrive too late to meet up with the Beothuk and their red canoes!"

Bjǫrn begins gathering up his hunting gear, but he is not one to easily let things go. Unexpectedly, he hurls his spear into the woods with such force that it quivers when it hits the ground.

"What do you want from me?" The boom of his voice reverberates through the forest as a leaf flutters down from the trees above. "By Óðinn's eye, I swear to you, I've tried my best, but we are lost."

"You didn't try your best," I say. "You tried to score another kill."

"Listen to me, Anja. I can't remember the route from a year ago. I never thought I'd have to come back alone."

"You should have returned with the other hunters when they left. You should have left me alone to die."

In the silence, a tiny bird releases a long, shrill chirp that echoes across the lonely beauty of the place. Bjǫrn turns and goes to retrieve his spear from the ground. I stare at it and remember how the river ate my pack, how it robbed me of my precious knife, the one with a grip made of walrus tusk. Bjǫrn's bow and arrows are lying on the ground where he has thrown them. Without another thought, I scoop them up.

"Going hunting?" the huntsman asks as he slides his eyes my way.

"We need to eat," I say churlishly. "I've a good aim, and I can hunt to kill."

A curse slithers out. He slaps a tree. "You'll be my death."

Ignoring him, I make my way to the opposite end of the clearing.

"Wait!" he calls. "It's too dangerous to go out on your own, especially at this time of night when the night prowlers start coming out." A gust of wind whisks through the trees, swishing branches, rattling leaves. "By Óðinn's beard, Anja, I'll come with you. Just wait for me."

I wipe a mosquito from my neck. The forest is growing dark and dim, and I feel a spirit presence in the air. Gathering my courage, I needle forward and duck into a copse of trees. I crave the taste of wild rabbit roasted on an outdoor fire and rosehip tea to wash it down.

Halfway down the winding path, I hear twigs snapping in the bush. When I look up, I catch sight of a bear hidden in the undergrowth. It romps between two black spruce trees, twitching its ears to dislodge the bugs.

"Back away slowly," Bjǫrn whispers as he comes up behind. There is a chill moving down my spine, a buzzing noise in my ears. My vision blurs. Bjǫrn takes my elbow and pulls me back.

"Move!" he mutters frantically. I step backwards and almost fall.

The huntsman drags me back down the path. As soon as we round a bend, we start to run. In the distance there is a clearing dotted with meagre shrubs and darkly silhouetted, north-facing cliffs. Through the trees, I spot a caribou picking its way around a stob. Wordlessly, I nock an arrow and release the shot.

With a twang, my arrow meets its mark. I feel the victory in my bones, the burst of joy that bubbles up. Bjørn says nothing. In silence, he begins to mutter the words to release the spirit of the animal, and I join in, and he looks up as if I am a ghost.

It is growing dark. In silence, we gut the kill and deal with the offal, and my sleeves get soaked in blood as we cut large strips of meat from the haunches. When I see the shanks that will go to waste, I curse myself and my arrogance. We would need two more weeks to properly use up all that the animal has to give. Tonight, the spoilage will only draw wild animals to our fire.

"We can leave the rest for the ravens and the wolves," Bjørn grunts as he wipes his bloody hands on a tuft of moss.

"I have no love for wolves," I sputter as I study the dappled moonlight shadowing the huntsman's face.

"The beasties would thank you for giving them a feast."

"And you? Will you thank me?"

"I'll thank you, Anja, when thanks is due, but tonight I wish to thank the Great Creator for gifting us with meat for a few more days."

"You'll thank your Creator, and I'll thank Thor. The God of Thunder was the one who protected me from the bear tonight."

Bjørn turns from me without a word. As the evening shadows begin to stretch, he helps me bury the carcass behind a bush. Then we set a fire and roast some meat. By the time we eat our fill, I can hardly keep my eyes open.

Bjørn tilts his neck back and peers up to where the stars are so numerous, they fill the sky and sparkle brilliantly in the black. In front of us, the fire crackles, and a log splits apart.

"Back in that cave, I promised I would offer protection until you healed. Now I'll make another promise." He lowers his head and studies me. His face is backlit by the dancing flames. "I promise to deliver you into caring hands."

He takes a stick and pokes the fire. Then he reaches into his pack and pulls out an elaborate brooch with raised runic inscriptions around the edges and golden knotwork cradling a giant purple jewel in the centre. The brooch glitters in the firelight.

"What is that?" I ask as I watch him finger the brooch pensively.

"This brooch was my *faðir*'s."

"You haven't told me about him."

"I know little," he says. A shadow moves across his face.

"Where is he now?"

"Gone," he whispers into the flames.

"Has he entered Valhalla's gates?"

Bjǫrn turns the brooch over in his hand until the campfire smoke drifts in his direction. Then he pulls back. "He died in a *holmgang* – an honour duel."

"What of your mother?" I yawn tiredly.

Bjǫrn winces as the fire sputters. With one eye shut against the smoke, he stirs the fire with his stick. "My mother is a feisty woman. She boxed my ears on several occasions when I was young. She wanted me to learn how to use a sword and shield, but I was more interested in learning how to hunt. When I had but four summers to my name, they say I downed my first rabbit." He chuckles, and the laughter sits low in his throat. "I was praised when I speared my first sea otter," he continues as I struggle not to fall asleep. "In a fold of skin underneath the otter's arm, I found its favourite rock – the one that it must have used for cracking open molluscs and clams. The Beothuk think it's good luck when one finds an otter's rock. It's a wonder that I wasn't named after the critter!"

"Who would call you Otter? That is no honourable Norseman's name."

"After my Norse *faðir* died, mother made a union with a Red Man," Bjǫrn whispers quietly. I snap awake. "Nashushuk, my *stepfaðir*, raised me as his own. He taught me the Beothuk ways and made me learn the Beothuk tongue. He was the one who taught me how to honour the animal's spirit when it dies, although mother also had a say in what I learned. She insisted on speaking to me in Norse. She made me learn the stories of the gods."

I sit up fully.

"'Tis a discussion for another day," Bjǫrn says when he sees my face.

"Our stories are much the same," I whisper carefully.

Bjǫrn falls silent. The fire highlights the contours of his face. "We must return to the Beothuk village before I take you back to Leifsbidur."

"Já," I say, swallowing deeply. "I am anxious to meet Raven's tribe." I don't tell him that I plan to stay with the Beothuk instead of returning to Leifsbidur. I don't have the courage yet.

Bjǫrn turns his head and looks at me. I take a breath. "Do you have any sisters or brothers?"

"Five half-sisters," he replies.

"All hail to Freya, the goddess of fertility. Your mother was blessed five times, not six!"

Bjǫrn chuckles softly before he lies back down and turns on his side and props himself up on one elbow. Through the coarse weaving of his open shirt, I see the smoothness of his suntanned chest.

"I have five sisters, but there is Huritt as well. He is Beothuk born. We are tied by friendship, not by blood. He is my hunting brother, and he is both strong and daring. He wears his courage on his sleeve. We did our vision quests together when we came of age."

I cock an eyebrow. The firelight dances across his face.

"A vision quest helps one find one's animal guardian spirit that will provide advice and protection throughout one's life. Huritt and I took our spirit journeys when we had but twelve summers to our name. The Beothuk left us in the wilderness to fend for ourselves for three whole days. It was a rite of passage. When we walked out of the bush, my *fosterfaðir* was very proud. Nashushuk acknowledged me as a man. He encouraged me to keep something from the spirit animal that I killed. I kept the raven's claw. Now it keeps me."

"It sounds similar to our *fylgja*," I murmur into the stars.

"It is," he says. "On my spirit quest, I found the raven. Huritt found the wolf." He sniffs and pulls out a raven's claw hanging from a worn leather neck-strap. "'Tis said that a man's spirit guide will come to him in his time of need." He holds out the raven claw for me to see. It is smooth and polished from excessive rubbing.

"Your raven's claw and your *faðir*'s brooch seem most worthy items to carry with you at all times."

"The brooch is a reminder of the Norseman who was my *faðir* but who is no longer," Bjǫrn says as he lies back down and crosses his arms behind his head. He stares up into the night sky. "The raven's claw is a reminder of Nashushuk, the Beothuk hunter who raised me."

I fiddle with a piece of grass and meet his eyes, the blue of them. The mosquitoes are biting. I swat at them and disperse the cloud. Bjǫrn's hair falls forward in his face; his fists fall clenched across his chest. For a long time after, I wonder if he is holding the raven's claw or the brooch, if he is holding neither, holding both.

Far off in the distance, an owl calls. We both glance up and search the magic of the sky, that pitch-black dome where the moon god reigns and the twinkling stars flicker like sky jewels. When a shooting star throws out a burst of light across the sky, I watch it explode in stardust and fizzle out, and I think of Freydis on Greenland shores.

Chapter Seventeen

WHEN THE BLIND CAN SEE

W e navigate a way forward, but the trees are dense, the sightlines poor. When we summit a ridge leading to a lookout point, I scan the land and feel the vastness of the place as the wind whistles past. Bjǫrn is ecstatic when we finally spot the wide expanse of ocean, but he soon despairs when we hit the beach edging a grand fjord where there are no canoes waiting, where there is nothing but waves washing into shore.

"If the Beothuk had been here, we'd see the charred remains from their fires," he says as he rubs the back of his sunburnt neck.

"It is past the summer solstice."

"They'll come," he says. "I know they will."

We wait, but Bjǫrn is impatient, and I get scared. He tries to reassure me, but I question the arrangements that were made, and he barks at me for pecking. After that, we don't speak about it anymore, and the days pass by in endless succession as the weather warms.

The ocean is teaming with capelins which we roast over a lazy campfire, popping them whole in our mouths, eating up the smoke of them. Then the crabs come in and we feast on them. When Bjørn goes out to collect quails' eggs, I go out to pick some berries which leave juice stains on my hands.

It seems like the work to feed our bellies is endless. Our only chance to rest is when we sit around the evening fire. Then Bjørn talks about his life, his hunting and what he hopes to accomplish before he dies, and I talk about my people back home and my life with the woman who raised me – my so-called mother – before all this.

On a Moon's-day when the sun is at its highest point and Bjørn is engrossed in carving some tool out of bone, he looks up and lets out a wild whoop of joy. Far up the fjord, I spot a group of boats, each half-moon in profile and riding low in the water with the gunwales rising in the middle to a smooth, curved hump. Paddling them are men with red ochre-coloured skin and long, black hair – strong hunter types. Before I can blink, Bjørn catapults off the boulder and wades into the water, frantically waving and shouting in the Beothuk tongue.

Wiping my clammy hands against my breeches, I force my heartbeat to settle down before I hobble forth to join the huntsman on the beach. Bjørn glances down, face beaming, and grabs my hand and holds it up as if I am his trophy prize. A shiver of annoyance thistles through me, and he laughs, almost affectionately.

"All praise to the great Creator, they've come at last!"

He splashes forward with a relentless cry of unbridled joy and expertly guides the lead canoe – full of hunting spoils and gear and men – into shore. Without a word, two agile *Skraelings* gracefully hop out. Instantly, Bjørn is lost to me.

The Red Men are foreboding, austere-looking hunters with flat, smooth faces. Some are covered in red ochre paint. Others have red tattoos branded on their skin. One has his long, raven-black hair tied back and adorned with a white feather that flutters in the wind. Another stares soberly at our makeshift camp as he adjusts his shoulder cassock, a handsome pelt lined with alternating strips of otter and marten. A third scrutinizes me from afar. This one must be the Medicine Man. His face has been painted white and he has red tattoos scrolling down half his cheek. He is dressed strangely with bones and shells hanging from his hides and what looks like a medicine pouch hanging from his belt.

I feel a rush of heat in my cheeks, thinking about how ragged I must look in my travel-stained leggings, my mannish garb, my plain and simple, scuffed-up hides. Perhaps they are scrutinizing all my scars. I wish I could fly away on eagle's wings.

"Bjǫrn?" I call. My heart is beating very fast. I yank my gaze from man to man, listening to the words rumbling from the hunters' mouths, gushing like fast-flowing waterfalls.

Bjǫrn is as animated as a squirrel finding nuts as he holds up a red fox pelt for his brothers to admire. A strange, lonely feeling niggles its way into my gut, and I blink back tears as I stand there listening to the alders creaking in the rising wind and the spruce trees tossing needles on the beach. I am a girl again, alone, ignored. These *Skraelings* – these Beothuk men – are Bjǫrn's long-lost friends, the huntsmen whom he has dearly missed, the men whom I have heard so much about. Sweet Óðinn, the huntsman is laughing. He never laughed like this with me.

I see a Red Man who is about my age staring at me curiously. His muscular arms are ringed by two red stripes, and they are as thick as tree trunks. His chiselled chest is smooth and flawless, and he is very tall. I marvel at the look of him, at the wolf tattoo on his arm, at his jet-black, braided hair which falls halfway down his back. There are tiny seashells woven into the ends.

"Huritt," he says, pointing to himself when he sees me staring. He repeats the name, and the strange, exotic nature of it tickles.

Above my head, a raven croaks. Glancing up, I see the black-winged creature soaring high above the trees. The Red Man spots it, too. He smiles with his perfect teeth.

"I am Anja Freydisdöttir," I sputter. In my periphery, I see some of the other Red Men moving closer, studying me with curious eyes, commenting to each other in a way that makes me shiver. It almost feels like blood is pooling in my lungs.

"Anja, the Beothuk are brazen, but don't be scared," Bjørn calls to me. "They are harmless. If you smile at them, they will smile back."

Some huntsman speaks to me in harsh, clipped tones. Bjørn responds. He draws a crowd.

"Wolf sees your raven-coloured locks and marvels at the whiteness of your clammy skin." Bjørn points out the man. Wolf is a sour-faced *Skraeling* with red triangles on his cheeks. The guttural sounds coming from his throat dip low and chomp on air before bouncing up into the blue. I glance at him uneasily. Bjørn chucks a smile.

"Wolf has offered me a ride in his canoe, but he is reluctant to take you."

"Why?" I manage as I try to control the jingling of my teeth.

"Wolf remembers that you were dead. He was there in the cave many moons ago. He saw you fight off fever spirits in the aftermath of your bear attack. He heard your moans and cries for help. He swears he saw your raven spirit walking among the dead."

"By Óðinn's beard, what nonsense talk is this?" I scoff. "Can't he see that I am alive and well?"

Bjǫrn releases a throaty chuckle. "You are most alive, but I won't tell them that you are well!" When he sees my sober expression, he wipes the smile off his face. "They don't trust you, Anja."

"I don't trust them!"

"It would help if you gave Wolf a lock of your hair."

"I won't," I spit. My voice is dead, flat, calm. Bjǫrn grins and winks.

"It would be wise to give him a strand. It will let him know that you walk in the land of the living. Trust me, Wolf would treasure that lock for his entire life."

I feel a rush of heat moving into my cheeks. Just then, a Red Man with a large, flat, oily nose gets too close. When he tries to touch me, Bjǫrn steps forward to block his hand. He reeks of fish and campfire smoke.

"I've told the men about your plight," the huntsman says. "Grey Owl wants to know more about your kin. He wants to know how you came to Vinland shores."

"I was shipwrecked, Bjǫrn. Tell him that my kin are dead."

Bjǫrn quickly translates, and Grey Owl frowns and spits out words.

"Grey Owl says your face tells lies."

"I'm not lying about the shipwreck, Bjǫrn. Tell him that."

"He wants to know more about the longboat. He wants to know the helmsman's name."

"Tell him the helmsman died." I feel like I am participating in a strange sort of dance where the tempo is picking up at a frenetic pace, twirling me into another dance with strange rhythms that I have never danced before.

Bjǫrn quickly scans my face before turning back. He speaks, and I am suddenly worried that these men – these *Skraelings* – will refuse to take me with them to their settlement. What would I do if I was left behind?

"Grey Owl won't take you unless you tell him the helmsman's name," Bjǫrn translates.

"Valbrand. I think he was Icelandic born."

There is a great exchange of words.

"Do you know your *faðir*'s name?" Bjǫrn finally asks. His jaw is twitching furiously. "Grey Owl wants to know."

There is a burst of panic laced with hope and edged with dread. I see myself through the *Skraelings'* eyes as just a simple maiden – a Norsewoman who came alive against all odds. Clearly, I am a stranger in this place. The sand flies are nipping at my ankles. I swat at them.

My mother's name is Raven. My mother, she is one of you. For some strange reason, I can't bring myself to say her name. I take a breath, knowing that avoidance only brings more suffering.

"My *faðir*'s name is Thorvard of Gardar," I start. There is a rush of astonished murmurs accompanied by a frenetic burst of excited chatter.

"Beg pardon, I did not hear?" Bjǫrn snaps. I drag my eyes back to him and see the confusion in his eyes. "Thorvard of Gardar? Is that the name I heard you say?"

"*Já*," I say. "That is my *faðir*'s name, but I was raised by Freydis Eiriksdóttir."

The *Skraelings* gasp. Most of them seem to recognize the names. I squirm under Bjǫrn's scrutiny.

"Thorvard used to live among the *Skraelings*, where he met Raven, my birth mother," I try again.

Bjǫrn's eyes glint steel. The one called Huritt steps in closer. He is so tall that he blocks out the sun. I feel the movement of the air above my head as he begins to address Bjǫrn as if I'm not there.

"Huritt has just ordered Grey Owl to row ahead and let Chief Achak know," Bjǫrn mutters. He can't bring himself to look at me.

"I was told to ask for Achak when I met with my mother's tribe."

Bjǫrn flicks a glance out to sea. There is an awkwardness about him. He hesitates before he squats down low in front of me and looks me squarely in the eyes. "May the gods reward me for my patience, Anja. I have walked with you between river valleys and mountain peaks, and not once did you mention Freydis or Achak. Not once did you tell me who you were! May the gods have mercy. It would have helped for me to know."

"I told you I needed to return to Raven's tribe," I say, confused.

"You didn't tell me the all of it. You didn't tell me you were raised by Freydis Eiriksdöttir!"

"You never asked," I say indignantly.

Bjǫrn glances at Huritt, as if he is hoping to get some help. Huritt is oblivious. Bjǫrn takes a breath: "Your *faðir* is not who you think. Truly, I tell you, you've got it all confused. Achak is the Chieftain of the Beothuk tribe, and he is your *faðir*! Freydis Eiriksdöttir was his lover. Thorvard took her away from Vinland against her will."

My chest constricts. "I am Raven's *döttir*," I repeat.

Bjǫrn picks up a stick and draws the outline of a raven in the sand. "Chief Achak is known as The Raven here on Vinland shores."

Above our heads, a seagull cries, shrill and loud. My hands start to shake.

"Thor give me strength," Bjǫrn continues. "If your mother is Freydis Eiriksdöttir, she is well loved by the Beothuk people. She and Achak were very happy when Freydis lived in the Beothuk village. You are their child."

"You lie!" I shout.

"Prithee, Anja, hear me out."

"I won't," I spit. "Just leave me be!"

I can't seem to catch my breath, to get things straight. Bjǫrn grows a serpent's head, a dragon's mouth that breathes out fire. He is Jormungand, the shapeshifter, who has crawled out of the ocean surrounding *Midgard*, the visible world. My eyes well up so that I can't see.

"My mother is dead and gone."

Bjǫrn looks at me and shakes his head. "Your mother is Freydis Eiriksdöttir. Your *faðir* is Achak of the Beothuk tribe."

"My *faðir* is Thorvard of Gardar!"

Bjǫrn quickly stands to address the huntsmen. My vision clouds; a headache pounds. Huritt responds in a flurry of staccatos, and I feel myself begin to sway. He holds out his hand to steady me, and I feel too many things all at once. Shock. Confusion. A wave of fear. When I step back, I knock into Bjǫrn's massive chest.

"Huritt formally welcomes you to these shores," Bjǫrn announces carefully. "He honours you as the chieftain's *döttir*. He wants you to travel in his canoe."

I itch to swat at him, to shut him up. He takes a breath.

"You are the chieftain's *döttir*. The Beothuk will treat you honourably."

Freydis's image butterflies into my mind, and I picture her sitting in her longhouse on Greenland shores. She is the mother whom I never accepted, whom I never knew. She is the mother who always was, who never was, who could have been so much more if I had only known. I didn't know. How could I have known?

"Just leave me be," I gurgle as I glance across the water to where the canoes are bobbing in the sea.

Chapter Eighteen

BLOOD OF MY BLOOD

I push my way through the *Skraelings* and walk into the bush to be alone, but Bjǫrn reaches out to stop me, cursing and angry-eyed. I refuse to accept the dung he spews. Everything I know – every story from my childhood – is contrary to what Bjǫrn has just disclosed.

"Anja, calm yourself!" Bjǫrn orders harshly. "You need to hear Freydis's saga from start to finish."

"I've heard her saga all my life."

"*Neinn!* Your people told you lies," he says, but he seems to lose his vehemence when he sees me crumbling, and I hate him for the pity he throws. "Someday you will accept the truth."

My stomach churns. Huritt flicks a curious glance between the two of us. When he speaks to Bjǫrn, his voice dips low and a flurry of words is exchanged. Huritt points to me, and Bjǫrn shakes his head and marches off without a word, as if I mean nothing, as if he is eager to relinquish the burden of having to care for me.

Huritt gestures for me to come with him, and when I stay frozen, he comes and gently takes me by the arm. I let him lead me back to his canoe where some of the *Skraelings* are busying themselves rearranging their hunting spoils to accommodate our supplies. They are careful to smile at me.

Huritt shows me how to grab hold of the gunwales and crouch down low and shuffle forward to find my seat in the canoe. He steadies the boat with his knees so that I can carefully manoeuvre myself into place. Without warning, our heads collide, and the canoe shimmies underneath my weight before grinding low into the sand. I am embarrassed and horrified all at once. My throat constricts. He is Beothuk and I am not, but then I am, but then I'm not.

Huritt calls out orders in a Beothuk gurgle that swirls around inside my head. The strange guttural sounds pop in bursts before fading into the humid air. When he is finished, he gestures for me to rest my back against a stack of furs. From my perch, I watch another group of men beetling around the beach. Like worker ants, they quickly dismantle our makeshift camp and shamelessly pull my life apart.. In the confusion, there is welling grief – a grief for what has come to pass, a grief that overshadows what could have been.

I finger the luscious seal pelts surrounding me and think of my Greenland home. Freydis, my mother, is lost to me. I try to remember the last conversation we ever had, but the only memories that I unwind are ones of Freydis spearing Jelani's chest. *O gods, she killed for me as any mother would.* I see her accompanying me down the path. I see her fading in the mist. I see her as I rub my eyes.

My chest cavity fills to bursting. A moan slips out. I want to lay my sword down and release the pain, but there is no one to speak to, no raven *fylgja* guiding me. When I wrench my injured arm from underneath a pelt, there is a jolt of pain before I look down and see the ugly scars that mark me – the white, ridged flesh. I hear Freydis's voice inside my head, calling forth our greatest gods. She must have offered sacrifices to Óðinn and Thor, asking them to keep me safe. I know it. I can feel it deeply in my bones.

I call to Huginn and Muninn, the sacred ravens, and beg them to come and carry a message back to Greenland. I must tell her that I am safe, that I am alive because of her sacrifice, that I know the truth. I must tell her that I know who I am, that I know who she is, that I am Raven's *döttir*, her moonbeam child. There are stardust tingles in my hands and feet.

As soon as the canoes are loaded, the *Skraelings* dig their oars into the sea, and we begin our journey underneath a clear blue sky. The fjord is soon left behind, and as the land falls away, the breeze blowing off the open water picks up. We hug the coast and keep the rocky shores in sight as we follow the birds out to sea.

It feels like I have a thousand bloodsuckers on my skin. When I start to shiver, Huritt stops paddling and immediately tucks me into furs. Later, when he spots two seals playing in the waves, he taps me on the shoulder so that I can share in the joy of watching them.

But there is no joy. All I feel is nothingness.

Bjǫrn sits cross-legged directly in front of me conversing with the lead paddler. His gurgled Beothuk words make him a stranger, and I lose him too. I am adrift in my own squall, weighed down by how I failed to see the truth. I try to sift through the memories of what the huntsman said, trying to remember everything and nothing all at once. Staring out across the sea, I see only a patch of white in her red hair, her final wave, the sweet sadness in her hardened face. By the gods, she was as loyal as the puffins coming back to breed on the same patch of land every year. She was as protective as a mother doe.

And I shunned her. I shunned her because Thorvard duped me. I rejected her because he told me to. I treated her like she was nothing to me. How could I have been such a fool?

Grief crests and rolls with the ocean swells. My stomach cramps, and I am reminded of my womanhood. I deserve the pain of everything.

The paddles dig in and drip, dig in and drip. I close my eyes. Bjǫrn doesn't turn to check on me. When he tries to rest his back against my knees, I shift in place to dislodge him and try to reassemble something of myself

When the Beothuk village comes into view, it is a dot on land, and I am as jittery as a freshly caught fish out of water, as focused as a bird learning how to fly. Bjǫrn repositions his large frame in the cramped canoe so that he can twist around to see my face.

"Your *faðir* is a good man, Anja. Chief Achak will take you in and welcome you to the tribe. After you meet him, swear to me that you'll ask me to explain everything."

I look out across the water. Behind me, Huritt shouts and the huntsman up front stops rowing and begins drawing out water from the bilge. Bjǫrn's eyes sweep across the land.

"The Beothuk will likely honour you with some type of solemn ritual when we arrive," he tells me in a solemn voice.

"I know little of being honoured," I say as I suck in a sob.

"Good manners are your gift," he says. "You'll find a way to thank them."

"How will I talk to them?" The question pops and skips across the water.

"I'll not abandon you," he says as he picks up his paddle and digs it into the water. "I'll stay in the village for a while before I return to Leifsbidur. I might even take part in the great caribou hunt. If the fates allow it, I hope to score a trophy kill."

The other canoes pull alongside, and there is a brief exchange. Huritt is bristling with excitement as he describes the welcoming ceremony with Bjǫrn translating. The two of them clearly share a bond. As I listen, I spread my palms, star-fish like, across my lap and try to imagine what it was like for my mother, the woman who was always so mysterious and private, the woman who kept herself from me.

Eventually, a very large, sheltered cove guarded by a series of craggy rocks opens on our right, and my vision blurs. I feel the prick of hope, the dread and joy of seeing him. I wonder if Freydis felt this same swell of fear when she first set foot in this Beothuk village. The sadness drags me down into the gloomy depths where my thoughts slowly drift back and forth in the filmy silt.

I hear drumbeats, booming sounds tumbling across the sea, pinging off the rocks in time to the swish of the oars, the call of a tern from the trees, the slosh of the water against the hull. Huritt and Bjǫrn toss words back and forth above my head. I have clammy palms, no raven earrings left to give.

"Chief Achak waits for you. He is over there." Bjǫrn's voice is fog and smoke.

"Where?" I ask, squinting. Bjǫrn points. "Please come with me."

"We'll drift in close," Bjørn reassures. "I'll help you get out."

"I'd rather stay here with you."

"His heart will break. You must go to him."

The canoe slows, and a bolt of pain shoots down my leg. Bjørn hops out, and the bottom of the canoe scratches rocks.

"Here," he says, "take my hand."

I throw a wobbly smile. "Is this the way you offer peace?"

"I'll sing no song to lure you forth, and my flute is packed away," he teases as he leans forward. For a moment, he holds my eyes, and I see into the depths of his knowing, where his tenderness is a moving tide.

"Careful, now," he cautions as he takes hold of the gunwale to steady the canoe so it doesn't move when I step out.

I feel them staring – these Beothuk with their red tattoos, these *Skraelings* whom I do not trust, this *faðir* whom I do not know. Bjørn leads me in his direction. My head is swimming, my attention piqued. I focus on the chieftain's face, but I need Bjørn to hold me up as we slosh through the shallows and wade into shore.

Halfway up the landwash, Bjørn stops and presents me to the chief. Raven is a regal-looking Beothuk man standing at the head of a gathered crowd. His medium-sized frame is heavy-set, and his eyes pierce mine. He is wearing a cape patterned with tiny shells that are so intricately placed, I can't help but stare at the brilliance of the design. I've never seen anything so finely made. On his head he wears a feathered headdress bowed to fit over and around his head. He has long, raven-coloured hair just like mine. For a moment, I stare at him as the sun beats down. Then I scan the faces in the crowd and see the red ochre paint on everyone and everything, shimmering in the summer sun.

"I am Raven," the chieftain says in Norse.

My thoughts are yelling. I've assumed all wrong. In my brokenness, I stagger under the weight of the realization that this is the Beothuk village where it all began. Where I began. Where mother lived.

"I am Anja Freydisdöttir."

"You are Raven's *döttir*," he replies.

There is a sage-like, smoky smell embedded in his hides and in his skin and in his hair. I am vaguely aware of his mantle being wrapped around me and the tinkling jingle of the many dangling shells. In his presence, I swallow stars.

When Raven releases me, I will my spine to iron up, but I have trouble seeing through my tears. Bjǫrn steps forward and with a gentle nudge, he takes my arm. Without thinking, I lean into him and listen as he translates what Chief Achak says. His tone reminds me of ash and herbs.

"I have counted every leaf and every rock since your mother left. I have wandered down many trails and journeyed down many streams. When the raven spirit guide asked what I had lost, I said I was looking for my family. Raven spread its wings and told me to take care of those who were already in the nest. I listened and came back and waited. I waited many moons, but you and your mother never returned to these shores." He glances at Bjǫrn, and I feel the heat rising in my face.

"Tell him I am here now," I say. I try to look up and smile, but Raven's voice nets me as though I am a fish, and I get lost in the strangeness of the sounds, the cadence and the beat.

"He wants to know about Freydis," Bjǫrn translates carefully. The air goes still.

"She is well," I manage shakily. "Tell him that she sacrificed much for me."

Bjǫrn studies me. "I'm sure he knows."

"Tell him anyway."

There is an exchange of words. Bjǫrn listens intently before he translates. "He wants to know what you are searching for."

"Tell him I have come home to listen to the stories of my people. Tell him that Freydis wanted me to learn."

In the distance, the drums start up, and the boom of them makes me jump. When a tall, sinewy woman comes towards me bearing gifts of foxes' fur and beaver pelts, a hush falls over the gathered crowd.

"Your *faðir* has many questions. He wants to know if you ever thought of him when you saw the moon."

An awareness dawns. Memories of Freydis slipping out at night crack, fizzle, pop. I snatch a breath. "We didn't always see the moon. Máni is elusive."

Bjǫrn waits for the woman to remove the seashell mantle from my shoulders. As she is replacing it with a fox's pelt, the poplars surrounding us begin swishing back and forth in the gentle wind.

"You must be tired," the huntsman says. "I'll tell the chief to question you another day." He clears his throat. Chief Achak listens carefully. When I look up, I catch the odour of campfire smoke and roasting meat.

"I told the chief that your leg is sore because you fought a black bear's spirit and you won."

For a moment, I am silent. When I go to speak, my muscles shake. "He should know that I had help. Tell him I conquered the animal's spirit with the help of his Beothuk hunters."

"I won't say that," Bjǫrn says carefully. "It was you. You were the one who took down that bear."

I look away. My eyes sweep across the sea. "I see that bear every day. I hear it and smell it. That bear is my agony."

The crowd is stirring. A baby cries. Bjǫrn turns from me and begins to speak in their throaty language. Their faces blur.

"I brought Anja's bear hide back with us," Bjǫrn announces to the crowd before he suddenly realizes he is speaking Norse. He blushes fiercely and repeats himself in the Beothuk tongue. The crowd emits a hearty laugh that builds and pops. Then he calls a hunter forth who carries in his arms the bear's bulked pelt. When he unrolls it, a murmur of awe rises like the flapping wings of a murder of crows.

In a blink, the bear seems to come alive. Terrified, I step back and brace myself to be attacked. My chest constricts. I cannot breathe. There are pins and needles in my hands and feet, a crushing pressure in my head.

I am strong enough. I am Raven's döttir. *I can conquer this vision bear!*

The chieftain speaks through mud in a bullfrog voice. I am drowning in a mix of words, all muddled by the gurgled sounds. I stare straight ahead, trying to focus on the chieftain's moving lips, but he grows bear claws that rip through flesh, incisors that puncture holes in limbs. The Medicine Man appears through fog. He reaches out to touch my hand, and the ritualistic bones dangling from his garb become my own.

The sea heaves with Thor's anger. Drowning, I feel my lungs about to burst until Bjǫrn reaches down and pulls me up. "Did I faint?" I gasp. His cheeks are red with shame. The chieftain speaks. Bjǫrn glances up and takes a breath. "He wants to know if you are well."

I bow my head. Bjǫrn hesitates. In front of us, the chief's shadow stretches in the sun. When he speaks, his eyes look kind, and Bjǫrn half-smiles.

"The chieftain would like to take you back to his fire. He

wants me to come as well. In the days to come, he will question me about your spirit bear and your visions."

I close my eyes.

"Come," he says. "They want you to see the gift they are giving me for the care of you."

"For the care of me?" I search his face then turn around.

They offer a set of new arrows in a red-ochred leather quiver with seashell motifs curving around the rim. Bjǫrn accepts the offering, but there is a pained expression on his face. For a moment, I wonder if he will speak, but then Chief Achak steps forward and his voice stirs poplar branches before the rumbles float into the cloudless sky.

"He is grateful that I stayed to look after you in the cave." Bjǫrn's eyes are bright. "What I did for you cannot be purchased, Anja."

The crowd pushes in, and Bjǫrn falls back. When I look down, a small hand grasps mine. The little girl has long black braids, and her face has been ochred red. I could have been just like her: an innocent valued by my kin, a Beothuk child with a song to sing.

The wind picks up. I feel Freydis's presence on a breath of wind, and our spirits touch. She whispers low: *To know love is to experience sorrow in the face of loss and joy in the face of reunion.*

Sorrow. Joy. Today I have experienced both.

Part Two

SHE FINDS HER WINGS

Chapter Nineteen

MY CLAN, MY TRIBE

Wasumaweeseek, 1014 AD

C hief Achak leads me in the direction of his village. As we
follow the winding path, the trill of a red-winged
blackbird is so long and sharp that the warbles tumbling out of
its beak rise above the din of voices, the swish of trees swaying
back and forth. I smell the poplars and reach down deeply and
find that lost part of myself – the joyful part, the part that feels
like I belong. It seems like the entire tribe is here to welcome me.

Someone trailing behind me reaches out to touch my hair. I
quickly turn, but I am caught off guard when I see the red grease-
paint smeared on the woman's face, on her long, flowing hair, on
the newborn infant she carries on her back. When I look around, I
am surrounded by a sea of laughing faces with smiling eyes.

The crowd presses in closely, and I smell the smoke wafting
off dozens of rose-coloured hides. There is a feeling that this can't
be real, that I stand alone even though I am surrounded and

smothered with attention, something I have yearned for my whole life, and yet all I want to do is to return to my turtle shell.

Chief Achak gestures for me to follow him. The pathway leading to the village is lined by silver birch. I am alive to everything – to the tweets of birds and the hum of flies, to the shuffling feet following close behind, to a howling baby at the back. The chief – my *faðir* – speaks in dulcet tones in a Norse accent that is very thick. He asks about my canoe ride. When I tell him that Bjǫrn and I were afraid that the canoes wouldn't come, he somehow manages to communicate that the seal hunt was late and he sent trackers out to scout for us as soon as the snows began to melt. We patch words together as we walk, building an understanding as fragile as a spider's web sitting in long grasses attacked by wind.

The village sits in a clearing surrounded by birch and black spruce trees. When I spot the large, conical dwellings, covered over with sheets of birchbark and banked with earth, that have been slightly sunk into the ground, I learn that the Beothuk call their homes *mamateeks*. I count twelve. They are as large as any longhouse, as grand as any chieftain's lodge.

"We sleep there," Raven says in Norse as he points to a house that fills the clearing. He flashes fingers. "Sixty men." This birchbark house must be bigger than it looks. I wonder if it houses his entire clan. Raven beckons me inside, and I feel my hands begin to shake. To enter means to begin life anew.

As I step into the dwelling, I see drying herbs hanging from the rafters and a dried, smoked fish attracting flies. There are bows and arrows, clubs and hatchets and a wide range of arrowheads and numerous hunting spears and other tools hanging in a well-ordered fashion from the walls. Raven offers me some type of fish – a piece of salmon so heavily smoked and succulent, I wish he would give me more. Directly in front of us, a second tent flap leads to another room with a firepit running down the centre. It makes me think of mother's hearth fire, and I feel a lump building in my throat. I push down ghosts.

Before I enter the gathering room, I glance into the shadows and see a shallow depression in the ground that holds a bed of luscious furs. Hanging from the rafters, there is a giant, circular carving etched in wood that depicts two ravens with their wings spread wide as they soar across a moonlit sky. Tingling, I gawk at it. The carving matches the raven earrings I have lost. I am suddenly tormented by the proof of who my parents are, of what I lost and what I've found.

"Look, *döttir*," Raven says as he points to it. "See moon and ravens."

"It is the same as mother's earrings," I say with the knowledge that he can't understand. My voice steps low. "I lost the earrings in the river on my journey here."

His eyes stay blank. "*Döttir*, come," he says in a stilted voice.

We enter another space where my Beothuk kin crowd into the *mamateek*. I copy the others by sitting cross-legged on the ground. From there, I can clearly see the oiled hide covering that serves as the door. A group of women wander in and sit down quietly on a mat. When I see that their foot coverings are patterned with tiny shells, I am suddenly embarrassed by my filthy boots and grimy smell.

My panic pearls. In the corner, Bjørn is standing with a group of huntsmen who are intimidating in appearance and scantily clad, with fearsome warpaint smudged underneath their eyes. The huntsman is avidly listening to what they say, but he acknowledges me with a tiny nod. The moment is as brief as a wisp of wind before his attention is ripped away by a beardless, austere-looking man with jet-black hair and muscled forearms sporting seal tattoos. The Red Man addresses Bjǫrn with a string of fierce, sharp words, and I quickly shift my gaze away.

I catch a whiff of acrid body odour, the smells of smoke and seal-skin fat. The cacophony of voices overwhelms, and I feel Chief Achak's red-ochred cloak with its fringes tickling me.

"Shaman comes," *Faðir* says.

I look up and see a tall, beardless man wearing several caribou skins sewn together in one large piece that he has wrapped around his body and one shoulder. The garment is held in place by a belt made from marten, otter and beaver skins. I try to still my thoughts, but my thudding heart will not slow down. Directly above my head, there are braided bundles of sage tied with hemp rope hanging from the rafters, surrounded on either side by bunches of yarrow and hawthorn berries and fleabane and various lichens and barks I don't recognize. I stare up in awe.

"Sage gives strength," Raven says in Norse as he follows my gaze. "Songbird. She burns sage."

I am turning the heavily accented words around in my head when a tall, lean youth arrives at Raven's side. He is wearing nothing but a loincloth, and I feel my cheeks grow hot. Warily, I watch him reverently place something covered in rabbit's fur into the chieftain's hands. When the bundle is unwrapped, an intricately carved, long-handled stick with a bulbous bottom is revealed. Raven senses my angst and turns to me.

"Pipe," he says. He runs his thumb over its smoothness before he gently puts it down and unwraps a second package containing what looks like dried grass. He spreads the contents flat and picks apart the clumpy bits before trickling strands into the pipe's bowl. He fills it to the top. Following this, he tamps it down with his thumb.

"We smoke," he says. He points to the men gathered round. "We smoke to welcome Raven's *döttir* to our fire."

More words rumble from his lips before he turns to the crowd and gestures for silence. Immediately, the din dies down. A baby cries at the back, but all eyes are fixed on us. Suddenly, I am very warm. I watch, transfixed.

Raven runs his thin, long finger down the length of the pipe before pinching some more of the dried grass between his thumb and index finger. I try to shift positions, try to move into his shadow, but he turns too soon. With gentle eyes, he looks at me and opens his palm. *"Tobacco,"* he says as he squats down and shows me the crushed herbs.

"Toe … back … o," I repeat, and he grins broadly at my attempt. Taking the pipe in his mouth, he nudges a long, slender stick into the fire and lights it. Then he circles the fire around the bowl. He takes a draw followed by a series of shallow puffs. On the third try, he inhales deeply before savouring the heady smoke. When he exhales the pungent fumes, I hold my breath.

"You are Raven's *döttir*," he says again, and a hush falls over the gathered crowd. The pipe continues to smoke as it sits idle in his hands. "We thank Creator."

His eager lips find the pipe again. He inhales deeply. Then he exhales, and an acrid scent fills the air. The people wait in silence as Raven takes another draw. Then he passes the pipe to the man sitting next to him. Soon the pipe is being passed ceremonially from man to man so that a cloud of smoke hangs suspended in the air. The children become restless. A trickle of sweat dots my hairline. I brush it off surreptitiously.

There is a mosquito hissing above my head. I can't see it, but the anticipation of it landing and slurping up my blood makes me squirm. Already, I dread the itchy welt that always forms.

The buzzing stops. I wait for the wee thing to bite, but nothing happens. The heat is stifling in the tent.

When the pipe finally finds its way back into Raven's hands, he turns and juts his chin at me. "Freydis lives. Our *döttir* lives."

In a panic, I search the crowd. Bjǫrn is standing at the back underneath a ladder leading to a sleeping loft. A group of boisterous children tug at his hunting shirt. He holds my eyes.

Someone whisks the pipe away and just like that, the ceremony is over. There is a communal sigh when someone lifts the tent flap to let the cooler air inside. In front of me, I study some girls my age who are wearing simple deer-skin robes in rosy hues. They seem given to laughter. I envy them.

Three fierce-looking warriors dressed in ceremonial cloaks are hovering at the back. One of them – a tall, muscular, middle-aged man with a stern countenance – studies me from a distance. His leggings have been elaborately decorated with fringes holding tiny rocks that jingle when he walks. His face looks fearsome. His eyes are the colour of iron ore. When he approaches *Faðir*, they embrace.

The Fearsome One points at me with his chiselled chin, and a shiver shimmies down my back. I look for Bjǫrn, but he is gone. At the end of the long firepit, Huritt is speaking with the Medicine Man, and his face looks animated. When he spots me, I throw a tiny smile. In front of me, the Beothuk girls are giggling amongst themselves, waiting patiently for Huritt to come to them. When he chooses me, their eyes hurl rocks.

"Raven's *döttir* …" Huritt begins. Before he can finish, Raven reaches out and clasps Huritt's neck and draws him in like a *faðir* would a son. Huritt smiles.

"Huritt is Askook's son," Raven says. He points to the Fearsome One.

My eyes flit between the three of them. There is a sharp pain in my injured leg, a weary feeling in my bones. Outside, the village children are squealing as they chase each other through the yard. I wish that I was one of them.

"Askook's *oosuck* – his wife – is Nuttah," my *faðir* says, but he is struggling to find the words. "They have big fire. Nuttah teach you Beothuk ways. She teach you Beothuk tongue. You go to her. Askook's fire."

I keep my face as still as stone. I glance at this chieftain who used to be our moon. *Far vel* mother. *Heil og sæl* moon.

There is a sudden noise from behind as two little boys come barging into the tent with carefree squeals. Taking a running jump, the smallest leaps into Raven's arms, and the chief's face comes alive as he tosses him high into the air. The other boy eyes me curiously. Slowly, Raven puts the youngest down.

"My sons – Nikiti and Miwok," he says, eyeing me.

I stare at them. "How old are they?"

Raven holds up two fingers for Nikiti and four fingers for Miwok. He is careful not to let his eyes leave my face. "Their mother is Wapun."

"Wapun," I repeat. The name floats in wisps of smoke. I think of Freydis. I see her face. I feel the warmth and strength of her hand in mine as she asks me to return to her and help her fill her lonely days. She is forwards and backwards and at my side. I shift in place.

A petite woman with long, black hair that has been plaited into two long braids steps forward from the shadows with her head lowered. Her leather foot coverings shuffle soundlessly across the woven mats. Without a word, she lifts her eyes and smiles at me. Then she gracefully steps behind Nikiti and Miwok and plucks them off each other with a firm but gentle hand. As she leans down, I am shocked to see that she is carrying an infant on her back.

"Weematin is littlest son," Raven tells me in a gentle voice that shows his pride. My eyes well up.

Wapun steps forward and gives a bow. My eyes fall to her bird-shaped earrings that brush her neck. She smiles again. I force a grin. Miwok, with his nut-brown eyes that are round and wide, wanders over and reaches up to touch my hair with hands that are tree-sap sticky. Nikiti remains firmly planted at his mother's side. Awkwardly, he stares at me. When I hold my hand out, Nikiti shies away, and I smile at him, knowing that I am not the only one feeling strange. Miwok pushes his face into mine, and I gather courage and find myself.

"You must go to Askook's fire," the chieftain says. He beckons, and I bite back tears not understanding why I have to leave. When I step outdoors, a ferocious gust of wind whips my hair into my face. Through a black curtain, I see Huritt gesturing for me to follow him and the Fearsome One – the man called Askook, the man whose fire is big.

On the outskirts of the village, there is a small dwelling with oiled skins for walls in a clearing surrounded by a grove of black spruce trees. Inside the tent, a golden-haired woman sits weaving long, thin, spruce roots into a basket. She has a willow-tree figure, and her face is a blend of hardened beauty and soft, welcoming gentleness. When I glance around, I see furs of every type – mink and raccoon, caribou and deer, fox and wolf. The pelts have been stacked in piles and placed in various depressions in the earth.

"You must be Anja Freydisdöttir," Nuttah says in Norse as she shuffles forward and kisses me gently on both cheeks. Nuttah gathers up her long, blonde hair and tosses the bundle of it over her shoulder. When she turns, I see her pregnant hump. All feels strange, and yet I feel something growing inside of me, as if I am a plant pushing its way up through soil.

"Come, my child, you have travelled far," she says in a voice as melodic as a lark in spring. I let her take me by the hand and lead me in the direction of the fire. "Surely you need to rest after such a momentous day."

I nod.

"Freydis was a friend," Nuttah says, blinking rapidly. "She suffered when she was forced to marry Thorvard of Gardar. That man was evil. Please tell me that he is dead."

I shake my head. Outside, the poplars moan.

"The last time I saw Freydis, I was pregnant and very ill," Nuttah continues, speaking fast. The weight of the memories seem to pull at her. Her fingers twitch. There is a sudden rustling behind us, and I feel Askook's presence at my back. Nuttah glances up and smiles.

"Askook was in Leifsbidur when your mother left Vinland shores. I was very ill. He saved my life," she whispers as he joins her side. "After he lost his wife and I lost my babe, he asked me to nurse Huritt, his little one. Now Huritt has become my son." She turns and studies me. Her smile sparkles as brilliantly as sunshine on lake water.

Huritt is leaning against a post. He fiddles with a hangnail on his thumb. When his gaze falls on me, I try to push the tiredness down.

"Your mother, Freydis, please tell me what became of her," Nuttah asks.

Mother's image flares. There are shadow memories in my bones. I snag a breath. "The story is a long one," I manage in a tired voice.

"Then you can tell it to me another day."

I force a tiny smile, gentle around the edges: "Will there be a moon tonight?" The question flutters out.

Nuttah points up through the smoke hole. Above our heads, a wisp of clouds is passing over a large strawberry moon spilling a red, golden glow into the night-time sky made out of Ymir's skull, the skull that holds the heavens high.

Chapter Twenty

GARGLED WORDS

I n the tent that night, Huritt keeps us all entertained. The children chatter like chipmunks and bounce around like rabbits. They treat me as though I am a treasured pearl inside a clam, while Askook stares at me as if I am a worm. Weirdly, his treatment feels familiar.

When Askook stands to bank the fire, he points to an empty pail and one of his little boys leaps up and disappears outside. Nuttah flicks a glance and says something in Beothuk, and Askook reaches out to gently touch her cheek. Then he follows his son out the door.

I take advantage of the lull to unkink my legs. In the process, a yawn escapes. From across the fire, Huritt tosses an impish grin and gestures to a depression in the ground.

"Huritt has given up his bed. He wants you to take it," Nuttah says in a tired voice as she begins to tuck her little ones into their sleeping hides.

Huritt's nut-brown eyes are soft and kind. When he stands, he is so tall and broad-shouldered that he needs to duck. At the door, he winks.

"Where will he sleep?"

"He is a hunter. Someone will take him in. I'm guessing he will go to Grey Owl's fire."

"And Askook? Will he return?"

"He is a night owl. He will stay out until we are all asleep."

When I finally settle for the night, I stare into the dying fire where the oranges, yellows and burnished reds are flickering in the charcoal black. Outside, the swooshing trees are wind-singing. My sleepy thoughts spin into the shadows where the smell of spruce and pine is thick.

In the dead of night when Askook slips into the tent, I spring awake. Outside the wind begins to moan while the black spruce trees begin dropping their plinking needles and hard, green cones on the roof. When I lift my head, I see only dappled tent shadows and a few live embers winking in the firepit.

I surface to the sound of squealing children crowding around my bed. Some are gingerly poking at my outstretched form. Some are huddled at my feet. When a little face pops into view directly above mine, I snap awake. Sunshine is streaming through the smoke hole, with dust particles snowing down gently in the filmy air.

Miwok's giggles are as loud as a harp seal pup, while the oldest – a girl with red ochre-coloured hair and scrolling red tattoos on her little hands – pulls me to my feet and leads me out into the empty yard where a crow is cawing incessantly. The children convince me to play a chasing game before we each take turns throwing rocks. I don't need to ask if I belong.

After a time, I sense that I am being watched. The children smile. The dogs begin to bark. When I creep around to the back of Nuttah's tent, I come face to face with Huritt.

"By Óðinn's beard, you scared me," I sputter.

Huritt throws an easy smile and points to the sun to show me I have slept in late. His grin widens at my scowl. Then he reaches for his water skin and casually takes a drink before offering the flask to me. Behind us, the children squeal. When a little one comes and tugs me by the hand and tries to convince me to resume the game, Huritt squats down beside her and talks to her. In my periphery, I catch sight of Nuttah carrying two heavy water pails down the path.

"May the great Creator give me the patience of spawning salmon," she huffs as I scramble forward to help her out. She calls to Huritt, "Where have you been?"

Huritt wipes the smile off his face.

"He should be out hunting," she mutters as she hands me the pails and reaches out to catch her little one before he runs off. She spits a string of Beothuk words in Huritt's direction as her fingers nimbly pluck a spoiled berry from the child's hands.

"Huritt has been told to follow you," Nuttah sighs when she straightens up. She rubs her back.

"Follow me? I don't need to be followed."

Huritt grins again.

"Chief Achak insists that Huritt must learn to speak Norse. In exchange, you are to learn the Beothuk tongue."

"From whom?" I ask, and Nuttah huffs. Huritt has a long blade of grass in his hand. He puts it in his mouth and begins to suck.

"From Huritt?" I ask, dumbfounded.

"'Tis so, I fear. Don't worry. I'll oversee the lessons."

"I am grateful."

Nuttah shrugs. "These days, I'm low on patience, I fatigue easily, and I am as swollen as a jellyfish. By the gods, I'm getting too old for all of this." She holds out a hand to her littlest one who is just learning how to walk. Simultaneously, she shouts to her oldest to come and help.

Huritt moves towards the firepit and leans down to start a fire. When he disappears inside the tent, Nuttah's eyes follow him.

"Freydis would want me to take good care of you."

I feel my lips begin to tremble. Thorvard's image flares. There is a sickening rise of nausea, a cresting wave of anger that kills sadness, squelches grief. "You asked before," I manage in a shaky voice. "I'll tell you now. Freydis returned to Greenland and moved to a separate farm where I was raised. I lived with her and saw Thorvard on feast days."

Nuttah hobbles over to a giant berry basket. She leans forward and dumps the contents onto a mat. A worm crawls out. "Thorvard was a maggot of a man."

I take a breath: "What was my mother like when she lived here on Vinland shores?"

"Freydis was fiercely independent," Nuttah says. She glances up. When she returns to cleaning berries, I lean over and begin to help. As the flies whiz past, I try to work up enough courage to ask the questions I must ask, but my throat is dry, my jaw locks up. What is wrong with me? Freydis, my real mother, isn't here. Thorvard is not the man I thought he was. My chieftain *faðir* wants to have nothing to do with me.

Nuttah's fingers pick through the berries one by one. "The fates were not kind to your mother. Freydis's life was cursed."

My hands are already stained purple from the berry juice. If I learn that Freydis was well loved, then the grief will be unbearable, and I will know that in my blindness, I missed out. But if the stories Thorvard's *skalds* shared about my mother's wickedness are true, I will know that I am cursed and all hope about the possibilities of having an honourable mother – all the stories I've created in my head about what a mother could be like – will be forever lost. What is worse, Freydis's wickedness will continue to follow me, breathing as though it is a living thing.

Nuttah inspects another berry before she flicks a glance at the children playing in the yard. "Toss away the mouldy ones," is all she says.

That afternoon, a girl wearing deer skins trimmed with marten fur comes to visit while Nuttah and I are teaching Huritt how to offer a proper greeting in Norse.

"This is Santu. She was married just last month," Nuttah says. The girl is about my age. She lowers her eyes and smiles shyly.

"*Góðan aptan*," Huritt's grin is one of pride. A slight frown feathers Santu's brow. When they continue speaking together in their tongue, I study her deer-skin robe which holds tiny, white seashells in the fringes. On her feet, she is wearing new leather slippers. I can smell the smoke wafting up from her soft leather hides.

"Santu will help you make yourself a new pair of shoes. The Beothuk call them *moccasins*," Nuttah says when she sees me staring at the foot coverings.

"I'd like that very much."

When Huritt speaks, Nuttah listens carefully. "Huritt says Santu should be the one to teach you the ancestral stories. She knows them best."

Santu looks at me expectantly. I turn to Santu and take a breath, knowing that to be familiar with the ancestral stories is to understand the Beothuk way of life. To share their history. To be worthy enough to belong. Santu smiles and says something. I catch the word "*Giwashuwet*".

"She calls you Bear Girl," Nuttah says, and I feel the flush of skin prickles as I draw in short, quick breaths.

"Please have her call me something else. Tell her my name is Anja."

Nuttah turns to Santu and rattles off a string of sharp-sounding words. The wind goes still, the birdsong stops. Afterwards, Santu comes to take me by both hands. She has the warmest of eyes the colour of earthen clay.

"She will call you Raven," Nuttah says.

Santu stays for the remainder of the afternoon. She is likeable and sweet and eager to try to speak with me. Nuttah translates, but Huritt soon gets bored. It is evident that his preference is to work with his hands, but he is so good-natured that when Nuttah insists he help me learn new words, he points out objects and identifies them by their Beothuk names. I start by learning the names of the animals, like *osweet* for the caribou and *odusweet* for the jackrabbit. Huritt mimes the actions of the animals in the bush. Very soon he has us giggling like laughing gulls. I watch his lips and listen to the way his throat pushes out the choppy sounds, and my courage grows, but I often stumble when I try to speak the simplest words.

"You'll learn in time," Nuttah says.

"Huritt hunts in winter," I try in Beothuk. My effort evokes a tired smile.

"Look, your *faðir* comes," she murmurs. Chief Achak holds himself erect with his shoulders squared. When he steps out from underneath a canopy of slouching trees, he grins at the sight of me sitting cross-legged on the ground. When he turns to Nuttah, the music of his voice is a rich and sonorous river, a gurgling stream of strange new words.

"He compliments you," Nuttah tells me afterwards. "He says that Anja Freydisdöttir carries the beauty of her mother's lineage."

I turn to him. "Nuttah is kind," I try in Beothuk, but my tongue gets knotted up, and I gurgle-gargle the phrase. The chieftain looks at me with knowing eyes. His Norse sounds like rustling grass.

Nuttah's voice rises with the wind as the sun peeks through the voluminous clouds that close together like curtains drawn. Santu quickly stands. Her agility is as graceful as the swiftest deer leaping through the meadowlands.

"Thank you," she says. She turns and respectfully takes her leave, and Nuttah chipmunk-chatters, and my chieftain *faðir* smiles. There are tingles moving up and down my sore leg. Behind me there is a raven croaking in the bush. I search for it, but it is an elusive spirit presence with its stark, distinctive croak, moving through the silver sky.

Around suppertime when we begin to smell the roasting meats, Raven invites me to walk back with him to his *mamateek*. We follow the winding path that skirts the village in single file, but I am as uncomfortable as a lamb being herded by a shepherd boy. The aspens shimmy as we pass, and the leaves rustle their applause.

Raven says nothing until we come to the place where two well-worn paths cross. When he points to a majestic eagle catching wind currents in the sky, I feign interest, but I am distracted by a group of *Skraeling* hunters, each as solidly built as a tree trunk. They are sitting around one of the communal firepits. I scan the group.

Bjǫrn is sitting on a fallen tree stump at the back, working a carving piece in his hands. Dappled black spruce-tree shadows are fluttering across his shoulders, shading half his face. Beside him sits a broad-shouldered man with a bold, upright posture and red ochre-coloured tattoos scrolling down his chest.

"We eat salmon at my fire tonight," Chief Achak says at my shoulder, startling me. I ignore the impulse to run to Bjǫrn even though the pull of his presence is as strong as a river current.

I express my gratitude in the Beothuk tongue and taste the feel of the words in my mouth.

"You learn well, *döttir*," my Raven-*faðir* grins. "To say thank you to our people is good. It means you treasure them."

When we arrive at the Raven's *mamateek*, the evening routine is much the same as the night before, but this time, there are more people. Wapun invites me to sit cross-legged next to her on a large reed mat. Her hair falls lower than her abdomen, and it is loose and straight and black and glossy and beautiful. All through dinner, I can't stop staring at her. When she smiles at me, I shift my gaze and scrutinize everything – the elders sitting around the fire holding the children in their laps, the laughing infants with their chubby legs, the dogs lazing by the fire, the feast of salmon berries, freshly picked. My *faðir* and his Beothuk wife have built a life, and I am part of it. How is it that I have slipped into this place so naturally? How is it that they seem to have accepted me?

At sunset, Raven walks me back to Nuttah's tent. I try to speak in Beothuk, but midway through, I give up. I can't help worrying that I will get the words wrong and that this *faðir* of mine will be displeased. An owl, perched high above us in the trees, releases a sequence of long hoots followed by a quick, ear-splitting screech. When I glance up, the owl flies off to look for mice.

"You did well today, *döttir*," Chief Achak says in Norse. Dusk's purple hues are smudged bruises along the horizon. A chorus of singing frogs are croaking noisily in the trees. "It is noble that you want to learn your people's tongue. To speak the language is to learn our ways."

"To speak the language is to belong."

He turns. The light is quickly fading. "Look up," he whispers. His voice is full of awe and stardust magic. I pinch myself. In the sky, there is a full moon rising.

"*Washewiush*. The word means 'moon'," he says so quietly, I barely hear.

"*Washewiush*," I repeat, and Freydis's image flares – her long, red hair, her glassy eyes, the way she frowns and tilts her head when I insist on going out into the meadowlands to look for herbs on my own It is like I am drowning in lakewater, holding my breath to the point my lungs will burst. Raven is oblivious.

As soon as we enter Nuttah's yard, we see Askook standing in front of a roaring campfire where the flames are leaping high and shooting sparks into the deep blue-black. Nuttah is rummaging inside the *mamateek*. I see her shadow smudging the walls of the dwelling.

Askook calls out a greeting. Chief Achak rumbles a short reply.

Today, I have learned. I can understand. In the Beothuk tongue, Askook greets just one of us.

I now know his words. I know my worth. I know my place. It is not with Askook at his big fire.

Chapter Twenty-One

STORY MEDICINE

Summer is at its peak when Santu invites me to go berry picking with her. As I hobble across the boglands, she points out herbs and gives them names. Then she takes me back along a coastal trail bordering a rocky beach pummelled by rushing waves. There we spot a gathering of eider ducks diving for molluscs in the swirling sea. As I am straining to follow their bobbing forms with my eyes, a gust of wind lifts my mantle. In my struggle to hold the garment down, Santu notices all my scars.

"A bear – a *giwashuwet* – bit me," I mutter into the wind.

We stand together staring out across the sea. Then she leans down and shows me her own ugly scar – a giant, purple, lumpy birthmark stretching up and down her right calf. When I ask to touch it, Santu smiles. The skin feels mushroom-like.

"You could red-ochre it," I say, pointing to the grease-paint smudges on her face and arms. She shakes her head.

"I like it," she says in Beothuk. She helps me up, and I ponder what she said until she points to the eider ducks again. They are taking flight over the landwash, swooping low as they press into the wind.

When we start to head inland, we encounter the carcass of a deer lying in a bank of grass surrounded by a swarm of flies. Santu squats. "It was likely killed by a *giwashuwet*," she breathes.

Reaching for my river rock, I close my eyes and struggle to push the bear memories down.

"It's hot out here," Santu says. She stands and scans my face. "You are sweating, sister. Are you feeling well?"

I nod as I feel for Bjørn's grounding rock in my pocket, the smooth warmth of it.

I get used to seeing Chief Achak in the afternoons when he comes to visit Askook's fire. We communicate in whatever language he prefers. He never stays for very long.

When Santu takes me fishing, she introduces me to a group of women who seem nice enough. When the silver capelin roll onto the beach, we haul them in, filling baskets. The women also show me how to set out woven funnel weirs to catch the cod. Sometimes we even venture out across the rocks in search of clams and oysters, taking care not to slip among the stinky, slippery, bug-covered strands of seaweed. These jaunts are hard on my injured leg. Santu gives me another poultice to try, and we share our knowledge of the healing herbs.

Bjørn comes to visit Askook's fire, but the distance between us widens when he spends more time talking to Nuttah and Santu's husband than he does to me. He and Huritt like to talk about their hunting spoils, about where they might try to go to spot the migrating herds of caribou. When they laugh together as they fix their fishing nets, I envy the ease they have with each other. It is evident they share a brotherhood.

One evening Nuttah asks Bjǫrn to stay late and play his flute, and the melody is a haunting one. When I think of the mother I never knew, tears pearl fatly before spilling down. I see Freydis sitting alone on Greenland shores pondering why the fates weren't kind. The darkness in me coils around my heart like snakes that hiss at me for being a fool, for shunning Freydis, for abandoning her. She called me "mole blind", and it was true.

"Raven's *döttir* is like the hawk," Askook says as soon as Bjǫrn finishes.

Bjǫrn looks at me. The sun is setting behind his golden head, slipping below the treeline, sending spears of light through the bush.

Askook sniffs. "Her eyes are keen. Her talons grip my son."

"Anja is no hawk," Bjǫrn says carefully.

Askook reaches for his pipe. "You do not see, huntsman."

Nuttah reaches out and steadies me with her hands. In the silence, the fire crackles, snaps. "Will you go hunting with Huritt and the others?" she asks Bjǫrn.

His brow contorts. "I have a mind to hunt for caribou."

"You should send word to Leifsbidur that you are back," Nuttah says as she takes up a stick and manoeuvres another log into place in the firepit. We watch in silence as the flames begin to lick the wood.

"I sent word to Leifsbidur. I told Nashushuk about the girl," Askook says. His eyes look flat.

"I, too, sent a message to my *fosterfaðir*," Bjǫrn quickly says. "Nashushuk will be surprised to hear from both of us." He sits up tall as the spruce trees encircling the yard sink into shadows. The sun is setting, bleeding out.

"Did you send word that Achak's Greenland child lives?" Nuttah breathes.

When Bjørn looks up, he nods his head, and our eyes connect. Askook grunts. Bjørn looks uncomfortable. "Will Anja continue to live with you?"

Askook slowly lights his pipe. Then he takes a hefty draw and releases a puff of heady smoke. "Raven's *döttir* should return with you to Leifsbidur."

My stomach drops.

Bjørn stands up. "I'll discuss it with the chieftain before I leave this autumn." He turns to me. His eyes blaze fire. "I am sure you'll have a say, Anja. Askook cannot decide your fate."

There is a confused expression on Santu's face. She stares at me. "Tell them you want to stay here among your people, where you belong."

There is a noise behind us. When I turn, Huritt is towering over us. He has a smell of seawind freshness. I notice the new eagle feather dangling from his long black hair.

"You must stay at our fire," he whispers as he squats down. His voice is garbled and mossy. I blink at him.

When I look up, Bjørn is halfway across the yard. He calls to me, and I raise my hand in *far vel* as some of Nuttah's children crowd around him, chattering like noisy squirrels. We hear their laughing, carefree squeals as they escort him quickly down the path.

After Santu and her husband take their leave, Askook grabs the pail to go fetch fresh drinking water and Nuttah leaves the fire to go and tuck her little ones into bed. In the peaceful silence of a warm summer night, I find myself staring into the fire.

"Do you like it here?" Huritt asks. His Beothuk is a mix of throat sounds rumbling around like tumbled rocks.

I nod my head. In the twilight, his handsome face breaks into another easy smile. "I have something for you, Raven's *döttir*." He scrambles up. In a few quick strides, he is across the yard. I watch him move, the stealth of him. The forest slurps him up in moonshadows, and as soon as he disappears from sight, I sit in silence listening to the crickets chirp.

When Huritt returns, he is carrying a huge stack of furs of every size and shape: mink and beaver, deer and rabbit, otter, fox, and caribou. There are pelts of many hues – browns and blacks and greys and reds. There are speckled hides as well: rich and thick, all tanned and ready for me to use. He has even brought a bundle of sinew thread.

"I give thanks to the animals for these pelts," he begins. He looks so solemn, I can't help but smile.

"They are very fine."

"You can make new shoes – some *moccasins*?"

"Surely these furs are not all for me?"

He smiles his impish smile. "Perhaps you can make me new *moccasins*?"

The moon shines down. The stars shine bright. He is standing so close, I am tempted to reach up and touch his cheek. The tears well up, unbidden. "It must have taken you many days to cure and smoke and treat these hides."

"These hides are a gift. Raven's *döttir* can make Beothuk clothes to wear." He winks. My face flushes hot.

"I always knew in my heart that I was worthy," I breathe, tilting my head up to the stars. I feel Huritt's eyes caress my face.

"You are Raven's *döttir*," he says. With the ease of a great hunter, he stands, and I see him differently. "These pelts are to honour you.".

He coughs, and the crickets chirp. Then he quickly takes his leave. At the trailhead, he pauses and turns back to me. It is too dark to see his teasing eyes, but his teeth flash white in the moonlight.

As soon as he is gone, I run my fingers across the furs and feel the sleek softness and the coarse bristles, dense and smooth. When an owl begins to hoot, I feel the presence of the ancestors in the earth and wind, in the black of night, in the rising moon.

By the time Nuttah emerges from the *mamateek*, the fire is roaring and the sap in the logs is crackling in a burst of snaps. When she sees Huritt's gift, her eyes search mine.

"Santu and Little Deer can help you sew the pelts together. You can start by making winter shoes. Three small caribou pieces is all you'll need to form the sole, vamp and cuff. The art of fashioning the cone-shaped projection at the heel took me a while to master when I first moved here, but I learned in time and you can, too. We will teach you how to secure the boot with a drawstring leather thong."

"I am grateful," I say shyly.

"You'll also need a festive dress for the *Mokoshan*, the Beothuk's greatest celebration of the year. It is the feast that marks the success of the great caribou hunt each autumn. You could make something from that fox's pelt in russet hues." Her eyes look bright. The moonbeams shine down and paint her hair silver in the firelight. "My son has been busy, by the looks of things. He honours you. I have never seen such luscious furs."

"You look tired," is all I say. She rubs her belly with her hand and smiles when she sees a ripple of activity when the baby moves.

"*Döttir*, you must help me sit," she mutters. There is perspiration on her lip. Instantly, I am at her side. Her hand clasps mine.

"You've been kind to take me in, considering that you are with child. It's extra work to feed another mouth."

Nuttah makes a noise in the back of her throat – a Beothuk sound, dismissive but noteworthy. "Anja Freydisdöttir, you are no burden," she softly says. "Rest assured, your mother would have been pleased we found each other."

Nuttah gives a little laugh, and I squeeze her hand. "I wish you didn't have to work so hard. I should go out hunting and bag a deer or two. I've got a good eye, or so they say. Mother taught me how to hunt when I was living in Greenland. She said it was an essential skill."

"She liked to hunt," Nuttah says, but there is something strange in her voice.

"I could go out hunting with the men. It might help you worry less about the winter food supply."

Nuttah stiffens. "You'll stay right here!"

I pull back. Her eyes look haunted; her voice is tight.

"Don't ever wander off on your own. I wouldn't like it, do you hear?"

"I could take Huritt or Bjǫrn."

"Askook wouldn't like it. He doesn't like to see you and Huritt together. As for me, I'd like to think that Huritt is different now that you are here."

"How so?" I ask in a careful voice.

"I have tried to teach him the importance of placing others before himself, and you bring out the best in him. In your presence, he is less self-focused, but there is a side to him you haven't seen. Truly, he is Askook's son."

I blink several times.

"Huritt is ambitious. He is a huntsman, yes, but he also has a fight in him. He will become a great warrior one day."

I snag a breath. The fire snaps. "He has been kind to me," is all I say.

"Huritt provided solace in my time of grief after I lost my firstborn son, but as an infant, he was difficult to manage. He never slept. Even as a wee bairn, he was a fighter. Now that he has grown into the fine hunter that he is, all the young women hope to catch his eye. They sing songs about him. I've heard them."

"Huritt has become a friend." The words slip out in gaspy breaths. When two dogs start growling at something in the bush, we both look up. "I'll stay away from him if Askook doesn't approve of me," I say, hoping she can't see the panic in my eyes.

"Askook doesn't trust you because you are Norse. He harbours resentments and nurtures wounds. Your arrival has reopened pain." In the firelight, her face looks pale. She rubs her back. "When he looks at you, he sees your mother and then the memories come flooding back."

At the far end of the yard, I hear Askook's deep, brittle laugh, the sounds of chirping crickets in the grass.

"I have been meaning to share this tale, but I worried that it would be too difficult for you to hear. The thunder god, Thor, might fill you with anger and despair."

"Tell me," I say miserably.

"It started when your mother was living here on Vinland shores and she left Leifsbidur to go out hunting on her own. Most of us were very sick. The winter gods had been cruel to us, and we were starving. She wanted to bring back meat, but there was a blizzard, and she didn't return. The whiteout was so severe, we thought that she had died. Even so, we sent out search parties to look for her. We didn't know Achak and Askook had found her and taken her back to this village."

The fire hisses, throws up sparks. Nuttah's eyes look glassy in the firelight.

"One whole winter passed. In the spring, Freydis decided to return to us. She had become Achak's lover, and she must have been pregnant with you at the time because Achak insisted on returning with her. Freydis asked Askook and his brothers, Megedagik and Abooksigun, to come back with them. She wanted them to carry meat back to her people." She pauses and runs the back of her hand across her brow.

"Perhaps we shouldn't speak of it," I quickly say when we overhear Askook talking to his men. Their voices rise over the long chirps of crickets and the fluttering wings of bats.

"I hate thinking about that brutal time," Nuttah whispers as if I'm not there. She chews the corner of her lip. "We were not prepared for the endless snowstorms that kept us from going out in search of food." She shivers despite the evening heat. Her face is lost in shadow, alive to grief.

"When Askook and his brothers arrived in Leifsbidur, Thorvard of Gardar appeared, as if out of nowhere. Your mother had banished him and his Greenlanders from the settlement, and they had wintered elsewhere. He blamed your mother for everything. What is more, Thorvard killed Abooksigun, Askook's little brother. Curse his bones, I say! Abooksigun was just a boy!"

When I hear her spit out Thorvard's name, I vow to make a runic stave, and the anger in me stirs to life.

"After Abooksigun's death, I heard Askook sing his brother's death song. He wouldn't stop. I lay in bed, sick and starved and crazed by grief after losing everything and everyone I had ever loved. I listened to that wretched song until I couldn't stand it anymore. Then I got up and stumbled out of the longhouse wearing a shawl dyed red. Askook was weeping in the yard, and my robe flew open. When he saw my pregnant mound, his eyes grew wide. Then I collapsed. I was very weak. When I came to, I was lying in Askook's arms, and he called me by another name: "'*Nuttah! Nuttah!*' is what he said."

"Askook saved you, then?"

She doesn't answer. In the silence, I find myself staring at her hands. Her fingers are laced together, motionless. She glances up.

"Thorvard of Gardar not only murdered Abooksigun, but he murdered many of the Norsemen who lay sick and dying in their beds."

"He raised me to think I was his by birth."

Her face is speckled grey and grief-stricken. "I lost the bairn that was in my womb because of him," she says, ignoring me. Her voice is icy; her breathing, strained.

"But Huritt became your little son."

"*Já,*" she says. Her lashes are wet. She pinches her sleeve and uses it to wipe her cheeks. "Out of all of us, Achak suffered most of all. He was robbed of a life with your mother, and then he lost you, too. Then there was Abooksigun."

I quickly stand.

"Achak's heart was ripped out by Thorvard, that skull-cleaver, that monstrous, hungry wolf. I was too weak to move."

A silence fogs between us, heavy and bloated.

"Did you ever get to say goodbye to Mother?"

Nuttah cannot look at me. I feel Mother's spirit presence whispering in the trees, stirring up moon shadows, slipping through the dew-soaked grass.

"My mother was not to blame for anything. She suffered too. I was raised to think Thorvard was my *faðir*, that he had a *Skraeling* lover, that Freydis killed her when I was born. I didn't know I was Freydis's child. She was my mother, and I didn't know!"

Nuttah slips into herself. For a moment we sit in the silence listening to the whisperings of the fire. I am aware of her ragged breathing and the sudden quiet in the yard. "I am sorry, Anja," she says, swallowing a whispered sob.

"Is this where the saga ends?"

Nuttah sighs. "You may think this surprising, but Askook is a good man. I remember the day a runner came to inform him that his wife had died in childbed but that his baby son was still alive. I felt for him. I had just lost my own newborn son, and in my grief, I wanted to end it all. Askook asked me to return with him to the Beothuk village to nurse his child. I felt I owed him. He had nursed me back to life."

There is a surge of heart pain, boom-thudding as I draw in air.

"When I recovered from my sickness, I learned that Thorvard had murdered my kinsmen," Nuttah continues, her voice dipping low. "I saw Thorvard for what he was – a man who stinks like the breath of fish, a man possessed by Fenrir, the monstrous wolf, a man worse than the son of Loki and the giantess, Angerboda. Only evil can be expected of him."

Each breath is a rolling wave. "The *skalds* tell stories back on Greenland shores. They say Mother was the murderer. They say she murdered you and that she stole your ship and sailed it back to Greenland shores. They say she stole your trading goods and kept the profits as her own."

"This isn't true, Anja Freydisdöttir!"

In the shadows, Askook bids his friends good night. Then he whistles for the dogs.

"Askook will never allow another Viking ship safe harbour here on Vinland shores," Nuttah says. "There is pure hatred in his heart for those who stole his brother's life. He hates the Norse. He resents Thorvard of Gardar most of all, but he also blames your mother for bringing evil to his tribe. He sees Freydis in you, and he worries that you have brought evil here as well."

"I am Raven's *döttir* in this Beothuk place."

"You are Freydis's *döttir* just as much."

"My mother's story is not mine to own. He cannot fault me for what Thorvard did."

In the shadows, I see Askook making his way towards the fire. I study his silhouette. At the woodpile, he stops to retrieve his spear.

"Why don't you return to Leifsbidur?" I ask as the campfire flickers and lights up her face.

"What for?" she snaps. "The place is dead. There are only a handful of womenfolk left, along with their Beothuk men. There were three Norsemen who were out hunting when Thorvard killed Abooksigun and stole our ship. Two of them are still living. The other died from a broken leg."

I glance up. Askook is towering above us. His eyes look hard. When he sees the stack of furs that Huritt left, he releases a rumble of Beothuk words, and Nuttah's voice rises in volume to touch the stars. She slides a glance my way. When he speaks again, Askook's face is cold. Nuttah rubs her belly and snuffs out his wind.

"I told him you must have something new for the *Mokoshan*," she says when he finally stomps off to bed.

I douse the fire, and there is a puff of smoke. For a moment, I stand there staring at the remaining embers crinkling orangey-yellow in the blackened pit. When I look up, the moon disappears in a frothy bank of clouds, as though it is ashamed and hiding and tired of its cycles.

I stand there staring. Then I swear.

I am sewing inside Nuttah's *mamateek*, when the crows start cawing in the yard and little feet come running past. One ... two ... I count ten children. Just then I hear a shout announcing the arrival of the chief. The children squeal and run to him, and I can almost picture the expression on Chief Achak's face.

"You should tell your *faðir* what Huritt did for you," Nuttah says as one of her little ones asks to be lifted. Nuttah is as patient as a big-eared bat waiting for a moth to flap its wings. I clear my throat and brush the sewing remnants off my lap. In silence, I leave the *mamateek*. Outside, the sun is bright, the weather warm. I find *Faðir* sitting on a log.

"Some elders talk," *Faðir* says as soon as I take a seat beside him. He pulls out his pipe and clamps the stem firmly between his teeth. "They want to throw a naming feast." He pauses to light the pipe and take a draw. I watch the wispy smoke rings rising in the stillness of the warm, summer air. "The naming ritual honours the Great Creator. We thank him for granting newborns life."

I find myself picking at a dried scab on my mangled arm. "I am not an infant anymore."

"Raven's *dóttir* will have to choose a Beothuk name," he says as he studies me.

"A name?" I ask, feeling dizzy. I smell the pungent odour of Raven's pipe as I bite the insides of my cheeks. "I'm grateful to be honoured," I finally say, "but I am a simple maiden. I don't need a naming feast."

"You were dead, my *döttir*, but now you live. There will be a naming feast."

I have the sudden urge to escape the yard, to escape this spectacle, this so-called life. There are too many expectations I can't meet. When I politely ask to be excused, Raven dismisses me with a smile. Through the trees, I catch a glimpse of Santu coming down the path. She calls to me, but I take a different route, ignoring her.

I follow a trail scattered over with spruce needles and dead, crumbled leaves and move in the direction of the marshlands, the place where the children are not allowed to go.

"By Óðinn's beard!" I curse out loud when I hit a section of heavy underbrush where it is slow going and I am forced to bat the tree branches out of my face. In the hot, humid air, the black flies are out in droves, buzzing noisily around my head. I swat at them, but they return for me.

Emerging from the tree-line, my breath catches when I see a wide-open space that offers a panoramic view of peat barrens with aspens, poplar, and new-growth spruce surrounding the area far off in the distance. Memories of Greenland and the vast meadowlands and green, rolling hills shimmy to the surface, calming me with earth medicine, until Mother's image rises through the mist of welling tears. I think of our ruined life, of how I treated her, of how fierce she was when it came to protecting me. I should have acknowledged her sacrifice.

Tilting my head back into the sun, I breathe in the smell of summer and the familiar fragrance of the earth: the wet, spongy mosses, the growing lichens, the green fuzz of pond scum, the bogland wet. As the wind rustles the sedges growing in tufts around the marsh, the angry tears spill down my cheeks and the anguish comes for my bones.

Freydis Eiriksdóttir was my mother! How I miss her – how I want her back!

When I breathe her name, I crumple, and the pain reroutes anguish into self-pity which flows into self-hate. All of a sudden I am on my knees, sinking to the ground, burying my head in my arms.

I feel something dark closing in on me, squelching hope and stopping air. I snag a breath, release a moan. In the silence, the crickets chirp. *Get up*, they say with a *tsssspppp*.

Cursing, I close myself off to my crumpled self and force myself to stand. To move. To begin to breathe. To sink into fear.

I begin by following a deer path and searching for clumps of marsh marigold and other healing herbs. When I find some, I squat down and check the undersides of the leaves and flowers for insects before I pinch off a few. The damselflies are plentiful, and I get lost in harvesting the herbs. The work helps stuff down the memories and squash the pain.

I am halfway around the marsh when I spot a mother deer flicking flies with her ears while chewing grass and scanning the area for signs of threat. When she darts behind a beaver-felled tree, I catch a glimpse of her little fawn struggling to keep up with her; its speckled body is hidden almost fully in the grass. There is clearly something wrong with the fawn's back-left leg as it hobbles through the swaying grass.

Watching her, I brace myself as a wicked cramp creeps down my injured leg. Two ravens are flying overhead, soaring majestically through the sky. As soon as they disappear into the trees, I feel the loneliness of the place. I am a lost wanderer abandoned by my people, abandoned by the gods. I have forgotten them, and this is their way of punishing me. I have stepped between two worlds, and I am alone and broken, cut in two.

There is a sudden bush snap behind me which alerts me to the arrival of something big. My bones freeze. I snag a breath. Goosebumps rise along the line of scars running up my arms.

"*Döttir*, where is your bow and arrow? You should not be in the bush without them. You know better." His voice is a boom-whisper ferreting through the trees.

"I came out here to be alone."

"I came to find you," he replies. He glances at the clippings in my hand. Then we hear another sound. Shading his eyes with his hand, Raven points to the mother deer across the bog. The summer sun beats down and peppers the deer in drizzled shade.

"Her fawn is injured," I say pitifully. "I think it has a broken leg. There could be a fox or coyote waiting in the bush to devour it. We should rescue that little fawn and help it heal."

"The mother deer is protective. She is trying to lure the predators away," Raven tells me quietly.

"Mother was like that."

The words hang heavily between us. The feather in Raven's braided hair stirs in the gentle breeze.

"Freydis killed a helmsman so that I could escape from Greenland shores. She only killed him to protect me."

Raven's back goes iron straight. The breeze stirs the tassels on his hides as he stares across the fen. Across the bog, there is a flicker of movement, and I catch sight of the little fawn struggling to stand. I follow the poor thing with my eyes, knowing that it won't survive out here on its own.

"You must let nature take its course, Anja Freydisdöttir."

We are attacked by a sudden swarm of bugs. Stepping

forward, Raven leans down and swats my legs. "Nuttah tells me many things," he says, glancing up. "She says you learn Beothuk fast like fox. She said you honour the sacred nature of our stories. She said you listened to your mother's story and you heard. She said you were deceived. I am sorry, *döttir*. I hope that listening to Freydis's story was good medicine."

Mother's face comes alive. Her image flickers, floats up high.

"I tried to bring the raven earrings you made for Mother back with me." The words stick on my tongue. "I lost the earrings in a stream."

"The loss of things means nothing. The loss of people matters more."

"You grieved for us," I say as the wind swishes through the marshes and eelgrass beds. We stand facing each other as *faðir* and *döttir* underneath the Great Creator's sky. *Faðir* squints one eye shut and looks directly at the sun.

"I found a way to live," he says.

There is a taste of wool inside my mouth. "Now it is my turn to do the same. Mother gave me up so I could come to you."

"I see how much you miss her, *döttir*. The huntsman told me you cried out for her in the cave."

I step back, embarrassed. "The huntsman helped me heal," I manage.

"His medicine soothed your pain."

"It kept me alive."

Faðir is silent for a moment. He scans the marsh. "We will celebrate your return to the tribe at your naming feast. My Beothuk brothers will honour you."

"Askook, too?" My spirit hums.

"Askook is like the *giwashuwet*. He roars after losing fish. His dead brother would not want him to roar so long."

The crickets clitter, and their stridulations are long and shrill.

"Askook has been generous to take me in."

"He will protect you."

"Once I had a mother to protect me," I mutter, looking down.

"You have a *faðir* now," he whispers softly in the wind.

Chapter Twenty-Two

THE AWAKENING

L ate summer brings with it a muggy heatwave that makes for easy living in the afternoons. The children and I go beachcombing and even Nuttah, who can hardly walk because of her pregnant bump, takes pleasure in cooling her swollen feet in the sea. All are talking about the arrival of the salmon run. There has been much debate about where to construct the fish weirs.

When the salmon finally come, I snag many with my spear. Askook barely acknowledges my success, but Nuttah beams.

"Your catch will make Chief Achak proud," she says, but I don't feel proud when, a few days later, I lose my spear.

"Perhaps you left it at your *faðir's* *mamateek* after visiting Wapun and her little ones," Nuttah suggests. She is sitting with a group of women minding the children in the yard.

"It's possible," I say, but I am as agitated as a squirrel digging for hidden nuts. "I'll retrace my steps."

"If you find Huritt, send him home," Nuttah calls, and I wave my hand in acknowledgement.

Oubee's husband stops me as I am heading down the path leading to *Faðir*'s *mamateek*. We exchange friendly greetings. He is an honourable man who likes to hunt and fish – a good provider to us all.

When I arrive in *Faðir*'s yard, there is no one sitting around the communal firepit, where the white ashes lie like powdered snow. The sun beats down. In the silence, a red-winged blackbird releases a prolonged screech as I approach the *mamateek*. Inside, two men are speaking low, and their voices are barely audible. At the entrance, I hesitate before I cock my ear and peer through the crack in the hides hanging from the door.

Faðir is sitting crosslegged on the ground, and his back is straight, his head is cocked slightly to one side. Bjǫrn is pacing in front of him.

"Huritt has given her most of the furs from my traplines. Those were my catches. He should be held accountable! I tanned the hides with urine, liver grease and wood-ash so they would be supple enough to make into clothes. Huritt stole from me!"

He pauses, and the shock puffs through me like stirred-up lakebed silt. *Faðir* says something I can't quite hear.

"*Neinn!*" the huntsman yells indignantly. "I hauled those pelts to She-is-Smiling so she could chew the edges to render the leather soft enough to sew. I did everything! What did Huritt do? Those pelts weren't his to give away!"

I can almost feel the softness of the caribou hide between my fingertips. I can almost see the mink, the marten and the fox hides, those precious pelts that were given as gifts to make me smile. Looking down, I wiggle my toes and feel the comfort of my new pair of *moccasins*, the ones that Santu helped me sew.

Bjǫrn suddenly kicks a pail, and there is another angry shout.

"What do you wish me to do, my son?" *Faðir* asks in an even tone. "Perhaps my *döttir* should return the pelts."

"*Neinn!*" Bjǫrn bellows. His voice rises like a colony of screeching bats. "During our hike back to the village, she lost her pack in a river. Those hides will replace her losses, but I should have been the one to give them to her."

"Huritt did not mean to dishonour you," *Faðir* begins. Before he can finish, Bjǫrn cuts him off.

"Huritt has deceived many. I've tried to tolerate his selfishness and arrogance, but I know he is jealous. He knows I am an honoured hunter. I've bagged more catches than he has this year. I also returned Anja to your care, and he was annoyed by that. He wanted the glory. He always does."

"Go talk to him," *Faðir* says.

Bjǫrn flicks his hair out of his eyes. "I won't," he says. "He insulted me when he called me stupid for staying behind with Anja in that cave. He wanted me to return with him to the village so that we could both take part in the great caribou hunt. If I would have left, Anja would have died."

My stomach falls.

"Bjǫrn, you must cool your blood."

"Chief Achak, I swear to you, if Huritt crosses me one more time, I'll gut him faster than any salmon catcher."

"I'll speak with Huritt. Until the autumn comes, stay away from him. When you go out hunting in the bush, take Grey Owl with you."

"I will gladly follow Grey Owl's *moccasins* down any path. He doesn't steal credit for his brother's work."

Faðir stands and begins to move towards the door. Instantly, I pull back and glance nervously around the yard. There is a round, leafy dwarf birch tree right outside the entrance to the *mamateek*. I dive for it.

"Huritt is young and headstrong," *Faðir* says in a gravelly voice as he pokes his head outside the door. Bjǫrn says something in reply. The words slip through the air, stifled like they are held in moss. *Faðir* tosses one last look outside before he retreats into the shadows of the *mamateek*.

Behind me there is a sudden shout as Fawn's little feet come running into the clearing. Her eyes are round and darkly lashed. When she sees me crouching behind the bush, she eyes me strangely.

"Come quickly, Anja. Grandmother is sitting at the big fire. She wants you."

I recast my face and climb out of the bush and gently steer the child back down the path. When she steals a sideways glance, I reach down and take her hand, and she smiles up at me and gives me sparkles that mean the world.

I am still shaking when I reach the old grandmother, who is roasting rabbit on a spit. She is so hunched over that she needs the support of her walking stick. When a puff of smoke drifts into her wizened face, she winces. Beside her, *grandfaðir* is nattering in her ear and Santu is trying to help them both.

"Wapun found your spear behind the smokehouse," Santu says in a gentle voice. "You must have left it there after your chasing games with your little brothers."

Grandmother *tsks* her tongue. She wants to show me how to make rabbit stew so that she can prove to me that the village is a place of great wealth with a bounty of food. I can't follow all her

Beothuk talk. My head feels like it is full of fire and smoke and seaweed and eelgrass. Now that I know what Huritt has done, all I can focus on is his trickery and arrogance, his lies and his deceit, his view of me as his trophy prize.

When I wake the next morning to a grey sky thick with fog, my mood is foul and my thoughts are as wiggly as weevils, as pesty as the vermin in the byre. In silence, I help Nuttah set a fire. When my chores are finished, I tell her that I have an errand to run for grandmother. She is distracted by her littlest one who is trying to bite a pinecone and swallow it. Amid the chaos, I scamper off.

At the spot where the hunters tan their hides, I meet Vipponah, who tells me that he saw Bjørn on the outskirts of the settlement with his pack in hand. Vipponah is working to skin a marten. The entrails lie in a bloodied clump beside him on the ground.

"When was this?" I demand.

"When the sun slipped behind the trees."

"He left last night at dusk? Where did he go?"

Vipponah shrugs. He is a slim man with a weathered face. "He likes to fish," he grins. "It is good catching at this time of year."

I walk down to the landwash to search for Bjørn, but when I can't find him, I watch the plovers eating the exposed worms on the sandbar. I have lost the joy I used to feel when I wandered off on my own. Now I constantly worry about the dangers I will face.

I look out across the sickly coloured green-grey sea touching the edges of the earth. In the distance, the village sounds are ones of life and connection: the sound of barking dogs and laughing children, of cookfires crackling and someone chopping wood, of men skinning the catches, of a baby crying at his mother's breast. As I listen, I hollow out space for my loneliness. There is bitterness over missing out on a life I yearned for and never found, a family life where I had a place. Even now, I can't seem to find myself.

When I return to the village, Santu and Nuttah and a group of women present me with a deerskin dress decorated along the edges with a zig-zag outline accentuated in raised relief by bird quills laid on the leather and then tightly oversewn with sinew to produce a corrugated edge. Santu has rubbed the robe with a mixture of grease and red ochre paint which gives the garment a beautiful rosy hue. The dress reminds me of the sky at dusk. Santu has even sewn some tiny seashells across the bodice in intricate flower patterns. A numb feeling lingers, spreading like ripples on a pond. Nuttah scrutinizes me with her gentle eyes.

"Many hands worked hard to make this dress. Why are you sad, *döttir*?"

I see the way she looks at me, like I mean something. Like I belong.

"I am truly grateful," I say, but the words sound hollow to my ears. From across the fire, Santu smiles.

"The chieftain told us to help you become one of us. He said we should start by making you a new dress."

Faðir *is behind all this*. The thought slithers through me before it comes to rest in my heaving chest.

Wapun motions for me to turn around and model the deerskin robe so that all can see. I do as she asks. Afterwards, she hands me a shell bracelet and a feather plume for my hair.

"Songbird wants to braid your locks," she says as she lifts my hair.

The attention is too much. I glance at the door, wishing that I could escape and be alone.

The women stay at our fire for a long time. Nuttah serves smoked fish and elderflower tea. It is a feast of sorts. When grandmother comes to sit with me, I let her natter and hold my hand. Her fingers are long and bony and elegant, but her skin is bramble-scratched and berry-stained. After I help her get re-settled on the hides, I study her bluish veins, her life wrinkles and ageing spots, this flesh story that speaks of her people and her way of life. Her hand squeezes mine as the women natter away like a gaggle of noisy geese.

"Imagine how it was for me," Nuttah sighs. She leans into me. "The first night I arrived in this village, I was taken straight to Askook's tent, and I was frightened. In the morning, I woke to a group of men standing over me." Her eyes are dancing sparks, alive with the remembering.

"Did they violate you?"

"*Neinn*, it was not like that. They came to eat, but I was still asleep. They sat themselves around the fire and helped themselves to my rosehip tea." She leans her back against the post and sticks out her baby bump to stretch her back. "Can you imagine how I felt when I was suddenly surrounded by a sea of red faces?" She gives a small chuckle. "Askook told me it was the way of his people."

"How did you manage it?"

"I had a little one to focus on so I didn't have time to care too much. Eventually, I found my place and learned their ways." She flicks a smile. "Your mother would have had it worse. I loved her like a sister, but she did not take kindly to being told what to do. I often wonder what it was like for her in this Beothuk village among these men. She was a headstrong woman."

My fingers pick at my tattered shawl. "Not always," I say quietly.

Grandmother speaks. Her voice sounds like water plinking over river rocks.

"Grandmother wants you to know that the Beothuk are a giving people," Nuttah sighs. "They will accept you in their own time."

I acknowledge grandmother with a smile and hold my hands towards the radiating heat spilling from the fire. "It must have been so strange for you when you first came here on your own," I whisper in Nuttah's ear.

"I had Askook," she mutters softly. "He helped me understand the importance of the circle stories and the worth of family."

"Do you miss the Norsemen who live in Leifsbidur?"

Nuttah clucks her tongue. "Truly, I tell you, I try not to worry about those I've left behind. It's better that way. Askook doesn't know, but I still give sacrifice to the gods. I still ask them to protect my kin back in Leifsbidur."

Nuttah's little one crawls into her lap. She has a sliver stuck in her thumb, and her cheeks are smudged with raindrop tears. The women's chatter fills the *mamateek*, and I lean back and listen as Nuttah busies herself trying to remove the sliver from her *döttir's* hand.

"I'm never lonely, Anja," she says as she pulls the hand closer to her eyes to better see in the firelight. "Living among Askook's kin has taught me much. I have built a life here."

Behind us, the door to the *mamateek* opens, and a rush of cool air slithers up my back as Miwok and Nikiti and four other children burst inside.

"We've seen Bjǫrn," Nikiti tells me as I catch him up in my arms.

"Where?" I ask. He tells me, but I can't decipher his mumbled words.

"At Grey Owl's fire," Nuttah says, translating. "You must go to him."

The children take me by the hand and lead me in a crisscross fashion through the village and down the path to Grey Owl's fire where the smoke is scattering in the wind.

"Your quiver is as long as you are tall," Grey Owl teases as soon as he spots Miwok in my company.

"Have you seen Bjǫrn?" I ask. Grey Owl's face is pox-marked. His eyes look stern.

"We saw him leave with Huritt," Hopi grunts.

"Stay here," I say to Miwok and Nikiti. "Don't wander off."

On the way to the smokehouse, I run into Santu's husband who is carrying a stick of roasted meat. When he sees me, his eyes twinkle like a lake in summer. I ask about Bjǫrn again.

"Try the smokehouse," Santu's husband says.

The path is lined with musk-sweet, scented poplars whose leaves are gently rustling in the wind. The three smokehouses, located on the outskirts of the village, are square in shape with wooden planks for walls and sharply pitched rooflines designed to capture the heat and smoke. Inside the first, Bjǫrn is cursing vehemently

I lose no time budging open the warped wooden door. It is dim inside, and I have to clamp my hand over my nose and mouth to manage breathing in the heavy scent of hickory smoke. When I push my way through the shanks of hanging meat, coated black, I find Bjǫrn and Huritt fighting at the back.

"You killer of mother cubs, come here!" Bjǫrn snarls. When he steps forward into the weird, filmy light, he knocks into a hefty piece of meat hanging from one of the ceiling hooks. The curing meat wobbles and twists and spins around. "Let me cleave your stupid skull in half."

There is a sudden roar and a chunk of meat swings past my head. I duck just as Bjǫrn delivers a crushing blow to Huritt's jaw. Just before he hits the ground, Huritt takes a sideways step and manages to right himself, blade in hand.

"Look out!" I shout as Bjǫrn releases a warrior's cry. In the dim, windowless shack where the animal spirits linger, Huritt's face is shaded black.

"If you've come to collect your choice of meat, Huritt can help you pull one down," Bjǫrn snaps as the shank of meat continues to swing back and forth. His face looks wild; the whites of his eyes pop wide in the smoky air.

Huritt spins around, and Bjǫrn quickly gives another block of meat a tremendous kick with his foot. The weight of it comes crashing down on Huritt's back.

"What's happening here?" I hiss as I half-duck to avoid the swinging chunk of meat.

"I didn't see you," Huritt croaks as he is pushed against the outer wall. When he turns, his face is slick with sweat, his hair is sticking to his neck, and there is a nasty cut running the length of his hunting arm.

"You're hurt!" I yelp.

Bjǫrn squeezes past. His jaw is bruised; his nose drips blood.

"For the love of Thor!" I protest. All around us, the hanging meats are like corpses, twisting and turning precariously.

Huritt steers me towards the door. When we stumble out onto the grass, the late afternoon sunlight is filtering through the trees, blinding us in a wash of light. Wincing, I search for Bjǫrn and find him standing a few paces from me. He runs his sleeve across his brow and then he leans down to retrieve his spear.

"Anja, your timing is impeccable," he mumbles without glancing up.

Huritt grabs my arm and pulls me close. His eyes look crazed; his grip is strong.

"Beware of Huritt. He is an unscrupulous hunter and a selfish rogue who cares more about himself than honouring you and your *faðir's* tribe."

I try to wiggle free from Huritt's grip.

"I'm warning you, Anja. Huritt will surely injure you. You can expect another bear attack."

"Let me go!" I yell. "Can't you see you are bruising me?"

Huritt drops my arm. "We must go home. Your naming ceremony will soon begin."

I crank my neck. Bjǫrn is slipping into the trees where some raven is croaking, as if to give a warning that a predator is near.

I scan the trees. There are no bears.

When we arrive back at Nuttah's *mamateek*, she lays a hand across her round, pregnant belly and throws Huritt a disappointed look. "Come, Anja. You must put on your ceremonial garb."

My heartbeat slows to a steady thump.

In silence, she helps me dress. I can't help but think about what I witnessed in the smokehouse. Bjǫrn was angry. Huritt seemed strange. I can't seem to make sense of it.

"You look Beothuk-born," Nuttah whispers as she admires me. One of her little girls has lost her front tooth; she throws a toothless grin as Nuttah continues to fix my hair. "You would make your mother proud. Come," she says impatiently. "We shouldn't keep your *faðir* waiting. He is anxious for the Naming Feast." I hear the quiver in her voice.

Askook and *Faðir*, dressed in all their regalia, are waiting for me by the entrance to the trail. *Faðir's* shell-fringed mantle tinkles gently in the wind, and the red-feathered headdress that marks his strength and bravery and represents all the great deeds he has done, trails down his back. His eyes soften when he sees me, and he acknowledges me formally in the Beothuk tongue.

"The moon is on the rise," *Faðir* says in a solemn voice.

At the base of the path, I turn and wave to Nuttah who has decided to stay behind because her feet are swollen, her legs are sore.

There is a sudden burst of pain. A jolt. An unexpected sting. I call on Mother's gods to give me strength, knowing that I am deceiving the Beothuk when I pretend to be joyful about this Naming Feast. The Beothuk honour me for *Faðir's* sake. The feast highlights my invisibility.

Chapter Twenty-Three

SHADOW VISITS

There is too much noise at the beach, where two hundred or more people have come to watch the procession Chief Achak leads. When Little Deer admires my dress, I'm hard pressed to find the right Beothuk words to express my gratitude. I try, but I can't speak for the rush of feelings ghosting me.

The ocean lisps. A shiver of wind ripples into shore. The water stills. I pick out the voices of young children and big, burly hunters greeting my *faðir* as we pass. Some of the Beothuk mist me with praise, but I retreat inside myself, wishing I was back on Greenland shores where I knew my place, where everything was familiar, where I was nobody. The Beothuk honour me because they want to celebrate a child who always was, who never was, who wants to be. They come to mark the birth of a *dóttir* who disappeared, who doesn't know how to be what they need, who is only half-Beothuk, Greenland born and raised.

When Huritt materializes from the crowd, I step back into *Faðir*'s shadow and shift the weight off my throbbing leg.

"Anja," someone calls. Behind me, Santu is pushing herself through the swell of people and holding out a small bouquet of wildflowers. She shoves them into my outstretched hands. "We give thanks to the Great Creator for bringing you to our tribe," she says as we get pulled along. I try to keep her by my side, but I am the sheaf and she is the seed, and we get separated.

The ceremony begins at dusk. There is a pulsating energy in the crowd. Grey Owl starts by formally welcoming me to the tribe. His forehead has been painted red and his black braid hangs down to his waist. What impresses most is his headdress with its spiked tuft of white feathers fading into red. I stare at it before my eyes come to rest on his missing tooth, and I wonder how he lost it. *Faðir* places a hand on his shoulder and formally greets him as I stand there saying nothing and feeling the weight of everything.

A group of men sitting in a circle start drumming. The booms are loud and rhythmic. Strong then weak. The ceremonial singers begin their songs and the dissonant sounds spilling from their throats rise with the bonfire smoke. Digging deep into the pocket of my dress, I find Bjǫrn's river rock and take comfort in the feel of it – this talisman from another life.

When Grey Owl draws my *faðir*'s attention, I find myself surrounded by the women of the tribe. She-is-Dancing has a skirt decorated with rows of cone-shaped hooves which jingle as the garment sways. Songbird has red fox fur lining the edges of her red-ochred dress. I feel a sting of jealousy that nips like a black-fly bite when I notice she is admired. I want to be like her, and yet I don't. I want to be buried, but I want them to know I am a seed.

When *Faðir* comes to escort me further down the beach to where a crowd has gathered by the washed-up skeleton of a whale, I iron up. We walk slowly, and I glance sideways and see that the Beothuk have prepared many dishes for this feast. There are birchbark bowls filled with salted cod, smoked meat and squash, dried capelins, and all my favourite berries. My little half-brother, Nikiti, is the first to raid the berry bowl. I watch him stuffing handfuls of the plump cloudberries into his mouth so that his cheeks puff out, round and pudgy. When Wapun catches sight of him, she grabs him firmly by the arm and he begins to wail.

"It is time," *Faðir* whispers.

I stare into the setting sun where the sparkles are bouncing through the waves. When I hear the Shaman praying to the Creator god, my feet feel heavy and all I want is to thieve away. With clammy hands, I pass through the parting sea of people who have come to witness my rebirth.

The crowd goes silent. The singing and the drum booms stop. The Shaman – a tall man dressed in a white pup-sealskin mantle – ends his prayer. Every part of him has been ochred red with the exception of his scalp which he has shaved and painted white. Around his legs, he wears an anklet made of bones, his necklace is a thick rope of seashells, and there are bone bracelets extending half-way up his thin, bony arms. In one hand, he carries a staff with the skull of some small animal at the top. In the other, he holds a shield covered in rabbit fur, the centre of which contains the outline of a bear stitched in black sinew thread. He is like a walking spirit, sullen and formidable, an unearthly presence in this outdoor space.

"*Döttir*, let the Shaman help you choose your name."

Faðir smiles, and I wonder what he sees – Mother's ghost, Nuttah's pupil, Askook's grief?

I shift my weight and inhale a whiff of woodsmoke in the

salty breeze as *Faðir* invokes the name of the Creator. The tide is quickly covering the barnacled rocks where the crabs like to hide. I envy them. If it were up to me, I, too, would scuttle underneath a rock.

A flock of geese flies overhead, honking noisily as the drums start up again. The booms punch loudly; the pulse rattles through my bones. When the Shaman loops behind me and whisks little Weematin from Wapun's arms, she freely relinquishes him, and I watch, transfixed. In the sunlight, the Shaman begins to dance and sway as if he is in a trance. I worry that he'll drop Weematin and that this naming feast will turn into something dire, but nothing happens. Weematin sleeps through everything. When the Shaman deposits him back into Wapun's waiting arms, *Faðir* leans in closely. His breath smells like crushed mint leaves. "Our people have cleared a path for us to walk along the water's edge."

Something is off, I can feel it. My leg is sore. A headache pounds. When I look up, a sea of red-ochred faces glitters in the setting sun.

Just breathe, I tell myself.

Faðir and I walk to where two canoes are gently bobbing in the shallows. Draped between them, suspended over the water, is the carcass of a dead bear with its head tied back so that all I see is its fearful, gaping maw frozen in a fanged growl. The corpse of the big black bear is attracting bugs as the two boats rhythmically bob up and down in the gentle waves.

For a moment, the world becomes a distant place full of stars and glittering icicles. I am pulled out into the wind currents, into the storm.

"That bear smells bad," some child says as my gorge rises and my knees begin to jiggle so that I can barely stand. I find myself staring down into the glassy waters of a flat grey-green sea, until there is a thunder-slap – a booming drum that yanks me back into myself again. My heart is pounding. I fear my ribs will crack.

"*Döttir*, look!" *Faðir* says. My pulse keeps time with the drums – the thwacking booms and steady beat.

The Shaman lifts his arms into the sky. When he speaks, I feel the bear's spirit come alive: *Raven's* döttir, *this is your naming feast*.

My tongue is tingling; my muscles twitch. I am sensitive to the sounds of shuffling feet, to the sounds of the moving sand, to the buzz of a fly zipping around my head.

"Creator, we thank you for this day and for the sun and moon and sky and earth," *Faðir* says in a booming voice that startles me as it echoes up and down the beach. "For all the drummers, singers, and dancers gathered here. For those who are not here. For our old ones and our young ones. For the newborns, especially. For Raven's *döttir* who returns to this, her Beothuk tribe. May she come to understand the ways of her ancestors, our family."

The Shaman dips his painted toes into the water. He sings, and his voice pitches high as he releases a mystical mix of pearly sounds that make his body shiver. He lifts his arms and one of his knobby knees and holds the pose. The crowd grows silent. In the background, another restless child begins to wail.

Three more times the Shaman performs this ritual before he makes his way towards the bear. His red-ochred face is illuminated by the setting sun as he turns and fixes his gaze upon the bear. When he begins to perform a water dance with his body bleeding red-ochre droplets into the sea, I draw in shallow breaths.

The Shaman is reverent when he takes up the dead bear's

paws in his hands and begins to thank it for its sacrifice. The trembles start when he points to me. I shy away.

Don't make me touch that bear. That bear. That bloated, blasted bear. That beast that besmirches everything!

Something slaps the ground, and the bear forcefully blows out air through its nose. I feel the vibrations in my bones and in the rumble of the surf pounding into shore. The salty waves leave a trail of sea foam on the beach that is tinged in red. Like blood.

All goes silent. In my head, there is nothing. *No ocean. No waves. No bear. No danger lurking in the shallows, or further up the beach …*

I shake my head. The cobwebs fall. I am with *Faðir*, and I am safe. The bear won't rise out of the water with its bleeding eyes. It can't. It won't. Please, not tonight.

"You are Raven's *döttir*," Chief Achak says from a distant place. The timbre of his voice brings me back to the bonfire smoke, to the peacefulness of a glorious sunset on Vinland shores, to this, my Beothuk home where the eyes of Raven's people are following me, where I am being honoured as the newly returned *döttir* of the chief. I have braved the wilds and found this place.

"We feast on bear tonight," *Faðir* says in broken Norse. I rub my stone.

"I'd rather not," I manage in a shaky voice.

Faðir stills. "The spirit of the bear visits you," he says. "The bear chooses you. Little Bear might be a good spirit name."

I pull away. By the gods, I don't want to be named after that bloody bear! This is stupid talk!

The Shaman has the attention of the people. When the ritual ends, everything seems less brilliant and I return to my broken self, all bear-consumed. *Faðir* leads me back to the landing where Santu and Wapun are waiting. Wapun's voice is as sweet as a partridge berry picked after the first frost of autumn when she speaks with *Faðir* and asks if I can sit with the women for a time.

For the remainder of the evening, I am not myself. My excitement fizzles out like campfire smoke, and I have trouble focusing on anything. I startle every time a dish is served.

When I return to *Faðir*, he leans in closely, and his shoulder brushes mine. "*Döttir*, we welcome you and honour you. The Shaman likes the name, Little Bear."

I find my voice and take a breath. The world stops. "I thought I might choose Raven as my spirit name."

"Meeting a bear is not for the weak of heart, *döttir*," he says. I blink. The air is too warm. "Bears teach respect. They humble hunters. The elders say you bent the bear's spirit when you survived that bear attack. You did not fly with ravens."

"I learned that bears are vicious animals. It is best to avoid them."

"A wise lesson you have learned," he says. "Now you must learn to respect the Beothuk ways, to respect your people, to allow them to celebrate your name. I am the Raven ..."

"You are the raven, and I heard the raven's call. I heard it in Greenland, and I have heard it here. The raven spoke to me when I was ill."

He looks at me. "You are Raven's *döttir*," he says.

I hear the gods laughing at me in this Beothuk place.

"*Döttir*, I will not force you. You must choose your own name. Your name must speak to you."

I am so desperate to please him and to be accepted in this Beothuk place that my lips start quivering, my stomach knots. Behind us, Askook's voice draws eyes.

"The Shaman waits," he says.

Faðir nods and extends his hand. When I take it, his grip is strong. The summer breeze blowing off the water stirs the eagle-feathers on his headdress that glisten in the setting sun.

I am escorted to the biggest bonfire I have ever seen. The flames leap up and lick the sky, throwing sparks into the air and tricking me into seeing dragons in this place where bears are stretched and the drumbeats move the singers to raise their voices to the sky. With effort, I focus on a group of dancers and watch as their footwork laces patterns in the dirt. As dusk falls, there is more singing and dancing, and the bats flying overhead become my friends. When the feasting bear is paraded through the crowd, I look past it, and the shivers come, and I feel my heart being drained of blood.

Bjǫrn is standing at the back. He is a foot taller than all the rest, and his face is illuminated in the firelight. His raven spirit glides close to mine, and I hear flapping wings in my periphery. I hold my breath.

Stay still. Try not to faint, Anja Freydisdóttir.

Bjǫrn holds my eyes.

"Look, *döttir*," *Faðir* says. Someone releases a harsh wail that startles me. Through the smoke, I see the outline of a man dressed like a bear whose body begins to dance and sway. To sway and dance.

I am in Loki's grip. The trickster god is playing tricks. *Neinn.* Not here. They have different gods. I get confused as I reach inside and fall into the spirit shadows, slipping and twisting and swirling so that I can barely see.

Bjǫrn is circling around the bonfire and trying to look for an opening in the crowd. I try to follow him with my eyes, but the crowd feasts on him and he gets slurped up. From underwater, I call for him as I begin to claw my way through the crowd. From far away, I hear myself pleading desperately for the men in front to step aside.

Huritt stops me with his hand. "Raven's *döttir*, do you like the feast?" he grins. Behind me, *Faðir*'s voice is a rumbling hum that crescendoes frenetically with the drums.

"I do," I lie.

"My hunting gift saved the day," Huritt boasts. I stand on tiptoes to search for Bjǫrn, but Huritt's tall frame blocks my view. The dance continues. The chanting climbs into the stars.

"The bear gave its life to honour Raven's *döttir*. Now the bear's spirit comes to honour her," Huritt announces in a booming voice. His chest puffs up. I gawk at him. The sheer weight of the anger I carry almost drops me.

"Were you the one who killed the bear?"

Huritt's eyes reflect the fire. He grins at me.

"I'm sure Bjǫrn told you that this bear would spoil my feast. Is that why the two of you were fighting in the smokehouse?"

"He didn't want to honour you. He doesn't want to make you a member of this tribe. He thinks you should return to Leifsbidur."

Behind me, a booming voice rings through the crowd, drawing eyes. The drums stop. The din dies down. When the Shaman calls Huritt forward and hands him something black, the bonfire illuminates the rugged features of his face. Huritt turns back to me, and in his face, I see pride.

"Raven's *döttir* killed a bear before she was reborn to us. She conquered its spirit. This is the hide it wore," Huritt announces to the purring crowd. There is a sudden pang, and my stomach drops. This is his glory, not mine. My spirit rails when I see the black fur stuffed underneath his arm.

"The bear spoke out, but Raven's *dóttir* fought it off. Now she takes its name at this, her naming feast!"

The bear's ghost forms, ethereal yet possessive, terrifying and horrendous. I am helpless to stop the memories from boiling up: the vicious roar; the smell of fear and piss; the feel of claws ripping through my skin; the gripping dread. I see the bear's fangs and hear its growl and smell its putrid breath upon my face. Huritt's toothy grin turns into bloodthirsty fangs. In his mouth, I see a lolling tongue.

Sinking down, I get buried in the throng of legs and feet as the bear's incisors rip through my flesh. I feel it chomping on my brittle bones, and I squirm to avoid a bloody death.

"O Great Creator, you guided our hunters well," some Red Man chants. The crowd goes silent. *Faðir* tries to help me up. He hooks his arm underneath my armpit, and his fingers dig into my skin.

"Thank you, bear," Huritt announces, oblivious. "You honour my sister at this, her naming feast." I can't seem to mute his voice. The hiss of it snakes into the grass. Another voice rises above all the noise. I search the crowd.

In the chaos, I dislodge myself from *Faðir*'s grip and stumble forward, but the Shaman is too quick. He reaches out and blocks me with his hand.

"Get away!" I moan as I wheel around. Bjǫrn grabs my hand, and I fall into his outstretched arms where I feel his warmth, his solid form. An instant later, he pulls me forward through the crowd and we are gobbled up and swallowed whole.

"Anja, concentrate! Look at the bonfire if you must. It has been lit for your naming feast." His voice sounds murky as though he is drowning, and I am caught up in seaweed. I gulp in water only to discover that it is air and I am drifting through clouds of heavy smoke. Slowly his face – his worried eyes – come into view. I love those blue ice-chip eyes.

"Let the bonfire burn off the memories of that great black bear," he murmurs in a soothing voice as we push our way through the gawking crowd.

From behind me, I catch the sound of Huritt's deep baritone calling out for me to stop. Askook shouts. I won't look back.

Bjørn and I snake our way up the bank and scurry quickly into the trees. When Bjørn turns and shouts to hold our pursuers off, his voice is a trembling boom, a thunderclap. He steadies me when I lean into him and I let him pull me, hand-clasped, in the direction of Nuttah's tent. The poplars whisper as we pass and then I hear the snapping of tree branches as though something large is moving through the bush in the dark, pursuing me. An instant later, I break free of Bjørn, half-dodging roots, half-limping, and half-running down the well-worn path, moaning and wailing as the trees close in.

"Wait, Anja!"

Behind us, the rumbling drums start up again and another moan slips from my lips. Bjørn is panting behind my back. He reaches out to slow me down, and I come to a grinding halt and almost trip. A branch has ripped the bodice of my dress and crushed some of the seashell work. There are leaves and brambles in my hair. I try to pick them out, and a sliver slices through my thumb. I moan again, and Bjørn catches me up around the waist. When he sees the panic in my face, he takes up my hand in his and tries to suck a sliver out, but he can hardly see. The black tree branches stretch out their twig claws, and I draw back and lean into his shoulder. He draws me into his arms.

"I know how much you wanted a Beothuk name, Anja," he

whispers quietly. I can feel my heartbeat in my throat. When I pull back, Bjǫrn's face is shadowed.

"They wouldn't let me choose my own," I say, choking up.

"I'll take you back to Nuttah's tent. She will know what to do. Tell her what you saw and where you've been. She'll understand. As you talk, remind yourself that you are strong and that you are the *dóttir* of a chief."

"I didn't want anything to do with that bear. I killed it long ago!"

"You didn't kill the feasting bear," Bjǫrn clarifies. He studies me. There is something burning brightly in his eyes.

"By the gods, I trusted you not to bring that blasted bear hide into the village, Bjǫrn. Why did you hand it over? You shouldn't have given it to the Shaman without asking me."

He stops himself from touching me and fills his lungs and looks away. "I didn't think," he says. "That bear mauled your skin and now it mauls your mind. I know how hard this is for you. You'll need to find a way to let the memories go."

"How can I?"

"Perhaps Nuttah will help set things right."

"She can't," I say pathetically.

He takes my hand, and we continue making our way down the path as the tree shadows wave to us. When we come to Nuttah's yard, the *mamateek* is a black smudge sitting underneath the stars, and Bjǫrn starts hooting like a snowy owl. There is no response.

"Wait for me. I'll go inside," I say as I slip past and part the hide covering on the door. In the shadows, I can see the shapes of the bed depressions in the ground and the silhouetted herbs hanging from the beams.

"How now, my girl? What has come to pass?" Nuttah clucks

as she draws herself up and rushes forward and presses me into a warm embrace.

I try to tell her. She strokes my hair.

"Hush now, *döttir*," Nuttah soothes. Her eyes dart to Bjǫrn. "I can see that she is not herself."

"*Neinn*," he says, "but she is where she belongs."

It seems to take forever before *Faðir* comes to breathe back life into my ghost. While Bjǫrn gives voice to what I face every time I see a bear, I sit in silence , and my eyes wander up and out of the smoke hole where I spot the moon and think of Mother and the name she gave me.

Chapter Twenty-Four

MOON CHILD

I am lying in *Faðir's mamateek*, disorientated and woozy, trying to remember how I got here, when I fully snap awake to the sound of drizzling rain tinkling against the roof. I catch the sound of muffled voices down below as a blast of fierce, blustery wind rips through the trees outside, bending them so that the branches scratch the birchbark walls. In the half-light of a cold, dark dawn, I rub my sore leg and listen to the voices drifting up into the loft. Wapun and Grandmother and the boys, along with some other women from Chief Achak's fire circle, are still asleep. Their forms are sprawled out across the floor.

There is a grumbled whisper. I cock my head and roll over and hoist myself out of bed, moving carefully so the boards don't creak. Bjǫrn's voice is bitterly angry, harsh and sharp. Holding my breath, I dress quickly in the crisp, cool air.

"I told you she would be upset!"

"He is *kavdiunait* – not one of us," Huritt hisses like a snake.

x

"The Beothuk ways are strange to him. He never learned them properly. Now he dishonours us."

There is a low rumbling of angry voices.

"Our naming ceremonies command a feast," someone boom-whispers. I can't recognize the voice.

"It is customary to kill a bear and roast the meat for a naming feast."

The elders' conversation waterfalls into a lively stream of voices that moves like the river, splitting off into arguments I can't understand. When a member of the tribal council criticizes Bjǫrn for taking me away from the naming feast, I am tempted to shimmy down the ladder and show my face. Instead, I force myself to breathe.

Outside there is another rush of wind that shakes the *mamateek*, announcing the arrival of a storm. As the wind dies down, the Shaman's pebbly voice trickles in and conjures up shadows that wriggle through me.

"Raven's firstborn needs a smudge to cleanse her spirit of the bear's sharp claws," he mutters in a mellifluous tone. The men are transfixed by his every word, but I feel like spitting on his shaven head. I count the men. There are twelve in all besides Bjǫrn.

"Raven's *döttir* feeds on memories of the dead," Grey Owl says.

"Your *döttir* is brave, but she lost herself."

"She never knew the story of her birth."

Faðir is pacing back and forth. "She must find her spirit guide," he says in a solemn voice. He glances up, and I pull back.

"Her spirit guide is the bear," the Shaman says with certainty.

The room erupts again. The men spew out scat. I shift in place so that I can better poke my head into the room. Askook is sitting cross-legged on the ground, and Huritt sits beside him, head bowed. Grey Owl wears a scowl. Santu's husband looks half-asleep. There is a sudden intake of breath as Bjǫrn steps into my line of sight.

"Huritt dishonoured the *döttir* of the chief," the huntsman says as his gaze sweeps across the room. I am struck by his way of hurling daggers without breaking bones. *Watch your step, Bjǫrn the brave.*

There is a flash of movement, and Bjǫrn points at Huritt with a look of pure anger on his face. "We used to be friends, brother! We hunted side by side. You were the wolf, and I was the raven. Where did you lose yourself?"

"Quiet!" Askook's voice flints fire.

"I challenge you to admit you've wronged Raven's *döttir* in front of your hunting brothers," Bjǫrn continues as if he didn't hear.

Huritt rises. The muscles in his jaw tense as he steps forward and glares at Bjǫrn. I suck in air. Askook stands as well, and the whisperings around the room erupt as tempers flare.

There is a sudden thwack, a shuffling of feet, a stumbling backwards into the wall of the *mamateek*. My eyes snap back just in time to see Huritt pouncing like a wolverine and pummelling Bjǫrn in the gut. There is too much chaos, too much noise. Behind me, the women and children stir awake. When Askook steps into the fray, the ladder to the loft gets bumped so that it wobbles precariously. With a little gasp, I reach out and grab it just before it gets knocked down.

Below, there is a horrendous crash as Bjǫrn falls backwards, reeling from another one of Huritt's blows. In a flash, he bounces back, growling fiercely as he jabs. With a vicious grunt, Huritt tumbles headlong into a line of reed baskets, and we hear a crash as the room erupts, and Grey Owl shouts. Huritt scrambles to get back up. He is supported by two burly men.

"Huritt ruined Anja's naming feast," Bjǫrn yells in the voice of a barking seal. He spits a wad of blood onto the ground before he throws a vicious swing, hitting the man beside him who falls amidst the sounds of scuffling feet and cursing men.

Behind me, the women crowd around, vying for a better view. Shaking them off, I scurry down the ladder just as Huritt delivers a punch to Bjǫrn's chiselled jaw.

"The Pale Face should be punished for the insolence he shows our tribe," Askook thunders as some hunters with muscled arms jump into the fray. Almost instantly, Bjǫrn is checked.

"Bjǫrn, my son," *Faðir* says as he eyes the crowd, "your anger won't solve anything."

Standing behind them, I clear my throat. Instantly, all chatter stops.

"Raven's *döttir*, we thought you were asleep," Huritt mumbles sheepishly.

Every part of me is vibrating. "I'm very much awake."

"Anja, the Shaman can redo the dance," Bjǫrn tells me in a breathless voice. His hair is tousled; his chin looks bruised.

Outside the rain slams against the conical roof and birchbark walls which have been covered up with skins and banked with soil on the outside and layered up with moss on the inside. *Faðir* turns to me. His eyes are giant pools of light.

"The Creator will help you choose your spirit guide."

Bjǫrn extracts himself from his captors' grip and moves into my line of sight. Before he speaks, I turn to address the elders of the tribe: "Bjǫrn was right. He knew that the bear would scare me at my naming feast. He tried to tell Huritt. I witnessed part of their exchange."

I see the smugness in Bjǫrn's smouldering eyes, the raven trickster in his face. Huritt steps forward from the back.

"I was ... bad ... to you," he says in Norse in front of the elders. His mendacity makes his words seem glib. Askook is standing behind him, but his posture is as stiff as the trunk of an old-growth tree. Huritt continues, ignoring him. "Please, Anja, I would like it for you to ... me ... forgive."

The elders' eyes fall on me, hard and unwavering. I feel the test. The waiting. The silence in the *mamateek*. The shrieking of the wind outside. Huritt tilts his head and looks at me. I know what it costs him to prostrate himself in front of the elders of the tribe and to speak to me in Norse.. Still, I am hesitant.

"The memory of the black bear's attack continues to haunt you, *döttir*," *Faðir* helps. "The only one to blame is the great black bear. His spirit lives inside of you. You must dislodge it with the Shaman's help." He pauses, and I feel his knowing look, the comfort that his presence brings.

"I am Raven's *döttir* now," I boldly state. "I am not bear's child anymore!"

The elders give me nothing, but there is a strange look on the Shaman's face.

"I am done with *giwashuwet*," I continue, struggling to find the right Beothuk word for "bear". "I will not speak of these salmon eaters anymore. Destroy that hide. Bring me proof that it is gone, for I am of Beothuk blood and I choose to live! I am Raven's *döttir* who won't eat or take the name of bear. Caribou is what I love."

The elders chuckle. *Faðir* smiles.

"To relinquish bear is to be reborn," the Shaman says from his corner of the room. His words shimmer like a will-o'-the-wisp. I see something unnerving in his wrinkled face, something that makes me shake inside.

"My *döttir* will come to live with me in my *mamateek*," *Faðir* says. "She will sit with me and Wapun at our fire. Our people will honour her. They will come to know her as the moon's child."

The room falls silent. The rain pummels the roof with an endless torrent of noisy plinks. I feel as though I am on the edge of a precipice looking down. One tiny step forward and I might find myself tumbling head over heels into the void.

The council asks one final question. They want to know about the bear hide that Bjørn lugged all the way from our cave. They want to know if the hide is still possessed by the spirit of the bear. The Shaman pokes his stick into the fire. He does not look up.

"Bear's spirit has been honoured. The hide's power is what you give it," he mumble-rasps.

"Anja wants us to get rid of the bear hide," Bjørn announces in the voice of a victor. He has won his battle, lost his fire.

"Is this what you truly want, *döttir*?" *Faðir* asks.

"I just want it gone," I whisper underneath my breath, but a weight is lifted, my spirit soars.

Bjørn clears his throat. "I'll dispose of the bear hide before this day is done. I'll tie some rocks to it and send it out to sea for some sea-monsters to gobble up." He walks over to where the hide sits in the shadows. Someone has folded it and bound it with rope, and the giant head looks devoid of body, devoid of strength. I watch in silence as Bjørn hoists it over his shoulder and lugs it over to the door. In silence, I follow him, and it seems as though a thousand eyes are following us. At the door, he turns.

"Anja, I never wanted you to be haunted by this bear," he murmurs so softly that the others cannot hear. "If I had known that the hide was cursed, I never would have taken it with us. I would have left it behind in our cave." He tries to smile, and tears well up.

"Just get rid of it," I manage, recognizing my strength in the struggle and knowing that I have lived despite the pain and suffering.

"When I throw it out to sea, I pray that the creature's blood-red eyes will see into the mouths of sharks. May it be cursed in Hel's underworld."

I catch his elbow. For a moment, he holds my eyes, and then he pulls back, shifting the weight on his shoulder.

"Bury the memories, Anja," he whispers. "Let yourself truly live. Chief Achak is worried. Just look at him."

I flick a glance over my shoulder. *Faðir* is with Askook, and the two of them are deep in conversation. The elders begin discussing the wisdom of smudging me, and a shiver shimmies down my back. The men start grumbling, and I block out the sound of their talk. Huritt is standing next to the loft ladder, watching me.

When I turn to leave, Bjǫrn is gone.

Chapter Twenty-Five

BUSH TROUBLE

In the following days, I keep to myself, feeling too embarrassed to speak with *Faðir* about how I wrecked my naming feast, feeling too angry to search out Huritt to confront him, and feeling too ashamed to speak much in Santu's company. The rain continues off and on, and I wonder whether Bjǫrn managed to sink the hide. The wondering makes me miserable. The village elders let me be, but there is talk. I hear She-Is-Dancing gossiping, and I wonder what she says about me. When I hear Songbird chirping like a little sparrow, I am tempted to migrate like the caribou and follow the path of the autumn geese.

The rains continue. Summer fades. I can smell autumn in the air. I continue to visit Nuttah every day, especially because her legs are swollen, and she can hardly walk. As her time draws near, I worry more and more. When I ask her about Huritt and Bjǫrn, she reassures me that they will work it out. She is one of the few who understands.

One day I come across Nuttah napping peacefully on a bed of

soft, white rabbit fur with her long blonde hair fanning out around her shoulders and her gentle breathing stirring the rabbit hairs. Leaning down, I slowly cover her sleeping form with another hide.

May the gods watch over her and keep the trolls away, I think as I retrieve a piece of flattened wood from the wood pile and a half-burnt stick of charcoal from the firepit. In a few quick strokes, I have drawn a stave on the piece of wood. When I go to stash the board under the hides at her feet, she stirs, and I step back..

I must remind her to always keep the fire lit and to keep an iron knife stashed beside her bed to prevent the child from being switched for a changeling, I think as she settles down.

Outside, I hear the high-pitched voices of Nuttah's little ones chattering excitedly as they try to figure out what to do with a wiggling worm. A moment later, they burst through the door, all dripping wet. I place a finger to my lips as they shake themselves off like playful pups.

When Nuttah addresses them in a sleepy voice, I spin around.

"I am sorry they woke you. I'll take them to *Faðir's mamateek.*" I grab for her youngest and hold her back.

"You are too kind," Nuttah yawns as she half-sits up. In the firelight, her cheeks look drawn, her face look old. One of her little girls has lost two front teeth since I saw her last. When she finds my hand and pulls me forth, I coax the rest of the children to follow us.

We leave the *mamateek* in a cold but gentle rain. The children pull me into the ditch to jump in puddles, and I laugh and splash and get soaking wet. We take a roundabout route back to *faðir's mamateek* and emerge at a place where the tall silver birch and black spruce trees sit guarding the entrance to his yard.

Miwok is the first to find an earthworm. Another boy finds a slug. When a little hand squishes a worm by mistake, Little Owl insists we pray Beothuk prayers. At five winters, he is learning well.

At the firepit, we pass a group of hunters hauling in game from their traplines. Their legs and *moccasins* are mucked with mud, and their red-ochred hair is plastered to their heads with sweat.

"Bird says that the caribou hunting is good this year," Nikiti lisps. "He says that I can go with him if I eat the seal stew that the women make. I don't like it."

I smile at him, this little brave. "What else does Bird put inside your head?"

He circles thrice around my legs while his sister sidles up next to me. She has long black hair as thick as a woodland beaver's coat flowing halfway down her back.

"Do you know Bjǫrn?" she asks. "Bjǫrn is Norse. You are too."

In the distance, I hear the voice of the frothing sea, the wildness of it calling out to me.

"Bjǫrn hunts fox and marten, too," the little girl continues as she tugs on my arm to get my attention. "He gave me a rabbit – the fur, not the meat. The pelt will warm my toes when winter comes. It is tan and white."

"Tan and white?" I repeat. I am careful to keep my own voice light.

"Bjǫrn is the best hunter of them all," she says, and I laugh with her.

"Bjǫrn plays the flute," her brother says. "He plays it well."

"He could teach you how to play," I suggest, remembering the music from the cave.

"Bjǫrn composed a song about you. He calls it 'Anja's Song'."

I draw my mantle tightly closed against the cold. "I'm glad," I say, although what I feel is not quite "glad".

"You should ask him to play it for you."

"I will," I say.

The sizzling smell of roasting fish nets us as soon as we arrive at *Faðir's mamateek*. After I remove a matted mess of wet leaves from a little hand, I herd them all towards the roaring fire where the heat draws puffs of steam from my deerskins. One of the little ones comes to take me by the hand, and I let her pull me over to the place of honour beside Chief Achak at the fire circle. As soon as I get comfortable sitting in a cross-legged position on the ground, the little girl crawls into my lap. Then she plops her thumb into her mouth and lifts her chin and looks up at me with her big bright eyes.

She knows her place better than I do, this little one.

The cod roll in late, and the Beothuk net them by the hundreds. The next time Santu invites me to go berry picking with her, she doesn't mention my naming feast.

"I spotted redcurrants near the creek," I say in a quiet voice.

"The frost is coming," she replies. "We need to harvest as many as we can."

We fill two birchbark baskets with berries and lug them back. After we have cleaned them, grandmother shows us how to harvest the bark of red willow by removing the outside layer with her thumbnail. She crisps the remaining inner bark before the fire and then Santu and I scoop up the shavings and store them in bags for smoking. All of us work from dawn to dusk preparing for the long winter months ahead, and I am as restless as the squawking geese heading south.

A second summer comes. We fish for trout and go out to collect enough clams and mussels to fill a hide sack of such a size that it requires two of us to haul it back. A few days later, Songbird teaches me how to make bird pudding stuffed in gut. It's a delicacy, or so she says, although from its smell, I disagree.

It strikes me that Bjǫrn still hasn't sought me out. The hunters tell me that he has gone deep into the bush to look for game. What if he returns to Leifsbidur without stopping in to say goodbye? What if he is reluctant to show his face at the communal fires? What if I have somehow shamed him and now he is avoiding me?

Nuttah tells me not to fret. When I still haven't seen him two weeks later, Nuttah releases a heavy sigh: "Your own mother was a wanderer," she says half-jokingly as she guts the fish. "Worry not. I'm sure he went out hunting in the bush. All of them will be out looking for caribou."

"I could go too," I say.

"You will stay with me, Anja Freydisdóttir. I'll need your help when the baby comes."

"Bjǫrn wants to return to Leifsbidur before the snows arrive," I say. "Is it far?"

"Leifsbidur is at least a three-day walk from here." She glances at me curiously.

I feel sadness brewing, almost like a storm of sorts. On the other end of the yard by the trailhead, the dogs begin to bark. When I look up, Huritt comes sauntering down the path with a string of rabbits slung over his shoulder for skinning. When he sees me, he smiles in the old way.

"They say you pick many berries for the tribe," he begins in Norse, but for the first time ever, he looks flustered.

"I have none for you," I say curtly, but then he grins, and I catch his butterflies.

"I looked for you," he simply says. "I wanted to give a simple gift – a gift to show you my sorrow." He smashes his fist against his heart. "I meant no harm."

"Have you seen Bjǫrn?" I ask. He studies my face and hesitates.

"The hunters wait for the arrival of the caribou. This year the herds are very large."

"And Bjǫrn? Is he waiting with the rest of them?"

Huritt shrugs. Somewhere through the trees, the geese are honking noisily as they pass over a saltwater marsh. Huritt deposits the rabbits in a heap by the firepit and rubs his hands together and shifts his weight. "Tomorrow, I return to the river. They expect me to bag many caribou. My aim is good. I can throw my spear further than all the rest."

"Shouldn't you be out there helping then?" Nuttah says as she glances up from her work.

Huritt grins. "I lost a draw and pulled the shortest stick. They made me come back here to grab another spear. Grey Owl broke his." He winks at me mischievously.

"I miss our learning," is all I say.

Huritt steals a berry from a basket and plops it in his mouth. Nuttah swats his hand, but there is an easiness about her, as though she knows that her time of holding on is gone.

"I need Anja's help to haul back drinking water," he says as he leans down and picks up the empty buckets.

I slowly stand and grab one of the pails. I expect Nuttah to say something, but she addresses Huritt in the Beothuk tongue instead. Her words fly fast and furious, and the speed is so quick, I can't follow the gist, but I hear the warning. Her voice is sharp.

The walk through the forest is peaceful enough. Huritt speaks in a gentle voice as he follows me down the winding trail towards the sound of trickling water. Just before we reach the riverbank, he reaches out to hold me back.

"Nuttah needs someone to stay with her in the *mamateek* when I return to the bush to hunt." An autumn leaf flutters down and lands on the pile that carpets the path underfoot.

"Is Askook worried about her?"

Huritt nods. He looks up into the golden peaks of swishing poplars.

"Her time is near," I say quietly. "You are right to be concerned, but you must remember she has given birth several times before."

"Askook says this time is different," he mutters in a serious voice. "Some say you are a seer, Raven's *döttir*. We want to know …"

"By the gods, who says this?" My cheeks feel hot.

"The squirrel never reveals where the nuts are hidden," Huritt replies with a brilliant smile. He shifts in place and kicks up a rock and picks it up. After inspecting it, he uses his throwing arm to chuck it far. When he turns back, he squints his eyes against the sun. "Please help Nuttah. She is mother for everyone."

Huritt fingers the fringes on his hides. When he looks at me, I nod my head, and our spirits touch.

"Raven's *döttir*, come see your gift," he murmurs unexpectedly.

"I don't need a gift," I say awkwardly.

"I did wrong at your naming feast."

"I've seen your tricks," I say uncomfortably as I glance in the direction of the *mamateek.*

"No tricks this time," he promises as he holds out his hand. "Fast like fox, come with me."

"I should go back."

Huritt's face crinkles into another lopsided grin, and we leave the pails, and Huritt pulls me down the hidden path that is half overgrown with weeds and brambles and tangles of twisted spruce rooted in mucky soil.

"Your *faðir* won't like it that we are alone," I try as I gingerly place my feet so that the twigs don't snap. Huritt places a finger to his lips and leads me to the marshlands where the land falls open and there is a blustery breeze. The clearing is full of stagnant ponds and dwarf birch trees and sweetgale that covers a landscape shaded in yellows and browns and brilliant reds. For just a moment, I breathe in the crisp autumn air and gaze at the carpet of foliage that greets the eye.

"Look over there," Huritt whispers as he points at something moving through the bush. The grasses shimmy in the wind in shades of mossy grey and vibrant green. In the distance, a mother deer is standing beside a fawn whose ears are twitching to fend off the flies.

"Majestic," I whisper. Huritt stands too close. I turn my face into the wind and gaze across the stillness where I feel myself falling into the depths of some great lake where my thoughts take the form of fish that talk.

"The mother deer and her fawn live on this land. They are the Creator's gift to us," Huritt says. He towers over me, and I can't help but admire the height of him and the way his black hair falls straight.

"Have you always been this curious about what nature brings?" I breathe. He slides a grin my way.

"Has your spirit always wandered with the wind?"

The grasses swish, and the doe looks up and spots us. She is wary, but she continues chewing a wad of grass. Huritt stands as still as stone. I feel the warmth of him in this sacred place where there is no need to prove ourselves, where we can fall back into being friends.

"I'll hunt caribou for you in the weeks to come," Huritt says.

I feel a smile forming on my lips. "In return, I'll sew you a deer-skin shirt."

"With shells, I hope."

"No shells," I say. "I haven't learned the art of sewing things onto hides."

Huritt turns to face me. He is so tall, he blocks out the sun. "The fawn needs its mother," he says, frowning. There is a pinch – a pop – of grief so profound that a swell of tears wells up and I am whisked away on a breath of wind that deposits me onto the back of a raven that spreads its wings.

Huritt points. The deer gracefully leaps into the tuckamore as a group of geese take flight in V-formation above our heads. Blinking, I tilt my head way back to watch the last bird struggling to keep up. Beside me, Huritt coughs.

"I killed a grouse yesterday," he mumbles as he squats down to examine some animal scat hidden in the grasses. I marvel when he speaks in Norse.

"Nuttah, she likes you," he continues. "She thinks you are a good *döttir*. She welcomes you at Askook's fire."

"I like her, too," is all I say. I glance uneasily behind my back.

"She thinks you should come back to my *mamateek*."

"And leave *Faðir*'s?"

"You could cook for me," he says. He grins again. "But I have to go back and hunt."

"I know," I say. Something has been said between us. Something as sticky as walking through cobwebs in the bush. My sore leg is throbbing; a headache pounds.

"When I saw the deer, I thought of you," Huritt says. "The doe finds her place among the herd. She mates with the dominant buck each year."

"We should go," I mutter underneath my breath.

For a moment, Huritt's eyes search mine. Then, without a word, he turns and ducks under some fallen branches before he slips through the silent woods like the natural-born hunter he was meant to be.

Even before we reach the yard, I hear Askook yelling. His voice echoes through the woods and pings against the peeling birchbark trees.

"I thought you said he was out hunting?" I say to Huritt's back. In my struggle to keep up with him, I almost trip.

Huritt stops, and I almost bump into him. Through the trees, we watch Askook stomping around the firepit. His face is contorted in an angry scowl, and he is dropping curses as naturally as animals drop their scat. Shaking, I try to hold Huritt back, but he easily unhooks himself and steps into Askook's line of sight.

"Come," he calls over his shoulder.

As soon as he sees us, Askook roars: "This *wobee* woman has you under some sort of spell!"

Alarmed, I shrink back and hide myself in the shadows of a black spruce tree.

"You call her a white woman when she is Beothuk born,"

Huritt responds in my defence. He throws a glance, and Askook mutters something underneath his breath.

"Raven's *döttir* is hiding from you in the bush," Huritt yells.

I suck in air.

"Husband, please," Nuttah calls in a desperate tone. From my hiding spot, I search for her, but the tears are spilling down my cheeks, falling like the autumn leaves.

"I won't let him come for you," Huritt yells, and my skin prickles to hear both his softness and his fighting fierceness. He comes to take me by the hand, and I let him pull me into the yard.

"*Washewiush* girl brings trouble to my fire," Askook spits when he sees us linked.

I am no moon girl! I am Raven's döttir! No words come out.

Askook's eyes narrow into slits. With a sudden shriek, he launches himself at me, and my body tenses; my hands fly up. Behind him, Nuttah screams before her cumbersome belly smashes up against his back. Horrified, I watch as her arms snake around his neck and she begins to tug and scratch like a wolverine. In the chaos, I turn to run, but Huritt steps in front of me.

"I'll protect you," he growls, but his face is a mixture of hurt, confusion, betrayal, shock. I go all bubbly, like I am floating in the sea, dog-paddling in heavy swells and trying to make it through a storm. Strong hands reach down and pull me up.

"Don't hit! Don't hit!" I scream as I lean into Huritt's bulk to protect my head and neck, my eyes, my face.

Nuttah's voice is clam-shell sharp. "Stop!" she yells. My ears catch the buzz of flies when I see her struggling to hold Askook back.

"Huritt should marry another," he rants. The words are

translated in my head in a swarming rush. *O gods,* I think. *He believes that Huritt and I want to marry!*

"Huritt has been a brother to me in this Beothuk place," I shout as soon as I collect myself.

"Raven's *döttir* tells the truth," Nuttah puffs as she doubles over and cradles her pregnant bump.

"'Twas an innocent walk in the bush," I insist. I hear my voice swelling, my heart knocking against my ribs. Askook gawks.

"Husband!" Nuttah tries again. "All is well. Huritt has befriended Raven's *döttir* and helped her learn the language, like we discussed."

"Raven's *döttir* is a scavenger, like her name suggests."

"She is honourable," Nuttah moans. "Look at her! She is an innocent in all of this."

"She needs to leave. Tell her to go back to the fox who raised her in that distant land."

I glance between them, feeling sick. Mother's ghost floats between us, hanging on a breath of air. There is an agonizing ache, a lonely grief, a living wound that festers, oozing green.

"Husband, listen to your words. Anja is the *döttir* of the chief! She is no longer one of them. She is Raven's *döttir*, and he is your good friend. Listen to me, husband! Your wrath burns for someone who no longer walks these shores. Thorvard of Gardar is the one to hate, but he isn't here for you to fight."

"This one has Freydis Eiriksdöttir's blood," Askook snaps. His battle scars – two vicious lines running along his right cheekbone – are popping out, white ridged against his red.

"Raven's *döttir* has already lost so much," Nuttah pleads. There is a sheen of sweat on her brow. With a sudden gasp, she clasps her belly and sinks to the ground.

"Nuttah, are you hurt?" I yelp with an anguished groan. I go to run to her, but Askook shoves me off.

"Raven's *döttir* is one of us," Huritt snaps as he catches up Nuttah in his arms.

"Her kinsmen took my brother's life," Askook counters, but his attention is focused on the pallor of Nuttah's face, her pregnant bump, her clammy skin. Nuttah bats her arms and tries to raise her neck to look for me.

"Anja can learn to live in this Beothuk place, like I have done. You cared for me, and I adopted the Beothuk ways. She can too! I tell you, husband, she is one of us!"

We hear the yelp of a dog barrelling down the path accompanied by the sound of men. When I glance up, I see *Faðir* and Grey Owl stepping into the yard.

"Otter says there is trouble here?" Grey Owl says as he studies the scene in front of him.

Faðir locks eyes with Askook, and his regal frame goes very still. "Brother," he says in a booming voice that punches trees. "You and I have been through much together. Our *moccasins* have seen much pain, but the storms have passed."

Askook shakes his head. "The Norsemen have returned," he says.

"Only my *döttir* returned to us," *Faðir* counters. "Freydis sent her."

"Raven, you are blind," Askook says as he helps Nuttah stand. He flicks a glance at me. "Thorvard of Gardar sent this *washewiush* girl."

"This *washewiush* girl is my moon child," *Faðir* replies in a voice that shakes the earth.

"Your moon child should hide her face behind the clouds."

Faðir glares.

"Paw! Can't you see, husband?" Nuttah says. "Anja is not Thorvard's *döttir* anymore. She is Raven's child because Freydis sent her back to us."

"Your *oosuck*, Nuttah, is very wise," *Faðir* says.

"Freydis follows the seagulls," Askook says.

"Be loyal, brother. My *döttir* is part of the circle. She has returned to me. She is a gift from the Creator. I cherish her."

I unwrap his words and find pieces of myself. *Faðir* stands as straight and tall as a cherry oak. He turns to me. "*Döttir*, you must stay away from Askook's fire."

"Your white-bird *döttir* has power over you, brother," Askook sniffs.

Nuttah splays her long, thin fingers across her belly, and I feel another pinch that heralds change. "Surely, she can visit me?"

I look between Askook and *Faðir*. When Askook says nothing, Nuttah reaches out to touch my cheek.

"I'll send word when Askook is not around," she says in a breezy whisper that is only loud enough for me to hear. Her hands are shaking, and it looks as though she is fighting to hold in a sob. "Promise to come back to me, Anja. My bairn needs you, and I do too."

That night, as I am sitting around *Faðir*'s fire surrounded by my half-brothers and the women of his clan, Grandmother frets about what to feed the men when they return from hunting. Food. Always there is talk of food. Is it not enough to just simply sit and talk? *Neinn*. Not here. Not in this *mamateek* where it is always necessary to keep working so that no one starves. The Beothuk month of *Wasumaweeseek* is soon approaching. Harvest month has always been a working month in any clan, in any tribe.

Faðir's face is aglow in the flickering firelight. When he glances up, it is almost like our thoughts touch:

Choose your path, my raven child. Choose to live among the Norse in Leifsbidur or choose my tribe, but choose before the snows come and cover the trails leading to the place where your mother's memory lives.

Chapter Twenty-Six

THERE ARE NO WORDS

The autumn weather turns colder, and a thin layer of frost stretches across the ground. When I go out with Santu to collect the last of the over-ripened blackberries that stain our teeth purple, the ease of being in her quiet company is a comfort. At night, when I can't sleep, I think of Askook, and thoughts of him get tangled up with thoughts of Thorvard, and then the nightmares come, and I am filled with hate.

I hear from Grey Owl's *oosuck* that Bjørn is out with the other hunters preparing for the caribou run. The women of the village are all a-buzz. Sitting by Nuttah's smoky fire, I listen for news and learn that the caribou fences are almost up.

"Have you seen Santu recently?" I ask Nuttah when we find ourselves sitting side-by-side sewing pelts together to make winter clothing for the little ones. She can't seem to get comfortable. Her belly is very large, and her feet are swollen and she is always tired.

"Santu is with child."

"With child?" I say, trying to make my voice sound cheerful. "I didn't know. I must wish her well."

"I'm surprised she didn't say," Nuttah sighs. She stops her work and rubs her neck, and the old feelings of loneliness come again, and I feel as though I am an outsider in this Beothuk tribe.

That evening I enjoy the company of the old clan mothers who sit around *Faðir's* hearth fire telling stories and sharing laughs, but all I can think about is Santu. She is moving on, and what am I doing? I don't even know my place. I am Raven's *döttir*. I should be pleased.

"Your face looks old tonight, *döttir*," Grandmother says as she studies me with her all-knowing eyes. "The Creator is here among us when we share our stories around the fire. You have lived a story of suffering, but if you tell it to yourself too frequently, you cannot love."

"I wish I was running free with the caribou," I sigh.

"Running can be lonely, *döttir*," she says with dancing eyes.

Wapun is trying to rock Weematin to sleep, but he is fussy. "Here," I say. "Give him to me. I'll try to settle him."

I find Santu sewing pelts inside her husband's *mamateek*. She leans into the light to better see, but the fire is smoking. When it drifts her way, she winces.

"You should sit outside," I say as I slip inside. When she sees me, her face lights up.

"It's too cold," she shrugs. She makes room for me to sit beside her on the mat, and I stretch out my toes to warm my feet in front of the fire.

"Nuttah's time is near," I say, feeling a lump building in my throat.

"Huritt wants you to stay with her. Did you see him? He came looking for you."

"I saw him," I mumble as I turn away to avoid the smoke.

Santu stops sewing. "Huritt looks out for those he loves," she says carefully. I glance at her. "He is an honourable hunter."

"I know," I say.

She takes a breath. "I should have told you long ago. Last spring, Huritt saw a lame fawn in the woods limping behind a mother deer. He worried about Bjǫrn. He knew he was in the cave with you."

I grit my teeth. I can't look at her. "What does the fawn have to do with me?"

"Huritt knew that if Bjǫrn was travelling with a lame woman, she, too, would be slow. In the big house, he shared his concerns. He insisted that he and a few others should go out in search of you."

"The huntsmen found us after the harp seal hunt," I say carefully.

"The harp seal hunt was long since done. It was Huritt who was your rescuer. He insisted on paddling to Bjǫrn's meeting spot several times. Askook didn't like it. He said he should be out hunting instead of looking for the dead."

I gawk at her. "I didn't know," I say. In front of us, the fire crackles as a log splits in two.

Santu returns to sewing. "I am with child," she breathes without looking up. She smiles into her work.

"Nuttah told me. Are you feeling well?"

She nods, eyes gleaming.

"I am glad for you."

"Thank you, sister." Her voice reminds me of the softness of rabbit fur. I shiver when she looks at me. "We must sit together for the *Mokoshan*. It is our biggest celebration of the year."

"I would like that very much," I say.

She tugs on a piece of sinew thread, and the fire spits, and she grins at me.

When I next visit Nuttah's fire, Huritt is there, chopping wood. "I expected you to be out in the bush, waiting for the caribou."

"I'm here instead," he says before returning to his work. Miwok and Nikiti hang on his every word. "The caribou are fast," he tells them, throwing a quick, charming smile so that the boys are drawn to him.

"Tell us about the caribou run again," Miwok pleads as I take up a string of rabbits and begin to skin them.

"At the top of the stakes, we tie birchbark strips," Huritt says as he drops his load. He beckons to Miwok, who brings his bow over. Huritt helps position it in the crook of Miwok's arm. "In the wind, the birchbark strips move back and forth and scare the caribou, so they try to bolt. The stakes prevent the animals from passing through the narrow exits in the fence, and they are forced downriver."

"That's where the greatest hunters catch them?" Miwok asks excitedly while his little brother, Nikiti, stabs the ground with a stick he is pretending to use as a spear.

Huritt corrects Miwok's placement of the bow as he continues speaking: "The hunters wait patiently in their canoes. The good hunters know how to aim their spears to take down the caribou. I'm a great hunter. I always spear the most."

Miwok looks up with reverence pooling in his eyes before he nocks his arrow and takes aim at a tree. Huritt nods in approval, and Miwok's shoulders swell with pride.

"Do the hunters use spears like mine with a wooden shaft and a fine bone point?" he asks after he releases an arrow that goes astray.

"Ours are made of stone," Huritt replies. "The killing is easier. Afterwards, we thank the Creator for the caribou's life. One day, you will come with me, and I will show you how to hunt."

Miwok's eyes grow as round as bog pools. "I hope to be just like you when I grown up," he chirps. "They say that your heels are silent in the bush and that your eye is very sharp."

Huritt laughs. "What they say is true," he says. He looks at me, waiting. When I say nothing, he points to his ears and directs his comment to my little step-brother. "I heard the whispers of caribou hooves gathering in the woods when I walked back here. I'll listen for them again when I return to the caribou run at dawn."

I try to suppress a burst of laughter, but it slips out. "We weren't expecting you back so soon," I finally say as soon as I manage to collect myself.

"I came back to check on Nuttah," he replies, and I have nothing to say to this. "You must stay with her until the baby comes."

"If Askook returns, he will be angry to see me at his fire."

Huritt says nothing. I return to skinning the rabbit meat, and I use all my strength and pull the rabbit fur outwards, and the legs come straight out of the pelt. Then I twist the head and break it off and toss it out. Under Huritt's scrutiny, I find myself fumbling.

"I think of you when I am in the bush."

"You shouldn't," I mutter self-consciously.

"I do," he says. I am tempted to tell him about Santu, but something holds me back. Huritt picks up his bow and arrows and saunters towards the path with Miwok following close behind. "Send word if the baby comes," he says before he disappears.

He has barely left when we are visited by the Shaman, who has his staff in hand. Despite the chilly air, the Shaman is wearing nothing but a loincloth with a necklace consisting of six decorated bone carvings and one large animal tooth. His whole body has been painted red.

"The Creator will soon give us caribou," he says as he leans in closely to scrutinize my work. I imagine him drinking the rabbits' blood. "I see you have been working hard. Your knife is sharp. You know how to use it well."

My head swivels, owl-like, when he speaks in Norse. His breath is putrid. He smells like fish. Just then, the Shaman catches sight of Nuttah emerging from the tent with her pregnant belly and her enlarged breasts.

"There are spirits here that could curse the hunt," he says to her in a singsong voice with nasal undertones. "The Powerful Monster walks among you." He breaks off suddenly, and I don't know where to put my eyes.

Nuttah slowly lowers herself onto the ground where she takes up her sewing. I watch, transfixed, as her needle pulls the sinew in and out.

"This Norsewoman – Raven's *döttir* – should come with me," the Shaman continues in a foreboding tone. "I will take her to the steam huts with the heated stones. I can smudge her there. She can release the bear."

Fear lodges in the pit of my stomach, and I draw back.

"There will be no smudging of my *döttir* today," Nuttah huffs protectively without bothering to look up. "'Tis not needed. She is fine."

I glance between the two of them and reach for my grounding rock.

"It is Chief Achak's wish that she be smudged," the Shaman replies in an eerie voice.

"Then I'll speak to Chief Achak first," Nuttah snaps.

"He left at dawn to join the huntsmen," the Shaman says. He blinks rapidly. "The Great Caribou Hunt will not go well if Raven's *döttir* isn't smudged. Raven would want you to give the girl to me."

"I'll not release her," Nuttah yips.

It strikes me that all I need to do is to turn and run, but Nuttah reaches out and grabs my arm. "Return to the *mamateek*," she whispers fiercely in my ear.

The Shaman's voice rises with the wind as he begins to chant in a raspy voice that echoes through the silver birch. As the wind swirls the autumn leaves around the yard, we hear the pitter-patter of approaching feet and two rambunctious boys burst into the clearing. Miwok and Nikiti are followed by Wapun. At the sight of her, the Shaman goes silent.

"You are wanted at Songbird's fire," Wapun sweetly says after she formally greets the Shaman. "She wants you to sing the ritualistic prayers in front of the communal firepit in preparation for the delivery of the caribou."

"Tell her that I am visiting Raven's *döttir*," the Shaman says.

Wapun lowers her eyes. "I am here now," she says, "and she is expecting you."

The Shaman mumbles something inaudible and then quickly turns and taps his staff with its tinkling shells on the ground. A moment later, he leaves the yard, and my bones relax.

"The Shaman rarely visits me," Nuttah smiles.

Very soon Nuttah and Wapun and I are giggling like a group of gaggling geese and talking about the *Mokoshan*. Little Nikiti looks scared. He tugs at my arm.

"I hope you didn't curse the hunt," he whispers in a quiet voice.

Three days later, the men come home. I am standing with Santu and Wapun watching the procession of hunters filing past when I spot Bjørn's tall frame pulling a travois behind him full of butchered meat. There is a carefree joyfulness about him I have rarely seen, and I am riveted to the sound of his laughter. When the other hunters praise him for bagging the most caribou, his humility sits on him like a well-worn hide.

The crowd presses in, and I stand back as he is hoisted high and thrown, prostrate, into the muscled arms of a group of hunters who carry him in front of the elders of the tribe. I walk behind. Bjørn's face is flushed. He has somehow changed. From the look of him, he has lost some of his seriousness and won the ability to smile an easy grin, and his laughter catches like wildfire.

"All of us worked hard to herd the caribou down the path," he announces to the villagers. "Nothing went wrong, but there was a scare when a yearling bull broke free of the fence. Huritt had my back. He saved the day."

A moment later, Huritt is swallowed by a moving swell of men whose thunderous voices drown him out. The little ones follow the procession in a pack as the line of heroes slowly snakes towards the smokehouses where the meat will be unpacked. Young and old point to the many caribou racks that Bjǫrn is responsible for bringing back. They call him "Great Catcher" or some such thing that I cannot decipher fast enough.

"Anja, I killed more than ten caribou in one day alone," Bjǫrn calls over the noisy din as soon as he spots me.

"I'll thank the gods on your behalf," I shout back. There is a sudden realization that the two of us are speaking Norse.

Grandmother, with her two white braids trailing down her back, tilts her head back and catches my eye. She grins as if she understands that nothing is more important than moments of connection. She doesn't need to understand the words. She knows the language of being human in this place.

The Beothuk prepare for the *Mokoshan* Feast with a frenetic energy that is infectious. From dawn till dusk, the women grind the caribou leg bones into a kind of mash which they boil in pots over roaring fires. As the bone marrow rises to the surface, they skim it off and press it into cakes. I feel useless until Songbird asks Santu and me to find a way to occupy the children so they don't get underfoot.

At suppertime, I am on my way back from Santu's *mamateek* when I come into the clearing where the hunters usually tan their hides. Bjǫrn is there, and I feel a sudden jolt. He is straining his shoulders as he attempts to de-hair a pelt.

"I never see you anymore," I call as I come up behind him, breathing hard. Slowly, he drags the scraper down. His blond hair falls forward in his eyes.

"I've been out hunting," he says, glancing up. There is perspiration beading on his brow.

"I miss your company," I say when he pauses to remove the hairs from his blade. "Perhaps you are avoiding me?"

I catch the beginning of a sheepish grin creeping into his handsome face. "I would never avoid you, Anja."

"I never miss your owly moods, Bjǫrn."

He smiles again. There is a new tattoo on his muscled arm. From where I stand, I can just make out the shape of it.

"Chief Achak has accepted you as his *döttir*. I hear the talk," he mutters as he pulls the scraper forward with a grunt.

"*Já*," I say.

"Are you pleased?"

"I have been reborn."

Bjǫrn's attention is half split between the hide and me. He fumbles with his blade. "Your *faðir* is like no other, Anja."

"His people have been good to me." My breathing slows. The trees that canopy the clearing are painted in brilliant shades of burnt orange and yellow and cherry red.

"Are you ready for the long winter months ahead?"

"I am," I say. "What of you? Will you journey home to Leifsbidur before it snows?"

He shrugs. The silence sits heavily between us. "I am a hunter, Anja. I need to do more hunting first."

He works the scraper away from him, angling the blade back before moving it forward and squeezing it against the beam.

Light from the setting sun filters through the trees, and Bjǫrn's silhouette changes shape, twisting and dancing on the ground. Somewhere in the forest, the children are laughing and yelling as they chase each other down the path. I live through them in this Beothuk place where I have been given the chance to start again and find myself, including all my broken parts. I bite my lip, knowing that if Bjǫrn had not rescued me and brought me here, I would never have discovered who I am, I would never have found this gratitude.

Bjǫrn stops his work and clucks his tongue when he sees my face. "You are sad?" he murmurs into the wind. He places his scraper on the ground, and in two long strides, he is by my side. As he lowers himself to the ground, he swats a mosquito off my leg.

"I have learned to own my sadness," I breathe. "It has shaped me."

It has been so long since we sat this close that I suddenly don't know what to say or where to look. Bjǫrn yanks a piece of grass out of the ground and twirls it between his work-hardened thumb and index finger.

"'Tis good that you are here, Anja Freydisdöttir." He tries to peer up into my downturned face.

"I am not Anja Freydisdöttir anymore," I say. "Now I am Anja of the Beothuk tribe."

"You are Raven's *döttir*," he says quietly.

"Raven's *döttir*, Greenland born," I clarify. Bjǫrn leans in so closely that I can smell his heady wood-smoke scent. Our shoulders touch, and we sit in silence, listening to the leaves dancing along the ground.

"You brought me here," I finally stammer awkwardly. "You delivered me safely to my *faðir*'s tribe."

"I said I would."

"I have tried to start again, but not everyone is welcoming. Askook and some of the elders do not seem pleased that I am here."

"That is not your responsibility. Just take care of yourself."

For a moment I am in the cave again, staring up into his sea-glass eyes as he rebandages my injured arm.

"You must thank the Great Creator. He has gifted you with family," Bjørn continues. His voice plummets low.

"I am grateful for all you did for me." The words slip out as the sun drops behind the trees. There is a sudden autumn chill, breezy and crisp and tinged with the odour of retted straw. Bjørn clears his throat.

"Tell me what this is all about." He looks at me with eyes as blue as a glacial fjord. I don't move when he leans in so closely that I can feel his breath against my cheek.

There is a yearning, hot as fire, swirling in my belly, a wave of tingles, a swell of joy as our noses touch.

Bjørn jerks back when there is the sudden sound of footfalls crunching leaves in the bush behind us.

"Raven's *döttir*, Nuttah needs you," Huritt calls in broken Norse as he runs into the clearing. He looks surprised when he catches the two of us pulling apart from each other.

"I was fetching water," I quickly say. Huritt's brow furls into a frown, and I can almost feel the heat of his shock and disappointment radiating off him. The weight of it is almost unbearable.

"You'd better go if it is Nuttah's time," Bjørn quickly says as he scrambles up. For a moment, I hesitate, but then Nuttah's image flashes, and I see her pregnant bump. Bjørn offers his hand to pull me up, and I take it, but Huritt's eyes burn my back.

Without a word, I collect my water-bucket and quickly head off down the trail, worrying about everything. Even from a distance, I can hear the sharpness in Huritt's voice as he snaps at Bjǫrn and criticizes him for the way in which he has scraped the hides. Bjǫrn lips back, and the two of them begin to fight. Even though my heart hurts for them in different ways, I don't have time to sort things out.

Nuttah is in labour when I arrive. Songbird parts the crowd to let me pass and then she ushers me into the *mamateek* that smells of sweat and hot seal oil and some strong herb.

"She won't let me in," she whispers fiercely. I gawk at her.

Someone has lit a fire, and the place is stuffy and way too warm. In the hazy, orange light filtering through the birchbark walls, Nuttah is bending over a sewing piece.

"The baby is coming," she calmly says. I catch a glimpse of her sweaty face and her black, raccoon eyes as the shadows of an autumn dusk flicker eerily on the walls.

"I'll call someone," I stammer awkwardly. I brace myself against a giant swell of panic and will myself to settle down.

"I need the presence of a Norsewoman who knows our gods and our stories and our songs," Nuttah pants. "I want this child to know both worlds."

My hands begin to shake. "The birthing process is the same for all women, is it not?"

"Please, Anja! By Óðinn's eye, this bairn is not like the others." She shifts in place. "This little one is coming fast!"

I can barely stomach to peek at the place where the baby's head is crowning. Nuttah startles me out of my reverie when she cries out loud. Immediately she scratches a runic inscription on the ground.

"Here is a rabbit's pelt to swaddle the babe when it comes

out," she breathes. When she flinches, I stand there helplessly gawking until she instructs me to bring a wad of deerhide to stuff inside her mouth. I do as I am told. Afterwards, I dab her head.

"You must not fret." The air sizzles through her teeth. "I've done this several times before, and there has only been one stillbirth. Now help me up. After the baby comes, you'll need to cut the cord and help me manage the afterbirth."

I gingerly ease her heavy weight into a semi-crouch before another contraction racks her spine.

"When I tell you, you must cradle the baby's head and then I'll push. There'll be muck, but you'll be fine. May Frigg, the goddess of motherhood, be with us." She grips my sweaty hand and squeezes hard. "Anja Freydisdöttir, please know this: You are a comfort in my time of need."

She closes her eyes and grits her teeth and pushes hard and grips my hand so hard, she almost breaks it. With the Queen of the Aesir's help, I will myself to find the courage to offer help.

It seems like a long time passes before the next contraction comes. Her shrill cry rips through the smoky dwelling, and a rush of footsteps approaches the *mamateek*. When I hear voices at the door, I get up to check.

"I'll break your bones if you let them in," Nuttah swears. She is squatting down. Her eyes are closed, her face is red, and she is grimacing. Once again, she pushes hard. There is perspiration dripping down her brow, trickling along her matted hairline. I shift my gaze and watch, transfixed, as something dark begins emerging from somewhere deep.

"Please tell me what I need to do," I breathe as Nuttah lets out another guttural groan.

"Give me another wad to bite," she cries before she gives another forceful push and reaches out to guide my hand.

The birthing happens surprisingly fast after that. I catch the infant as she slips out, all white and slimy with hair matted and mucked and sticking to her tiny head. Nuttah tells me to cut the cord and use the hide to clean the bairn, just as the infant releases a healthy cry.

When I have finally finished swaddling her, I cradle the tiny bundle in my arms. She has tiny, perfect, little hands and tiny, perfect, little feet.

"Go tell Askook we have a *döttir*," Nuttah says weakly. "I want her to grow up to be just like you."

Her words are like falling stars that fizzle out too quickly. I stare at the little one and brace myself when the shaking starts.

"I'll tell Askook," I whisper softly in her ear when I finally manage to get her propped up against a stack of hides so that the bairn can suckle at her breast.

"Tell him that she is healthy because you helped," she says, and I squeeze her shoulder in gratitude.

When I step outside into the windless night, I am met by a sea of faces backlit by a giant bonfire shooting up flames into the star-studded sky. It is not the first time that I have marvelled at the Beothuk ways. In Greenland, men would not wait around for fear of encountering the trolls that steal the bairns and replace them with changeling lookalikes. Here, the men gather round.

"Does my *oosuck* live?" comes a panicked voice that I recognize all too well. Askook's face looks wild.

"Nuttah is safe," I say cautiously, "and you have a healthy *döttir* whose lungs work well."

Behind us, there is a sudden, joyful whoop, and the booms of a drum start up, and the singers begin throat-singing the songs of the ancestors. In Askook's presence, I feel like a deer targeted by a hunter with keen, sharp eyes.

"Anja Freydisdöttir, you help my *oosuck* well."

He holds my eyes. The vibrating drums drown out the sound of the crackling fire and the mutterings of the gathered crowd. A warmth spreads through me as I square my shoulders and lift my chin. Then the shock sets in. Askook has spoken to me in the language of my people. He has spoken to me in Norse.

I would laugh if I was not so tired.

Chapter Twenty-Seven

BONE MARROW CAKES

It snows on the day of the *Mokoshan*. The large white flakes flutter down and melt almost immediately so that the potholes fill up with a slush-like soup that thinly ices over. In the cold, my old bear injuries throb. The gods could have inflicted worse burdens on a girl who has forgotten them.

Faðir tells me that there is surplus caribou meat that has been divested of bones and packaged into bark boxes. It needs to be taken to the storehouses, and he asks me to help carry the boxes. There are ten in all. A moment passes between us, a test of sorts, as if *Faðir* knows I will help despite my injured leg, just because he asked.

"We must thank the Great Creator for the winter meat," he says with a gentle smile that carves itself into his cheeks. "Your huntsman killed the greatest number of caribou. He will sit in a place of honour at my side during the *Mokoshan*. He has earned the right."

"He will be pleased," I say, dipping my chin in deference.

I am kept busy throughout the day fetching and transferring foods to *Faðir*'s *mamateek*. Central to the celebration will be the serving of marrow cakes coupled with ceremonial tastings of the succulent caribou meat pieces that have been slowly roasted over a smoking fire. The tribe will pay tribute to the spirit of the caribou that gave its antlers, its bones, its hide, its fat and grease, its sinew and its meat. We will honour the caribou for everything.

Just before the celebration begins, I find myself with Wapun and the aunties standing near the bed depressions where a giant circular carving of the ravens soaring across a moonlit sky hangs suspended from a beam. The room is stifling hot, and the children are so restless that the aunties have difficulty holding them back and preventing them from prematurely entering the feasting room. A little one cries. Santu reaches out to comfort her, and I get pulled into translating in my head, listening to the ebbs and flows of everyone speaking all at once. When I steal a glance into the gathering room aglow with firelight, I look for Huritt and Bjǫrn, but I can't immediately spot them in the crowd.

Wapun addresses me in a gentle voice. She has a way of quietly honouring me, of slipping into the shadows to give me a chance to find the words to speak, of letting me just be Raven's *döttir*, of encouraging me to be myself. Her caribou-skin cloak with its hairy side turned inwards to give her warmth is a work of great skill and talent. I admire how the fringes have been decorated with pieces of antler bone and tiny, shiny, polished stones. The lavish use of powdered hematite has turned the garment a brilliant shade of red. It is too red, I think, but Wapun likes the colour, and it suits her well.

She hands me a birchbark container edged in pink, decorated

with traditional chevron designs. When I cock my head and accept the gift, Weematin lets out a startled cry. Wapun coos to him as she reaches for his little flailing fists, and he squirms in the carrier on her back.

"It comes from Huritt," she eventually says. I consider the meaning of the gift. Wapun is careful not to stare.

I turn away from the women and gingerly lift the birchbark lid. Inside there is a necklace made of caribou-bone triangles, some of which have been meticulously painted with red ochre, some of which have been left white. Huritt's gift is beautiful.

"You should put it on," Santu says as she comes up behind me. I lift my hair and she helps me wiggle the necklace into place.

When, at last, we are called into the gathering place for the feast, the place is at capacity. There are bodies pushing up against the walls and a throng of people spilling out the door. In the centre of the room, the Shaman sits cedar-trunk-straight in all his regalia with the fire shadows flickering across his painted face. When he spots me, he throws an icy look.

We pass Askook and Nuttah, and she smiles up at me as she cradles the sleeping bairn in her arms. Their other children are all sitting cross-legged beside them on the ground with Huritt flanking Askook on the right. I can't look at him. Not yet. Not now.

There is ordered chaos in the gathering place where the Beothuk talk amongst themselves and the fire flares and pops and snaps, where everything is infused with a strong smell of woodsmoke and the enticing odours of cooking meat. When I look around and see all the families gathered, leaning against each other's backs, there is a strange tingling sensation and I feel at peace. I am finally home. My spirit smiles.

I follow Wapun as she picks her way over to where *Faðir* sits, with Nikiti and Miwok trailing close behind. Bjǫrn is sitting crosslegged on the ground. When I pass by, he looks up and smiles.

"Chief Achak said to leave room for you," he says as his eyes take in my fancy dress.

"I see you have new buckskin leggings," I reply. Bjǫrn tosses me a lopsided grin. Then he shifts to make room for me. The Shaman rises. The people settle. The hum dies down.

The Shaman's voice is as big as thunder. He acknowledges the gift of the caribou and thanks the Great Creator with his ritualistic prayers. I can't understand all of it and my thoughts wander, my eyes drift up. When I blink, a carved stone figurine sitting in the rafters flickers in the hazy light before the image wavers and goes up in smoke. When I look up, Huritt is staring at me from across the fire. His dancing eyes wander down my neck, and as soon as he spots the necklace, he winks at me mischievously. A strange feeling bubbles up. I suddenly have difficulty getting air.

Wapun turns around. "Sit closer to me to avoid the smoke."

Huritt flashes another brilliant smile.

When the meal begins, I can hardly eat. I give my bone-mash cakes to Miwok and barely touch the rest of the caribou and the other dishes that have been prepared. When the drums begin again and the dancing stars, the feast seems to come to an official end. Soon the room is buzzing with voices and pulsating with the sound of the booming drums.

"Huritt is waiting for you," Wapun says as she leans across my step-brothers and tugs at my sleeve. The guilt slips into that soft place, that empty void, that place of nothingness I thought I'd filled. The realization that I could never circle him – that

Huritt would always need to be in charge – sits inside, all gritty like sand in mussels.

I get lost watching the footwork of the dancers moving to the steady rhythm of the drums.

"*Döttir*, did you enjoy the bone-mash cakes?" My eyes slowly lift to meet *Faðir*'s gaze. Something about his countenance comforts me. There is kindness in his eyes – something more precious than pearls found in oysters.

"The Great Creator is with us," *Faðir* says. I lean in closer to better hear as the room erupts in a burst of laughter and another group of hunters get up and begin to dance. Huritt is among them. He throws his caribou skins over his muscled shoulders with a wild whoop, and the crowd erupts. They call out to him as his plaited hair swings and thumps his back. His dancing is reckless and wild and free and complicated as he moves through intricate patterns, weaving together fancy footwork. His full body gyrates in honour of the caribou.

"I thank the Great Creator for many things," *Faðir* tells me above all the noise as the two of us sit watching Huritt circling around the fire.

"I, too, am grateful," I say distractedly.

"The hunters praise their *oosucks* for preparing all this food. Having an *oosuck* is important to a hunter," *Faðir* says. He pauses. "I know of one hunter who wants to share his *mamateek* with a woman who will help him eat his caribou."

I glance at Bjǫrn who is sitting with his back to me. He is talking with Santu's husband, but he ends the conversation and sits up straight and cocks his ear to better hear. It is so hot in here that I can hardly breathe.

"Huritt came to visit me at my fire," *Faðir* continues in a solemn voice. "We spoke so long, the fire died."

I eye the door. Bjǫrn shifts in place so he can get a better look. Our eyes connect. His face is ashen. He looks like he has just been fish-gutted. *Faðir* glances up just as Huritt leaves the dance circle to speak with Grey Wolf.

"Huritt is a great hunter. He is well respected by our tribe. You would make him a fine *oosuck, döttir.*"

I have the urge to bolt, to disappear. To fly away on raven's wings.

"Huritt will build you a new *mamateek,*" *Faðir* continues in a steady voice. I lower my eyes to avoid Bjǫrn's stare. My tongue won't work. There are a thousand butterflies behind my eyes.

"We must inspect Huritt's gifts. He presented two large caribou. Their skins and antlers are very fine, and they will give our clan a lot of meat. By the first new moon of summer next year, Huritt promises to harpoon a whale when the pods swim in close to our village during the great migration. Huritt will honour you. You should be proud."

May the gods help me! Which god? Óðinn? Thor? There are no Norse gods here.

"Askook proposes a different mate for his son. It will not be easy, but I will convince him to approve the match."

The smell of meat and grease and smoke and sweat is strong, and my stomach turns when Bjǫrn quickly stands. As he does, his plateful of caribou bones and congealed grease falls into the firepit. There is a hissing sound as the fat sizzles and a log bursts apart, popping and spitting. The fire-burst is so loud and unexpected that I pull back just as Bjǫrn pushes past.

Bjǫrn picks his way over to where Huritt is sitting and hauls him up. I gasp, but it is as though I am watching from a riverbank where the water is rushing past, swishing and swirling downriver at breakneck speed, separating me from everyone who matters most. I shout, but my voice is drowned out by the drums and the singers and the thumping beats: *Strong, weak, weak. Strong, weak, weak.*

When Huritt and Bjǫrn get swallowed up by the crowd, I feel someone tugging at my arm. When I look down, Miwok begins nattering in his boy-man voice. I shake him off and begin tackling the labyrinth of hands and feet that block my path.

I am unexpectedly waylaid when Askook grasps me firmly by the arm. The noises blur. Helplessly, I watch Bjǫrn forcing Huritt out the door.

"Nuttah is well pleased with you," Askook stammers. His grip is strong. I glance over my shoulder to where *Faðir* is standing. Our eyes connect. I see the confusion in his face. He knows how much I want to leave.

"My *oosuck* says the birthing went well because of you," Askook says. His words stir up an awkwardness that makes me blush. "She says Raven's *döttir* should be praised."

His scrutiny is disquieting. I stare at the moths helplessly hurling themselves against the walls as the *Mokoshan* festivities build to a peak.

"Nuttah has been a great comfort to me in my time of need."

"Nuttah wants the *döttir* of the Beothuk Chief to name our child," Askook says. "You are worthy of this honour. I have agreed."

There are too many voices, too many words spilling out of Askook's mouth. He smiles his wolfman smile after muttering a bunch of sweet-nothings in the Beothuk tongue. My mind is so addled that I go numb. He has honoured me, and yet there is no satisfaction, joy, or pride.

"In the forest, the raven is a fierce and cunning bird," Askook slowly says.

"The raven also is intelligent," *Faðir* says.

"The raven was turned black forever because of his mischievousness, but he symbolizes knowledge, truth, and transformation," Askook announces as he turns to me. I steady myself and he smiles again. "I see you, Raven. I see the value of your name."

Raven. My name is Raven! I have a name!

"The Creator has been good to your family," I manage with the sudden realization that even though I have earned Askook's respect, I don't need it anymore. I take a breath. "I will ask the ancestors about the name."

Faðir steps between us and whispers fiercely in my ear: "Go before Huritt and Bjǫrn's jealousy destroys them both. The dogs are howling. Go before the storm sets in."

I lose no time retrieving my mantle and picking my way through the crowd. When I finally make it to the door and throw it open, I am met with a blast of icy-cold wind that makes me pull my mantle high around my ears.

The celebrations have moved outdoors. I hear the laughter as I half-jump over the shallow potholes, each covered over by a thin crust of ice. It is very dark, but there is a full moon rising, nested between thin wisps of cloud. Songbird's family huddles around the communal firepit with their birchbark cups in hand. In front of them, the flames shoot backwards in the hissing wind.

"Come drink with us," one hunter calls as I scan their group, looking for Huritt and Bjǫrn's familiar forms.

"Soon," I say with a wave.

It begins to snow, and I try to recall all of Huritt's familiar haunts. Peering into the darkness of the nearby bush, I try to will my feet to move. I hesitate when two bats come whirling past.

Inhaling deeply, I flick one last glance towards the fire and gather up my courage and quickly scamper into the woods.

There is building terror by the time I reach the first bend in the path, covered over by wind-bent trees. I am alert to every sound, vigilant when an owl swooshes down just ahead. I can't shake the thought of trolls moving through the bush with yellow eyes, of all sorts of dangers lurking in the trees. I half-run, half-limp down the winding path where the dark blobs of trees morph into imagined forms waiting and ready to attack.

When I finally enter the clearing where Bjǫrn likes to tan his hides, the place is deserted. A shimmering, evanescent moon breaks out from behind a bank of clouds, casting branch shadow strips across the path. The darkness pushes in around me, stifling any desire to continue moving towards the field that holds the brook. I pull out my knife and hold it out in front of me defensively, forcing myself to follow the sound of the moving water, forcing myself to swallow fear, the stab of it. I snag a breath, and the imaginings come in a rush: the bobcat's sharpened claws, the stealthy way it hugs the trees, its tendency to drop quickly and unexpectedly when it stalks its prey.

In front of me, I hear a blood-curdling howl, a vicious shout, a loud and ugly curse. When I emerge from the treeline, I am standing on a bank staring across a snow-covered field. Just below me, the moonbeams are bouncing off the snow, illuminating the dark silhouettes of two grappling forms in the slush.

I break into a run and slip and slide down the bank. At the bottom, I spot a trail of blood in the snow. When I see the red on white, my breath comes out in ragged gasps, pluming in the bitter cold.

"Stop it!" I yell as Bjǫrn lunges forward with the surprise

attack of a right-hook uppercut. The blow is snappy, and Huritt reels backwards, and I scream so loudly that I almost fall. Bjǫrn turns his head, and I scream again, but I am a distraction – a costly one. Huritt throws a series of punches, hard and fast, as I lunge towards them, sucking in frost that burns my lungs.

The two of them are very fast. In an instant, they have moved away from me, and Huritt flays Bjǫrn with a branch before falling backwards on a patch of ice. He has barely managed to right himself when Bjǫrn plants himself firmly in the mud and successfully delivers some hard body shots.

"Don't!" I yell. I can't reach them fast enough.

Huritt is a warrior. He jabs his fist up and manages to deliver a violent punch. Bjǫrn reels backwards, holding his jaw, his shouts echoing through the frosty air.

"Stay back, Anja!" he yells as Huritt charges.

Screaming incoherently, I cringe when Bjǫrn finds an opening at a very awkward angle and punches Huritt in the eye.

Huritt's cry reverberates through the frosty air. In stunned silence, I watch in horror as he suddenly drops to one knee. With a warrior's cry, Bjǫrn begins doggedly pummelling him in the face. When his fists collide with Huritt's eye for a second time, Huritt yelps and teeters before passing out.

I scream so loudly that Bjǫrn jolts to attention as if dream-startled. When he turns to look at me, his eyes are vacant, and I suck in air and feel blood trickling down my throat. It's almost like I don't know him. There is a garish knife wound on his cheek, shallow flesh wounds on his arm. I blink in horror, stop mid-flight.

Almost instantly, a flock of black-winged birds ascends into the night-time sky and flies off into the black shadowed trees illuminated by a silver moon. When I look back, Bjǫrn is staring at me in a daze.

"Where did you come from, Anja Freydisdöttir?" he mutters as if he is afraid of me and of himself, as if he is suddenly tasting the bitter berries of sweet revenge, as if he is suddenly registering my presence in this field of snowy slush and muck.

"Where did you go?" is all I say.

Chapter Twenty-Eight

MOON SPARKLES

"Huritt?" I mumble, rushing forth. He has an injured eye, and one of his back teeth is missing. I kneel beside him. *O gods!* I had hoped that it wouldn't come to this. With a heavy grunt, I manage to roll him onto his side, but when I see his eye, I almost puke. The haemorrhaging has left bright-red patches spreading into the whites, and the slashes on his face make him almost unrecognizable.

"Careful, Anja," Bjǫrn pants from behind my back.

Huritt stirs in a state of dull wakefulness before passing out again in the muddy snow. I feel useless even after I bind up Huritt's bleeding fist with a strip of leather from his festive garb. Anger, hot and fierce, rises like steam from a boiling cauldron, scalding reason, interfering with my ability to think things through. There is an ugly tickle frogging in my throat, and I feel like tossing a murderous stave into someone's tracks.

"When he wakes, you'll have to answer to my *faðir* for this," I sputter, directing my words to the huntsman's back. I hear a low, guttural grunt, a scornful huff as Bjǫrn bends down to retrieve his knife. In the snow, he slips and his feet cross sideways and he reaches low to touch the ground, but he maintains his balance even though his arms splay wide.

"If I were you, I'd leave him for dead," Bjǫrn says gruffly as he rights himself and starts to make for higher ground.

"That isn't what you taught me." It comes out in a whisper, but Bjǫrn stops dead in his tracks. He slowly turns. The clearing is ominously quiet. I can smell the pungent odour of rotting leaves, of something decaying in the woods. A wave of shivers shimmies down my back. My feet are tingling. My sore leg throbs.

"I need to return to my people," Bjǫrn mumbles, spitting out a gob of blood. "I'll leave for Leifsbidur within the week."

"Coward!" I spit in his face.

"That I'm not. You, of all people, should know it!"

Huritt moans in pain. I cradle his head in my hands and gently lift him off my lap so that I can stand. For a minute I am tempted to stay with him, but my heart won't let me.

I follow Bjǫrn's shadowed form and pick my way across the frozen ground before I carefully take a stab at climbing up the icy bank to higher ground. Several times I almost fall. Bjǫrn ignores me as he collects his weapons and finds his furs.

"How dare you leave me!" I hiss as I draw the wolverine into my voice and grab for him and drag him back. I am close enough to see a sheen of sweat on his furrowed brow and the nasty slash across his cheek. The cut is oozing blood.

"Anja, you are betrothed," he says with thick emotion. "I overheard your conversation. There is no reason for me to stay here any longer. I need to return to my kin."

"You can't leave! Not like this."

"It's time, *hjarta mitt*." His term of endearment is a moonbeam twinkle, a falling star, a lacy snowflake against my cheek.

Bjørn leans in closely. Using his dirty thumb to wipe off a spot of blood from my cheek, he tries to smile. Unexpectedly, the smell of him draws me in, and I fall into the softness of his chest where the weight of the past few months comes crashing down. Sorrow, heavier than a ballast rock, sucks my breath away and I feel my eyes brimming. Another moan escapes, cradled in a heavy sigh.

"I can't endure another loss. I can't. I won't. It would be too hard," I say. I feel the warmth of him seeping into me as he rubs my back. His heart thuds loudly as he presses me against his furs, the scratch of them.

"*Hjarta mitt* ..." Bjørn begins. The moon peeks through the trees, and the wind slithers through the silver birch. "You and I have been through much." He swallows hard. "In that cave, I would have died for you rather than seeing you suffer all alone." His words come out in starts and stops. "You were the *döttir* of a Beothuk chief and I didn't even know. Even if I had, I wouldn't have cared."

I feel a big, fat tear trickling down my cheek. I brush it off.

"You were so brave," he says as he takes up my hand. "You fought a bear and you survived. A bear, no less! I've killed many blacks and browns, but I've never seen one the size of yours." He laughs a little, and I glance up at the stubble on his chin, at the clotting blood on his injured cheek.

"Anja, it was no hardship to stay with you in that cave. Remember how we talked for long hours into the night? Remember how I played the flute for you? Remember how I recited the sagas of the gods? I tell you this: you were my muse. As you healed, I softened and came alive! You taught me how to laugh and how to put down my bow and arrows and my shield. You taught me that misfortune lies heavy upon everyone, but I also helped you discover that it is better to live in the moment than to live where the shadows dwell.

"When I brought you to your *faðir*'s *mamateek* and he paid me for the care of you, I felt the insult fiercely in my gut, especially because my sole motivation had been to care for you so that you survived. For my efforts, your *faðir* handed me new weapons – new killing tools. By Óðinn's beard, I cared for you! I made you whole again. All I wanted was for you to live."

"I survived because of you," I manage weakly. "You rescued me and brought me home. I found my *faðir* with your help."

"You saved me too," Bjǫrn quickly says. He pulls me closer into him. The moon leaks sparkles onto the snow.

"On that momentous day when I saw you safely delivered into your *faðir*'s arms, I saw your joy, and I was proud to be a part of that. Don't you see? Before you, I was just a simple hunter. Now I am someone else – someone better – a protector who sees beyond himself."

He pauses, and I see the man I've missed for many weeks, the whole of him.

"You belong with your people, Anja of the Beothuk tribe."

I try to speak but it is difficult to find the words. "I don't love Huritt," I whisper miserably. I can feel my lips quivering. "Huritt asked my *faðir* if I wanted to be his *oosuck*, but Huritt means nothing to me. He is like a brother and nothing more. I do not love him. I never did."

Bjǫrn's jaw is twitching. He turns his head, and his silhouette is backlit by a silver moon. "You were a foolish knave for fighting Huritt because of me!" I continue pathetically. "You assumed that I loved Huritt and that I was willing to make the match."

"How can I ask you to come back with me to Leifsbidur?" he stammers.

"Let me choose," I breathe.

"*Þú ert hjarta mitt!* Did you hear?"

I lean into him and wait for a few moments. The words sink in. "I am your heart?"

"*Þú ert hjarta mitt!*" he repeats. "I've done my duty and kept my word. I beg of you, please let me go."

Behind us, Huritt groans. Bjǫrn, the protector – my protector – slowly lifts my chin. I feel the heat of him, the strength of him as he draws me in to his waiting lips. His kiss falls deeply on my mouth so that the world twinkles and sparkles and glitters silver-gold.

We pull apart.

There is a glow-in-the-dark phosphorescence about him that attracts me to his brilliant smile. He leans in again. This time I catch butterflies and taste his sweetness, the breath of him. I let the feelings take me to a rocky ledge where my stomach drops as he nibbles at my hungry lips. I feel the glow in my belly that moves lower until my whole body yearns for him. The moment lingers, gleaming like crystals, and I shiver in the frosty cold. When he wraps his mantle around my shoulders, the heat of him still lingers in the folds, and I get all jumbled and tipsy breathing in his scent.

Below us, Huritt cries out in agony, sending shivers of panic down my spine. Glancing sideways, I see him writhing in the muddy snow.

"Let's get him up," I say as the moment we shared withers like wildflowers in the first frost of autumn.

"Anja, please believe me. I had to protect myself! I had no choice. Huritt attacked me first. He forced me to draw my knife."

There is a flush of red creeping down his neck, and I am torn about what to think and who to comfort first. Huritt emits another anguished cry as he cups his eye and claws at his face.

"We need to get him back to Nuttah's tent," I say more urgently.

Bjǫrn begins making his way down the bank, and I scramble to follow him, but halfway down, I start to slip. Shrieking, I land on my bum at Huritt's side.

Huritt mumbles, blurting out some stupid talk. I stroke my hand across his good cheek, but in a confused state, he swats at me and I draw back, feeling a rush of hot, stinging tears.

"By the gods, he can't see. You blinded him!"

Bjǫrn releases a string of curses. "He blinded me! He tried to steal you away from me."

"We must get him back to Nuttah's *mamateek*." I whisper as I lean down and try to comfort him. Just as I take up his hand in mine, he almost passes out.

The two of us struggle to lift Huritt up and keep him steady on his feet. He is heavier than I thought, and I am panting and sweating by the time we are done.

Huritt is only half-awake as the three of us slowly begin making our way back up the bank. The ground is slick and muddy and treacherous, and the temperature is falling fast. Huritt can barely walk, can barely see, and I am not strong enough to help him move.

"Perhaps you should talk to him," Bjǫrn mutters as we struggle to drag him down the path. Huritt is moaning like an injured cow. His *mukluks* are a muddy mess, and it is slippery, and I am struggling with my own injured leg. I glance ahead through the shadowy tunnel of black spruce trees, arched over like stooped old men. When Bjørn almost slips on an icy patch, our hands lock together behind Huritt's back.

"One of us should run ahead and find some help," Bjørn grunts as he repositions Huritt's weight.

"Not me," I say. "You'd kill each other if I wasn't here."

I examine the gashes on Huritt's face. The cuts run deep. The blood has clotted and crusted over. But it is his eye – his slashed-up eye – that looks the worst.

Bjørn labours to keep Huritt upright as the moon breaks through the pregnant clouds. Tonight, I ask Máni to give us light so that we can get Huritt safely home, but Máni is a fickle god who once again disappears behind a wall of clouds.

When we finally reach Nuttah's yard, I am so exhausted I can hardly stand, and my injured leg is in agony. The spasms shooting down my back affect my leg and waves of pain rip through my hip. As we gently ease Huritt to the ground, he moans and Bjørn shoots me a worried look.

Someone has built a bonfire in Nuttah's yard, and the flames are wildly flickering back and forth in a cold wind. There are a group of huntsmen still celebrating the *Mokoshan*, and they are huddled around the fire, talking amongst themselves. There is a burst of laughter, and the fire flares. Nuttah has the baby in her arms, and Askook is deep in conversation with the Shaman, whose white pup-seal mantle is glowing in the firelight.

"Wait here. I'll go for help," Bjørn mutters in my ear. He slowly stands, but before he can move, Nuttah spots Huritt lying in a heap. Without a word, she thrusts the baby into Askook's arms, and everything around me blurs.

In moments, she is scurrying across the yard and making her way over to where the three of us are hidden in tree shadows.

"What happened here?" she pants as she crouches down. She flicks a glance between the two of us.

"Huritt and I were in a fight," Bjǫrn mutters stupidly.

When she sees Huritt's bloody face and swollen eye, her brow constricts. "By the gods, why ever did you hit him, Bjǫrn? His eye looks bad!"

"In my defence, he hit me first."

Huritt moans in agony, and Nuttah turns and calls out to Grey Owl. There is too much commotion, too much noise. When the Shaman spots us, his body stills. Without a word, Bjǫrn takes up my hand, and we begin to slink back into the trees where the darkness lurks.

I feel as if we move as one, as if I am a part of him. In my periphery, I see Askook bending over Huritt's form. Beside me, Bjǫrn knocks into a spindly branch and a dusting of snow flutters down. When I see the lacy specks of white settling into the folds of his hides, something shifts inside.

"The Shaman will blame you," I mutter urgently. "We must leave!" Panic oozes like octopus ink when Nuttah begins to scream for help.

"They'll carry him to the healer's tent," Bjǫrn says stiffly as he pulls me down the path. He is tugging at me urgently and breathing hard.

"Will he lose his eye?"

"He is a hunter. He cannot lose his eye," Bjǫrn snaps, but his voice is shaking, his palms are wet.

We cut through the underbrush where the weeds and grasses lick my legs and the snowy slush gets in my shoe. Behind us we hear cracking branches, a rush of feet.

"Stop!" Nuttah cries as soon as she spots us trying to slink behind a copse of trees. We skirt another group of *Mokoshan* revellers sitting around a blazing fire. Behind us, Nuttah calls out to us: "I know a hiding place!"

"This is madness," I say, breathing heavily. "I need to stop." Turning, I see Nuttah beckoning to us frantically.

"I don't trust her," Bjǫrn says. "She will betray us."

"She is safe," I pant as I listen to the ticking of my racing heart.

Reluctantly, we follow her. When the three of us reach an alcove hollowed out in a grove of pungent spruce, we stop and huddle together. The place is dark shadows and crouching trolls and hidden rodents scurrying through a pile of leaves, the brown wetness of them.

"Raven's child, if you were part of this," Nuttah gasps, "you must go back with Bjǫrn to Leifsbidur."

"It wasn't her fault," Bjǫrn whispers urgently.

"It doesn't matter whose fault it was, she will be blamed."

I feel a bolt of fear as powerful as a lightning strike. "I am Raven's *döttir*! I'll tell the elders what happened, and my story will clear Bjǫrn's good name."

Nuttah laughs. "I had hoped that Askook would embrace you, Anja Freydisdöttir. I had hoped that Huritt would be the bridge."

I move towards her, but she pulls back. "I thought my son was good to you?"

"I did nothing to encourage Huritt. He never told me what he was all about. It came as a surprise when I learned that he wanted me to be his *oosuck*."

For a moment, we stand in the penetrating darkness listening to the little sounds of creepers slithering through the undergrowth.

"Askook would have accepted you, *döttir*," Nuttah sighs, but she seems colder. I can feel Bjǫrn's heat at my back. The mist from his breath rises in a cloud above our heads.

"It was your acceptance I needed most," I murmur to her in the dark.

"I wish it was so simple," she says. "Tonight, I see what you are all about. You have made your choice."

Bjǫrn reaches out and clasps my hand. The shadows flicker as the wind picks up.

"The two of you must leave the village. Go tonight!" Nuttah urges. She seems more sad than angry, more tired than she's ever been. "If Huritt's wounds were inflicted in a fight, Askook will try to seek revenge. May Thor protect you. He'll kill you both! I know my husband. I know his hate! Chief Achak will not be able to protect you. This saga started well before your time, and what happened here tonight will only fan the flames of a long-burning hate." She glances over her shoulder. Her voice dips low. "Bjǫrn, you have been Anja's guardian from the very start. Because you cared for her, I'll let you go."

The words hang between us, suspended in the frosty cold. I think of Mother and her dealings with Thorvard of Gardar. I think of her strength and the love she had for *Faðir*, the love she had for me, the love she had for the Greenlanders and Icelanders who accompanied her to Vinland shores.

"As Chief Achak's *dóttir*, I'm certain I can make the council understand," I whisper. "Bjǫrn meant no harm. He was only trying to win my hand and protect himself."

"Anja, you don't know this place," Nuttah whispers fiercely. "The Beothuk elders will wonder why you didn't want to become Huritt's *oosuck*. They might even think you ordered Bjǫrn to inflict the injuries on Huritt's good hunting eye to destroy his chances of marrying you. Oh, *dóttir*, it doesn't look good for you!

They'll blame you. They'll hold you accountable for harming Huritt, who held such promise for this tribe."

"It's not her fault!" Bjǫrn says indignantly as he steps between us. In the distance, we hear a shout. We hear the dogs. We hear the drums.

Nuttah reaches out and grasps my hand. Nothing feels right anymore. I use my free hand to brush off the tears. In the rising wind, the pinecones drop in a quick rush of plinks and thunks as the black spruce shimmy and the poplars groan.

"Will you wish Santu good health from me?"

"I will," she says as she studies me. "Your mother left me behind in Leifsbidur. You are just like her. Both of you are wanderers." She throws a glance behind her back. "You must take care of her, huntsman. Promise me."

The clouds suddenly break apart and the moon comes out and covers Nuttah's face in flickering stripes. Bjǫrn towers over both of us. When he speaks, I watch the movement in the protrusion on his throat.

"I'll take her back to Leifsbidur."

"You have chosen the man who knows you best," Nuttah says, and I feel the pinch of Mother's spirit presence as the moon shines down. My breath climbs and catches. I bite back tears.

"I won't forget you," I manage in the language she taught me, the language that somersaults down my throat and tumbles across my tongue. It is the language of my ancestors, the language I have come to know.

Chapter Twenty-Nine

HANDCLASPED

Bjǫrn takes a circuitous route, skirting the campfires where everyone continues to celebrate the *Mokoshan*. Through the trees, the bonfires shoot up sparks into the night-time sky, and snippets of conversation are punctuated by bursts of laughter and thumping drums. Bjǫrn pulls me forward impatiently. We circle the village and come to a clearing where he has pitched his tent, a dark and lonely dwelling set into a grove of trees. Outside the entrance, Bjǫrn stops and turns and slips his arms around my waist. When he pulls me close, I sink into him and feel the softness of his kiss.

"Come inside," he whispers gruffly when he finally pulls away. "I need to collect my gear."

As my eyes adjust to the dim shadows, I recall the first time I saw *Faðir's* red-ochred face, and then the memories come flooding in as quickly as rabbits scampering through the underbrush. I fall through thoughts, dropping fast.

Bjǫrn hastily collects his bow and arrows. He is but a dark

shadow inside the tent. In the distance, the Beothuk are singing traditional songs in honour of the caribou.

"I am a burden," I murmur quietly, thinking that Bjǫrn is now a hunted man because of me. "What if we are forced to run? What if my leg slows us down?"

"Word hasn't spread yet. Listen. The celebrations are at their height. We must get going. They won't expect us to leave tonight."

"I need to find the courage to let you go," I say quietly.

Bjǫrn pauses and turns his head. "*Neinn*, you need to come with me, *hjarta mitt*. I need you. You mean the world to me."

I blink, and the grief peels like a flimsy piece of birchbark, and I get stuck holding it and puzzling over it and watching it curl. Bjǫrn leans in and kisses me, and there is a blissful, helpless feeling. When he pulls back, I am still revelling in the feel of him.

Hastily, he collects his *faðir*'s sword, a sleeping hide, an extra shirt, and some *pemmican*. When his body brushes close to mine, he finds my hand before leaning across me to grab his tanning tools.

"I, too, need to get my things," I choke. "I also want to see my *faðir* one last time."

Bjǫrn fumbles with his scraper. When he recovers, his breath is warm against my cheek. "I'll come with you," is all he says.

"I'll need to change into my seal skins. I can't wear this."

"Your feasting dress is very fine."

We kiss again. "Santu helped make it."

"Do you want to see your *faðir* on your own?"

Tears are brimming. I feel them spilling down my cheek. "Please come with me."

He lifts my chin and holds my eyes, and I catch a strong whiff of smoke and pine and sweat and blood wafting off his hides. This time his kiss is rough and quick.

We leave his tent as silently as we came and make our way back along the winding path with the wind hissing at our backs. As soon as we reach *Faðir*'s yard, I stop.

"He will know by now. He might see me differently."

"If he does, I am here."

The moon – a white, misshapen orb – throws light across the firepit where the embers are barely glowing in the black. The *mamateek* is dark, and all is quiet in the dark.

"His household has retired to bed," Bjǫrn mutters as he shifts the sack he carries on his back. I shiver in the frosty air. Above, the dwarf Dvalinn star found in the deer constellation is a burning beacon of light that sits high above the *mamateek*.

"I'll not wake Wapun or her little ones. Weematin often sleeps between his parents. If I wake him, he'll start to wail."

"Go around the back," Bjǫrn murmurs, gesturing with his chin.

As soon as I am halfway around the *mamateek*, I catch sight of *Faðir* standing by the trees. He is peering up into the wonders of the night-time sky, and he is still dressed in all his regalia.

"He waits for us," I whisper, and my voice catches.

The wind moans and hisses as if the gods are groaning, as if the woods are preparing for a troll attack. For a moment, I cannot move, but then I slowly start making my way across the yard in the slushy snow, adding to the wealth of footprints that are freezing solid in the mud. Halfway to him, *Faðir* turns.

"Songbird came," he says in Beothuk without greeting me. His eyes arrow through Bjǫrn. "She brought news from the Shaman's tent where Huritt lies. Huntsman, you have blinded Huritt."

"O gods!" I gasp. Bjǫrn and I are handclasped. A tremor travels up my arm. I long to tell *Faðir* everything – that Huritt took joy in provoking Bjǫrn, that Bjǫrn was injured too, that jealousy was the cause of everything, that the fight was a long time coming, that Bjǫrn did not see the situation for what it was.

"The rooster will give the morning call and your pale-faced Norseman will be punished, *döttir*."

His voice wind-rumbles as if piped through a hollow, burned-out tree stump. There is a burning sensation in my throat. In the quiet, Bjǫrn drops my hand.

"This *pushaman* beside you – this whiteman we have honoured and brought into our fold from the time he was a child – has done bad things, *döttir*. You must make a choice. You must choose to stay in this village or leave with him."

It will be my choice. My choice! It must be my choice.

"My hand was forced!" Bjǫrn says indignantly.

"Please hear his side!" My thoughts churn and whirl and I begin to sway. I am floundering in a no-man's-land, struggling and gutted, hesitant to choose my mother's people over my *faðir's* tribe. I don't know if I should see myself as Anja Freydisdöttir or Raven's child.

To stay. To leave.

I shouldn't leave.

I cannot stay.

"I have become someone new in this village," I say quietly. All I see is *Faðir's* crooked nose, the placement of the red-ochre markings on his broad cheeks. "If I choose Bjǫrn, I will lose you."

To leave.

To stay.

Bjǫrn is stomping his feet on the ground to keep them warm.

"*Döttir*, I will always be alive in you," *Faðir* says. The wind

359

flings his words towards the moon. I hear Mother's laughter in the gusty breeze. When I look around, there are only shadows dancing through the leafless silver birch, shimmying this way and that.

"My old hawk eyes see many truths," *Faðir* murmurs. "The huntsman will take you with him, and you will go."

"Bjǫrn fought Huritt to win my hand," I say defensively. *Faðir* cuts me off.

"If your huntsman had only spat out words like he spits out chokecherry seeds, he would not have had to blind our best hunter to win your heart."

There is a swooshing hiss in my ears, a tingling sensation moving down my back.

"Bjǫrn has a Viking temper," *Faðir* continues. "He follows you like he follows the caribou."

"The ravens speak to him."

Faðir flicks a glance at Bjǫrn. "You are of value to me, *döttir*, but your huntsman failed our clan. Songbird believes Bjǫrn should pay a price like our ways demand. She is preparing to sing his death song when morning comes."

"Huritt provoked Bjǫrn!" I yelp.

"Your huntsman has stolen Huritt's life. He has blinded him. Askook will seek revenge."

"Bjǫrn protected me! I would have died without him in that cave."

"Your heart will bleed, *döttir*, if your *moccasins* do not follow your huntsman. I know it. I have lived your story. You must follow him or get lost in grief and lose yourself."

"When you lost Mother, you didn't lose yourself."

"Many moons came and went before I visited the Sweat Lodge and released your mother to the healing smoke.

Afterwards I asked the Shaman to read the bones. He told me many things. The Shaman predicted that no pale-faced Norseman would rule me again, but one day a raven would come and take away a gift that was meant for me."

Overhead, the tallest silver birch sways back and forth in a rhythmic dance while the poplar branches creak noisily in the rising wind. Bjǫrn looks reluctant to approach. "Anja, it is time to leave," he calls out worriedly.

"Go to him," *Faðir* says.

"I just found you, *Faðir*! How can I leave? It is not so easy."

"You and he are linked by raven spirits, and ravens are known to mate for life. I would have grown wings to follow your mother back to the land of the *pushaman*, but it wasn't possible. Now I live with her memory, and even that is fading."

"We need to leave," Bjǫrn says again as he steps in closer. A gust of wind suddenly pelts ice against my face, and I quickly lift the hood of my mantle against the cold. When I look up, Bjǫrn and *Faðir* are standing face-to-face.

"You caused trouble in this Beothuk tribe," *Faðir* whispers. "Your Viking blood now makes you a *kavdiunait*, a 'foreigner'. Beware, my son."

"Askook always hated me," Bjǫrn mutters underneath his breath.

"His hatred grows."

Bjǫrn shifts in place. "Huritt was my brother."

"You have changed all that."

"Do you hate me, too?"

I glance between the two of them.

"Your caribou will feed us through the winter, and you, alone, saved my *dóttir*'s life. For that, I thank you, and I will grant you life. But I fear for my people, and I fear for you.

Tonight, you have stirred up old resentments. You have started war, my son."

"It is the mischief-maker's, *Wisakedjak*'s fault," Bjǫrn mumbles almost incoherently. He struggles to contain himself. "I didn't think before I hit Huritt and knocked him out. I fought to win back Anja's heart. I wouldn't let Huritt cheat me like he did before."

"Huritt would take down a man's canoe if he felt others were getting too close to his," *Faðir* sniffs as he draws his brows into a frown.

"I didn't want to be loved by Huritt, not like that," I say. "He was my brother in this Beothuk place."

Bjǫrn steps behind my back to block out the wind. When I turn, I see him tugging on the cord around his neck. In silence, he draws out his raven's claw and holds it up into the moonlight.

"I am no raven," he says, directing his words to *Faðir*. "Both you and Nashushuk taught me that the raven is mischievous and curious, a creature symbolizing transformation, knowledge, and the complexity of nature and the subtlety of truths. Anja is the raven."

I shift my weight and look down at my feet. There are lacy snowflakes sitting in the frozen footprints on the ground.

"*Döttir*, you are like the sun to me," *Faðir* whispers quietly.

My throat chokes up. "You, *Faðir* – you have always been my moon."

In the distance, I hear Mother's voice, weighted down by worry, telling me to be back before the moon is on the rise. Her image sparkles and shivers and fizzles out.

Faðir reaches inside his festive cloak and brings forth an ornately carved pendant inlaid with walrus ivory and red rock crystal. The design depicts the face of a raven with wings wrapping around the circle. The pendant is hanging from a deerskin cord.

"This circular pendant has no set beginning and no end. It is much like us," he says as he places the necklace over my head. "One day you will return."

For a moment I hold the pendant in my palm and feel its warmth.

"I see the raven," I murmur as the wind picks up.

"You, alone, must see the raven inside yourself."

It is my choice.

"Raven's *döttir* is grateful for her *faðir's* acceptance in this Beothuk tribe."

Chief Achak smiles a sad smile. I peer into his tired eyes and see the two of us as separate, yet together. He makes me feel like I belong.

When I look up into the nighttime sky, the moon god winks and tells me that I am Raven's *döttir* who has chosen to live and love like *Faðir* does.

Chapter Thirty

DEER SKINS AND APRON SKIRTS

B jǫrn and I lay out our sleeping hides underneath an ocean of stars in a cloudless sky. It is chilly, but I am warm enough in my winter sealskins, snuggled up against Bjǫrn's warm chest. I fall asleep breathing in the fresh outdoor air and listening to the distant tides rolling into shore.

In the morning, I wake with a start to the sound of seagulls screeching overhead. For a moment I think that Askook has found us, but then I realize where we are, and my heart slows. The frost shimmers in the first rays of sunlight, and it is so cold that I can see my breath. Bjǫrn is curled up next to me, and it is a struggle to resist the urge to touch his stubbled beard, to kiss his sleeping face.

When I sit up slowly, I notice that the fire is out and there is a dusting of snow covering everything. A flock of honking geese flies past, and the noise of them is soon muffled by the hiss of waves crashing into shore. Soon I am thinking about Greenland, about Mother's hearth fire, about our Norse longhouses, about the Beothuk *mamateeks*, about Nuttah and Santu, about all that I have left behind.

The cries of the seagulls pull me back just as the sun begins to show her crimson face in bursts of yellow, in flares of tangerine orange where the rays bleed into the churning sea. Up the beach, a steady stream of icebergs is jiggling into place, locking us in for the winter months. The ice will prevent the Beothuk from easily pursuing us by canoe.

"You are awake at an ungodly hour, *hjarta mitt,*" Bjørn mutters huskily as he rolls over on his side. I pluck out my raven necklace and glance out across the sea.

"I couldn't sleep. We should go, Bjørn."

He props himself up onto one elbow and flashes me a sleepy, lopsided grin before rubbing a hand across his dimpled face. When I lie back down and peer up at him, desire burns hotly, a tingling moves through me, my belly swirls. Bjørn pulls me in.

"You are hungry for my kisses," he teases as he nibbles at my neck. I feel the heat of him against me as I curl into him. When he lifts my furs and gently kisses the parallel bear scars across my breasts, the goosebumps rise, my nipples pucker, and I give in. He moves lower, but our hides are bulky, and we are clumsy with each other. Bjørn looks at me with his sea-blue eyes, and I float in them.

When we pull apart, he runs his fingers through his hair so that tufts stick up. Chuckling, I go to pluck the hair out of his eyes, but he catches up my wrist and holds me steady so that he can study the pendant hanging around my neck.

"Your *faðir* has a carving gift," he mutters as he reaches forth and gently pulls the pendant towards him. The rock crystals glitter in the morning sun; the sparkles float, tickling the raven's wings. With speed, Bjørn yanks out his own raven talisman, and I lean in closely to inspect it. The black of it has been worn smooth, but the tuft of feathers at the top remains fuzzy after all this time. When I go to replace it underneath his tunic, my fingers linger on his chest. Bjørn responds by nuzzling his stubbled chin into my face and planting little kisses all over me. Gasping, I ease back slowly and arch my back as his well-built body hovers above mine.

"*Hjarta mitt …*" he whispers against my ear. I taste him fully, and he releases another groan as his hands probe low. A moment later, I feel his warmth driving its way inside, and we come together, gathering momentum, listening to the crashing surf. Afterwards, we stare up into the pale-blue sky.

"I never knew it could be like this," I murmur as I cuddle against him and listen to his racing heart. He smiles, and his dimples pop.

"It will always be like this for us. I know it," he says with a trickster grin.

"Always?" I say, dreamily.

"Ravens mate for life," is all he says, but instead of reaching for his raven talisman, he digs into his pocket and pulls out the Norse brooch his birth *faðir* left him – the one he showed me long ago. It is oval in shape and there is a giant purple jewel in the centre, edged in gold.

"This means the world to me. I want you to hide it for safe-keeping," he whispers fiercely. "You are mine now, *hjarta mitt.*"

Over the next few days, Bjørn speaks to me more about his family as we hike up the rocky shoreline leading back to Leifsbidur. He lets me know that he is anxious for me to meet his mother, and I let him know that meeting her will bring me joy. His reassurances give me hope that his mother will embrace me and that she will be pleased for the two of us. I feel building excitement and an eagerness to return to the life I once knew on Greenland shores.

As we travel over bleak terrain where everything is brown and dead, where the blackberries are shrivelled on the bushes, where the frost lying in the bog grasses is thick and lacy and the cattails rattle in the chilly wind, there are more moments of intimacy. When a brood of ducks skid to a landing and break through the thin layer of ice on a marsh we pass, Bjǫrn picks up his pace, forgetting all about my leg. When I complain, he comes back for me and pulls me in and kisses me firmly on the lips.

"I will thank sweet Freya when we arrive back in Leifsbidur," I tell Bjǫrn. "I will give her sacrifice. She helped us find each other."

"May our lady keep brushing us with her cloak of falcon feathers, and may the Great Creator lead our *moccasins* to safe shores," he sighs as the wind rips through his furs, tousling his long, blond hair.

Bjǫrn grabs my hand, and I am so happy that my throat chokes up. Who will I be when I arrive in Leifsbidur? Will I be the chieftain's niece, Bjǫrn's young wife, my mother's child or Raven's *döttir*, now displaced? Bjǫrn sees the worry in my eyes and he caresses my cheek with his thumb.

"We must be grateful for all we've been given in this life. We have faced much together, and we will survive what is to come. I will protect you, Anja Freydisdöttir."

It is late in the afternoon of the third day when the settlement of Leifsbidur comes into view. When I see the beginnings of a cluster of longhouses, I hold my breath. Childhood memories filter in, stirring dust, until Bjǫrn cups his hands around his mouth and begins to shout. His greetings travel with the wind.

There is a burst of noise and suddenly we see a group of barefoot children running towards us, shouting ecstatically as they wave their arms. Their suntanned faces are a combination of Norse and Beothuk, just like mine; their hair is long; and they are dressed in plain and simple clothes made from the softest deer skin hides.

"Bjǫrn is home!" they cry in their high-pitched voices as their little hands reach out to us. I lean down to greet them with a smile, listening to all their chattering. Soon they are crowding around us and dragging us with them up the path.

When one of Bjǫrn's kinsmen sticks his head out of a longhouse door and sees us, he calls out a greeting, and the good people of Leifsbidur come running. In the chaos, Bjǫrn grasps my hand and pulls me close, and all I can think to do is to bob my head and try to smile.

Bjǫrn does his best to introduce me. In the excitement, I feel a flush of hot embarrassment, an awkwardness. For a moment, I wonder if I belong.

It's not long before I spot a tall, thin, elegant-looking woman standing all alone inside the longhouse door, eyeing Bjǫrn. She wears an ankle-length linen under-dress with the neck closed in by a silver brooch of elaborate design. Over this, she wears a *hangerock*, the shorter-length woollen dress suspended by shoulder straps and fastened by another set of brooches. At the familiar sight of the apron skirt, my throat chokes up, and I remember Mother and our hasty parting and her sacrifice.

"Praise Óðinn!" the elegant-looking woman says as Bjǫrn's face breaks into an easy smile. She steps towards him and turns him around to admire his healthy form.

"Bring the ale!" someone shouts.

"What happened to your face?" the woman frets as she holds him back to study him. Bjǫrn shrugs dismissively. When he turns to me, I am shy.

"This is Anja from Greenland," he proudly says. "On her journey here, her longboat was shipwrecked in a storm."

"Anja?" she says as she turns to me. "Did you say you sailed from Greenland shores?"

"I did," I say.

"I heard tell of you. Bjǫrn's uncle was with you in the cave. He told me that you came on a *vyking* ship and that my son felt obliged to stay with you while you recovered from a bear attack."

"What you heard is true," I politely say as I feel the beginnings of a rumbling and shaking in my bones. She studies me.

"What about your clan?" she asks. "We had a message from the Beothuk village – from your *faðir*, Chief Achak. He always thought you lived."

"My *faðir* is well," I say, shooting Bjǫrn a panicked look.

"Your uncle must be Leif Eiriksson."

I nod.

"Then you know that this settlement was founded by your family," the woman continues a little stiffly. "Leif came here only once before. His sister, Freydis, soon followed him. I knew her well."

I glance up quickly just as Bjǫrn discreetly reaches for my hand, which is buried underneath my mantle folds. The grin of hopeful pride is still evident on his handsome face.

Bjǫrn's mother speaks again. Her voice is silky smooth:

"I am Logatha. Welcome, Anja Freydisdóttir."

Acknowledgments

Thank you to my brilliant editor, Jennifer Kaddoura, whose passion for her work inspires me to be the best writer I can be. Your structural edits made me stay up into the wee hours of the night, and I will forevermore have your voice in my head, but I will always be grateful. You are truly a gem of a person, and I feel blessed to have you as my friend.

To my amazing agent, Emmy Nordstrom Higdon, who is always there to answer all my questions and who has truly been a guiding light. Thank you also to the team at Westwood Creative Artists as well as to The Rights Factory and Sam Hiyate, who had a vision and who believed that the Vinland sagas were worth retelling.

Thanks to my fabulous team at One More Chapter, HarperCollins. I am immensely grateful to Charlotte Ledger and Bethan Morgan for believing in me as a new writer and for fostering new interest in the Old Norse sagas. Bethan, I owe you a deep debt of gratitude for being as passionate as I am about

Nordic mythology and saga retellings and for allowing me to take creative liberties as I attempt to weave present day societal issues into the past using Old Norse story threads. I am also grateful to Lauren Morocco for publicity support in Canada and to Simon Fox, Dushi Horti, and Tony Russell for their editorial expertise, their insights, and their careful reads of earlier drafts of this novel. Thank you for your attention to detail and for your ability to make it look like I can spell. I am also thrilled to have had the talented Andrew Davis design the covers for the Vinland Viking series. Thanks also to Savannah Tenderfoot for raising awareness about Beothuk mamateeks.

There are many writers and academics who share my passion for the Old Norse Sagas. I am especially grateful to Nancy Marie Brown and Jackson Crawford, whose work inspired me to learn more about the Viking Age. The world building in this novel also would not have been possible without a visit to several Viking heritage sites, including L'Anse aux Meadows National Historic Site and Norstead Viking Village in Newfoundland, Canada. I am grateful to the re-enactors and *skalds*, especially Paul Njolstad, Mark Pilgrim, and Kevin Young. To Karen Ledrew-Day at the Beothuk Interpretation Centre Provincial Historic Site in Boyd's Cove and to the staff of The Mary March Provincial Museum in Grand Falls-Windsor, which details the life of Demasduit and the history of the Beothuk in Newfoundland. Thank you for answering all my questions with such enthusiasm.

The support of early readers helped shape this novel. I am particularly grateful to: Megan C., Heather McEwen, Lise McLewin, Bev Rach, and Barb Rogers for slogging through earlier drafts and to Bill Rogers, who passed away before he had a chance to see this novel in print. He wanted the first signed copy, and I am grateful for his encouragement. Thanks as well to

Tiziana Hespe, Lee B. and Michael G., Ann Garside, Laura Gerlinsky, Tom Hughes, Sheri Miller, Anne-Marie Casavant-Turner, Wayne Lehman and Shawn Davis, Victor and Patricia Saavedra, Barbara Yopyk, Guy Fuller, Rick Murza, Tiffany Irwin, Jonathan Penner, Blane Morgan, and all of my cheerleaders. Your friendship means the world. I know that my writing has sometimes interfered with my ability to connect with all of you regularly, but I thank you for your ever-faithful friendship and for championing my work.

Heartfelt thanks to my family, including my brother, John Goranson, my sister-in-law, Seoyoung Ryu, and my nephews, Yohan and Jaewon, whose excitement at seeing my books in print always makes me smile. I also want to thank my parents, Alan and Elaine Goranson, who have supported me in all my endeavors, who continue to celebrate all of my achievements, and who have inspired me to be a lifelong learner.

I am profoundly grateful to my two girls, Tavania and Taralyn, who have grown up so quickly while I have been drafting novels and taking flight into another mother's world. Finally, to my spouse, Doug, who has cooked all meals while I wrote. You are my *hjarta mitt* whose love and support and sacrifice have provided me with a sense of belonging and connection. Thank you for this messy, busy, frenetic family life we have created together.

Author's Note

The Vinland Sagas were written in Iceland in the 13th and 14th centuries. They contain two works – the *Saga of the Greenlanders* and *Eirik the Red's Saga* – which summarize the life story of Freydis Eiriksdöttir, the first and only woman to lead a Viking expedition across the North Atlantic around 1000 AD. In the sagas, Freydis is described as a nefarious character who murders her Icelandic companions during her expedition to Vinland (modern-day Newfoundland, Canada). She then steals and loads the Icelandic ship with all the goods and produce that the ship can carry in the hold, and she sails it back to Eiriksfjord in Greenland. After she returns to her farm and livestock, she rewards her friends richly in order to have her misdeeds concealed. In time, however, the truth about what had transpired in Vinland reaches the ears of Leif, her brother, who tortures three of Freydis's men to learn the truth. According to the sagas, Leif does not punish his sister, but he predicts that her descendants will not get along well in the world.

What is fascinating is that Freydis's saga was initially told in the oral tradition by storytellers who were skilled at weaving fact and fiction together to entertain their listening audiences. In all likelihood, they bent truths for political reasons in order to foster or divide clan alliances. As a result, it is likely that the actual history – the truth about what happened to Freydis in Vinland – has been lost. What if Freydis did not murder her companions? What if she was falsely blamed for the wicked deeds that were performed in Vinland by the males in her company? What if she was the victim of character defamation because she was a strong woman who came from a powerful family?

In this novel, we enter Freydis's story after she has returned to Greenland and her brother, Leif, is pressing her companions under torture to learn the truth. She is portrayed as an innocent who was forced to lie to protect her unborn child – a child whom she conceived with her Beothuk lover on Vinland shores – in order to avoid the charge of adultery that would have led to her banishment and much scandal and shame. Freydis's pregnancy in the opening scenes of this novel mirrors what we know about her in *Eirik the Red's Saga*. In the Old Norse stories, we learn that right before she left Vinland, Freydis brazenly confronted a group of Beothuk in a pregnant state, that she freed one of her breasts from her shift, and that she smacked it with her sword. According to the sagas, the Beothuk were frightened to see a female warrior who was pregnant, and they turned and ran back to their boats.

While Freydis is a real character in the Vinland Sagas, her daughter, Anja, is an imagined one. The Beothuk characters in this novel are also fictional. My motivation was to present the customs and culture of the Beothuk people in a respectful and non-pejorative manner. Any language and descriptions used were not meant to offend. I am grateful for the insights and new awarenesses that Ms. Savannah Tenderfoot provided in earlier correspondence concerning my writings about the Beothuk.

Although we will never be certain about what transpired when the Vikings first met a now extinct Beothuk tribe in Vinland around 1000 AD, I took creative liberty to imagine a world where there were some peaceful exchanges between the Beothuk and the Norse and where children who were born into interethnic relationships were treasured. This differs from the actual history described in the Vinland Sagas. In the Vinland Sagas, the Norse and the Beothuk are portrayed as not being able to get along well because of mutual feelings of distrust and suspicion. In fact, the exchanges the two groups had with one another often were described as being violent. In contrast, my attempt at creating an alternate history where Anja, who was raised Norse but accepted by her Beothuk family, stresses the bonds between all people – the strength, perseverance, and love that runs through every human's veins and connects us all.

As a psychologist, I have spent my career working with clients who suffer anguish as a result of living through traumatic incidents. Shock, grief, helplessness, and powerlessness are experienced at the time of trauma in a swirl of horror that impacts emotional wellbeing and functioning for months and years afterwards. Anja's struggles with post-traumatic re-experiencing, avoidance, and hyperarousal symptomology represent the experiences of all trauma survivors. Anja lives in a state of fear and distress, worrying about unexpectedly becoming trapped in trauma memories. Her situation is truly tragic and heartbreaking, but she learns to live life beyond the trauma of the bear attack with the help and support of others. Belonging and acceptance allow her to be reborn and to learn how to live life in the now.

In this novel, Anja also yearns to learn more about her early beginnings. Her quest to find her roots mirrors the experience of many who have not been raised by their birth parents. It is part of our humanity to want to know about our parentage, our ancestral history, our cultural background, and heritage. Anja believed that finding her kin would allow her to find acceptance and self-worth, but in the end, her greatest lesson was that she had to belong to herself first before she could deeply connect with others.

While the hope is that I was able to make the experience of someone who suffers from post-traumatic stress live for my readers, a deeper motivation was to give voice to the importance of finding connections. Over the years of practice as a Clinical Psychologist, I have learned that one of the fundamental components of healing involves finding social supports. Connections provide the energy, strength, and sustenance to transcend suffering, to see ourselves and our situation differently, and to rewrite our own personal histories. Anja's flight led her on a journey of self-discovery, but in the end, it was the belonging and connections she found that made her whole.